Stories from Lone Moon Creek

Book Two: Ripples

Teresa Millias

Teresa Millias

Brighton Publishing LLC
435 N. Harris Drive
Mesa, AZ 85203

Stories from Lone Moon Creek

Book Two: Ripples

Teresa Millias

Brighton Publishing LLC
435 N. Harris Drive
Mesa, AZ 85203
www.BrightonPublishing.com

ISBN13: 978-1-62183-356-7
ISBN 10: 1-62183-356-9

Printed in the United States of America

First Edition

Cover Design: Tom Rodriguez

⟡Table of Contents⟡

Dedication

TO THE HOLY SPIRIT AND TO YOU, THE READER.

Prologue

The bubbling and rippling of Lone Moon Creek continues, just as do the stories which meander through the valley and up into the hills. The flow of water has never been known to completely cease, even though each summer brings onlookers to stare at the bald-headed, dry, rocks.

Lone Moon Creek waxes and wanes with tales just as sure as the spring floods and winter blizzards come and go.

Agnes and Marjory continue monitoring the happenings and surmise they know the answers, being about as successful as Claudia Taylor, who thinks she knows how many mustard plants are in Ike Lincoln's hay field.

I'll see you at the other end of the furrow.

.

"WE DON'T KNOW WHERE YOUR MOTHER AND FATHER ARE, MARJORY. No, MISS APRIL HASN'T RETURNED TO LONE MOON CREEK EITHER," AGNES ANSWERED SADLY.

◦⁄ᎭChapter One◦᠙᠌᠍

ON THE OTHER SIDE OF PEACEFUL

The canyon went on forever.

"Listen," Genevieve whispered to Glen as she nestled her hand into his.

Glen knew exactly what she meant but asked, "Listen to what?" He merely nodded as his eyes stretched the length of the stone corridor. Together they assessed their beautiful lives in silence, letting nature's backdrop outshine the sets of Broadway.

"Haven't we had the most wonderful life imaginable?" Genevieve again whispered, not wanting to disturb even one molecule of air.

His strong arm around her shoulder said it all. They stood on the highest precipice looking past their childhood, past the college years to their wedding, where it all began. It wasn't long before the profitable jobs, the house, and the vacations followed suit. What would be next in their future?

Glen and Genevieve descended their pinnacle slowly and carefully, following the trail leading to the lower level of the canyon where soon they would be at the hotel preparing for a sumptuous dinner in their favorite restaurant.

"Glen!" His wife screamed as she saw him trip and fall forward onto the path. He wasn't able to scream as she also careened face forward to lay on the million-year-old structure, no longer thinking of their beautiful lives.

They didn't feel the grit go under the skin of their legs and elbows and didn't feel the rough hands pull on their arms to the point of breaking. They didn't know that there were tight rags tied over their eyes or bristled ropes that cinched their feet and hands. Just that morning they had been in the spa being massaged with rose-scented oils and aloe cream. Genevieve had selected "plum orchard" nail polish for her manicure and pedicure. Glen had navigated the equipment in the gym as he waited for his wife.

Genevieve's head lolled from side to side as she sat in the back of a smelly, rank truck. The canvas straps held her upward. Her compromised mind took her to Cancun where she and Glen had vacationed the year before. They were sailing on the azure diamonds of the sea as she gleamed like bronze sunshine. Her sleek captain took her into never-never land. The waves lulled her thoughts until they began to catapult, making her stomach stretch upward to leave the body. She told Glen she needed to return to the shore.

Glen lay cinched to the filthy floorboards. His mind was unsettled as he thought of the two of them in Austria, no—on a rickshaw in the Orient. Maybe their Alaskan trip with the dogsled races? Had his legs been caught in the dogs' leashes or had his foot gotten wedged in the ski lift? Why couldn't he hang on to the rickshaw? He was tipping out. He tried to call for Gen to help him. Why couldn't he call out her name?

Wait, wait! Glen's panicked thoughts pierced the reasoning center of his brain but ended as once again the needle thrust into his flesh.

Genevieve began rocking, wondering what possibly could be restraining the motion of the wooden antique chair that sat by their beautiful fireplace. She tried again and again to rock the chair. *Something must be blocking it,* she thought. *Oh! The marble statuary in St. Peter's! Of course!* She felt relieved and ceased trying to force the chair. "Come here, little one. Don't be frightened. You are precious," she'd uttered to the child in the orphanage. Glen kissed the child and suddenly they were canoeing through the wild rapids of the Amazon. The baby was not in the vessel! "Glen!

Glen!" The straining against the bondage caused Genevieve to receive another dose of sedation.

The truck rumbled on for miles, Glen and Genevieve were unaware of their travels. But why would this be of any concern? They were frequently traveling somewhere, often sound asleep with complete trust in the commander of the vessel. Now, hundreds of miles from the canyon, the abductors did not care if the two came out of their stupor. In fact, they were antsy for some excitement, something to laugh about.

They watched Glen, who came to reality before his beautiful wife even stirred. He struggled and squirmed, moaned through the gag, and lifted his head to look at Genevieve's shoes. He heard his neck crack as he tried to see all of his beloved. The three men were satisfied with their entertainment—they laughed. One poked Glen with the end of a rifle. Beads of sweat poured from Glen; they were nothing like the luxurious beads of dew through which they'd marveled when in the Hawaiian orchid fields.

Genevieve lurched forward, to no avail. She grunted and moaned, calling all nonblindfolded eyes to be on her. Glen grunted to her. Back and forth they communicated much like the African baboons they had observed during an anniversary trip.

She wouldn't get anymore sedation either—for now. Fortunately for Genevieve, the truck came to a stop.

The blindfolds were harshly yanked from their eyes. Glen was uncinched and raised himself to his knees. The husband and wife looked into each other's eyes; not like on their wedding day, but as if looking into a deep well that had no bottom. Glen had never before seen the fear that he saw in those green eyes, and Gen never knew her husband could be frightened.

What made them look away from each other? To the left and to the right were faces—children's faces! There were children crammed together on benches that lined the sides of the truck. All the little eyes were focused on the woman and the man. The children did not look at the guards. No one spoke. Genevieve looked at their dirty, tear-stained faces, their matted hair, and the fear in their eyes. Glen saw no shoes, only bare feet with ragged clothes, and fear.

The children were herded down a ramp like cattle while the bondages were removed from the big people. Genevieve literally jumped into Glen's arms. Neither one of them knew what was happening or why.

A guard had an inkling that they would run and quickly encircled them with a thick, bristled rope. He pulled them into a building.

"Sit," he commanded as he knocked on an adjoining door.

How many times before had Glen and Genevieve felt their arms pressed together as they sat side by side? It was a natural occurrence for them. They had pictures of themselves sitting just so on the riverboat cruising the Mississippi, at an outdoor coffee table in Paris, in the crowd waiting for the bullfight to begin in Madrid, and fishing off the pier in Orlando, but never one with a rope holding them in position.

Glen could read the fear in his wife's eyes and vowed to do anything to get them out of the nightmare. He lowered his stature to whisper into her ear when the wooden door swung open. A man in an unfamiliar uniform stood scowling at them.

"Stand," he ordered.

The two rose as one.

"You'll do," he scoffed and walked out of the room.

They felt the rope yank across their bodies as the guard said, "Come."

The guard shoved the couple into a long wooden building, making them both fall to the floor. The rifles were pointed at them as the rope was removed. Again, in their peripheral vision, they could see children lined against the walls.

"You are here to watch them, and if one even tries to escape, it will be you who gets the first bullet."

4

That was the point when Genevieve totally fell apart and sobbed in her husband's arms. "What's happening? Why are we here? When are we going to get out of here? We've got to get help. Who can help us? Where are the police?"

"Shh," Glen warned as he tried to comfort her. He wished he could keep her from going through another moment of the insanity.

Genevieve jumped as she felt a hand on the back of her arm. She swung around to look into eyes sadder than hers on the day she couldn't go to the class picnic in fourth grade because she'd had the measles. The eyes were even sadder than her own when Jimmy Owens took Ellen to the dance and not her and sadder than the day she was told her grandfather had passed away. The girl wore the eyes of the eternal angels who had to watch the ruination of souls.

"Oh my dear child," Genevieve cried as she reached to hug the girl who was bringing compassion to her.

But Nova jumped back saying quietly, "Don't cry, they'll take you away." She quickly ran back to her place in the line.

Gen looked up at Glen with pleading eyes. "I'll think of something," he whispered. "I'll get us out of here." He gave that promise with all his heart and soul; she could feel it.

As if there had been a gust of wind, the children all sat in one fell swoop. They stared at the American couple, the couple who once had it all and as far as the children could see, still had it all.

"What are we supposed to do?" Genevieve whispered just as the door blasted open with two men carrying large bowls of— food? The other two men holding rifles stayed by the door.

Again in unison, the children rose and marched in single file to the first bowl. With a bare hand, each reached into the "mush" and carried it back to his or her spot. When all were served, their heads lowered to eat out of their hand-troughs. Glen thought about the dinner he and his wife had been planning to share at their favorite restaurant.

5

The "waiter" sailed the remains of the second bowl across the floor to the newcomers and left with the others. The two starving Americans looked at each other and then, like the children, sank a hand into their "dinner."

Just as before, the door opened with the force of a geyser, and the boys immediately stood and filed out of the building.

"You," a guard punctuated the word as he jabbed Glen in the back. "You, too. Go with them."

"I will not," Glen retaliated as he swung around to face the dictator. "I will not leave my wife alone."

"She will stay here with the girls; you will go to watch the boys."

"I will not leave my—" Glen took the butt of the rifle against his jaw.

"Glen, Glen." Genevieve knelt over her bloodied husband.

Two soldiers grabbed his arms and dragged him out as Genevieve scooched on her knees, thinking she could rescue him. She leaned against the door and cried into her hands. She didn't notice the routine that the girls were methodically going through. She never saw them rise, use the attached outhouse, take a blanket from the pile, and lie down. All in perfect rows. It wasn't until Nova nudged her arm with a blanket did Genevieve look beyond her misery.

"For you," Nova said. "You sleep now."

Genevieve spread her blanket identical to the girls and noticed that each one was facing and looking at her. *Oh, you dear children*, she thought as she looked into the eyes of each one. *What is this? Why are you here? Why am I here? Where have they taken my husband? Is this for real?*

One by one she saw their little eyes close. Little eyes that must have mothers somewhere, fathers who cry for their child each night, brothers and sisters, families that don't know where their little girls are. Genevieve wadded the corner of the blanket against her mouth to try and muffle her sobs. Her shoulders quaked and pounded against her crucified soul. Was this the "agony in the garden" or the "scourging at the pillar?" She lurched forward when she thought Glen might be killed. She started to pray—something that she hadn't done in a long, long time. After all, she'd had no need for prayer. She'd had the idyllic life.

As she prayed, she heard the whimpering and the apparent nightmares sporadically resounding through the room. Her heart was breaking, but maybe not so much for herself as for the children.

She must have fallen asleep. Somehow exhaustion is always the victor. Gen awoke to a noise. She couldn't think where she was or remember any of the previous days. It wasn't until she felt two little bodies nuzzled close to hers did she remember. On the right was a tiny girl with a thumb half in and half out of her mouth and on the left was someone holding on to her arm.

Nova began running as if the place was on fire. She quickly roused the two girls and almost dragged them back to their blankets just as the door burst open. All the girls rose, folded their blankets, used the outhouse, walked past the rising mountain of blankets to add their own, and then sat along the walls. Genevieve followed suit. The female guard merely stationed herself at the door. She kicked the door with the back of her boot and the boys filed in with two soldiers carrying the two big wooden bowls of mush.

Genevieve ran to the door when she saw Glen. She wanted to hug him, as she always did, but she couldn't on that day. He held up his hand like a crossing guard and she immediately stopped. She stared at his face, his beautiful face contorted with swollen tissue and dried blood. One eye was red, black, and blue. Barely able to enunciate the words, Glen quietly asked, "Are you all right?"

Whack. He fell to his knees.

Genevieve turned, ready to assault the assailant when Glen reached out and grabbed her foot. "No, Gen, no; they'll hurt you."

Genevieve listened.

They ate out of their hands in silence, trying to ask and answer all the questions that registered in their eyes.

Genevieve covered her mouth with her clean hand to mask her sobs when she looked into the bowl of mush to read the message that Glen had inscribed: I love you.

"Watch them!" the commander snapped at Genevieve as she and the girls entered a different building filled with machines. She looked over her shoulder to see Glen go to another location with the boys.

The girls walked directly to their stations. No one moved until the commander threw a switch that set the gears and levers and wheels and pulleys in motion with such an overwhelming noise that Genevieve jumped backward. Her look of horror was apparently entertaining to the commander, as he slapped his thighs and laughed uproariously.

Again, his directive of, "Watch them," assaulted her ears.

What does he mean, watch them? What should I do?

Genevieve responded to a girl in the third row who was motioning her to come.

As she approached, she saw that the lever the girl was trying to pull down was not moving. The girl began to cry.

"There, there, honey, let me help you," Gen said gently as she put her arm around the girl's shaking shoulders. Genevieve sighed, knowing she had no idea about fixing machinery; her Glen would usually take care of any such matters for her. But with the pleading eyes of the girl, Gen smiled with pseudo confidence and began looking at the various parts of the machine.

Suddenly she looked over at the next row when she heard a tapping sound. Without saying a word, the girl doing the tapping pointed to a latch underneath the lever and mimed how to turn it to release the lever. Genevieve followed the instructions and... Success! A look of sheer gratitude spread across the face of the girl in crisis.

Genevieve began walking up and down the rows just as her teachers used to do. She watched and tried to learn, but she didn't know what she was watching or what she was learning.

Why on earth do they have these children doing this work? Why am I here? Where are their parents? Where are my parents?

For the first time since the nightmare began, Genevieve thought about her parents and Glen's parents. They would help them! They would find them and come for them. Yes! They would come!

Without even thinking, Genevieve jumped in the air and twirled and shouted and hugged the first girl she came to.

"Don't make noise, don't talk," the girl whispered.

"Oh, I'm sorry," she whispered in return but couldn't rid herself of the newfound joy.

Many hours later, a siren sounded. The machines suddenly stopped, which created a silence that hurt everyone's ears. No one covered their ears except Genevieve. The boys' and girls' groups marched outside to the rear of the building where there were wooden tables with benches and trays of fruits, vegetables, meats, pastries, and milk. Glen and Genevieve looked at each other, thoroughly baffled, and then they knew: the inspectors and a suited man with many medals on his chest were there to observe. They walked around the tables, smiling at the children and jokingly taking a piece of fruit or meat and rubbing their stomachs. Never did they pause to converse with a child or ask, "How are you today?" They knew better.

The American couple watched the children devour the food. What a treat for them to have peaches and mangoes, uncooked peas and cucumbers, sliced turkey and beef, with desserts and milk! Glen and Genevieve, too, ate like starving dogs and tasted food that surpassed that from any highly praised restaurant they'd patronized in the past. With a dribble of mango juice careening along her chin line, Gen wiped it away and noticed Glen's swollen fingers.

9

She pointed to his hand and let her furrowed brow and worried face speak for her. He merely shook his head as if to say, "Don't wonder and don't worry."

The delicious tastes of her lunch soon were substituted with rotting sorrow, sorrow for her husband who undoubtedly was fighting for his life and hers inside the boys' building.

The inspectors stared at the couple. One nudged a guard and asked, "Where'd you get those two?"

"America."

"America!" The inspector laughed hideously. "Funny."

Genevieve watched Glen grab the edge of the table with his good hand; she saw the veins in his temples pulsate. He stood.

"No, Glen, no," she spoke aloud.

Every eye turned to look. The flippant chatter from the hierarchy ceased.

Glen sat.

Suppertime brought the customary bowls of mush. The days of "fine dining" were over. Gen noticed the red welt on her husband's neck and buried her face in her hands. It was in that position that the word "parents" reenter her brain. She looked left and right before writing the word in the gruel. Her partner quickly lifted his head with eyes wide. His fingers pulled through the word to delete it as a guard neared, but the sparkle and hope in his eyes made Genevieve feel a smattering of relief. They both knew that their parents would get to the bottom of this; they had connections in high places, and they had the money to cause action.

Genevieve looked past Glen's neck wound to the children. *Who was going to help them? Would their parents have the means to start an international search? Would their parents know how to get the government involved?* Tears dripped into her supper.

Later Glen lay awake with his boys spaced methodically around the edges of their dormitory. He had never seen a dormitory before except in the old army movies. In college he'd had a suite with three other guys. He didn't think there were huge dorms like the one he was currently living in anymore. *Where did all these boys come from?* Glen thought. Some were Asian, some Latino, some as blond as can be, some black, some white. *Their parents must be frantic, just as mine must be. This has to be stopped. We need help. God, please, we need help. Help us, please.*

Glen's prayers were suddenly interrupted by screams and thrashing that emanated from the fifth blanket to his right. He quickly ran to the boy who was fighting a war in his dreams.

"Shh," Glen whispered to the little fellow.

The boy woke out of his dream and flung his arms around Glen's shoulders. "You're OK. It's all right," the American consoled the trembling victim. "Lay back down." Glen didn't know that at least twenty other victims received comfort that night by watching the kindness shown to the screamer.

Genevieve, too, became a lantern in a wretched, heinous night.

Glen's job during the day was similar to Genevieve's. "Watch them" was his only directive. The magnitude of the machines, the power, the adeptness needed to operate them was startling. The danger and the lack of safety were glaring.

He watched as each station became occupied. Now he knew not to jump when the switch was thrown. The noise, the repetition, the motion—*How could they stand it? Has anyone tried to escape? How can they do this for hours?*

Glen's theorizing came to a sudden halt when he heard a scream. He ran to a boy who already had three others around him. They were all desperately trying to pull his shirttail out of the press. Glen quickly pulled the buttons away from the holes, and sure enough, the rotor pulled it under the press and deposited it into a box on the back of the machine. The boy stood shirtless and bawled. Glen knelt in front of him and guided his trembling arms back into the flattened shirt. He gently buttoned each button that had survived while the boy tucked it in. Glen started to get up when the boy lurched at him with a hug.

All over the world, people know about love. Whoever would have thought that I would be in this strange place today being hugged by a victim of trafficking? Glen wiped the tears from his eyes.

The American walked between the rows. He began to sense that the boys were working harder than the machines. They had to pull or rotate or force some of the moving parts to either keep them running or to get them moving. *Hmm, oil. Where would the oil be?* Glen thought. He began opening cupboards and drawers. He swung around when he felt someone tapping his back. A boy crouched low, fearing the door might open and he would be caught away from his station. He pointed to the end cabinet. Sure enough, there were dozens of oil cans, none of which had been opened. The American began the trek around the room, giving each parched, emaciated machine the drink it had been longing for. The noise level steadily decreased as each machine received its fill. The machines were nicely whirring and not grinding and thumping. The boys' spirits lifted as if they had taken the oil. For the first time, Glen saw smiles.

Glen wished he could share the moment of joy with his wife. Never had they been denied the chance to share. How much for granted had they taken their opportunities, their luxurious side of peaceful?

The siren blasted. Could it be? Were they going to be treated to another spread of real food? Every stomach growled with the thought of juicy fruit and crunchy vegetables. The marching feet walked with an easier gait and almost glided like the oiled machines. The shortest children bobbed left and right to look around the taller children. Where was the food? Everyone sat at the outdoor tables. Stomachs growled. Genevieve looked at Glen; his excited eyes were trying to tell her something but what she did not know.

After a time, a panel truck drove to the site and trays of food were placed on the tables. Then followed two cars of inspectors and uniformed soldiers.

"Eat! Eat!" a man hollered.

Little fingers darted back and forth faster than bird's beaks feeding their young. Gen closed her eyes as she savored every bite. Glen couldn't take his eyes off of her beautiful face. The food brought them something that they desperately needed: the memories of days past. The children felt it, too. Some began to cry while they ate. For some reason, the pastries brought about the most nostalgia of home.

The truck, that truck! Genevieve gasped as she grabbed for Glen's arm. The same truck that they had been in pulled onto the lot. Soldiers jumped out and herded fifteen children out of the back of the truck and into the sunlight. As they stood huddled together, the soldiers grabbed the same number of "picnicking" children and corralled them onto the truck. In that evil place, screams and crying ascended to the high heavens.

"Back to work. Back to work!" a guard ordered.

The machines in the boys' work camp might have been working in good order, but the gloom of the world settled upon the children and the adult.

At nighttime there were cries from the newcomers and those who missed and worried about the fifteen who had been removed. Genevieve and Glen went from blanket to blanket administering what comfort they could. It must have been the wee small hours of the morning when the whimpering and sobbing slowly lessened.

Lord, I'm serious. This has to stop. Where are my parents? Where is the help? How can I get the word out to the government? Glen continued to pray until daybreak.

Please, Lord! My girls need help.

Genevieve bolted upright. *Did I say my girls? I did say "my girls!" Lord, I hope that was OK. I waited so long to have a child and you presented me with all of these?* She had to smile, in all the quagmire of despair; she just had to smile as she looked across the sea of blankets and of course cried.

Was someone crying with me? She held her breath to keep in the sob and listened. It wasn't crying, it was singing. Some little soul out there was singing herself to sleep. She remembered her mother doing the same thing for her. Of course! She could do that for "her girls." She began the lullaby:

Sleep my child and peace attend thee,

All through the night.

Maybe the next night she would be able to sing without crying.

The word had gotten around that Glen knew how to fix machines, creating increased production. He was told to accomplish in the girls' work camp what he had in the boys' camp. Genevieve could barely breathe, as she was overwhelmed by her husband's presence in the building. It was the only time they'd been together outside of mealtime. The guards never took their eyes off the man and his wife. Twice the couple luxuriated in a just-by-chance glance that allowed their eyes to meet.

Over the days, Glen solved other problems in production and mechanics. Genevieve gratefully noticed that he wasn't showing fresh wounds anymore.

The days and the nights became colder. The guards couldn't keep the coal stoves burning. Everyone shivered most of the time because of the inadequacies of the "stove men." One night Glen quickly dug the word "plan" into his bowl of gruel. Genevieve gouged her fingers through it to destroy the evidence, as they used to say in the movies. Her eyes were asking, "What? What is it?" She knew he couldn't answer.

Glen brought warmth to the barren souls. He fixed the stoves, convinced the guards that tall, tall chimneys were needed or the whole complex would catch on fire and showed others how to stoke the fires. The warmth meant comfort and security in an odd sort of way; it meant that they at least had something. Genevieve knew Glen was doing those things for his boys, his girls, and his wife.

We're his family now, she pondered, *and he will do anything for us.*

The days droned on. Glen inscribed the number twenty-one in their supper. Genevieve was bewildered as to why he would write that number; it certainly didn't depict the number of days since they'd been abducted from the canyon. She thought that perhaps they had been there about ninety days, but she didn't know. Gen had lost many of her days to depression or fear or a type of "unconsciousness to life." The next night Gen scrawled twenty-two in the gruel. She had no idea.

Thirty-one was to be the next number, but the bowls of supper didn't arrive. The boys and girls waited in complete silence, but they had learned to communicate nevertheless. Glen would wink, and whoever he was looking at would return the wink. Genevieve would wave with her pinky finger and someone would wave back. These mannerisms were monumental to the children. They were a link to humanity, to love, and to all that had been taken away.

Suddenly the doors opened, bringing with it an inside picnic! In came trays of delicacies that would have impressed the wealthy. The children started squealing with delight. Some stood and jumped, some hugged the person next to him or her, and some merely stared in amazement. Did Genevieve and Glen dare to hug each other? They did, they did, they did!

All the troubles left the world during that meal. Tummies were full; everyone felt fat and happy.

"Silence!" screamed a commander.

He began walking in front of the children, his heavy boots pounding with each step. He stopped, pointed, and shouted, "Stand!" He walked on, stopped, pointed, and shouted again.

The ritual continued as Genevieve murmured, "Oh no!"

Glen closed his eyes and whispered, "Oh no." Some of the children started whimpering, they knew.

"There." The uniformed one regaled in his appointments. Glen counted fourteen children. The commander swaggered over to Genevieve and shouted, "And you!"

Genevieve gasped; Glen sprang to his feet.

"Take her," the commander directed.

"No!" yelled every boy and girl in the building as they ran to protect their lady and man.

The commander knew better than to kill his workers. He called off the guards. "Let it go, never mind. Let them have their stupid Christmas."

Glen and Genevieve looked at each other in disbelief. Gen was so traumatized, she couldn't stand. She sank to the floor as she saw the little faces staring at her.

"Glen, did you know it was Christmas?"

"I had no idea. Merry Christmas, dear heart."

It was the thirty-eighth of whatever Glen was counting. At least they could now use Christmas as a guide for a calendar they had to hold in their heads. They knew New Years' Day would be the next week.

The following week, captives learned that New Year's was apparently important to the guards, because they began celebrating on New Year's Eve day and they celebrated far into the night.

It was just at daybreak that Genevieve and the girls woke to a thunderstorm.

"What a way to start the New Year," she moaned.

Glen and the boys also awoke to... *Wait a minute*, Glen thought, *that's not thunder!*

Glen jumped up from his blanket and ran to the door. The guard was sleeping soundly from his celebratory reveling. The American ran outside to see helicopters landing and soldiers running.

"My father!" Glen ran to the arms of his father. "Dad, quick, we've got to go in and get Genevieve."

"Genevieve, Genevieve, I knew they would come! They're here; they're here to rescue us! Come!"

Genevieve ran into the arms of her husband as she laughed and cried, "Thank God. Oh thank God!" She hugged her father-in-law as he wept after months and months of trying to find them. He couldn't imagine what they had been through; he saw how skinny they had both become.

They started for the door when Genevieve suddenly flung around and there, not making a sound, were the girls huddled in the farthest corner, not knowing what to think about what was to become of them. They knew their lady was going away.

"Come," she called across the building as she motioned with her hand. "Come!"

Slowly they walked to her as she turned to her husband and said, "I'm not going if they don't go."

"Same here, Dad. My boys and I are all going together."

"Your boys?"

"Come with me, I'll show you."

It took days and days to evacuate everyone and, unfortunately, years to locate the children's next of kin. In fact, Glen and Genevieve have a houseful of children living with them in a little rural town where there's lots of love for them all.

Every so often, one of the children would ask their Papa Glen to tell them the story about how he regulated the flew on the coal stoves in order to send the SOS smoke signals every day for thirty-eight days.

"I'm going out this afternoon, Marjory. Betty is coming to stay with you; you know how much fun the two of you have! And, oh yes, she's bringing you a piece of Mulberry pie—your favorite!

No, I don't think this adult education class would be anything you'd be interested in.

Yes, I'll take you to the library tomorrow so you can choose new books."

ᑕᔆ᠎Chapter Two᠎ᑐᔆ

And All the King's Men Couldn't...

"I just wish there was a pill..." Ashley stopped as she looked from face-to-face. She saw eyes like her own—helpless, hopeless, frustrated.

"Me too," said a barely audible voice from the corner. All heads turned to Marie who had never before contributed a word to the support group discussions.

The silence of "death thoughts" spread throughout the room of baby boomers much in contrast to the spread of life that permeated the nurseries after World War II. The young soldiers and their new wives now waited on the firing lines across from their children; the children who were supposed to bring fresh hope to the civilization.

"Are you people crazy?" The question blared across the room much like an air raid. "People die when they're supposed to die!" George went on then mopped his forehead with a handkerchief.

"Do you like to see your father suffer?" Ashley retaliated with eyes of fire.

"No, of course not," he stammered with beads of sweat pooling into the spaces where hair had once been.

"Well? Why can't we put a stop to this nonsense? They're living like captives in their own bodies," a woman snarled at George. Her bathing beauty figure had been replaced with thicker hips, and she'd transposed her emerging grays with hair color.

"Ashley! Think what you're saying!" George panted as he rose to his feet, showing his protruding stomach. He was the little boy depicted in a picture frame at his father's bedside, dressed in an army uniform, of course. To his left was his dad, home from the war, and to his right, his beautiful, smiling mother. "Do you think our parents went through the war to have their lives ended by their children?"

Ashley rose to her feet, reminding Marie of the prize winning debating club team from high school - the club she never had enough nerve to join.

Kids had started to be different after the war; they were indulged with "things" and they were prompted to "speak out." But that didn't apply to those like Marie, whose father hadn't returned from the war. She wanted to have the courage to speak out, but she inherited her mother's shyness, she guessed.

"We love them! That's why we can't stand to see them like that! God, our childhood was filled with vacations and birthday parties and home movies. They gave us so many good times," Ashley continued her defense.

Marie didn't remember vacations, but her mother always baked a birthday cake for her. Mrs. Stebbins from across the hall and Mrs. Ranleafe and Agnes from next door would come every year to make her day special.

George's big belly was now two feet away from Becca's less-than-size-six prom queen figure. The flashing between their eyes could have been synonymous with the sight their dads saw coming from the fighter planes.

"All right, folks!" came a startling command from Jacqueline. "Time's up for today. See you next week, same time, same station."

The two A-bomb baby boomers slowly exhaled to defuse their boiling adrenaline.

"No, Ma, it's Ashley, not Barbara. Barbara passed away when she was two years old, you know that."

"Oh? Where's Scott, is he here?"

"No, Daddy is not here, Ma, you know that."

"Is he coming today?"

"No he's not; he died three years ago, you know that."

"Where's Izzy?"

"Who? I don't know who that is, Ma."

"I used to walk to school with her."

"You used to walk to school with her? Well, how on earth would I know her? I wasn't even born then!"

"Oh, Barbara, you don't remember anything!"

"I'm not Barbara, Ma. I'm Ashley! Do you remember a daughter named Ashley?"

"Do you have a doll named 'Cuddles'?"

"I don't have a doll, Ma."

"Aw, you poor thing, I'll get you one."

"You're going to get me one? No, Ma I don't need a doll."

"Is Scott in the other room?"

"No, Daddy is not in the other room."

"Well, I better get up and fix dinner; he'll be home soon."

"You don't have to fix dinner, Ma. They do it for you, remember?"

"They do?"

"Yes, you'll go into the dining room later with all the rest. Do you remember going into the big dining room?"

"Hmm, not really, Barbara."

"It's Becca, Ma."

George took a deep breath as he pushed back the white hospital curtain. The eyelet rings never failed to be noisy. He stared at the gaunt man who had more attachments on his body than the combat gear he carried during the war. Another operation—how many had there been? George didn't know. The doctor said it would be a 50 percent chance this time and the major ordered, "Let's go for it."

George never knew anyone who wanted to live more than his dad. His father *was* life, George deduced as he watched the thin chest rise and lower.

George was staring at the intravenous bandage when the major abruptly said, "George!"

George felt his body snap to attention as he would do as a child.

"At ease, soldier," the old man murmured. "You're staring like there is a situation here."

"No, sir, no," George stammered, knowing he never had the composure of the major.

"Victory is coming, son. One way or another, victory is coming," the major whispered as he gritted his teeth against the pain.

"I know it is, Dad," George responded. He ordered his tears to stay in hiding.

"Mama," Marie whispered to the breathing statue, "I'm here. It's me Mama, its Marie. How are you today?"

Marie took her mother's hand and placed it between her own. "I'm here, today is Tuesday, and tomorrow will be Wednesday. Yesterday was Monday. It's still August, it's summer, Mama. Do you remember summer? It was hot in Lone Moon Creek during August, wasn't it? Do you remember how we'd go out on the back landing to get the cooler night air? And you'd show me all the stars? They were beautiful weren't they?"

Marie thought she could feel her mother's hand pulsate, but she probably didn't; her mother hadn't voluntarily moved for six years.

"And somehow I'd fall asleep listening to you tell me about the stars. You used to say that we were going to go to one of those stars, live there and be so happy. Do you think about that now, Mama? Do you think about going to a star?

I wish I could help you get there. Is it time, Mama? Is it time for you to go?"

Marie drew her mother's hand close to her face and cried into the old fingers.

"Wanting Them to Be Something That They're Not" was written across the whiteboard. The group took their Styrofoam coffee cups to their seats and looked at Jacqueline. She pointed to the board and said, "That's it. Who would like to start?"

Why was she so cold and pragmatic? thought Ashley. *Couldn't she just once welcome us and speak for the first five minutes?*

"Well," interjected Sally after a long pause, "I guess I can start. I suppose you're trying to get us to think how we want our parents to be like they used to be instead of who they are now."

Sally waited for a response from Jacqueline who only replied, "Could be."

I hate her, Ashley thought as she glared at Jacqueline.

"Yeah, I know I do that," Sally continued. "I hate the way my parents are now; I'd give anything to get them back the way they used to be. Man," she said as she shook her head, "they used to be so much fun. And I'm sure they don't like themselves anymore either. Some days my father will sit for hours and just stare at Ma. What is he thinking? Does he wish she would go away? Is he sorry he ever married her?"

"I don't know," Jacqueline said coolly. "Who wants to be next?"

"Maybe we always do that," Jerry said pensively. "When we're little we want to be one of the big kids. When we're a teenager we want to be out on our own. When we're struggling we want to go back as a kid. When we're old we want to be young. So maybe it's normal to want our folks to be young again."

"Did any of those scenarios ever come to fruition?" Jacqueline asked dryly.

"No," Jerry admitted. "I don't know why we waste time even thinking about it."

"But we can do something about it!" Ashley announced loudly as she slammed her hand on the desktop. "We can put them out of their misery. They can't do it, but we're still in our right minds; we can do it!"

"But how do we know if they're ready?" the little voice from the corner asked.

"Because we're their children. We know!"

"We don't know!" George exploded as he wiped his sweaty hands on his pant legs.

"Why can't 'old age' be a position of honor?" Jacqueline asked with no expression.

"Honor?" Ashley sailed the word at her nemesis. "There is no honor in old age."

"Why not?"

"Are you from this planet?" Ashley asked.

"I believe I am," Jacqueline replied.

"My mother doesn't even know who I am!" screamed Becca." Is that a place of honor? I need to help her leave this honorless world. There is no honor for her here."

The group listened to Becca sob as she rummaged through her satchel for a tissue.

"Why can't we love them?" Jacqueline asked emotionlessly.

"We do love them," came a quick retort from Marie. Marie who wished she'd been in the debating club. "It's just that… well… like with me… my mother has been in a comatose state for six years, and she… she… can't love me back. I'm getting nothing back from her! Doesn't that mean it's time for her to go … to go… to her star?"

The group listened to Marie sniffle as Ashley passed a tissue around the circle to her.

"Well, my dad is not ready," George spoke to rid the room of the sound of the sniffling. "He will never be ready!"

"Never?" Jacqueline inquired.

George's mouth opened to speak but froze with no sound exiting.

Ashley's allegiance strangely embraced her new ally— George. Jacqueline was definitely the enemy.

"No, Ma it's not Barbara, its Ashley.

"I'm your daughter, your daughter. Do you remember having a daughter? Ma, don't cry, I'm sorry, I'm sorry. I didn't mean to yell at you."

"Barbara wouldn't talk to me like that."

"No, I suppose she wouldn't. Who am I, Ma?"

"No, I'm not Shirley's girl. I'm your girl, Ma. I'm your girl!"

"I've got to go, Ma."

George slowly swept the curtain back, trying not to make the metal rings ping against each other. His dad had taught him how to go on maneuvers in their backyard without making a sound. "Your life may depend upon it, son."

Now the enemy was death. Was George as cautious of not rattling the cage of death? He wasn't sure; he just felt he needed to be quiet. The major sensed a presence; his eyes snapped open with a noticeable fear, probably the same fear that he knew in the South Pacific and then later in Korea.

He smiled at George; he seemed relieved.

"Son, I've made a decision!" he spoke firmly as he would have done to his troops. "There has been a surprising turn of events in my life."

George swallowed.

The major continued, "The fear of death has been conquered! I don't know how or when or who did it, but I'll be damned if I don't find out and give them my gratitude!"

George visualized his dad being celebratory with his fellow officers: slapping each other on the back, raising their shot glasses, and lighting their cigars.

"It'll be any day now, son. I'll be shipping out any day now. I'm ready. I'm ready now."

The major and George saluted each other just as they had when George was a small boy.

※

"It's Sunday, Mama. I prayed for you in church today. I know God was listening to me, but why is He waiting? Why won't He take you now? You're not happy on this earth, are you?"

Marie stared at her mother's statuesque profile. "Remember how you always took me to church, Mama? I know what a good person you are. When Daddy didn't come home from the war, you brought me up all by yourself. God knows how good you are. Why doesn't He take you now?"

Marie wished she could leave the nursing home just once without tears in her eyes.

※

"Do They Have the Right to Live?" was scrawled across the board.

"Oh, for God's sake!" Ashley mumbled to herself as she slammed her satchel onto the desk.

"Do they?" Jacqueline asked when the group had settled in.

What the hell is the matter with that woman? Becca thought. *Doesn't she have any compassion for us? Doesn't she feel sorry for us? Some support we're getting here!*

"Ashley, would you like to start? It looks like you have a lot on your mind."

"What kind of question is that?" she asked as she pointed to the underscored jottings. "I would like to know," the ticking time bomb pronounced distinctly as she shuffled papers in and out of the bag to keep her angry hands busy.

"Are you having a problem with it?" Jacqueline asked.

"A problem? What do you know about rights? My father served in the war so we'd have rights. He risked his life for his new bride, my mother, who keeps searching for him. He gave her the right to live, damn it!"

When Ashley's words caught up to her reasoning powers, she halted and covered her mouth with her hand. "Oh my God," she whispered.

George broke the icy silence when he said, "You know, I got the hell scared out of me the other day when my father said he was ready. It was like he was planning his last maneuver. He was confident; he'd conquered his fears, and he was ready. And he'd done it himself. No one stepped in and did it their way. He had the privilege of using the natural right he'd fought for. I don't know why I was shocked."

"But my mother can't decide anything for herself," Marie timidly uttered. "I think I will have to end her life myself."

"Doesn't she have the right to live?" Jacqueline asked quietly.

"But that's no way to live!"

"Are you sure?"

"I imagine it's no way to live. How could it be?"

"It's a way of life. It may not be your way of life or mine, but it's a way."

"Well, I don't know, I just don't know anymore."

27

"Hi Ma, its Ashley."

"No, not Barbara. Ashley! But you know what, Ma? If you want to call me Barbara, it's OK... yes... it's really OK."

"Ma, do you want me to tell you a funny story that happened many years ago?"

Without any hesitation her mother said, "I sure do, Ashley."

"When can we go on the mountain again?"
"You like it up there, don't you?"
"Yes, I like to look out and see the whole world!"

⟶Chapter Three⟵

Picture Perfect

There sat the nephew, there stood the pastor, and there were her ashes—two earthly beings and one living elsewhere.

The "ashes person"—Noel Joy Larkin—was the only person who lived on her mountain. She'd liked it that way. Now she was downtown in a building, with company. But fear not Noel, you're soon to be released—returned to your mountain.

"Hurry it up, Pastor, I don't like air conditioned, downtown living," Noel voiced, but she was certainly not heard.

Peter thanked the pastor, gave him a donation, and carried Aunt Noel to the car.

Peter remembered the road, the curves, the trees, and the bridge. When he was a boy, it was there that his father would take him to see Aunt Noel. She was cool with her wild hair and her denim and flannel shirts and ratty shoes. She was nothing like his mother, who didn't come to visit Aunt Noel.

Peter gave her a quick glance as he maneuvered the car on top of the ridges and tried to stay out of the ruts.

"Your last ride up the hill, Auntie, even though I know you didn't take many trips off this mountain."

They passed her house on the right, the dirt driveway almost completely filled with grass, and the chicken coop. They passed the blackberry bushes along the road and the fence that kept in Old Babe and Dolly; he could see the pond that he once called a lake and the grove of Christmas trees where he always picked the one he wanted but for some reason never came to get it. His mother would have a tree delivered to their house; it didn't come from the mountain.

"We are almost at the top," Peter reassured Auntie.

The two left the modernism of the vehicular age as they stepped out "on top of the world." Peter could see where the three counties converged, just as Noel had pointed out many summers ago.

"Why would she leave this mountain?" Peter asked himself as he slowly rotated in full circle, not realizing that with Aunt Noel in his arms, he was letting her enjoy the view with him.

"Are you anxious to get out of these confines?" he whispered.

Peter couldn't say he actually saw the ashes sail with the wind and settle to the earth because his tears blurred the event; but the urn was empty, so he knew he had done what had been requested of him.

Peter sat on the mountaintop for a long time, not wanting to leave Noel alone on her first day.

He stroked the grass and tossed some pebbles at a log and let some stray tears water the earth.

Peter left the mountain to stay downtown for the night. Morning would be soon enough to enter Aunt Noel's domicile.

"Where do I start?" the young man wondered.

He walked from room to room noticing the same system: cabinets and filing cabinets. *What on earth has she been filing for the last ten years?* He hadn't noticed them when his dad brought him there as a boy.

There were cameras and more cameras! *When did she get so interested in cameras?* he thought, even though he knew she always had them pose for a picture before going home. Tripods? Camera cases? Lenses? Lots of books on photography. More equipment? More instructional books. Her own dark room? He did remember that room always being dark but never thought anything of it.

Peter opened the top drawer of a metal filing cabinet then the second drawer and the third. In the next room, Peter opened drawers to reveal more folders, more alphabetizing; it was the same in each room. Under each letter and in each folder there were photos. Peter leafed through the first folder, barely breathing. *How could this be?* One photograph was more beautiful than the last! *When did she take all of these? This represents years and years of work! Where were they taken? She never went on any vacations. She was always on this moun... this mountain! That's it!*

Peter returned to his room at the boarding house with as many boxes as he could carry.

"Who is that guy?"

"He's a nephew of the hermit lady."

"What do you think he's got in those boxes?"

"I don't know; I hope it's not dead critters."

Peter fell asleep looking through photographs.

The next day, the people watched as the car blazed up the mountain.

By the time he returned with another carload, three strangers were waiting for him in the foyer. They immediately helped with the boxes and went to Peter's room.

"What do you think is going on?"

"I have no idea."

"He's bringing something back from the old hermit's house."

"Maybe those men are from the Secret Service. Maybe she was making counterfeit money up on the hill!"

The next day, Peter's Jeep was followed by a covered pickup truck.

"Man oh man, there must be lots of it, whatever it is."

"You don't think she was making drugs up there, do you?"

"No, that's not a police vehicle."

"But it could be an undercover truck."

"I guess we'll never know; the nephew is checking out today."

It wasn't until six months later that Peter returned to Lone Moon Creek, but he didn't come alone. Five rooms were rented; the crew departed early in the morning and didn't return until dusk. That went on for three days.

"Do you think she murdered people and has their bodies buried up there?"

"She did something underhanded. Why else wouldn't she come downtown and mingle with us?"

"She didn't want us to know what she was up to."

Peter was given the daunting task of writing a short synopsis of each picture, at least those chosen by the producer.

Peter wished with all his heart that he had been more alert and interested in the days past when he and his dad and Aunt Noel walked the mountainside. She was a natural teacher, a natural environmentalist and during those walks, she probably gave more lessons than Peter received during a semester of school; but he was young and free to explore and to run ahead.

Peter stared at a photo of a nest completely tucked into a bush. *How did she capture the sun as it spotlighted just the baby birds? How did she know the time, maybe only seconds, when this occurrence would take place? Had she watched birds going in and out of their hiding place?* Aunt Noel could immediately identify baby birds and the type of bush they were in.

Peter sighed. How could he do justice to these photos? Maybe he could hire enough people to research each and every photograph to find the names of the ... "Wait a minute," he yelled aloud. "Aunt Noel was organized; she had reams of information in her file cabinets. Of course! She would have labeled everything!" Peter started studying her system; after four hours, he began doubting the validity of his college education, his master's degree.

It wasn't until he saw the speckled doe trying to catch raindrops with its tongue did he remember where he saw the synopsis. The numbers and letters matched! This was it—this was her system!

Peter raised his eyes when the sun flickered it's reflection upon a framed picture on the wall: Where There Is Goodness, There Is God—Because God Is Goodness.

Hmm, Peter thought. *Interesting.*

"Long time no see."

"Yes, hello, I'm back for a while."

"Going to take more things out of your aunt's house?"

"Actually, yes. I'm making good progress. But it's easier for me to take everything home and work on it there."

"Work on it?"

"Yes, it's a doozy! I'll be here for one more day. Good night."

"Yeah, he said what he's working on is a doozy!"

"I bet she found a stash of gold coins hidden years ago when the English or maybe the French trampled through these grounds."

"But they brought many boxes out of there."

"Maybe some were jewels and some were maps and some were gun powder!

"My God, she could have blown away the whole mountain! I don't think she had many brains the way she didn't come downtown to associate with us; she was probably embarrassed about her non- intelligence."

"Yeah, probably."

"You've got to get those cameras up there now," the director explained to his crew. "I was there with Peter last week— I've never seen anything like it!"

It was autumn, one of Noel Joy Larkin's favorite seasons; the other three favorites being winter, spring, and summer.

The downtown people watched as a van filled with cases and people left the boarding house and then left the valley. The crew assembled themselves and their equipment on the highest mound of Noel's land, but the cameras didn't roll. The cameras were as paralyzed as the humans. The only movement occurred in one-degree increments. That's how slowly the humans rotated to take in the breathtaking foliage of the world below.

"If I lived here, I would never leave either," one of the crew uttered.

It wasn't until the director drove in that the work began.

The documentary on Noel's photography and mountain was going to be a beauty.

"See it as Noel would see it, slow down. Think with your eyes. Look for the unique; she saw nothing in the ordinary. Look past, look into, look beyond," the orders bounded and rebounded around the mountain.

"All right, Peter, have you found Noel's notes on each photograph the staff has selected for the documentary?"

"There are just a few that I can't seem to find, but I'm on it. I'll go through everything again."

"OK, I'll call you in the winter when we come back for our seasonal change."

"You must be kidding! You guys will never make it up here in the wintertime."

"We'll get here even if we have to come in by helicopter."

"Keep a room for me; I won't see you until the wintertime, and oh yes, don't be surprised if you see a helicopter fly in."

"Did you hear that?"

"They're going to take something out by helicopter?

"Holy Moses, it must be something big!"

"She must have something important like, like maybe George Washington's desk."

"Maybe it's a trunk full of Indian relics or a china closet full of silver tea sets and dishes from the British."

"How about those Spaniards? Didn't they have a lot of gold and swords?"

When the time came, a helicopter wasn't necessary; the four-wheel-drive vehicles were capable of the challenge. Drivers with experience in winter rural travel were hired. The camera crew stepped out of their vehicles as if they were Eskimos; they were prepared. Surprisingly, within half an hour, they shed their jackets while they trudged through the brilliant snow. They found the perfect winter day, a Noel day, whereby walking in the wild was the culmination of what life was all about. She had captured that very concept with her camera, and now her protégés were setting the mountain to motion. The film would zoom in and out on the mountain while the announcer, the storyteller, would speak about the close up photographs. A book was also in the works and would be ready for sale when the documentary was aired.

"There it is!" Peter yelled. "There's my Christmas tree!" That was the year when Peter went home with his mountain tree.

One more season—spring! Newness, rebirth, hope, a poet's plethora of plethoras. Peter couldn't stop looking at the pictures of the newborn animals. *How could she have gotten this close? Trust! They trusted her! They knew her!*

There were pictures of plants awakening, plants being born, winter ice melting on the periphery; she knew how to capture spring. But how could she select an ordinary subject and portray it in a way that made the observer wonder why he or she had never seen it like that before?

On the last day of filming, the camera crew almost frolicked on the mountaintop. Their seriousness had lightened. Was it the spring air or was it just knowing that this was the last season of filming?

⟨❧⟩

"They're here again."

"I can't believe they're still coming around."

"Maybe we'd better take a little drive up that mountain and find out what's going on."

"You're right, this is our town; we should know what's happening."

A carload of downtowners slowly crept up the hillside.

"OK, this is far enough; we'll walk the rest of the way."

"What the hell?"

"Get down everybody; they've got guns."

36

"Run! Let's get out of here."

It wasn't long before three sheriff cars and two state police cars ascended Noel's mountain.

The policemen watched blue paint splatter onto someone's shirt and orange paint drip from someone's shoulder while green paint ran down the back of a stocky man's neck. They police watched grown men running through the woods and fields laughing and cavorting like school kids.

"All right, men, we're out of here, and the sirens never had to screech, much to the delight of the blue jays."

Peter and the crew returned to town.

"I'm sorry Peter, but you and your friends are not welcome here any longer."

"Do you mean because we're paint splattered and dirty? We were just having a little fun playing paintball."

"Well paintball or no paintball, we've had it with the likes of you guys; we don't know what you're up to. We just want you out of here."

"I'm sorry you feel that way. We'll leave right away," Peter said.

"There! We don't need the likes of them; maybe now we can get back to normal."

Things were pretty quiet around town until...

Sandra LeRoy went through town putting posters in every shop and on every bulletin board she could find.

"What does this mean? ' Tune in to Channel 8 on Friday, June 8 at 8 p.m. and watch *God's Mountain*.'"

"Beats me. I won't be watching it; that's my night to watch wrestling."

"You know, I've been seeing ads about that on the TV. I don't know much about it. It looked kinda nice though."

"My Lord, now it's in our local paper. What does it have to do with us?"

"Says here that <u>God's Mountain</u> is our mountain, you know, the old hermit's mountain."

"What!"

"Yeah, somebody must have been up there taking movie pictures."

"Do you suppose that was what those people who came with Peter were doing?"

"Could be."

The time came. Everyone in Lone Moon Creek was tuned in to channel 8. The music came up, the title rolled across the screen with the mountain behind it. "Photographs by Noel Joy Larkin" nearly jumped out of the screen to land with a punch in the chests of the inhabitants. "Special thanks to Peter Larkin" also brought about a jolt, especially to those at Bart's Boarding House.

For fifty minutes, the air didn't move in Lone Moon Creek. If the cat cried to come in, no one satisfied its demand. Anyone who had to be at work at nine o'clock was an hour late. The kids didn't have to go to bed at eight. No one thought about popcorn or chips.

The bass voice of the narrator made the women silently swoon and the men sit taller as they realized they were living in one of the most beautiful areas of the country, maybe even the world. Little kids would tilt their heads as they looked into burrows and nests and dens and hollow logs. Smiles would come across their faces when they saw what lived in the lair. Teenagers had expressions of shock when they realized the snowy utopia was right in their town, not in Aspen or Taos or that the wild-flowered woods and fields were "right here" and not in Augusta, Maine, or Lansing.

The production fluctuated between the close-ups of Noel's photos and the broader views of the four-seasons mountain. The "oohs" and "ahs" of the viewing audience were the only utterances necessary; they said it all. The autumn portrayal probably brought the most profuse responses.

The credits zipped by with no one able to focus on any of the names except the men at the boarding house; they had an idea who they were. The announcer gave information about the new book that was just released, while countless people jotted it on notepads next to their chairs.

"Hi, everybody!"

"Peter! You're back!"

"Yeah, I'll be living up on the mountain within the year."

"No kidding? That's great!"

"Do you think you'll come down and visit with us once in a while?"

"Sure."

Remember when I was on a team and I played baseball?"
"I sure do."
"Was I good?"
"You were terrific!"

ᥕ᷾Chapter Four᷾ᥕ

Worn Grass

J ohnnie swiped her foot back and forth in the worn grass, the grass that was now dirt, the dirt that was the pitcher's mound.

Benjamin J. Beckwith always wanted nine sons for a baseball team, and as far as he was concerned, that's what he got, even though the youngest and last child was a girl.

Baptized Josephine Mary, the little girl with the blond ringlets and the scores of pretty dresses with matching hair ribbons soon could be seen toddling behind her brothers out to their baseball diamond, the only one in their part of town. Mrs. Beckwith had long given up the idea of having beautiful flowers with garden benches and gliders and umbrellas in her backyard; she knew the love her husband had for baseball and his desire to someday have the best baseball team in town.

As the boys grew, and one by one was added to the team, Ben's Boys became "the team to watch." Weeknights had the team practicing on their backyard diamond, but Saturday afternoon brought the town teams to the back of the school for the *real* games.

For several years, Josephine Mary and her mother joined the moms group nestled comfortably in the shade far to the side of the playing field so as not to get hit by a foul ball. But as Mrs. Beckwith feared, one day Josephine Mary demanded that she be allowed to stand by her dad at the bench. Mrs. B. could see her husband grinning from ear to ear as the blond curls bounced under Johnnie's baseball cap when she ran, pounding her hand into the little baseball glove.

"Come on, Johnnie, dig!" the abandoned mom heard him say.

Now Mrs. B. sat in the stands with the other spectators. Occasionally she would look in the direction of the babies and toddlers and youngsters, but she enjoyed, too, finally getting to see her boys play a full game; she was surprised by how good they were!

"When's little Johnnie gunna be allowed to play?" Old Jeb Walker asked.

"Oh not for a long, long time, Mr. Walker; she's a girl, you know."

"Tain't no matter. I watch 'em over the fence at your place and she's gettin' good."

"She is?" Mrs. B. asked worriedly. She had no idea that her husband had her daughter involved with practice except for handing her brothers a bat or running off to get the foul balls. "What exactly have you seen her do?"

"Geez, all Friday, it was last week when Charlie there fumbled the ball and Johnnie scooped it up and flung it to first base. I 'bout laughed my head off when Leo caught it and got the Gipper out."

"The Gipper?" Who's that?"

"It's your husband!"

"Be quiet, old man, and watch the game," Jeb's wife poked him as she spoke.

41

"The Gip won't have to play once your little one gets on the team, right Jean?"

"Mmm," Jean sighed, "I suppose you're right."

"They're really good, Jean, you must be proud of them," a lady seated in back of Jean interjected.

"Oh I am. I just worry about Josephine Mary."

"Who?"

"Johnnie," she professed reluctantly.

Jean started looking through the window more and more as she did the supper dishes. Josephine Mary looked like she was in seventh heaven; she was always moving. Even when she was in the outfield, she didn't stand still; it was like she was hunched over marching in place. And always pounding that glove. Jean shook her head. She didn't know what was to become of her girl. Maybe she should just tell Ben that their daughter should be in the house more, learning what all girls learn, not sliding into second base and getting... "Josephine! Oh dear Lord!" Jean cried as she ran from the backdoor.

All the Beckwith boys were standing around their little sister by the time Jean got there. "Ow," Johnnie said with a laugh as she rubbed her head, "that'll be the last pop fly I'll ever miss."

"That's my girl," Ben exclaimed as he darted a quick look at his wife.

Jean couldn't help but hear the spectators conversing in the stands:

"Yeah, the little one is playing in today's game."

"Well, she's got to start somewhere."

"Start?" howled Jeb Walker. "You're gunna be surprised when you see that little spitfire play ball."

"Be quiet, old man, and watch the game," his wife commandeered.

Jean looked to the sky. *Dear God, keep my little girl safe,* she prayed. When her eyes returned to the field, every nerve in her body tightened. *Oh, why is that big boy pitching the ball so hard? Can't he see how little she is?*

"There's two strikes on her; she's probably nervous being up at bat for the first time," someone whispered from behind Jean. Jean held her breath.

"What did I tell you," Jeb screamed as he jumped to his feet. "Go, little spitfire, go," he continued to scream as he waved her on to second, even though she was watching the Gipper, who gave her the same signal. Jean was on her feet along with everyone else as Johnnie slid into second and was safe! All the Beckwith brothers were off the bench jumping and hooting for their sister.

Oh no, why does he have her there at shortstop? She could get creamed if a fastball comes at her!

"Double play! Double play!" Old Jeb Walker hollered as he rose from his seat, not knowing yet if it was to be. Johnnie caught "the bullet," threw it dead on to the first baseman, who threw it to second for Jeb's prediction of a double play.

"Eeeeeeeeeeeeee!" Jean exclaimed as she peered out from her hands mask.

The pitcher, catcher, first baseman, and second baseman brothers gave Johnnie a shout of "Good job."

Jean could hear her husband directing, "Get your heads back in the game."

Johnnie got walked to first. "Good eye, good eye, spitfire."

Jason had a single, Winston got on by an error. Charlie popped out, Ed popped out, the ball got away from the catcher and Johnnie took off. This time it was old Jed who moaned, "Oh no."

Instantaneously, every other person was uttering the same: "Oh no." Jean took it as a bad, bad sign. Her eyes grew big as baseballs as she watched her little Josephine careening toward home plate while the catcher threw the ball to the boy who ran to cover the plate, the ump was crouched over as he eyeballed the play.

The settling dust made more noise than anyone on or off the field. The moms looked up from their shade haven, noticing that all was quiet. Only after the ball had been fumbled again and the umpire yelled, "Safe," did the brothers and the Gipper breathe. Jean collapsed onto the bleacher.

They really did become the team to watch. Attendance increased as the family's reputation spread far and wide. A few novice entrepreneurs capitalized on the situation and did well with their hot dogs and drinks. But, as with everything, things changed. The oldest boys were on the school varsity team, the next oldest on the JV team, and it was just Larry, Lance, Mark, and Johnnie practicing on the yard that wasn't as grass worn as it had once been. Jean thought that maybe the back part of the "outfield" could now be developed into the rose garden that she always wanted. And yes, with a white wrought iron table and chairs.

"But, dear, we're still going to have all the boys here for the summer, and we'll need to practice for the town team games; a rose garden would not be safe. You know them; they can hit the ball a country mile!" Ben tried to be jovial as he faced his disappointed wife. "Things are going to change, however, when Charlie goes off to college, then the twins, who'll go the next year; we're going to be losing them fast." This time it was Jean who saw the disappointed look on her husband's face.

After two years, the Gipper joined up with another dad and his kids, but the team didn't sparkle and dazzle as his original team had. The Beckwith's couldn't predict the moves and thoughts of the other players like they had with their brothers. It was probably more of a "normal" team, but not a spectacular one. Then Johnnie was on the girls' varsity team at school, entirely skipping the junior varsity. When summer came, she was selected to attend a softball camp a 150 miles away.

Jean and Ben spent most of their time going from game to game to game. Three of their children went to college on baseball scholarships, including Johnnie. They were traveling farther and farther to see the games.

"Wouldn't it be nice sometime to stay home and work on our backyard? The grass is coming in nicely to cover the dirt," Jean said

"Don't worry, someday we'll have lots of time for that," Ben answered.

Johnnie was called up to the next higher league. "Come on, dear, we have to go to her first game!"

"OK, get the airline tickets."

"I'm glad we came," Jean whispered to Ben as they sat in the huge stadium. "What a feeling this is to be here because of Josephine Mary!"

"Yes," he nodded, "because of Josephine Mary, and thank you for letting me have little Josephine Mary on my team."

"It really was a team, wasn't it?"

"It sure was," Ben concurred just as the organ music came on loud and clear through the speakers and the visiting team was announced.

"First base—Josephine Mary Beckwith."

Jean gasped, "She's using her real name!"

Ben responded nonchalantly. "Of course, she's a girl." They both laughed.

Johnnie's talent was evident. Her parents didn't mind hearing the murmurings around the crowd of nothing but praise for her. Jean came to the realization that flower gardens, lawn umbrellas, and white wrought iron furniture didn't matter when she had a devoted husband who raised a team of Beckwiths.

The home team was fighting hard to break the tie. The throw to first was not on target, and Johnnie had to step off to catch the ball but only had to take two steps to be back on and have the out. What happened?

45

The home team girl got up and dusted off her pants, but Johnnie lay on the ground, not moving.

"Ben!"

"Give her a minute, she'll be all right."

Jean remembered the same silence that took over the game when Johnnie stole home as a little girl. And she was all right, then. *Come on, Johnnie, get up.*

"Ben?"

"She'll be all right. The coach is going out to check her." The coach signaled to his manager.

"Why isn't she getting up?" Jean persisted.

"Sometimes it's better to keep someone still for a while." Ben controlled his quivering voice.

"Come on, play ball!" someone yelled from the top deck. Ben turned so quickly that Jean grabbed his arm for fear there was going to be an altercation.

A man to their left pointed and yelled, "The ambulance is coming!"

"Oh dear God," Jean cried as Ben encircled her shoulders with his muscular baseball arm.

"No! I don't want to sit outside, just take me to my room," Josephine answered with a scowl.

Jean and Ben sat at the kitchen table staring at each other. It was six months after the last ball game and there they were with the "player of the year" in a wheelchair, never to walk again.

"No, I just want to watch another baseball game, nothing else. Please leave me in peace."

Day after day, Johnnie sat in front of the TV watching baseball. Her brothers and their wives and kids would stop by, but even they couldn't lure her out of her doldrums.

"Damn, damn, damn," Jean could hear her daughter screaming.

"What's the matter, honey?"

"There's not one baseball game on until tonight," she yelled as she flung the remote.

"That does it. You're going outside, and we're going to play ball."

"*We* are going to play ball?" Johnnie reiterated.

"Yes, we are, and you're going to like it," Jean said with such determination and anger that Johnnie never said a word in rebuttal.

⬲

"All right, now you catch this ball."

The daughter had never seen her mother throw a ball, and now she knew why. The ball sailed downward to Johnnie's feet.

"Ma, you throw like a girl," Johnnie laughed.

"Well, I'm mad," her mother retorted as she bent over to retrieve the ball and then walked backward to get into position. Again she threw the ball to the ground with even more of a contorted face and more awkward body movements. So much so that Johnnie couldn't contain herself. She sat in her wheelchair and roared with laughter. Suddenly Jean realized that it was the first time she'd heard her daughter laugh in over six months. She twisted her baseball cap so that the brim was to the side and imitated an exaggerated wind up with her tongue showing out the side of her mouth while Johnnie almost went hysterical with laughter.

"Ma, stop, stop, please," she howled. "You are so funny!"

"OK, you throw to me and I'll catch it."

Johnnie tossed the ball at her mother.

"Whoa! I'm not one of your big shot players, you know," Jean called as she ducked then ran back for the ball.

"Sorry, Ma. I'll throw it easier this time."

"Can I play?"

The two women looked to the fence to see Old Jeb Walker.

Jean could see her daughter tense up, but she jumped right in with. "Sure, if you think you can keep up with me," she said while she tossed the ball surprisingly straight up and then caught it on its return.

"Wow! Mom! I can't believe you did that!"

⟨⦚⟩

"Why do I see a ball going back and forth out there?" Ben asked as he sat at the table having a cup of coffee.

"It's one of your children with Old Jeb," Jean said.

"Oh, who's here?"

"Go look out the window."

Jean gave him the background story as he laughed. "I wish I had been here to see that!"

"OK, Spitfire, let's add a little speed to that ball; you're throwin' like an old lady."

"I'm rusty, you know," Johnnie said.

"You're rusty all right. Your mother could throw harder than you," Jeb Walker said.

"Oh yeah, watch this."

"That's it. Now you're gettin' your ole punch back. How 'bout battin' a little?"

"Are you crazy? I can't bat sitting in this contraption."

48

"Sure you can. Give it a try."

Time after time, Johnnie missed the ball. "Forget it," she screamed. "I can't do it."

"Yes you can. I have a little runt of a grandson who's in one of those chairs and he can hit the ball. What's the matter with you?"

"Here's what the matter is with me," she yelled as she vehemently flung the bat at Jeb to make him hit the dirt for safety.

Up popped his head like a woodchuck. "Dang, somebody's got a temper."

"Yeah, me, and don't come back here again."

"I'll see you tomorrow," Old Jeb hailed as he sauntered off across the not-so-worn grass.

"No way. I'm not going out there with him."

"Josephine, he's just trying to be nice. Be kind to him—he's an old man."

"Forget it." Josephine punctuated her statement by crossing her arms.

"OK never mind. I'll go out there myself and play ball with Old Jeb. I'm just as good as you are anyway."

"Fine! Have a great time!"

"Oh no," Jean muttered to herself. "What have I gotten myself into? Hi, Jeb, I guess it's you and me today."

"That's OK, ma'am. You're never too young or too old to play ball."

Johnnie peered between the slats of the blinds for as long as she could stand it. "Oh my God, this is pathetic," she mumbled as she rolled her "buggy" out and down the ramp. "Never mind, Ma, I'll do it."

"Thank God," Johnnie heard her mother say as she sailed a ball into Jeb's glove that almost knocked him backward.

"That a girl," he said and howled with laughter.

For the rest of the week, Johnnie and Jeb could be seen "doing the best they could do under the circumstances."

"See you over the weekend?" Jeb asked.

"Some of my family is coming."

"Great! Get those brothers out here with ya and play some ball!"

"No way. I don't want them to see me fumbling around like a kid," Johnnie said.

"They watched you once as a kid, did they ever make fun of you?"

"Well, no, but this is different."

"See ya Monday?"

"No, sorry, I've got to go see that worthless shrink of mine."

"Tuesday?"

"Yes, Tuesday."

∽

"So, how was the shrink?"

"The shrinketh did stinketh," Johnnie proclaimed as she threw the ball into Jeb's glove.

"Most of them do," Jeb said with a laugh as he threw a little harder. "They think they know you, but they don't; they don't know you until you tell them about yourself, and then they know you."

"Yeah, and then they try to fix you. You know what? I feel like bunting the ball."

"There! I bet your shrink didn't know that about you, did he?"

"No, he didn't." Johnnie laughed as she popped a good one.

"Can I bring my grandson over tomorrow?" Jeb asked.

"You mean the one in the wheelchair?"

"Yeah."

"I don't know, Jeb. I'm such a beginner myself," Johnnie answered slowly.

"But you've been there; you were on the top. You know the feeling."

"And now I'm on the bottom!"

Jeb watched the tears form. "Johnnie, you have so much to give to the kids. Help them get some success."

"Let me think about it."

"Sure."

The next day, Jean and Ben watched their daughter peer out the window, wheel herself into her bedroom, wheel herself out, peer out the window again, go back into her room, and come out once more.

"Are you thinking?"

"Yes, I'm thinking."

After fifteen minutes, Johnnie saw the old man and his grandson leaving. "Oh, for Lord's sake, I can't take this!" she moaned. She hollered out the backdoor. "Wait!"

That moment, that word, that directive changed her life. Jean and Ben clasped hands in thanksgiving; Old Jeb sighed a sigh of thankfulness, and Billy grinned from ear to ear.

Jean never got her backyard gardens with the white stone pathways or the trellises or the outdoor furniture, but she didn't care. She got her daughter back. The highly respected teacher of handicapped children, children who came from all around the country. And she got to see her husband playing ball again as Johnnie's assistant. Soon her Beckwith boys were helping with the students whenever they came home to visit. And if that wasn't enough, she got to wave at Old Jeb peering over the fence, not even noticing her worn grass.

"REMEMBER WHEN YOU TOLD ME THAT SISTER AGATHA HAD BEEN A FOSTER KID?"

"YES."

"AND YOU TOLD ME I WASN'T A FOSTER KID?"

"YES."

"CAN WE GO OVER TO JACQUI'S HOUSE AND VISIT WITH THEM? I LIKE THOSE KIDS."

"I SUPPOSE SO."

"CAN I WEAR MY FOSTER GRANT SUNGLASSES? GRANDMA, DON'T YOU GET THE JOKE?"

Chapter Five

THE COVER UP

"Let me tell you one more time before Mrs. Calderon gets here. Be a good girl and be respectful; use your manners. Be helpful... Oh, here she is. I love you."

McKenna stood at the door with her worn, brown satchel and clothes to match—old and tired. Inside, her heart coordinated perfectly: it was dismal and far too aged to be in the body of a young girl.

"Are you ready, McKenna?" The caseworker asked.

The girl didn't speak, only nodded.

"You'll get her back if you can get yourself straightened out and stick to it," Mrs. Calderon snarled at Meredith for the sake of the gawking neighbors.

The mother looked at her daughter. "I will, baby, I will." Meredith cried theatrically and McKenna knew that was her cue to put on "the best performance of her life" also.

"I love you, Mommy. I love you Mommy," she cried as Mrs. Calderon nudged her into the car.

Meredith waved from the window, wiping her tears just long enough to see the car drive away from the house.

She immediately pulled the ratty coverlets off of the new furniture and quickly dispersed the carefully selected accessories around the room. The mirrors and paintings were hung, and McKenna's picture was lovingly placed on the new side table. That afternoon, Meredith planned to purchase a fresh floral arrangement for the coffee table as her reward for getting her daughter her next "job."

"Ah, yes," she said as she exhaled then sat on the beautiful couch surveying the room. But she knew her work wasn't over. Each room had to be resurrected, and she excitedly jumped up to get it accomplished. Never knowing how much of the house a child services person was going to inspect, Meredith made sure it looked like a poor woman's hovel when one of them was to appear. One time, a caseworker walked clear upstairs to look into the bedrooms.

The old tattered quilts came off the beds as she sailed the new satin ones clear across in one flutter. Out of the closets came the lamps and the pillow shams and the landscape artwork for the walls.

"Much better, much better," she chirped as she hung the pretty draperies on the rods.

The kitchen was her dilemma. How could she possibly modernize it? Mrs. Calderon always looked into the kitchen, as did the others; they would immediately notice a new range or a big, beautiful refrigerator. A dishwasher would really set one of them on their heels. Even replacing the old, chipped, yellowed sink would cause one to wonder where the extra money was coming from.

Luckily, the bathrooms were so-so. They had been somewhat modernized when Meredith and McKenna moved in.

"Do good out there, baby. Mama needs you," Meredith sang as she ran upstairs to change out of her secondhand clothes. She was going shopping.

"Come in, dear. I'm so glad you're here. It's McKenna, right?"

"Yes, Mrs. Derby."

"Oh, call me Jacqui or Mama Jacqui."

"Yes, ma'am."

"Well, I'm going to be running along," Mrs. Calderon announced. "I'll check in with you both after two weeks. Give me a call if you need to."

McKenna stood in the entranceway surveying her new "home away from home."

"Come, sweetheart, I'll show you your room. You won't mind having two roommates, will you?"

"No, ma'am."

"Come now, Jacqui or Mama Jacqui," she reminded the newcomer.

"Oh, sorry, Jacqui."

"There you go. Here's your room."

McKenna saw the three single beds, the three dressers, and the one closet.

Pretty plain, but clean, she thought.

"There are four more bedrooms on this floor; some are filled and others will be soon."

"You must take in a lot of children," McKenna said sweetly.

"My husband and I love doing it. Now, are you going to be needing any new clothes or personal products?"

McKenna opened her satchel. "This is all I have, Jacqui."

"That's OK, don't you worry. We can go out right now and purchase what you need. We'll be back before the kids get home from school."

"Oh, that's very nice of you, Mama Jacqui." McKenna remembered her mother's words: be polite and respectful.

McKenna quickly learned the names and habits of all twelve people living in the Derby household. It was the perfect zoo! McKenna laughed to herself as she lay in her humble little bed. The place was going to be like taking candy from a baby. *There is so much stuff around here; it'll take months before they know anything is missing!*

Of all the children, the real Derby's and the foster Derby's, McKenna was the most helpful. She knew where everything went and often put things away for the others; she told them that she enjoyed doing it.

When Mrs. Calderon made her two-week visit, Mrs. Derby couldn't give enough praise concerning McKenna.

"I'm glad to hear that, Jacqui; that's the kind of report we like to get."

"Keep up the good work, McKenna," Mrs. Calderon whispered to her as she left.

◯◝◝◞◝

"How's my baby?" Meredith asked as she sat across from Mrs. Calderon in the busy train station.

"She's fine, she's fine. You don't have to worry about her; you've brought her up as a pro."

"Yes, I have, haven't I," Meredith swooned as she checked her makeup in her *acquired* gold compact.

Meredith gave it two more weeks before she checked her post office box in the train station. The key seemed to glow with excitement as Meredith let out a "whoop" of exhilaration when she saw the envelope. She stuffed it inside her coat and hurried home.

"OK, baby, show Mommy what you've got for her!" Meredith sang as she kissed the envelope.

"Ooo," she fawned as she held the locket up to the light. "Nice, very nice." She knew what a real gold chain looked like— this was one of them. She looked at the gold filigree around the heart locket; she saw the tiny diamonds placed systematically around the heart. She opened the locket and immediately took out two pictures, one of a man and one of a woman. She threw them into her wastepaper basket.

"Anything else?" she asked as she spread open the envelope.

"Ah, baby girl, you never fail to amaze me!" she squealed as she pulled out ones, fives, and tens. A quick count yielded $49. She knew the difficulty of finding money laying around a house filled with foster kids—there was usually no money. This must have come from Mr. Derby's dresser or from the pants pockets in the laundry room. She had taught McKenna to always volunteer to do the laundry. Maybe Mrs. Derby, too, throws money in the bottom of her purse. McKenna loves to straighten closets, especially closets that hold purses.

~

"Hello, it's Meredith. Are you going to your sister's this weekend? Good. I have something for you to take to the jewelry shop. I'll meet you in the park. See you in one hour. Yes, Mrs. Calderon, you'll get your twenty percent."

"I can't imagine what has happened to your locket, Daisy. Please don't cry, Daisy. We'll find it. OK everyone, we're on a search. Everyone look for Daisy's locket. It has to be here somewhere," Mama Jacqui announced.

"Where did you last see it, Daisy?" McKenna asked as she put her arm around the crying girl's shoulder.

"I always keep it wrapped in a handkerchief in the back of my second drawer," sobbed the girl.

"This drawer?"

"Yes."

"But, Daisy, this is the third drawer. Are you confused?"

"Well, I meant third drawer. My mother and father's pictures were in that locket, and the locket once belonged to my grandmother. I have to find it," she wailed as she started tearing everything out of the dresser drawers.

"We'll search the house. Don't you worry," McKenna said with all honesty.

The search was perfect for McKenna; she saw all sorts of things tucked away in little hiding places.

"Thank you for being so nice to Daisy during this very difficult time for her. You are such a dear person," Mama Jacqui whispered to McKenna with all earnestness.

McKenna half smiled.

"Mrs. Calderon called today, McKenna. She said next weekend you'll be able to go home for a visitation. Isn't that great? Your mother must be feeling better."

They thought they knew what "feeling better" meant.

"Oh! That is good news, Mr. Derby."

McKenna knew she'd better step up the program. She knew better than to go home empty handed.

Meredith ran out onto the porch when she saw the car stop. "McKenna! Oh, I'm so happy to see you! Thank you for bringing her over, Jacqui. Yes, seven o'clock will be fine. She'll be ready. Bye."

"Wow! When did you get the new chair?" McKenna asked.

"Sit in it! It goes back!"

"Nice!"

"So, how are things going at the Derby's?"

"Oh, you know, all those kids in one house—it's a zoo."

"Yeah, I can just imagine. So what did you bring me? Oh, by the way, I like your new outfit," Meredith said.

"Yeah, she bought me all sorts of stuff."

"See, I brought you up right. You be nice to people and they will be nice to you."

McKenna reached into her designer tote and handed a bag to her mother.

Meredith began wriggling, jiggling, and giggling like a child at Christmas. McKenna sat back in the recliner and silently watched her mother. Maybe her mother was still a child. Maybe she never had a childhood.

"Glorious girl! Look at this!"

"I know, Ma, I brought it here."

"Oh yeah," Meredith said with a laugh as she tried the ring on each finger." Too bad it's so big, but I can wear it on my thumb! Wait, a minute." Her exuberance suddenly ceased. "Taking a diamond ring? Is that smart? Who wouldn't miss a diamond ring?" She sounded panicked.

"Mama Jacqui, that's who. She has a whole pot of play jewelry for the kids and guess what? That's where I spotted it!"

"What?"

"Yeah, apparently she didn't even know this was a real diamond!"

"The kids were playing with it?"

"Yes! But I could tell immediately."

"You have that *eye* for fine jewelry, like I do!" Meredith proclaimed proudly. "We'll get a bundle for this," she murmured as she held it up to see the sparkles fly. "Anything else?"

"Some cards."

"What's this junk?"

"Do you know how valuable those baseball cards are?" McKenna seemed insulted that her mother would think she would bring home junk.

"I guess I don't," she answered with uncustomary meekness.

"I sat with Mr. Derby and Wilson every time they went through Wilson's card collection, and I listened to the evaluations."

"Wow, you are really impressing me."

"Thanks."

"But, McKenna, that Wilson boy will definitely notice that some of his cards are missing."

"One evening he asked me to help pack them to be shipped home to his real dad."

"And?"

"I helped him."

"Well, well, well. I have never dealt in baseball cards before!"

"And... I want to come home soon, so tell Calderon that you're better."

"Why?" Meredith asked.

"I'm getting bored over there. I wouldn't say there is much more of anything valuable in the house, plus there is a girl at school who is really bugging me."

"OK. I see that I have some wheeling and dealing to do."

"Oh, I'm so sad that you're leaving, but I'm happy for you, sweetheart. You want to be with your mother, don't you?"

"Yes, but you'll always be Mama Jacqui to me." *There, I was respectful right up to my last words.*

"I'll be crying for days, McKenna."

Mrs. Calderon pulled away as the whole crew stood on the sidewalk waving and crying.

McKenna stared at the fleeting landscape wondering why she felt sad.

"OK, here you are. Give me a call when you're ready to go to your next gig."

"Welcome home! Why so gloomy?" Meredith asked.

"How'd the baseball cards pan out?"

"We made a killing! Thanks to you!"

"Yeah, aren't I just great," McKenna uttered as she ran upstairs.

"Feeling better?"

"I'm OK."

"You're going to be A-OK when you hear this. We are taking off for the islands tomorrow!"

"Our islands?"

"Yes! You and I definitely need a break. I have booked everything; pack your bags."

"Wow, those baseball cards must have been golden!" McKenna said with only one little thought of Wilson. *Too bad you missed out, Wilson. But I didn't!*

The young girl marveled at how her mother could work the crowd; she was like a sly fox. With her allure and beauty, she could nuzzle up to people and pick their pockets while they felt honored to have such a charmer even give them the time of day. Of course, she never gave them "the time of day," but rather tantalizing giggles and rolling, seductive made-up eyes and lovely, soft touches from her manicured fingertips.

Because of this *art*, they enjoyed everything that the islands had to offer. McKenna realized that she did need to unwind. After all, living in with strangers and securing their trust while stealing from them was hard work. Her mother knew.

Her mother also knew when it was time to move on; people in one location can't be fooled forever.

Mrs. Calderon received the call. "Find a foster home for McKenna."

McKenna didn't balk, she knew the routine. Her mother could only "work" for a short duration, then it was her turn.

"Find her a place where they aren't all dirt poor," directed the mother.

Within two weeks, McKenna was on the doorstep of the Abernathy's.

"Mmm, nice house," she whispered to Mrs. Calderon.

"I thought you would like it," the collator said with a smile.

The door was opened by a fashion model. "Hello, McKenna, I'm so pleased to meet you," Janine said sincerely as she extended her hand drenched in rings and bracelets.

McKenna quickly surveyed the gold before she lifted her eyes and graciously thanked Mrs. Abernathy for her cordiality. Again, the waif appeared in old, worn clothes with a small satchel.

"Let me show you the house, dear. Good-bye, Mrs. Calderon."

"Wow," the foster child murmured as she looked from top to bottom, knowing it paled in comparison to what she'd experienced in the islands. "I've never seen anything like this before," she fibbed.

"Come, sweetie. You're going to love your room."

"Am I going to be in here all by myself?"

"For a few days. There will be others coming shortly. Now, relax and unpack. Mr. Abernathy will be home from work soon and then we'll eat. Ta-ta."

~

"Welcome to our home, McKenna."

"Thank you, Mr. Abernathy."

"You are here just until your mother feels better? Is that correct?"

"Yes, sir."

"There will be some housemates here in a few days, right Janine?"

"Yes, we have already talked about that. Isn't it exciting, McKenna?"

"Oh yes," she answered, hoping they didn't notice her look past their faces to the buffet, which was laden with silver serving pieces.

"Here, sweetie. Have another pork chop."

"No thank you, Mrs. Abernathy," she answered politely as the sparkle from her host's earrings almost caused her fork to fall from her hand.

"Please call me Janine. Honey, why don't you show McKenna some of our collections while I clear the table?"

"I can do that for you, Janine," McKenna offered.

"Oh no, no. Not on your first night anyway," she said with a laugh.

"Come quickly, before she changes her mind," Mr. Abernathy exclaimed. "Let's start over here with our marble collection. I'll show you which ones are very, very valuable."

"Marbles have value?" she questioned, legitimately surprised.

"I should say so! Hold some of these up to the light. Aren't they exquisite?"

"Which ones are the most valuable? Wow, pretty!" Her photographic memory clicked.

"Let's go into the family room. I know you won't be interested in my baseball cards, but you might like to see our collection of glass sailboats."

"Baseball cards? No, I don't know a thing about them but I want to learn," she said naively.

"Well, this one I guard with my life," he grinned as he held it to his chest. Click again—saved to her memory.

"Having fun?" Janine asked as she glided into the room." Oh, boring old baseball cards! McKenna, wouldn't you rather look through my antique jewelry box?"

"I guess I would!"

Later, McKenna lay in her foster bed letting her mind bounce from one collection to the next. She could have been overwhelmed, if she was inclined to be that way.

Over the next few days, McKenna realized that the house was a treasure trove! To have precious things exposed as they were was a mystery to her. Her accessibility was unfettered. There would be no need for creeping and crawling through closets and blackened corners. What was this? Trust? They should know better; nobody can be trusted. McKenna had heard her mother say that a thousand times, so it must be true.

Janine and Scott were thrilled to have her proceed from one collection to the next, carefully handling each item, carefully returning each novelty just as she'd found it. She seemed to have a special affinity for the colored glass sailboats, the antique buttons, the diamond-studded tie tacks, and the coins dating back to the 1700s.

Both foster parents were glad to answer any questions she had. McKenna learned about the most valuable pieces and calculated which piece she would abscond with first.

It was two in the morning when McKenna awoke to voices downstairs. She put on her robe and tiptoed to the stairs. She quickly stifled her gasp as she looked down to see Daisy and a caseworker at the door. She tried to duck back but it too late.

"McKenna, McKenna," Daisy screamed as she ran to her. "I'm so glad to see you," she continued.

Most of McKenna's fears dissipated with that warm greeting, and she rushed to Daisy.

They both said, "What are you doing here?" at the same time.

"You first," Daisy interjected.

"My mother had a relapse, so I have to stay away while she gets better," McKenna fibbed. "And you?"

"When I went home for a visit, my mother asked about the necklace."

McKenna gulped.

"And I had to tell her it had been stolen. She beat me pretty bad, but I promised I would find who took it and get it back."

"And did you?"

"No, but I am sure it was DiDi."

"I remember DiDi."

"Yeah, so she caught me going through her stuff last night and called the police. Jacqui thought it would be best if I moved to a different house and away from DiDi. I'm so glad I'm here with you, McKenna."

"Um, me too, Daisy," she muttered sheepishly as they hugged again.

"Oh, Scott, look at our two nice girls," Janine cooed as she smiled at her husband.

"Hello, Mrs. Calderon, come in. Is there something I can do for you?" Janine asked.

"Just checking on McKenna. Could I speak with her?"

"Sure."

"Do you have any mail or packages for your mother? You know she loves hearing from you."

"Sorry, I've been very busy. I'll try to get something together soon," McKenna said.

What's the matter with me? Is it because Daisy is here? Is it because Janine and Scott are so trusting? I don't like this 'trusting' business, McKenna concluded as she tried to sleep.

"Psst, McKenna, are you asleep?"

"No, what's the matter?"

"I want to ask you something," Daisy whispered.

"What?"

"Would you go with me to the Derby's? You can visit with them while I sneak into DiDi's room and look for the necklace."

McKenna didn't respond.

"McKenna? Did you hear me?"

"I did hear you. I was thinking."

"And?"

"We'll talk about it tomorrow."

How can she tell Daisy that it will be futile to search any longer? What can she tell her?

"Good morning, ladies. Did you have a good sleep?"

"Yes," they both lied.

"Your breakfast is ready, and I'll be back in an hour," Janine said.

"Daisy, what if you gave your mother a bunch of money instead of the necklace? Would she let you off the hook?"

"Mm." Daisy thought about the question as she snapped off a piece of bacon. "She'd still be mad, but money does work wonders on my mother."

"Strange you should say that! Same with my mother."

"But that is a hopeless case. I'd be luckier finding the necklace than being able to come up with money."

"What if I gave you the money? Would that do?" McKenna asked.

"Where would you get money?"

"Never mind about me. I have my ways."

Ah, now I'm back to normal! I'll swipe something tonight and give orders to Mrs. Calderon that I'm working solo—she is to give me the money, not my mother.

McKenna walked from the silver tea service to the sailboats to the tie tacks to the marbles. There! Her decision!

She wrapped the marble in tissues.

"McKenna!" Scott's voice shot through the room.

"Oh, sorry, Scott. I hope I didn't wake you. I had to come downstairs to get tissues," she said as she held them to her nose and dabbed a few times.

"You're not coming down with a cold are you?"

"I hope not. Good night."

"Good night."

McKenna's hands shook as she hid the marble in her closet.

"Guess who I saw in school today? It was Wilson."

"Who's Wilson?"

"Remember that boy who lived in our last house with the Derby's? The boy with the baseball cards."

McKenna's hands froze over top of her keyboard.

"Don't you remember Wilson?"

"Um, I'm not sure."

"He remembers you."

"What do you mean?" McKenna asked, deliberately not making eye contact with Daisy.

"He said you were nice. I told him you and I were together in this house. He said to say hi."

"Say hi right back."

"Poor kid, I feel sorry for him."

"Why?"

"When I asked him why he was using crutches, he said his father went ballistic when he discovered some of his best baseball cards were missing. His father is in jail now."

"Oh my God."

"Sounds like you feel sorry, too," Daisy said.

"McKenna, Mrs. Calderon is here to see you. We'll go into the other room so you can visit."

"Your mother is furious with you!" the caseworker whispered with eyes flashing.

"I can't help it. I have to wait for an opportunity," McKenna said.

"Well, you better get yourself an opportunity."

"OK, I've got something, but you are to give the money to me, not her."

"You must be joking!" Mrs. Calderon.

"No, I'm serious. I have to have the money."

"You have to have the money? Well, in that case, you'll pay me twenty-five percent commission or no deal."

"OK, OK. Meet me in front of the school tomorrow at three, and I'll give you what I have."

"How was your visit, dear? How is your mother; is she feeling better?"

"She's not that good."

McKenna's thoughts raced from the marble to the twenty-five percent to her mother to Daisy to Wilson. Oh, poor Wilson. She could never repay him, and he took a beating because of her. And Daisy would never get her grandmother's necklace back, and she also became a punching bag because of McKenna.

I can at least help Daisy.

She got out of bed to get the marble; she wanted to hold it in her hand for the duration of the night.

The marble. Where was it? Where was it?

She bolted downstairs and ran directly to the marble collection. There it was in its special wooden holder!

"Are you surprised to see it there?" Scott asked.

McKenna swung around to face her future.

Janine stepped into the light. "It's OK, McKenna, you can tell us."

I can tell you? I can tell you that I am a thief? I can tell you how my mother has trained me to steal? I can tell you how we can abscond with people's belongings without blinking an eyelash?

The young girl whose body encapsulated a heart that had been tortured with guilt until it became hardened and encrusted enough to allow her to do whatever her mother asked suddenly felt something begin to weep inside of her. She stood staring like a statue, but she felt something pouring out of her heart; she felt something gushing in. Her outer composure would not break; from childhood she had learned how to do this. It wasn't until Janine encircled her with her compassionate arms did McKenna release the flood. Could three hours of crying eradicate her lifetime of wrongdoings?

Scott waited patiently for the final sigh. Both Janine and McKenna leaned back against the couch after what felt like a grueling day of hard labor.

"McKenna, this may be a surprise, but we already knew most of what you told us," Scott said.

Again appeared the statue with the stare.

"What are you a cop?" McKenna asked.

"I'm an investigator and Mrs. Calderon has been under investigation for quite some time now. I have an idea that the marble was going to go to her?"

"Yes, but the money was going to come to me so I could pay Daisy back for the necklace. I felt bad that she got into so much trouble with her mother." Again McKenna cried into the arms of Janine. "And... and poor Wilson. He's... he's... he's on crutches because of me." McKenna sobbed uncontrollably.

"You know what's so good about all this, sweetheart?" Janine asked as she stroked McKenna's hair.

"Good? What could be good?" she managed to ask in a little, tiny voice.

"You still have feelings. I'm hearing sorrow and compassion and empathy. Those are good things."

"They are?"

"Oh yes, you never want to lose those."

"Wait!" McKenna jumped up from the couch.

"My mother isn't going to be in trouble, is she?"

Janine and McKenna looked at Scott.

"Well," he started slowly, "the judge will have to decide that. But you know what, McKenna? You will always be welcome here until your mother *gets better.*"

"Yeah," she said with one remaining sob coming to the surface.

"Here," he said as he handed her the marble. "I want you to meet Mrs. Calderon as you had planned. When we see you make the handoff, we're going in. Can you handle that?"

McKenna thought about it and said, "I don't think you can make anything stick until she hands me the money."

"Wow," Janine interjected as she looked at the girl, "you are good."

"You're right, I'll just video the encounter, and we'll wait until she gets back to you."

"What's everybody doing up so early in the morning?" Daisy chirped as she looked over the stair rail.

"Just watching the sun come up," Scott replied.

The next day McKenna waited for Mrs. Calderon in front of the school. She handed her a small cardboard box. "Here it is."

"Good! It's about time you got some kind of action going." Mrs. Calderon seemed to be almost giddy. "And remember, I get twenty-five percent of whatever I can get out of it. Oh, by the way, your mother is furious that you haven't sent her anything. I'll let you know when the transaction has been finalized."

As she walked away, McKenna looked across the street to see Scott giving her the thumbs-up sign. She turned back and she was suddenly grabbed and yanked by the arm. "Mom! What are you doing here?"

"What have you been doing all this time at the Abernathy's, and why was Calderon talking to you?"

"I've been the only kid in the house, and they watch me like a hawk," she said, improvising. "And Mrs. Calderon wanted to tell me that you were furious with me and that I better get moving."

"Well, OK, but hurry up. Bye for now."

"Psst, Daisy, are you asleep?"

"No. Are you?"

McKenna laughed.

"Have you ever done anything wrong, Daisy?"

"Um, I don't think so, why?"

"Just wondering."

"Psst, McKenna, are you asleep?"

"No. Are you?"

Daisy laughed.

"Have you ever done anything wrong, McKenna?"

"Yes, why?"

"Just wondering."

"Good night."

"Good night."

McKenna couldn't look into Mrs. Calderon's eyes when the undercover agent read her her rights and escorted the irate woman to the vehicle.

"You'll be sorry for this," she screamed from the car.

Another agent wrote "Threatening a minor" in his notebook.

The case was held up in the courts for months. It seemed that Mrs. Calderon had also been involved with other people in the same unlawful practices; she waited in jail. Meredith waited in jail, and McKenna was on probation at the Abernathy's house.

Scott came home one evening with an uncustomary special lightness to his step.

"Girls, sit down for a minute. No, wait a minute. Daisy, you sit down, and McKenna, you get the camera. Now, when I hand this bag to Daisy, you take her picture. I mean, when she takes the something out of the bag, you take her picture. OK?"

McKenna was poised to take the shot as Daisy put her hand into the bag. She pulled out the necklace! Daisy and McKenna whirled around and around screaming and hugging.

"How did you get it back?"

"Months ago, we put out an APB on Mrs. Calderon and anything she sold. The vendors turned in anything she disposed of."

"Wait," McKenna interrupted, "you must have Wilson's baseball cards!"

"And our marble," Janine laughed.

Out of his vest pocket came the cards and out of his shirt pocket came the marble.

"Ah!" screamed the three females as they twirled in dance.

"How about these?"

Scott brought forth a diamond bracelet.

"Nope, not mine," exclaimed McKenna.

"Gold cuff links."

"Not mine."

"A signed golf ball."

"No."

"A diamond ring."

"Oh! That's the kids' play jewelry from Jacqui's!"

McKenna didn't recognize any of the remaining items in the box, and she was relieved about that.

Years later, when McKenna's daughter asked her if she'd ever done anything wrong, she could honestly answer, "Yes."

"I'M SLOWING DOWN SO WE CAN LOOK AT THIS BEAUTIFUL ESTATE.
IT'S A SHAME THAT MORE PEOPLE CAN'T ENJOY IT. I DON'T KNOW WHY THAT
OLD WOMAN DOESN'T SELL ALL THIS; I CAN'T IMAGINE WHY SHE'S HANGING ON
TO IT. MARJORY! YOU'RE NOT EVEN LOOKING THIS WAY. WHAT ARE YOU
LOOKING AT?"

"THE COWS ON A THOUSAND HILLS."

Chapter Six

BONES ON THE SIDEWALK

Jesse muttered as she turned the newspaper so the dry part was over her left ear. She didn't want another earache; she'd had, too many of those when she was a kid.

As she saw the first rays of sunshine creeping along the sidewalk, past the first bench, across the huge grate, on the base of the barber's pole and now ten inches from her face, she took her hand out from under her coat and put her fingers into the light. She touched the shade, the light, the shade, the light. As the morning minutes passed, she could feel the heat settle into the lighted part of the sidewalk. She let her hand remain in the sunshine as the rest of her lay in the cold.

She thought of her mother putting warm drops of something into her aching ear then blowing in smoke from her father's cigarette. "There, that'll deaden the pain."

Jesse thought maybe it had.

She took the newspaper off of her head; the sidewalk, which she was staring at sideways, was almost dry. A faint rise of steam came out of the concrete pores.

Jesse thought of steam that came out of a wet garden, permeating the tomatoes and cucumbers, making them warm, fresh, and delicious. Her mother would let her eat vegetables the way she liked best: tomatoes dipped in sugar and cucumbers sprinkled with salt. Nothing fancy.

Jesse's mouth watered a little—which was pleasurable; it had been tacky dry. She promised herself to remember the little trick of thinking about mouthwatering garden vegetables when in desperate straits of dryness.

She needed to get her bones off the sidewalk. The ones on the right side of her body felt like they had flattened during the night and had, by the process of osmosis, melded with the concrete; they ached, therefore the sidewalk ached.

"Therefore the sidewalk ached?" she repeated the thought to herself.

What was that class in college where everything was: if this was true, then that was true, or if this happened then that was going to happen? "Probabilities?

"I don't know," Jesse muttered to her leg bone. She did remember the professor being handsome with dark hair and so relaxed. She remembered thinking, what an easy way to earn a living: conduct class of if this/then that and go home to your wife and children—all beautiful of course.

I'm sure the class would have concluded that if an old lady laid on the cold sidewalk all night, then no, she would not be able to get up.

Well, you college brats, this old lady has to get up somehow. I just have to get my bones out of the concrete and reshape them. That's all.

"This is how I earn my living, Professor Probabilities," Jess muttered as she looked at her one warm hand.

"Hey, you little critter, come over here. Your day has started, hasn't it? Where are you off to so fast? That's it, crawl on my hand. Are you out looking for breakfast? I will be soon, also. You like my warm hand, don't you? What are you, some kind of an ant? I think so. Ants are very industrious workers. Are you industrious? It doesn't look like it now, the way you're lolling around. Maybe you're on your coffee break already this morning. You're a pretty cute little fellow. Oh, good-bye! Have a nice day," Jesse whispered to her little friend as he scurried across the concrete slab and disappeared into a crack.

"Don't step on a crack or you'll break your mother's back." Those were words we lived by. All of us walked to school in syncopated rhythm as we avoided the cracks. Not one of us ever, ever wanted one of our mother's backs to be broken.

It didn't count, thank goodness, if a wiseacre who intentionally wanted you to step on a crack pushed you.

Sometimes we would sit on somebody's grass and tell heartrending-dying-mother stories; we worked ourselves up into a bawling session. None of us ever wanted our mothers to die. I guess they all have by this time, however.

Jesse turned her stiff-as-a-telephone-pole neck so she could look upward. "God, you've got yourself a bunch of good women up there; all those mothers who wore aprons and set the milk bottles out on the porch and made Jell-O. They were the best! Take good care of them."

A tear trickled out of one eye and rolled down her cheek to fall with a little *splat*. Jesse pulled back a few inches to look at the wet spot. She wished her little critter would come back; he could have a drink. *Would I be too salty for him? Ah yes, dear old science class.*

She remembered the cows going over to the salt lick in the field and the one time she imitated them! Ah, to be a kid.

She loved the morning quietness, the sunshine, and the ant.

Her uncle's farm in Lone Moon Creek was pretty much the same. The quietness in the mornings went on forever—up the hill and over through the woods and down the hill and over the creek and up the lane and over to the pond and across the fence. Then the birds began their chirping as the dew started to sparkle; the cobwebs glittered their dewy strings; the flower petals opened and blades of grass stood up straighter. After that, it was a full orchestra with all of the farm animals each sounding out the new day.

Jesse lay there with her bones in a heap thinking of the farm when she heard the familiar steps. Her telephone pole neck bent forward to see Joe's familiar shiny, black shoes.

He stopped at Maggie's spot. They "good morninged" each other.

The meeting of his thick patrolman's shoes with the sidewalk became more pronounced as he approached Lester's spot. Lester must have had too much Chianti the night before; Joe was having a hard time waking him. The nights Lester doesn't drink too much he wakes immediately with a loud, "Good morning, Vietnam," which makes Maggie cackle.

"Hey, Mr. Vietnam," Joe said, "you going to sleep all day?"

"Uh?" muttered Lester.

"I know, I know. Get yourself over to the Legion Hall; they'll give you some breakfast. And Sarge, don't drink like there's no tomorrow."

"Yes, sir," Lester replied with a feeble attempt at a salute.

"Jesse," my mom would call, "are you going to get up today?"

"In a few minutes," I would call back and then sleep for another hour. Summer days, how delicious. I would sleep until ten or eleven, eat, sunbathe, and gab with my friends all afternoon. Then eat and gather with my friends for the evening. I remember carnivals and jukeboxes and movies. Psychologists say children need hours of pleasant "nothings" in order to develop emotionally.

"Say, Jesse, you still in dreamland?" Joe asked as he looked downward. Usually Jesse watched his shoes come closer, looking to see if he was going to step on the crack or perhaps estimate how many steps he was going to take or think about what sneakers he wore as a boy.

"Oh no. I was just thinking about when I was a teen."

"Few years ago?" Joe said with a wink.

"A few."

"This place will be bustling in another hour. Better move along for the day," Joe spoke in a fatherly tone.

"I know, just been waiting for you to go by."

"Have a good day, Jesse."

My mother used to say the same thing as I hurried off to school with my Roy Rogers and Dale Evans's lunch box and a little bouquet of newly picked flowers for the teacher. I knew she would be there when I returned wearing her pretty apron ironed and starched and a big bouquet of flowers in the cobalt-blue vase centered on the dining room table.

Let me pull my knees up first. Ah, the fetal position; it's a good position, a comforting position, something we know about before we are born.

It must be quite pleasant in the womb.

She plays wonderful music. I can tell she loves it. It calms her and soothes her and soothes me.

She reads love poems so I can hear them, too. Her voice is sweet; it relaxes me.

Every afternoon she and I go to special places... nice places, quiet places. She tells me about the paintings or the lake or the trees.

She is good to me. Someday when people ask why I love things from her era, I'll tell them.

Now I need to push until I can get on my hands and knees, much like the salt licking position.

All right, straighten my back. Well, God, you've got me on my knees now! I'll pray for the same thing that I do every day: Watch over my children and my husband. Amen.

"Now, one knee up, press on that knee and pull myself up." Standing but still hunched over, Jesse watched two men walk by and look. *Expressionless, that's good. I can handle expressionless,* Jesse thought to herself.

"Expressions, girls, expressions," our vocal music teacher would peal.

Her eyes now lined up horizontally with the world five feet six inches above the ground. Well, maybe not five feet six inches anymore. Jesse really didn't know, maybe she had shrunk a little. "Osteoporosis is as much a problem to us street people as it is to non-street people," she mused. "The only difference is that we don't have a shelf to put the bottle of calcium on!"

Jesse chuckled at her own humor and said to herself, "Jesse, you're so funny!"

"I know, I know," she answered herself.

Now I've got a routine going here.

"Good morning, everyone. Have you heard about the street woman and the ant?"

Lester's thick, hungover voice broke the stage-show mood as he hollered out, "What the hell you doin' over there, Jess? Talkin' to yourself like a mad woman?"

"Darn you, Lester. You made me forget the punch line," she bellowed back.

Cleaning her spot was easy. She folded her blanket with the singe marks, put it in her bag, picked up the bag, and walked. One foot and then the other, just like other people.

Jesse remembered her daughter's first steps.

"Get the camera," she squealed, "get the camera."

Molly was taking her first step. Her tiny foot with the pristine white baby shoe and the pink-laced sock went ahead and then the other tiny foot with the pristine white baby shoe and the pink-laced sock moved ahead.

Jesse loved Molly's adorable little feet with the teeny, tiny toes and dimples—such softness.

"Watch where the hell you're walking, old lady," screamed a young man on his bicycle.

Maggie never let a retort go by and rallied to the occasion with, "No bicycles on the sidewalk, you moron!"

Maggie looked a mess.

"Oh no, Lord, don't let me laugh," Jesse prayed as she got closer to her.

Maggie's gray hair stuck out like corkscrews. She had safety pinned the red rose she found yesterday into her hair. Her lime-green scarf was wrapped three or four times around her neck, and the strap of her denim overalls hung off her shoulder.

"How are you today, Maggie?" Jesse chirped, remembering Mrs. Hanson, her fourth grade teacher, giving lessons on common courtesy. *I wonder if they teach common courtesy anymore.*

"How the hell do you think I am?" Maggie snapped. Maggie hadn't gone to the same school.

"You got any money left, Jesse?" Maggie suddenly changed her tone and smiled through her crossword-puzzle teeth.

"Yes, I do, and please join me for breakfast," Jess replied quickly. She never wanted to put Maggie into a position where she had to beg; she did that enough throughout each day.

The best part of going into a restaurant, a cheap restaurant, was the bathroom. Maggie and Jesse didn't drink at night like Lester, because they didn't want to pee on themselves.

Jesse suddenly thought of herself on a talk show:

"Tell us, Mrs. Schwartz, what made you stop drinking? Was it the famous Betty Ford Clinic?"

"No, it was the fear of peeing on myself."

(Laughter, applause)

"Morning, girls, how are you today?" asked Marla, who always opened the diner during the week.

"Fine, thank you."

"Why don't you ask Joe, he woke me up this morning," Maggie kidded.

"You're such a cut up, Maggie," Marla laughed." What'll it be?

"We'll split whatever Maggie orders," Jesse directed.

Mmm, butter and syrup on warm pancakes with coffee and orange juice.

Jess reached into her bag and pulled out the bottle of calcium pills. She placed one on Maggie's place mat and one on her own.

"Oh my God, here we go again," Mag cackled! "My bones press so hard into the sidewalk now! Why do you want me to make them harder? So they can hurt more?" she squawked as syrup dribbled down her chin.

"Take your pill and not another word out of you," Jesse smiled.

Mom used to say basically the same thing except not "pill" but "vegetables." I couldn't understand how anything good could be harbored in vegetables, except the ones right from the garden. She really was up to date on nutrition; the good mother of the '40s, '50s, and '60s who stayed home with her children to see that they ate properly.

Jesse, too, had made sure her children had nutritious foods and learned that children would eat better if there was no stress at mealtime and it was fun! I remember Danny, Isaac, and Molly being delighted with the carrot and celery stick, raisin, apple, peanut clowns, mashed potato, and meatloaf ski slopes. We had fun conversations; those were Jacob's specialty. All of us loved going to the table.

"Jesse? Are you in there?" Maggie asked as she cocked her head pretending to look into Jesse's brain.

"Oh, sorry. Did you take your calcium?"

"Yeah, yeah. I was asking you what your plans were for the day."

"Let me think," Jesse muttered, resting her chin on her clasped hands.

"Of course, you know I have to go to the park for a while."

"God, you would think you were born there the way you visit every day."

"I was born in a place similar to the park..."

I walked through the woods in the winter... cold and deep. I walked through the woods in the spring... wet and new. I walked through the woods in the summer... cool and thick.

I ruled the woods.

I was the queen until the day the woods jumped out, and I stood still in the autumn and said, "Yes, your majesty."

"Hey, Old Stogey!" shouted Maggie when her friend walked in.

"Sorry, Jesse, honey, got to go. Thanks for the breakfast. I'll run into you later."

"Stay well." The words trailed off as Maggie put her arm around Old Stogey.

Oh, my favorite place, with my favorite bench, with my favorite God. You are something, Lord. How you created all this. May peace come into this old body, Lord. Let me do some good for someone today.

I can't even imagine how long these trees have been here or who planted them. Or were they saplings from former trees? The maple will always be my favorite. We would play in our woods for hours, so snug, so protected.

It rained on top of our woods. We could hear it tippy-tap-tapping way up high. The thick, thick leaves made a roof that kept us dry far under on the crunchy crackly floor...

We played all afternoon, listening to the pitter-patter, with us below, snug and warm and dry.

From our maples we did the "sapping" the old-fashioned way with the big iron pot outside to boil the sap to syrup. What fun, feeling so important doing the small tasks such as putting more sticks on the fire—fire.

Jesse softly touched the blanket inside her bag.

"So maple trees. I wonder if Maggie knew the syrup she had this morning originally came from you."

The ducks look well this morning... especially the Nilly family—there's Willy, Tillie, Lillie, Silly, and Frilly. I like Willy Nilly the best!

"Oh, Mommy, you're so funny."

"I know, I know."

One more hour and I'll have to get out of this Florida sunshine; it's going to be a hot one today.

The seventh, hot, dry, scorched day in a row... We had cleared two fields.

And had stacked in what seemed like a million bales... Now out to the third field...

We walked to the tractors and the wagons and the baler without talking... We braced ourselves against the thought of a long, long, hot, parched-throat day... With hayseeds sticking to sweat,

and hands sore again from baler twine.

Mounting the tractor... With one foot on the hitch...

And one foot still on the ground... He stopped as if paralyzed...

The rest of us stopped, suspicious of a standstill.

No one spoke... then, slower to move than the caterpillar

that had decided to perch on my work shoe... He turned to us and asked, "Who wants to go to the creek for a swim?"

We didn't know about Florida hot.

"Hey squirrels, quit your squabbling over there. You're driving me nuts. Get it squirrels?"

Jess started to fix up for the children. She took her comb from her jeans pocket and ran it through her hair, smoothed down her Pepsi T-shirt and sat up a little straighter. Yes, here comes the morning brigade of little ones.

Older children have been gotten off to school, beds have been made, dishes washed, and laundry done and put away. Now it's to the park! Later, they'll return back home for lunch and nap time. It's a good routine; it works well. Nutrition, work, play, exercise, rest—all good for children.

Oh my, look at her in that little outfit—how adorable.

There are the twins!

Here comes big brother holding on to the side of the carriage with the new baby.

Lots and lots of children climbing, running, jumping.

I remember playing out in the snow. My mom forming a huge circle by going baby step over baby step in the snow and then crisscrossing into pie wedges. She then taught us how to play Fox and Geese with the center of the pie being safe. She could run!

Here comes a mother running now. Her little boy was very fast, but she caught up to him. As she grabbed him, I heard her scold, "No, you are not to go over to that woman. We don't know her; she might hurt you. Do you understand me?"

"Yes, Mommy, yes, Mommy."

I stared at a Florida version of a black-capped chickadee while tears formed in my eyes.

"I would never hurt you, little fellow," I whispered as I saw the boy by the teeter-totter looking over at me.

"I need to see the rose garden," Jesse said to herself as she put her coat over her arm and grabbed her bag. Going along the path, she thought of the paths they used to take to get to the berry bushes. Mothers knew what would taste good next winter. Every berry crop and fruit crop was utilized to the fullest. "I never heard anyone of the neighborhood mothers saying, 'Don't go near her, she might be dangerous.' There was no one around who was ever dangerous."

Well, times change.

Oh, it's a sea, an ocean of roses!

Drawing nearer, she lowered herself to her knees; she wanted to be face-to-face with the blossoms, to smell their wonderful aroma.

Jacob once brought her roses.

She recalled her mother who tended her roses as well as she did her family. Winters were long and hard on the folks who loved to be in their gardens.

Jesse gently used both hands to draw the rose closer to her face.

She always wore roses... I snuggled into roses... Cried into roses... Slept on roses... Took walks with roses... Hung onto roses... Fought my nightmares into roses... Spilled cereal on roses... Said my prayers into roses... Bled bloody knees into roses... Hid pennies into pockets of roses... And spun roses around and around until we both fell down, and I laughed and laughed into roses.

"Hey, lady. Can't you read the sign? Don't touch!"

He scared the rose admirer so vehemently, she yanked the rose off its stem!

"Oh, I'm sorry, I'm sorry," Jesse pleaded.

"Get out of here," he hollered.

Jesse slid her arm through the handles of her bag and hurried away, only daring to look at the roses out of the corners of her eyes.

When she got far enough away, she sat down in the grass and opened her clenched hand, displaying a wad of rose petals. The old fingers flattened each one the best she could. She reached into her bag for the small wooden box and inside, with her locket, she placed four rose petals.

"What are you doing?"

Jesse looked up to see a little girl and her younger brother both dressed in sailor outfits with white shoes and socks.

"Oh, I'm setting up a little game with these rose petals. I have the circle formed and the lines to crisscross the circle almost finished." She placed a penny in the center.

"Who's going to play?" the girl asked.

"I think the ants will play when they get up from their naps," she answered, half serious and half comical, just as she would to her own children.

"Daddy, this lady is funny." The little girl directed her statement to the man who'd paused to hear the conversation.

87

"I hope the ants have a good time. And since they're still taking their naps, we'd better tiptoe out of here because Mommy is waiting at the hospital to show you our new baby."

"Bye."

"Bye," Jesse said.

The three of them left the park pretending to tiptoe and of course being very careful not to step on any cracks.

Jess rolled onto her knees and used the side of the tree to balance herself while getting up. She left the petal game with the penny. Some little folks may find it and think they've found something to bring them good luck, she mused.

"Jesse? Is that you?"

"Gwen?"

"My holy good night. I haven't seen you in a dog's age. How's life been treatin' you, Jesse?"

"Not bad at all. And yourself?"

"My son tracked me down again. Remember me telling you about Doug in South Carolina? I went kicking and a screaming. This time he brought two men with him after the fight I put up last time. So they got me there, and I admit, I calmed down. Damn, he's got a swell house and everything to go with it. Highfalutin he is, and his wife and his kids, my grandkids, highfalutin, can you imagine? I didn't raise him like that. Everything we had was modest. Ray was out of work a lot with his back, and I worked where I could. Well, hot shot Douglas said he'd never, ever live that way again. It wasn't much, Jesse, but it was clean and it was all ours. We even shared what we had with those who had nothing, and I mean nothing. So I settle in, start living high off the hog. Joan gets me all fixed up with the hair, the nails, the clothes, the shoes, the jewelry. I set back like Astor's pet nanny goat feeling like a damn fish out of water. You know what I mean?"

"I do, Gwen."

"So one night I ups and leaves."

"That's some pretty nice jewelry you're sporting there!" Jesse said.

"Yeah, I took everything they bought for me. Figured it was mine. If I was there, I'd be wearing it. Right?"

"You're right. What if Doug finds you again?"

"Naw. He said that was the last time. He knows I can't live like them. What you been up to?"

"Just hangin' out, as the kids say, trying to make sense of this world," Jesse said.

"Well, good luck, honey. You picked an awful hard way to find the answer."

"It is a hard way, but you know, I'm learning a lot more about life out here than I did in my sheltered world."

"Well, God bless ya, sister. Write a book about it before your eyes go bad like mine are doing. I'm over on the West Side if you ever need me," Gwen said.

"Thanks, Gwen. Take care."

"I will, I will," she replied as she bustled away in her sling-back shoes with matching purse.

Jesse dug into her bag for the Cub Scout change purse. Ah, just enough for the city bus. She needed to get to the train station.

She bent over so nobody could see and gave the change purse a little kiss before putting it away.

It was cool on the bus, cool but smelly. Oh well, it was a lot better than hot and smelly. They drove through the business district. Jacob used to work in a business district: Air-conditioned offices, suits and ties, briefcases, very sterile she always thought. They were good to other people, however. Lester claims you can always go there and people will dig into their pockets for a few dollars. I know Jake would. They didn't seem to mind either if their doorways were utilized during the nighttime as long as everybody was cleared out by 8:00 a.m.

The most difficult places to inhabit are in the poorer sections where the people inside are only a step ahead of the people outside. There's a lot of anger among poor people who aren't quite sure where they stand in this life.

Jesse surmised that was why she liked her street. There were only stores, no one's residence close by, nothing open to attract people at night, and it was well lit. She was surprised Lester had enough sense to habitat there. Maggie—sometimes she was there and sometimes not. There were a few others down the street; if they stayed around, she'd go and meet them.

Do I sound like my mother or what? She chuckled to herself. I can just see us walking down the street with our decent clothes on and our basket of goodies for the new neighbors. I always had the job of making the card. My mother was right. It did make me feel better and the new people, too. She called us the "Welcome Wagon." Neighborhood people used to look out after each other in Lone Moon Creek.

"The Newly Refurbished Train Station" read the sign in front of the building.

"Get over here," a woman snapped at her son as he stopped to pick up Jesse's coat, which had slipped from her arm. His gentle smile and compassionate eyes were as refreshing to the street lady as lemonade on a hot day.

Jesse didn't feel uncomfortable carrying her bag in there; everyone was carrying some sort of bag. She walked to the room of locked storage boxes, going over to the smallest ones. She retrieved the key out of the sock that was stuffed into the toe of a sneaker, opened the box, and took out the envelope.

Jesse hid everything quickly in her bag's designated spot and walked out. "Thanks, Jacob," Jesse whispered to her beloved as she raised her eyes to heaven.

I'm so glad people have the foresight to save old, historic buildings like this one. Jake's folks did a tremendous job in saving half of their town, spearheading fund drives for refurbishment.

"What were you brought up in? A barn? Don't stand there like a fence post, move your stuff out of the way. Can't you see people want to get through?" a man in a polyester plaid suit yelled after banging into her.

Jesse looked around; there was no one close by. What people wanted to get through?

He scowled at her as he flew on to his destination with his shirttail fluttering out from underneath his jacket.

Let's see, lemonade and maybe a sandwich. She was hungry. *What a sweet little restaurant,* she thought.

Mommy, can we have ice cream?

Of course you can, my darlings. You have been so good.

"Ma'am?"

"Oh, I'm sorry. A small lemonade and a tuna on rye, please."

She could hear the ladies at the next table say, "her kind" and then whisper and "mental institution" and whisper some more.

After paying, Jess picked up her paper cup and plate with the sandwich, her other baggage, and walked out to the main terminal.

Maybe I should be in a mental institution; maybe they were right. Jesse used the napkin to clean off the small blob of tuna that had dropped to her Pepsi shirt. She knew it wasn't normal to live the way she did, but she couldn't live the other way either. "I'm halfway between the devil and the deep blue sea. Wasn't there a song like that way back?"

Maybe Gwen hit upon something when she said to write a book. "Maybe that's what I should do. Yeah, right."

The sandwich was pretty good. Not like Mom made or not like I made for my family, but beggars can't be choosers.

Wait a minute; I'm not that bad. I get my allotment every month. And speaking of payday! It's a tradition that I go to the movies on payday!

Another bus to stay out of the heat and into the theater I go. Yes, certainly popcorn!

I remember my first movie! The theater on Main Street with the balcony and the hanging chandeliers and the soft-cushioned seats were unprecedented for charm and magic. I would look up at my mother every now and again to be sure I wasn't dreaming.

This should be a good movie; I saw the previews at the Sears store on all fifty TV sets at once. I wonder what God thinks when he sees our extravagance.

Oh, here's the movie!

"I love you, Miranda. I have always loved you. Ever since I first saw you help your grandmother with the horses. How lovely..."

"Hey!" Jesse shouted." Let go of my bag! Let go."

Jesse stood up to get a better grip on the handle while she beat on the boy's arm with her other hand.

"Let go," she screamed louder. She felt her fingernails dig into his arm.

"You old bitch," he hissed as he released the bag to touch his arm.

"All right, all right, get out, the both of you," the attendant squealed as he put the beam of light on them.

"I'll get you, old lady," the boy hollered across the row as he ran out flinging his jacket over his shoulder.

Jesse's popcorn had completely torpedoed into the laps and hair of the people in front of her. She stumbled over the feet of the people who wouldn't stand to let her through.

"Damn old bag ladies," she heard someone mumble as she left the theater. It certainly wasn't the magical experience she had experienced with her mom.

Jess slowly trudged down the street; the heat hit her whole body, robbing every milligram of air-conditioned theater coolness out of her pores. *Maybe I should go north just for the summer*, she thought.

Up north I could sit on the cool green grass shaded by the maple trees and even lie on a velvety cushion to take a nap while the birds sing to me.

I would let Danny and Isaac and Molly take their naps outside sometimes; they loved it. Molly would be in her carriage with the netting pulled over, and Isaac and Danny would crawl up onto the chaise lounge chairs. I would sit and read and be on guard for bugs. As I watched their little chests rise and fall, I would thank God that they had perfectly pure air to breathe.

"Jesse! What's shaking?"

Oh no, here comes Simon. He's such a... a...

"Couldn't miss that wiggle just a walking down the street," he sang.

Simon, a tall man with a full beard, clad in a long duster, excelled in off-color innuendos, thinking he was debonair.

He swooped back one-half of the duster, put his hand on his waist, and did some sort of a hip rotation. Jesse looked down to see his big, filthy feet sticking out of his sandals.

"Are you coming to the shelter any night soon, Jess-Bess?"

"Not if you're going to be there," Jesse said as she glared at him while he walked faster.

"Maybe we can, you know, find out what life is all about," he said as he tried to "purr" his voice.

"Don't even think about it," Jesse snapped. She swallowed hard after a sensation of tuna fish rising startled her.

"Ah, St. Luke's!"

"Where you going to? A fire?" he bellowed as his smell traveled as fast as his long legs.

Jesse swirled toward him with daggers in her eyes and uttered each word separately, "Don't. Ever. Say. Fire. To. Me!"

"OK, OK, you sassy little lady. Where ya goin'?"

"Into the church."

"Whoa, this is where we part company."

"Good.

"You think God is going to help you?"

"He just has," Jesse said.

"Baaah," Simon growled. "You're going to hell like the rest of us."

I breathed heavily as I leaned on the closed door. I let my bag fall to the floor as I shut my eyes and let the coolness of the huge stone church permeate my skin. The scents of church trickled into my brain, and I identified them as incense, candles, and flowers. Cool, dark, and quiet—three ingredients I could live with forever. The holy water felt refreshing on my hot forehead.

Ah, so calming, so quiet. A few candles twinkled in front of the Blessed Virgin Mary, a few in front of St. Anthony, St. Joseph, and the Sacred Heart of Jesus. The ceilings were so high and the stained glass was a million pieces and a hundred colors; the Stations of the Cross was mounted on the walls. The pews were smooth, so smooth. I rubbed my hand gently on the polished wood, sometimes following the grain, sometimes not. I sat for a long time soaking in the peace, the safety.

I don't remember falling asleep, just pretty colors coming down on my green grass with my children and I picking them up to show Daddy. We danced outside with the fireflies.

"Jesse, Jesse."

I can't wake up now; I have to finish dancing with Jacob.

"Jesse," someone persisted.

I opened my eyes to see Father Benito.

"Jesse, I have to lock the church now. Do you need a place to sleep?"

"Oh no, Father, thank you. I didn't realize I had fallen asleep."

"Can I drive you someplace?" he asked.

"No, I can catch the bus out front. Thanks anyway, Father."

I gathered my belongings. Feeling rested, I made my departing sign of the cross a lot easier than my initial one.

I wondered what time it was. It was starting to get dark.

There's my bus!

I'm usually home by this time. I hope no one has taken my spot.

Ah, my street.

I hurried down the aisle of the bus when some kid yelled out, "Hey, old lady, you forgot your bag!"

I panicked, swung around in horror, and started back to my seat.

"You've got it in your hand, stupid old lady," the boy howled with laughter as his companions slapped their knees and high-fived each other.

I could see the bus driver scowling at them in the rear view mirror; that wouldn't straighten them out.

"Have a nice night," the driver said as I disembarked.

I turned to say, "You, too," but the door closed and the brakes released to send the bus off to its nightly prowl around the city.

95

"Well, Southern fried succotash, where you been, Jesse?" Maggie cackled when she saw her with bag and baggage lumbering along.

"Had business, that's all," she replied, anxious to get settled.

Lester wasn't home yet. Not surprising.

"Ah," the tired lady breathed a sigh of relief. "Home Sweet Home." She pulled out her patchwork blanket and carefully laid it under her palm tree. Sometimes palms have to replace maples.

Jesse donned her coat for extra padding, took out a rolled sweatshirt for her pillow, checked on her envelope, checked on the locket with the four new rose petals, and checked on the Cub Scout purse. Later after Lester got back from his carousing and was asleep, she would transfer her money into fifteen different hiding places.

She wasn't tired after her St. Luke's retreat.

Jesse looked up through the palm fronds at the night sky.

"What do you see, Jesse?" Mama would ask. And I would tell her all the dot-to-dot animals or ships or dolls I could see in the night sky.

"What do you see, Mama?"

Isaac was a lot better at it than anyone. He came up with the most incredible objects that the sky could ever hold. Danny would say, "You don't see that, Isaac."

"Oh yes I do," Isaac would insist.

"Where is it?" Danny would insist harder.

Isaac's little pointer finger would line up with his line of vision and he would say, "Right there!"

Who could dispute him? Maybe it was right there.

Jesse could hear Maggie talking to someone; Maggie loved to have company.

Jesse rolled to her side; her old backbone couldn't stand too much star gazing anymore.

Her lonely fingers touched the pink, calico, flower patch of her quilt, then the red, white, and blue stripped one and on to the yellow daisy patch, pausing at her darling Sunbonnet Sue. She ran her fingers over the mint green and yellow seersucker patch. The little ripples used to tickle her fingertips, but they don't anymore, guessing her hands were too rough now. The pink calico pattern would start again. The patches had come from her childhood dresses that she had outgrown. Her mother had stitched the quilt together.

Years later, it was Molly's blanket. Jesse pulled the corner up to her face trying to smell Molly, her sweet girl.

Mommy, tell me what I did today!"

The wind combed your hair today... The dewdrops tickled your neck... The sun blushed your cheeks... The lake cooled your feet... The grass skittered across your back... The trees sang songs to you... The moon told you a story... And the stars tucked you in.

"Mommy, tell me again."

Jesse couldn't detect her scent anymore; she hadn't been able to for a long time, she just pretended she did. She laid her arm across the singed spot so she wouldn't have to look at it.

The concrete had gathered a lot of heat during the day; it would stay warm way into the night. The wayfarer wouldn't be a bit surprised if the northerners didn't feel a chilly forty to fifty degrees by morning.

Where are you, Mr. Ant? Are you sleeping? You probably had a busy day. Oh no, here he comes, singing his head off.

"Way down yonder in the paw-paw patch / Pickin' up paw paws / Put 'em in your pocket / Pickin' pup paw paws put pem... Damn, I can't even sing straight," Lester howled.

"Moon over Miami / Cheese and salami." He laughed to himself.

97

"The moon is as high as an eagle's eye." Lester trilled his falsetto voice.

Jesse could hear Maggie cackling up a storm.

"When your baby's done gone stick her in the eye with a big pizza pie." Lester ended his concert with low, gravely notes. "There, that's over for the night. Oh no."

"You ain't nothin' but a hound dog / A waltzin' with my darlin' to the Tennessee Waltz," he bayed at the night sky.

Jess pulled the sweatshirt over her mouth and laughed until her sides hurt.

Oh, Lester, you funny old goose. I haven't laughed like this since the slumber parties at Marybeth's house.

Jesse listened until she knew he was asleep. It wasn't hard to discern. Just as she knew the sound of the oscillating wringer washer with its methodical pulse, she knew Lester's snoring. Jacob, who never snored, must be rolling over in his grave knowing I now sleep on a sidewalk, down from a man who snores like a locomotive!

Oh no, Maggie is starting up! Her snore is always a high-pitched two noter.

"OK, let's get in rhythm here," the concertgoer thought out loud. "There! There it is! Oom pah, oom pah."

Jesse began humming the "Blue Danube Waltz" as the orchestra played.

I think it's safe to get my money situated now, Jesse reasoned. OK, toe of old sock in sneaker, wooden box, change purse—Jesse kissed it and said, "Thank you, Danny, I love it"— pants pocket, shirt pocket, another sock, old calcium bottle, inside magazine, lining of coat, other sneaker, lining of bag, inside tear of blanket, in…

Jesse stopped; somebody was near. Lester was snoring again, so was Maggie, but not in Waltz rhythm. She peered down to Maggie's spot—someone was hovering over her!

"Hey! Get away from her," she bellowed in an imitated low toned man's voice. She pulled out the cord that was always around her neck and blew the whistle for all she was worth.

The person ran off into the night. Lester stopped snoring. All Jesse could hear was Maggie's "pah pah."

Jesse tucked the remaining money into the envelope and laid back to listen with fox ears.

Is that Joe already this morning? It feels as if I just got to sleep. It is. He and Maggie are laughing again.

She must have had a happy childhood the way she cackles with everybody. I wanted my children to be happy, too. Jacob and I worked hard to keep a happy home just as our mothers had. Jesse remembered some of her friends who never wanted to go home. How sad.

Jesse chuckled as Joe gently but persistently persuaded Lester to wake up. "Oh, I don't think I slept a wink," he muttered, "with Jesse over there snoring like a thunder cloud."

"What?" I yelled back.

"Is that true, Jesse?" Joe asked and winked.

"I don't know; I didn't stay awake to listen!"

"Oh, Mommy, you're so funny."

"I know, I know."

She quietly told Joe about the visitor from the previous night. He said he would have the graveyard shift drive down the street more often.

"Thanks, Joe."

I wish I had some of the horse liniment Uncle rubbed onto Old Babe. Someday they'll put me into a nursing home, and I'll have a pill for everything that ails me. I guess that won't be so bad.

"Robber, Robber!" Maggie screeched louder than northern blue jays.

"What's the matter?" Lester hollered down the street.

"My things, my things!" I could see her on all fours moving around and around like a cat.

By the time I got down there, she was motionless sitting cross-legged on her blanket.

"What was taken, Maggie?"

"My red rose, my rose for my hair." She began to cry.

I knelt, hoping my knees could take it, and wrapped my arms around her. "It's OK, Maggie; we'll get you another one."

She sobbed harder than ever as her corkscrew curls bounded to the sobs.

"Would you like to have something delicious for breakfast?" I asked her. The tactic always worked on me and then later, on my kids.

"Yes," she answered, wiping her nose on her embroidered handkerchief.

"This is wash day, too. Would you like to go to the Laundromat with me?" I asked gaily, still working on the "get you out of the dumps tactic."

"OK!" Maggie smiled.

"Women!" Lester bellowed, disgruntled. He apparently had been watching the consolation scene the entire time.

Marla served us French toast, bacon, coffee, and orange juice. I served up the calcium pills, while Maggie shook her head knowing that this was part of the deal, no sense arguing.

I changed into a clean shirt and pants after freshening up in the ladies room. Maggie went in next. I read the entire paper, well the parts I was interested in, while I wondered what was taking her so long.

When the door opened, Marla exclaimed, "Well, I'll be!"

Maggie, as if modeling on the runway, swirled to show us her new dress, new shoes, and necklace.

"You look beautiful," I told her. "Where did you get all that?"

"Off a dead woman," she answered matter-of-factly.

"A dead woman? What dead woman?"

"I don't know, she couldn't tell me her name."

"You're pretty funny, Maggie," I said as I gave her "the eye." Every person who has dealt with children knows what "the eye" is; my children surely knew.

"You better tell the truth Isaac, or Mommy will give you 'the eye,'" Danny would say to his brother.

"Well, you see, I know this undertaker," Maggie began, "and if he thinks it's possible, he gets the outfit off and gives it to me," she answered proudly.

"Maggie, aren't you embarrassed to do that?" I asked wide eyed.

"Embarrassed? I'd be bare assed without it!"

Marla and the two men at the counter laughed until I thought they would choke.

I reached for the check, but Maggie grabbed it first.

"On me today," she said proudly.

"Why, thank you," I uttered my fourth grade teacher's words of etiquette while I thought, *I'm not even going to think about where she came up with the money.*

The droning sounds in the Laundromat almost put me to sleep. I thought I nodded a few times.

I know I kept my eyes closed when I heard a woman say to her friend, "Watch which machine you use, you don't want to put your clothes into one they've used."

I folded my warm, fresh, clean clothes as lovingly as my mom had. The same way I did for my children.

Women have jobs that are so completely satisfying, if they would allow it, Jesse thought to herself as she worked. Jobs like this absolutely torment some women. They never feel the satisfaction or the worth to their family or the peace it can bring.

"Hey, Sweet Pea, look at you! Va va boom." Charlie ogled Maggie lustfully. "Want to stroll with me?"

"Sure do. Do you mind, Jesse?"

"Of course not. Go on. Have fun."

It was OK. I liked the solitude of the park.

"No, go on, dear. I don't mind being home by myself," my mom would say.

I knew it was true. Her home was her sanctuary, her refuge. She could fuss around for hours or merely sit in her favorite chair and read or go outside and putter around or just sit and soak in the peace.

I was like that, too. Jacob would feel badly that he had to leave me and go to work. It took him a long time to realize that I was absolutely truthful when I told him I loved being home. Once he realized the truth, it removed a lot of stress from him.

As Jess continued folding, she thought of her little sundresses her mom had made on her treadle machine, another task she loved.

Little sundresses with wide straps on tiny shoulders... Sashes tied around little waists with big billowy bows... Ruffles swirled around tanned legs... With tiny toes peeking out of sandals...

Crisp pink and white stripes with tiny embroidered rosettes... Or red country gingham with white pinafores or blue calicos drenched in flowers... Or maybe sailor-looking suits...

sometimes with pockets... sometimes with smocking... or with matching bonnets... all gathered so petite under huge maple trees to hear Mommy read afternoon stories.

Jesse reached into her bag to draw comfort from her patchwork quilt.

"What do you have in the bag?"

She snapped open her eyes to see a present-day Shirley Temple.

She wished Maggie was there to see her curls.

"Oh honey, would you like to see something pretty?"

She nodded as her curls bounced.

Jesse gently pulled out her blanket.

"I used to have dresses like this," Jesse told her.

"It's pretty," she spoke as she touched the blanket.

"Do you know which one?"

"Cheryl! My Mary in heaven, why do you wander away from me? Mother of God, don't you know this lady could hurt you?"

"She wouldn't hurt me," Cheryl proclaimed just as Shirley Temple would do by putting her little hands on her hips and sticking out her bottom lip.

"Well, mother of Jesus, you never know." The woman sounded exasperated as she pulled Cheryl away.

Jesse closed her eyes again as she directed her thoughts heavenward. "Well, Mary in heaven, mother of God, and mother of Jesus—what do you think?"

"Yes, me too." She nodded slowly.

Jess walked the path toward the rose garden, wondering if the pathway to eternity would be this beautiful. She thought of the little sailor-suit children with their new baby. Boy or girl, she didn't know, but hopefully loved as much as Molly was loved when she joined her family.

There were a few of the rose petals left from the game. The penny was gone. "You're going to have good luck," some mother or father undoubtedly said as their child picked up the coin.

Jesse didn't see the man who yelled at her yesterday; she was glad. She made her way to the shaded bench. With bag and baggage, she sat on a bench with crossed arms in front and stretched out old legs even more in front. She knew she shouldn't do this, but this was her comfortable pose the I-could-go-right-to-sleep-sitting-like-this pose.

Rose perfume anointed her while the breeze feathered her hair.

"Mommy, let's plant it here. Here, Mommy, and one over here and one over here!" We planted rose bushes all over our yard as we skipped with hoes and watering pails. Daddy came home and we served him supper with roses in all the bowls and platters and cups and plates and he lifted all the children and gave them piggyback rides.

I woke with a start. I reflected on my dream; it had been a nice dream. I smiled as I sat trying to remember every bit and piece.

Fresh fruit came to her mind: pears, peaches, grapes! She needed to have a piece of fruit!

She reached for her bag. She reached to the other side. "Dear God, no," she cried aloud. Jesse jolted upright and flung around. Ah, she had completely forgotten about sliding it under the bench.

The wanderer's heart raced as she lumbered out of the park.

This farmers' market had its similarities to the northern cornucopias she'd patronized in the past.

Oh look at these, so perfect. The color! How can one choose? I'm going to select one of each species!

"Yeah, right, Jesse," she said to herself, "how are you going to carry all that?"

"Don't touch the fruit," a woman wearing a bandanna commanded.

The patron looked to see what other people were doing to select fruit; they were all touching the fruit.

Jesse picked up another plum.

Again, "Don't touch the fruit."

"I'm purchasing these."

"OK, hurry it up," she snarled as the sweat ran out from under her bandanna.

"I plan on selecting a few more pieces."

"I'm watching you every minute so you don't steal nothing and don't put your paws all over everything."

Jesse left. She didn't need the fruit.

"Excuse me, excuse me," a young man running up behind her called. "I want you to have this."

I looked into the bag—fruit. I looked up at him.

"That was inexcusable behavior from that woman, please take this."

"Are you sure?" I asked, studying his face.

"Certainly."

"Excuse me for staring, but you look so much like my husband's friend, Doug. They worked together up north."

"My father's name was Doug, and he worked in Connecticut and New York. Doug Grissum."

"That's it!" Jesse blurted out. "Doug Grissum!"

"Did you know my dad?"

"Jake talked about him all the time. He brought him home for dinner a lot. Real nice man. Is he still in Connecticut?"

"Yes, he is. Whom shall I say was asking for him?"

"Jesse, Jesse Schwartz," I said contemplatively, "Jacob's wife."

"OK, will do. Sorry I have to run. Enjoy the fruit!"

"Oh, I will, and thanks," I yelled down the street as he hailed a cab.

I guess Doug finally got married and had a son. Jacob would be happy for him.

As Jesse bit into the juicy plum, her tears washed its shiny top and dripped with the juice from the bottom. Lone Moon Creek, our beautiful home, our maple trees, our flower gardens, our friends.

That night I thought of how Doug Grissum's son would be younger than my children. After all, when Doug came to the house he played with my three. How they loved it. He was "Uncle Doug" to them. I would have grandchildren by now.

Sobs came out of her gullet.

"God, come to my rescue, please. Don't let me come undone. I'm slipping—help me, Lord. Protect my mind." She began gulping.

A heavy hand came down on her shoulder. Jesse panicked. She twisted quickly to see Lester.

"What's the matter over here?" He looked worried. "You OK?" he uttered in a fairly sober voice.

"I'm sorry, Lester, I got to thinking about my family." When she said *family*, she broke down again.

"Do you want a slug?" he asked as he presented his brown bag to her.

"No, I gave that up long ago. I just hope I don't go insane. It's on my side of the family, you know."

"Well, I didn't know, but every family has some of that."

"Does yours? Jesse asked shyly.

"Yeah, it's me!" He laughed so robustly, Jesse started laughing too.

"Oh, Lester, you're just what the doctor ordered."

"I don't know about any doctoring, but you, young lady, better get some sleep."

"I will, Lester, I will and thank you."

"Don't mention it," he muttered as he went back to his spot. I heard the paper bag rattling.

"Easy does it, Lester," I whispered.

"Up! Up! Now! Right Now!"

What on earth? I thought.

"Move it, lady!"

I heard Maggie screech, "OK, give me a chance, will ya, you big baboon?"

His steps were heavy and fast on the sidewalk.

"Quick, Lord, unstick my bones from the sidewalk."

He pounded his billy club very near Lester's ear. I could see Lester's head bolt upward like a shot.

"What the hell?" were Lester's only words.

He knew right away—it wasn't Joe.

By the time he got to me, I was standing. Unfortunately, like a bag of bones, my bones felt like they were not in their correct places.

He looked at me and asked, "Why don't you people get yourselves into some kind of institution?"

He waited but received no answer then kept moving.

"I saw the one-man Gestapo go through," Marla confided to us as we sat in a booth.

"I hate him," whispered Maggie as she might have done of her least favorite teacher years ago.

The word, Gestapo had rendered me into a bowl of putty. I recalled my in-law's stories of the war.

"What an awful way to wake up," I said quietly.

Maggie clucked. "The next time he's on duty I'm going to—" She got up to use the bathroom. "I'll tell ya later."

She must have finished her story while I was using the ladies room, as I heard Marla and several others whooping it up with fits of laughter.

To me, the day was doomed. How many millions of children have to start their school day with a knot in their stomachs the size of a basketball and heavy as prejudice?

"Jesse Irene McCullah." My mother would sail my three names up the stairway with her orders, but I never felt fear; in fact, she was a great disciple of, "Start you morning out happy and the day will follow suit."

How did Jacob's morning start that dreaded day? I should have been there.

"Jesse! You look as white as a ghost," Maggie pealed out a concern. "I'm going to the park with you today. In fact, Simon is going to meet us there."

"Oh, uh, sorry, Maggie. I've made, uh, other plans for today," Jesse uttered weakly, hoping her friend wouldn't detect her lie.

"What? You always go to the park in the morning?" Maggie insisted.

"Well, not today," Jesse said angrily.

She threw some money on the table and hurried out.

Oh, I hate myself right now; I cannot face my problems.

Jesse refused to sit in the park with Simon, that pig. He would scare all the mothers and the kids forever; they would never trust her again.

It's people like him who give the rest of us a bad reputation. Maybe I'm as prejudiced as anyone else.

"No, I'm not, I'm not," Jesse cried." I would never burn someone's house down."

Jesse fell to her knees on the sidewalk, wrapped her arms up around her head, and cried like a baby.

Who walked by?

She had no idea.

As the last tear sneaked out, Jesse opened her eyes to see an ant seemingly looking at her.

"Some sight, huh?"

It turned and ran down into a crack.

"Well, ever onward," she said to herself as her old muscles hunched and lurched to get up.

⁂

"Yes, I have a library card," Jesse Swartz blankly uttered to the scrutinizing librarian.

In the card catalog, Jesse saw where the bird books were housed and spent the next several hours perusing beautifully colored volumes of birds. It wasn't like being in the park, but it was interesting.

Jesse paused on the massive front steps on the way out to look at the approaching black clouds; thunder was rumbling. She noticed the pedestrians had quickened their pace, even though it wasn't yet raining. Like insurance, they were anticipating that something might happen. Did Jacob think something might happen? Is that why he had such a large policy?

Here it comes. One drop, two, four, sixteen, thirty-two, sixty-four—Isaac could count like this to infinity. He was a smart little kid.

Jesse pulled herself up the steps of the bus. With the air conditioner running, she was nearly frozen when she reached the train station. The hot, humid air felt good as she stepped off the bus. She remained outside under the platform awning to get warm.

She watched the rain; a nice gentle rain. All the farmers up north would have a day off. A rainy day liberation is good when you work seven days a week. Tomorrow would bring extra work, however, because the wet hay that had been cut would have to be turned to dry.

"Don't tell me I'm going to spend the night in the shelter?" Jesse questioned aloud.

"Excuse me? Were you talking to me?" Asked a man standing close by.

"No, sorry," she murmured.

While she sat staring blankly at the people in the station, a thought came to her like a locomotive: God is going to punish me for my thoughts about Simon. Now I *will* have to stay in the shelter if the rain keeps up.

My mother always said, "Jesse Irene McCullah, God will know your unkind thoughts and will punish you for them."

I didn't threaten my children with ideas like that; it was too much of a burden on children, she always thought.

"Please, please, please," Jesse did a litany as she went out to check the weather. "Oh no."

"Jesse, here, come over by me," Gwen hollered and flung her arm around in the air. Her bracelets clinked and jangled as she did so. "I've been saving this cot for you."

"Oh, thanks, Gwen," she mumbled, quickly looking around to survey the placements.

All seemed in order, so Jesse felt relatively safe in giving Gwen her attention. Gwen had a pink robe on over her clothes.

"That's a beautiful robe, Gwen," Jesse told her, knowing she wanted a compliment by the way she straightened and patted it.

"Why, thank you. It's another item my daughter-in-law picked out for me."

"Are you sure you don't want to live with your family? They'll give you everything."

"I need my freedom, Jesse, my independence. I need to be free."

"You sound like a flower child."

"I was one of those once, long ago," Gwen said as she reminisced. "We didn't even know what freedom and independence were, but we sang about it," she continued with a laugh.

"Do you think this," Jesse stated as she pointed to encompass the room, "is freedom?"

"It sure is, honey. And where is your home that you don't go to?"

"My house is gone, Gwen."

"Gone?"

"Gone."

I turned my back to Gwen, so unlike me, so unfriendly. At slumber parties I could talk for hours; with Jacob I could talk for hours. I could hear Gwen starting a conversation with the woman on her other side. The cot I was facing was empty. Good.

I heard Maggie's familiar cackle from somewhere across the room. I didn't see anything of Lester. I hoped he was all right and not sleeping in the rain. I dozed and woke all night. The intermittent coughing and snoring almost heralded fear. My in-laws' barracks stories from the war wove in and out of my dreams.

As Jesse stepped out into the morning sunshine, she heard a woman say, "Ladies, this is the shelter I've been telling you about. It's a wonderful place, so don't forget Saturday night at the country club our annual dinner/dance fund drive to keep this place open."

I guess it was a pretty nice place, I thought as I walked up the street.

Jesse took the bus to her street just to be sure Lester wasn't there.

I'm sure he wouldn't get so inebriated that he would lie out in the rain all night. Of course there were days and nights that I had no idea where I was or what I had done; those were awful times.

What?! That's him lying on the sidewalk.

"Bus driver! Bus driver! I have to get out."

He wouldn't stop until the bus reached the corner. From there to Lester, Jesse's heart beat much faster than her legs could travel. Her bag continued to bump her leg like a prodder on a horse. Why didn't Joe wake him up? Joe wouldn't let him sleep this late. Oh, wait a minute; the tyrant officer wouldn't care about Lester.

I began calling Lester's name as I drew closer. He didn't respond. I lowered myself to shake his shoulder.

"Lester, for heaven's sake, wake up. You've got to change out of these wet clothes; you'll catch your death. Lester."

Jesse pushed his upward shoulder to roll him onto his back. She couldn't turn him, but she only managed to rock him slightly. The rocking, however, made Jesse see blood coming from his head.

"Hang on, Lester, I'll get help!"

Marla called 911. Jesse hobbled quickly back to Lester.

"Are you even breathing?" Jesse couldn't see that he was.

"I'm going with him," Jesse Schwartz spoke assertively to the rescue crew.

"Jesse, what happened?" the uniformed police officer asked as he ran toward her at the hospital.

"I don't know, Joe," I muttered into his shoulder, so relieved to see a familiar face.

"I just heard," he said then frowned. "How long have you been here?"

"About seven hours, I think."

"Have you heard how he is?"

"No. Nobody talks to me."

"I'll see what I can find out."

After quite a stretch, Joe came back with coffee, pies in wedge shaped boxes, creamers, sugars, and two plastic spoons.

"He's having extensive surgery on his head, Jess."

"Did he fall?" Jesse asked.

"No, it appears, they say, he was hit with a blunt object."

"A blunt object?"

"Yeah, looks like assault."

"Can they tell how long ago it happened?"

"Oh, I'm sure they can. Why?"

"What time did Officer Gestapo walk through?"

Joe looked at Jesse rather horrified. "Jesse, you don't think?"

I looked down and cut into my pie with the plastic spoon.

Maggie was just about on top of my spot when I returned in the evening.

"Jesse, can I be here by you? I'm afraid to be so far away after what happened to Lester."

"Sure, Maggie," I answered wearily.

"How is he?" Maggie propped herself up on her elbow and asked.

"Not good; he's in ICU."

"If you wake up early, Jess, wake me, will you? I want to be out of here before the baboon goes through."

"What makes you think he did it?"

"Word travels fast through my underground connections, you know." Her voice cracked as she peered out from under her blanket sounding like a wild witch from Salem.

Jesse lay awake listening to Maggie's "pah, pah," but without Lester's "oom," it didn't complete the cycle.

I recalled the morning years ago when I was hysterical, asking Pop Schwartz what time it had happened.

"As far as they could figure," he sobbed, about three in the morning."

"Good morning, my two best women. Let me see your bright eyes," Joe called out.

Maggie and Jesse both lurched forward.

"Ah, Joe," they sang in unison as grins spread across their faces.

"Hot dang, I'm glad it's you," Maggie cackled, "and not that horse's ass."

"Oh, Mag, you're such a flatterer." Joe laughed as he extended his hand to help her up.

"The doc asked me to get some of Lester's friends to go in and visit, you know, talk to him while he's in the coma. Doc says people in a coma can hear what's being said. What do you say, girls?"

"I can do that," I answered while using Joe's arm for a boost.

"Not me, Joe, sorry," Maggie piped up. "Can't go near hospitals; they give me the willies. They'd have to hog tie me to get me in one."

"Do you want me to send a patrol car around for you this afternoon, Jesse?"

"No thanks, I'll take the bus, Joe."

"Good enough. See you tomorrow morning, girls."

"Do you want breakfast, Mag?" Jesse asked.

"I would, but I have to be at the funeral parlor before eight o'clock."

"The funeral parlor? Oh, I remember. A new outfit coming down the pike?"

"I don't know about coming down the pike; I'd say my Santa's coming down the chimney!" Maggie cackled as she sashayed off with her curls bouncing.

There he lay, not snoring, not snorting, not singing, not grumbling, not rattling his brown paper bag, not anything. Well—breathing. Lester, so clean, shaven, quiet, sleeping, hair combed that wasn't bandaged, sterile sheets, a pillowcase, a bed, a ceiling, a window, a door, a floor, electricity, and temperature control.

Lester, you look like a duck out of water, I thought.

I had never seen him elevated to that level; when I looked down at him, he was right there, so close.

At any second I expected him to snort or thrash or yell out some of his Esperanto, in street vernacular of course.

I looked at every nail on his hands, which rested on his chest—so posed. Ten fingernails. I never thought of Lester having fingernails. Let me see if he has those little moons. By golly he does!

Lester, you sly old devil, having moons.

His hands displayed many scars. I began scrutinizing them, thinking about what they might have come from. I compared the size of his hands to mine. I put my hand over his to compare, but I didn't touch him. He must have worked hard once upon a time to develop such a hand size or maybe his father was big like this.

I didn't know a thing about Lester and nothing about his father.

Someone did a pretty good job shaving him; only a few whiskers stuck out on his neck. I tipped my head sideways and lowered it to look at Lester's profile. I stood hunched over for a long time, looking at and tracing his silhouette in my mind. His face was almost like a statute. The profile could be that of a general or a president or a chef or a movie director. Who knows? Who was this man? What has he done in his lifetime? He has a history; everyone has a history.

I looked at his ear, I looked inside his ear which embarrassed me; looking inside the ear is kind of private. It's just something you don't do, not on purpose anyway.

I slowly walked around to the other side of the bed; he looked the same but different. Was it the profile of an architect? A circus trainer? A priest? An oil driller? Again, the ear—the channel that would carry my message to his brain.

There was no indication of response, only a channel for voice transportation. My voice was supposed to take a voyage into Lester's brain and maybe stimulate or unlock something that has been deemed frozen.

"Lester," I whispered. "Lester, its Jesse. You know, from-the-sidewalk Jesse. Down the street from you. How are you? I'm awfully sorry this happened to you. I came back from the shelter to check on you and your head was bleeding. I'm real sorry, Lester."

I stopped talking and looked at his lips, waiting for the slightest movement. I never noticed his lips before either. What purpose do lips have anyway?

"Lester, why do people have lips? Is it to keep the food in? Maybe to make a seal so air won't come out when it's supposed to go out the nose? I know we have to lick our lips when they're dry or to get food off. Oh, I know! For talking, for speaking correctly. Right? What else? Maybe to protect our teeth. Teeth—do you have teeth Lester? I never really noticed. I'm not a very observant person, am I?

"Well, let's get back to lips. This is sort of fun thinking about uses, isn't it Lester? Oh! To whistle, how could we whistle without lips or drink through a straw? We're doing pretty well at this Lester; I think they'll put us at the head of the class, don't you? OK, Lester, you can laugh now, that was a joke. I bet you're laughing up in your brain, aren't you?

"Excuse me, ma'am," said a nurse coming into the room, "we have to take Mr. Lester for tests now. Can you come back tomorrow?"

"Yes."

I turned back to "Mr. Lester" and whispered, "See you tomorrow. We'll work on something new. How about hair—all the uses for hair? Now you be thinking. See you later alligator."

He didn't come back with any response about a crocodile, so Jesse left. On her way home, she noticed ears and lips and fingernails.

When the bus stopped suddenly, Jesse stretched her neck to look out just as everyone else did. Something was going on out on the street.

"Oh, for God's sake," someone from the front said, "another demonstration."

"What is it this time?" a lady to the right and center asked.

"What difference does it make?" retorted a man making his way to the door. "Now I'm going to be late."

Jesse could see him running up the sidewalk trying to dodge the people.

"Ha! I don't believe it!" laughed the bus driver, "The cabbies are on strike!"

"The city is going to be a mess," groaned someone behind me.

"Yeah, worse than it usually is, if that's possible," the yammering went on.

When Jesse finally got "home," there was no Maggie, only a piece of paper with a stone on top of it: *Jesse, it got so late and you did not come. I went to the shelter. Hope your OK. Mag.*

Well, I guess I'll have to be OK. I'll just get my old bones down here on the sidewalk. I should have taken the time to meet my neighbors from down below. What did my mother say about a helping hand or a helping heart or helping neighbors? Something, I don't know. Thank God she never lived to see how I turned out; the truth would have shocked the starch right out of her apron, I'm sure!

God, please talk to Lester while I'm not there. Thanks. And, God, watch over Jacob and Danny and Isaac and Molly. Amen. Oh, get *them* busy! Yes! They can visit with Lester for a while! Amen

Good idea, Jesse.

I know, I know.

⟨❦⟩

"Maggie! What are you doing here so early?" Jesse asked as she saw her friend walking toward her.

"I wanted to be sure you was all right," she smiled through her crossword puzzle teeth.

"Oh yes, and thanks for caring; that was nice of you. Say, Mag, that's a beautiful suit and pin you're sporting this morning."

"Ain't it though? I love it!"

"What would happen if a family member spotted you wearing the clothes of the dead?"

She stopped moving and cocked her head to the side making her corkscrews bounce to the left. "Huh?"

She was thinking. Her bottom lip went into her mouth (another reason to have lips, Lester, to think.)

"Well," she finally said, "I'd just tell 'em I shop at the same store they do and run like hell!"

"Oh, Mag, you're too much," I said with a laugh.

"Ain't I though?" she declared as proud as a peacock.

"Did those new sneakers come with the suit?" I asked curiously.

"Yeah, kind of weird, ain't it? Seeing how I'll be the one running like blue blazes." She cackled while putting her hand impishly over her mouth.

"You want to go eat?" Jesse asked.

"Sure, we'll tell Joe we're OK when he checks the diner."

In the afternoon, streams of people waited at the bus stop with Jesse, a lot of cab people.

The heat bore down, the kind of heat that penetrates the irritability center of the brain. Standing so close with no one speaking was a show of bravery and stamina against heat, Jesse presumed.

Then it broke.

"God damn bag lady up there probably will use two seats. Don't know why they're even allowed on the bus with a bag full of garbage. Sleeping half the time, putting their feet out in the aisles."

Jesse felt the sweat trickle down the back of her neck.

"Hey! Shut up. She has as much right on a bus as you do," snapped another voice from behind.

"Don't tell me to shut up you damned hippie. You're just like her—freeloading on the rest of us."

The hand Jesse held the bag with started to shake.

"For God's sake, leave her alone, she's an old lady, you fat Jew."

I didn't need to ride; I could walk.

Well, God, it's interesting how your name comes up when people are angry. Do you think that man wants bag ladies and hippies to be damned by you? I don't think so. And the division of the ranks—what do you think of that? Christians against Jews, Jews against Christians? People create such dilemmas. It was so simple for us. I loved Jacob and Jacob loved me.

Jesse found another bus stop with shorter lines.

❧

"Lester, it's me, Jesse."

Clean, everything was clean, sterile.

He was on his left side with only one ear available.

"Do you want to talk about hair today, Lester? Oh, I almost forgot, there's another reason for lips; Maggie brought it to my attention. It's so you can think—you tuck your bottom lip into your mouth. Doesn't make much sense, does it?

"It's hot out there today. No surprise, right? The cabbies are on strike, so it's a mess. I hope the bus drivers don't strike now.

"Oh guess what? You might get some little visitors and one big one! Yeah, I asked God if maybe they could visit you while you're here. You'll get a big kick out of them—they're full of it!

"The big one is Jacob, Jacob Schwartz; he's my husband. You'll like him; he's so kind and interesting and fun. If you need anything, he'll be sure you get it. He has a lot of connections, knows a lot of important people, if you know what I mean.

"The biggest boy is Danny. He has freckles across his nose like me with blond hair. He can talk your ear off about baseball; he lives for it. He's got those long legs; it was hard to keep him in pants that were the right length. I hated seeing him in those high waters. He sure can run the bases. He can tell you about his and his dad's baseball cards. They have some from back in your day, Lester. Did you play ball?"

I paused to look at his still body; he was so still, I thought maybe he was waiting for the pitcher to throw the ball as the hush settled upon the crowd.

"Then you'll see Isaac, the middle child—dark curly hair, dark eyes like Jacob. He'll keep things interesting! He's our little walking encyclopedia. We have no idea how he learned so much about everything. He is so interested in absolutely everything! He wants to know why and how and where and when and what for! I don't know how he can retain it all.

"Isaac will tell you all about the ocean or outer space or— you name it! But you know what Isaac would like, Lester? He would be fascinated with what you have seen and experienced throughout your lifetime. He loves history. I think he puts it all together in his mind like a puzzle.

"Are you sorting things out in your mind right now?" I wondered as I heard the faint breath going in and out of Lester's nostrils.

"I wonder if you can smell things. Maybe tomorrow I'll bring in a hot dog with mustard and relish and onions; that might stimulate you.

"Then, Lester, you'll see my little girl, Molly. You'll love her; she's such a sweetie—has red curly hair like me. No, not as curly as Maggie's corkscrews! Aren't they funny? I love looking at them. Molly just has nice curls and blue eyes. What a doll and does she ever have her daddy wrapped around her little finger! She's taking tap dance lessons, so she'll want to perform for you. She'll melt your heart with her goodness and sincerity. She wants to grow up and be a teacher."

I couldn't go on. I managed to squeak out, "Bye, see you tomorrow," and then stumbled into the hallway. I sat on a bench and covered my face with my blanket to muffle the sobs.

"Sweet cheeks, is that you?" a voice in front of her asked.

Oh no, it's Simon. I'll pretend I didn't hear him and keep my face buried.

"Jesse girl, what's happening?"

I knew he wouldn't go away. I lowered the blanket.

"Oh! I thought you were someone else," I remarked, looking at a stranger.

"It's me, Simon."

I knew the voice was Simon's, but this was a nice looking man with short hair, no beard, no soiled long duster, and no filthy feet in sandals. No dirt anywhere!

This man in a wheelchair with hospital clothes was Simon.

"What are you doing here, Simon?" I asked.

"I'm in here to die," he answered matter-of-factly.

"To die?"

"Yeah, I have no home to go to, so Doc said I could stay here to die. You wanna meet me in the linen closet for a little one-on-one resuscitation?"

It was Simon all right.

Just as I announced I was leaving, four men came down the hallway. The big one said, "Simon, my main man, we got to have us a little game of pool upstairs. I'll let you break."

Simon went, apparently unaware of the ploy to get him back to the psych ward.

I remembered the psychiatric hospital I was in.

I hurried to get out into the fresh air. When was the last time I'd eaten?

I stopped at a sidewalk café that was in the shade.

"Would you care for a drink today, ma'am?"

"Just iced tea and a pastrami on rye, please."

A drink, I thought as I laughed to myself. There was a time when that was all I wanted.

After I ate, I knew I had to get up or I would doze in the chair.

I should call Mother Schwartz; I haven't talked to her in several months. Oh, I just can't today; I don't have the strength.

Ah, to be in the womb again, I thought as I jiggled on the bus seat. I sat with my bag in my lap so as not to take up space; I couldn't see forward. It wasn't long before the cross hatching design on my bag blurred and blurred and blu—

I woke up to "I don't know. I've been on the bus for, let me see, fifty-four minutes, and she's been sleeping since I got on. Well, what else do they have to do? They don't have any lives, don't know how to work, and don't care if other people might need a seat."

"They're all self-centered. If the city were smart, it would put them all in a work camp—make them live there and do something constructive. I tell you, their families must be disgusted with them."

I focused on the cross-hatching. My mother had beautiful roses on a trellis like this—so lovely. I had a trellis similar to hers. Jacob had it specially built for me as a Mother's Day present. I don't think my family would be disgusted with me; I think they miss me. I know I miss them.

When the bus stopped, Jess got off and walked to the cool section of the sidewalk where she saw, just before the line of shade, something sparkly. She stooped to see a small Star of David medallion. After she picked it up, she whispered softly into her hand, "I love you, Jacob."

"Just keep it, just keep it," a woman in a jewelry store said curtly after hearing the story. "Nobody will even think of finding it or looking for it, not in this city of thieves."

Looking up abruptly, Jesse retorted, "I'm not a thief."

"All right, all right, trust me, just keep it and go on your way now," she dismissed Jesse nervously.

Out on the sidewalk, Jesse fumbled through her bag for the wooden box. She put her new star in with her locket and four rose petals.

Jesse looked around. Where was she?

"Sir, can you help me?"

"Excuse me, can you—"

"Ma'am, do you know where—"

"Sir, which way is the—"

"Excuse me, ma'am, do you know where St. Luke's is?"

"Why yes. You're quite a ways from it, but if you cross the street and take the next bus, it'll get you to St. Pete's."

"Thank you."

"You're very welcome."

She could see the crowd gathering at the corner.

Give me courage and strength, Lord.

"Jesse, wake up. Jesse!"

She awoke to Maggie's corkscrews bounding toward her face.

"What's the matter?"

"There's a car that's actin' mighty suspicious."

"What do you mean?"

"I've been watching it. Goes up the street, pretty soon it goes back, slows down right by us. What do you think, Jesse?" Maggie asked nervously.

"Let's get out of here before they turn around, Maggie. Now! No! We don't have time to gather our things, let's go." They interlocked arms and fled into the alleyway.

In total darkness, they panted in night air and panted out scared air; the two of them intertwined like scotch and soda in a smoke-filled bar. Jesse felt the cold bricks release their frigidity into her back.

"I hope we're not standing next to someone out here," Maggie whispered as she squeezed closer. She was thinking her foot might be next to someone's head.

"Shh."

Jesse thought of her belongings out on the sidewalk, exposed to the world, without her there to guard them.

They stood, two pillars in the night, two souls; POW's as Jacob's mother and father were years ago.

"I hear Joe coming," Jess whispered to Maggie.

"You do?"

The leader tugged on Maggie's arm, prompting her to follow.

She tugged back.

"Joe," Jesse called abruptly.

His flashlight beamed them in the face.

"Jesse! Maggie! My God, what happened?"

While listening to their story, he helped gather their things. Everything had been ransacked. Jesse's blanket was lying half in the street. The envelope was gone. The wooden box was empty. Clothes were all over the sidewalk. She found the Cub Scout change purse that Danny had made; it was over by Maggie's things. Joe spotted the Star of David.

Jesse's grief culminated when she realized that her locket was gone.

"My three children are in that locket! Joe, help me, help me, it's a locket, a gold heart-shaped locket. We have to find it," Jesse cried as she crawled in circles on the sidewalk.

***

"Marla, set these ladies up with a breakfast on me," Joe dictated. "They've had a rough night."

"Good glory, you two look terrible. What happened?" Marla asked as she poured the coffee.

"You know," Joe began as he settled into their booth, "I don't want you two living out on the street anymore. See if you can make other arrangements someplace. If you can't, I'll get someone to help you. What do you say? Is it a deal?"

Maggie and Jesse looked at each other.

"It's a deal," Maggie said.

"Deal," Jesse replied.

***

I walked into the room of the almost dead. I wondered about "almost dead." Could it be when you look back at your life for the last time? Is it a reconciliation time? A chat time with God? A planning for eternity time? All of a sudden it piqued my interest.

"Lester, its Jess. Its tomorrow, I mean it's really today but, never mind. I'll get you more confused than you already are. But maybe you're not confused at all; maybe everything is crystal clear to you. Is it Lester?" Jess asked as she looked at him with his right ear up—the tunnel from mixed up Jesse to crystal clear Lester.

"I guess I have to move, Lester. Maggie, too. They're kicking us out. Oh well, what are we going to do? The accommodations weren't that great anyhow. I'm feeling real bad about losing my locket. Oh well, what are you going to do? That's life, right, Lester?

"Sorry I ran out on you yesterday. I get a little sentimental talking about my family, you know. Did they come to visit you? I hope so. Did they tell you why Mommy is down here and they're up there? Some bad men come during the night and set our house on fire, Lester.

"Oh, here I go again. Wait until I can find my tissues.

"Can you imagine that? I can't fathom doing such a thing, can you? They're in jail now. They set our house on fire because Jacob was a Jew, can you imagine? They claimed they didn't know anyone was in the house. A man and his three children were in the house and they didn't know!

"Sorry, Lester," I sobbed.

"And me, you ask? Where was I? I was at a spa on Long Island! Can you believe it?"

I waited for Lester to answer.

"For my birthday, Jacob had purchased a weekend spa retreat. I tried to tell him, 'Jacob, I don't need that,' but he insisted I needed to get away and relax. 'I always did so much for my family,' he said; he wanted me to take a break. Well, by the second night, I left early in order to be home in time to prepare their breakfast; I missed them so much.

"Sorry, Lester."

Again Jesse was out in the hall with the blanket over her face.

Maybe I shouldn't come here anymore. I'm not doing Lester any good; I'm not doing myself any good. I'll be upstairs with Simon pretty soon. Good grief!

I think it's time I visited the church.

"Father, do the Sisters of Charity have any rooms left?"

"I don't really know but I can find out for you."

Well, God, what do you think? Some people are waiting for your first coming and some are waiting for your second return. The day you come for me will be a happy day. Why are people fighting and killing over how many times you've come back or have not come at all?

You show yourself in different ways to different people, right? And, as far as I know, the people who see you differently are as intelligent as other groups—they know what they know.

Goodness must prevail over evil. Isn't that what you really want from all of your groups?

"Jess," Father Benito interrupted quietly. "Sister Agnes wants you to go on over."

"Thanks, Father, I will. And Father?"

"Yes?"

"Does God love Jacob as much as he loves me?"

"Yes, Jesse, absolutely."

There was a cross over the bed, a statue of Mary on the dresser, a closet, curtains on the windows, and a beautiful old bed.

"Thank you, Sister."

She gave me a hug.

I sat on the edge of the bed looking through the lace curtains at the garden. How peaceful. Why had I been persecuting myself out on the street? All that expensive psychiatric care, had it done any good? Oh, I'm sure it did. I was so far gone with alcohol and self-destruction. I know they helped me—now I have to do the rest with God's help.

I scooched up on the bed and lay down; how comfortable, how nice. I looked at the upside down cross and said, "You'll come back again for all of us, won't you?"

I closed my eyes for sleep.

Maggie! I bolted upright! I have to see if Maggie has found a place to stay.

Jesse swayed and swaggered around the room trying to think where she had seen the lamp. She hurried to the door and started down the hallway when she heard "cackling." She followed the cackling to the living room.

"Maggie!"

"Jesse! I'll be damned, oops, sorry, sisters. When did you get here? Holy shit, oops, sorry, sisters."

Before Maggie was through, they were all laughing as hard as Maggie's corkscrews were bouncing.

"Lester, I'm here! You won't believe what an excellent cook Maggie is! She can bake, too! She sent these warm blueberry muffins for you to smell. I'm going to put them right on you bedside stand. Now let that wonderful scent go up into your brain. Isn't it heavenly? It reminds me of my mom and me out picking blueberries in the warm air of Lone Moon Creek. My favorite recipe was simple: sugar and warm milk on a dish of blueberries. It was Molly's favorite, too. Keep smelling them, Lester. Do you remember warm blueberry pie with vanilla ice cream?

"Lester, can you imagine Maggie and myself living in with the nuns; we've got it awfully good there. I tend to the flowers and vegetable gardens while Mag cooks. You might imagine that things are pretty lively in the kitchen! I'm going to give my monthly allotment to the sisters. They don't want to take it, but I will insist.

"I wonder if Jacob had a premonition that something might happen to him. He had a huge life insurance policy on himself. Of course, the house was insured, too. I went through half of it, however, in all of my craziness. It costs a lot of money to straighten up. I had to get my mind back plus I needed help to stop drinking.

"Fortunately, Jacob's father hired a lawyer to manage my money; I wasn't capable. That's why I get money each month. For years I was angry with Pop Schwartz for controlling my money, but he really knew best.

I've been out of the loony bin for a long time now. I thought of buying a new house, furniture, a dog, but I never could come to grips with it; I never wanted my own property again. Did you have a house once, Lester? Someday you'll tell me your story, won't you?

"My little munchkins will probably tell you all about their rooms, the tree house, the tire swing, and the paths through our woods. They'll talk you ear off!"

"Mmm, smells good in here," said a nurse who came in to turn Lester. "Blueberries?"

"Yes, help yourself," I offered.

"See you tomorrow, Lester."

Oh, it feels so good to care for flowers again. I love pulling weeds and making the gardens beautiful. "Water, water, water, everything needs water."

"Is that you singing a song about water?"

Jesse turned, "Joe! Come here and give me a hug."

"How do you like it here, Jesse?"

"I love it! Look at my gardens!"

"I have been, they're fantastic," Joe said.

"I'm going to start training some of the other women in gardening. I'm going to be a teacher like Molly wanted to be."

"Who's Molly?"

"Molly was my daughter."

"Oh."

"Joe! Do you want to see Maggie? Knock on that window there."

Maggie pushed up the window and leaned out. "Well bust my britches. How the hell are you, Joe? Oops, sorry, sisters."

"Great, and you look happy!"

"Happier than an escapee in a—" she quickly covered her mouth and laughed. "Yikes, I better get back to my cream puffs before they burn. Stop by again, Joe."

"She's fantastic in the kitchen," Jesse said.

"Whoever would have thought," he replied.

"Who knows what lives any of the street people had?"

"You're right. Oh, I almost forgot."

"My locket! Where did you find it?"

Jesse checked inside to see if the pictures were still there. They were!

"Someone found it and turned it in to Marla. They your family?" Joe asked.

"Yes, that's Jacob and these are my three kids."

"Where are they?"

"Oh, they're all over doing special assignments for God."

"Oh?"

"Yes, he's got them visiting with Lester now. They'll get Lester to come out of his coma."

"That's good. You probably heard Simon is in for a little R&R," Joe said.

"Yes, I saw him one day at the hospital."

"Gwen has gone to her son's again."

"Willingly?" Jesse asked.

"No, she's too much of a free spirit for that. She'll be back."

"I'm sure."

"Well, Jess, I'm glad you and Maggie are here; it's one of the nicest places in the city."

"It surely is. Thanks for everything, Joe. Oh, and Joe?"

"Yes?"

"Is it Joseph? May I call you that?"

"You may."

Jesse and Joseph hugged good-bye.

"I brought you roses, Lester. Smell."

I put the roses under his nose. I expected his nose to twitch, but it didn't.

"Soon your whole room will smell like roses and strawberries, Les. Maggie sent strawberries in for you. Smell the delicious, red, ripe juicy strawberries, Lester.

"Did you ever pick strawberries? We used to pick—"

Something caught Jesse's eye. She turned to look at the bottom of the bed. Had Lester's foot moved? She didn't know?

"How are you able to go so many days without your alcohol? Are you having withdrawals? Is your brain getting messages that there is no alcohol? I know I had a hard time stopping. Of course, I never wanted to face reality either. Do you want to face reality, Lester? I can get you a nice place to stay if you'd like, unless you want to stay outside. That's your choice.

"I brought this in for you, too, Lester. It's a baseball. I'm going to put it in your hand. There, that's it. Keep your fingers around it. Squeeze it once in a while. Has Danny been sharing all his baseball stories with you? I had the greatest picture of him and Jacob when Dan was about two years old. Danny was sitting on Jake's shoulders, both with their baseball caps on, both with mitts, posed to catch a ball. I kept it on the mantle with the other pictures. I had some great shots—my hobby. What was your hobby, Lester?

"Has Jacob had a chance to tell you how much in love we were? Probably not, with all the kids jabbering on and on. Well, he'll get around to it. We could have been the poster couple for happiness. I just adored him; he was my best friend and confidant. He made everything better.

"He let me breathe and caught me when I fell. We promised to love the only God that there is and always, always respect God by putting good before evil. Have you been in love, Lester? Isn't it glorious? The feeling is the highest high on earth, don't you think? We fall apart when love is gone, don't we?

"I've got to go now, Lester. I'll see you tomorrow. Warm up that baseball."

"What do we have today?" a nurse asked.

"Help yourself to the strawberries," I commented as I closed the door.

∽

I used the phone in the living room to call my mother-in-law.

"Hello, Mother Schwartz?"

"Jesse Irene?"

"Yes, how are you?"

"I'm old, how can I be?"

"Have you gotten a housekeeper yet?"

"Oh yes."

"Good. That big house is much too much for you to handle by yourself."

"Tell me how you are, dear?"

"I'm really doing well. I live in a wonderful home with many talented ladies. I work in the gardens and visit sick people in the hospital."

"That sounds wonderful, Jesse. When are you coming home to see me?"

"I don't know, Mother Schwartz. I don't know if I can go back to that town; I don't want to break down anymore."

"I understand."

"Maybe, however, I should stop thinking about myself all the time and think of you. You suffered horribly: First escaping from your homeland and then coming to America to lose your only son and three grandchildren. Plus, you had to stay in that town, to drive past Jacob's and my property every day."

I could hear Leah crying.

"I'm sorry, Mother Schwartz, I didn't mean to make you cry."

"I'll be OK."

"You know what! I am going to visit you, and we're going to look through all your old pictures. Would you like that?"

"I would love that, dear."

"Let me give you the phone number here, and you call whenever you want to talk. I'll set a date for our visit, and I'll let you know. I love you, Jacob's mother."

"I love you, Jacob's wife."

"Come in."

"Jesse, can I talk to you?"

"Of course, Maggie, come in."

I put my book down and pointed to a chair Mag could use.

"What is it, Maggie?"

"I think I'm going to leave here, Jesse."

"But why?" I sat forward in my chair.

"Something's calling me, Jess, I can't explain it really. I need to be out and free, I guess. I know it's stupid with all we got here; this is like a damn palace. Why do I want to go? I must be crazy, but I miss the excitement and the thrill of it all. I miss my buddies, I don't know."

"But what about your cooking and baking? Don't you love that?" Jesse asked.

"I do, but the newness is wearing off; it's getting to feel too much like hard work now."

"I know it is hard work, but you could train some of the other women to do a lot of the chores."

My mind was racing to think of reasons for her to stay.

"It's dangerous out there, Mag, you know that."

"I do, but I guess it's a call of the wild, and you know how wild I am," she said then cackled.

"Let's think about this in a few more days before you make any final decisions, OK?"

"OK."

I lay down on my bed.

"Jacob, see if you can get St. Anthony to speak to God about this, will you?"

"Lester, the good sisters donated this radio for you! Let me see, I'll get something good on here. I know you like music; I heard you singing many a night! Yes, you.

"I remember being on the farm and we could get one station. So guess what? Yup, that's all we listened to!

"How about jazz? Country western? Rap? Rock and roll? Classical? New age? Rock? Easy listening? Swing? That's it—swing.

"My mother had this music on all the time. I love it even though it's not my generation. I'll bet your mother listened to it, too. Oh, here's a great song."

As the melody sashayed around Lester's room, Jess peeled oranges and broke the sections open to release the aroma into the air.

Maggie sent in just-baked brownies. The nurses will love them.

"Do you remember dancing, Lester? I have an idea you could sway to this music—listen." She took his hand and gently led it back and forth to the rhythm, singing along to the radio.

The crooner hadn't realized a doctor had come into the room and observed for a while.

"You know what we had in our school, Lester? Every Friday morning the kindergarten through sixth grade classes met in the auditorium to sing. Together we sang the old standards like 'America,' 'Erie Canal,' 'Bicycle Built for Two,' 'I've Been Workin' on the Railroad,' 'Skip To My Lou,' 'When Johnny Comes Marchin' Home'—great stuff, right? I used to teach my kids lots of songs. I heard you singing, 'Way Down Yonder in the Paw-Paw Patch' one night. We used to sing that.

"Well, I'm going to leave the radio on for you, and don't eat all the brownies in one sitting! Maggie sends her love. See you tomorrow.

"Oops, I always bend down to pick up my bag and there is no bag! Now that is freedom!"

"Hey, sweet cakes, what's cookin'?"

Oh no.

"Hello, Simon, what are you doing on this floor?"

"Getting bored up there. Those guys are dense, dumber than a fence post, most of them."

"So, your therapy is going well?"

"Oh, yeah. I know the routine; I play the games."

"What are you talking about, Simon?"

"I go through this every once in a while to give me a break from the streets. The streets can be grueling sometimes. I come in here, have three squares a day, nice clean bed, get shaved, washed, and get lots of attention. Get to talk to some of the docs. Now that I enjoy! Some of them are really smart; I love it. It's a damn good day when I can stay one step ahead of them!"

"So, this is all an act?" Jesses asked.

"Shh, don't blow my cover; it's too hot to hit the streets. Another two weeks and the heat wave will be over."

"You're something else, Simon."

"Aren't I though?" He laughed as he bopped down the hall.

❧

It wasn't until Jesse started weeding around the lily patch did it come to her: if Simon could "pretend" a situation to get his own way, maybe they could "pretend" in order to keep Maggie there.

After some "tall persuading," Sister Agnes consented to her scheme.

It all started at supper time.

"What in heaven's name is this?" questioned Sister Mary Margaret.

"I haven't the slightest notion," said Sister Lucia, pitching in.

Maggie looked from one to the other in bewilderment, as the dish in question was merely meatloaf.

"Here, I'll drown mine in catsup," Annie exclaimed as she grabbed the bottle.

"If you three don't like it, I'm not even going to try it!" Liz chirped.

"Now ladies," Sister Agnes interjected, "just think of the garbage the people in India are forced to eat."

"What's the matter?" Maggie asked, overtly flabbergasted.

"It's OK, dear," Sister Veronica remarked consolingly, "we all have our bad days."

This went on again at breakfast, lunch, and supper for five days.

Sister Agnes announced to Maggie that she would have to be replaced with Suzanne.

"Suzanne!?" Maggie squawked so hard her corkscrews almost hit the ceiling. "She only knows how to make sandwiches!

"Sister, if you give me another chance I'll get it together. I think I was just having a bad week. I'll train some of the ladies to help with the lesser tasks, and then I can concentrate more. Maybe my freakin' brain was on hold. Oops, sorry, Sister."

So Maggie decided to stay.

Thanks, Jacob, for getting the ball rolling.

"Oh, my God! Lester! You're awake!" I cried all over his arm.

"Yeah, how ya doin', Jesse?"

Suddenly the room was filled with hospital staff clapping and hugging me. I heard remarks like, "You did it, Jesse," "The human touch works wonders; we need more volunteers like you, Jesse."

I didn't want to take time for well wishes, although I didn't want to be rude either; I wanted to ask Lester about my family.

In much wanted solitude, I finally asked, "Did you see my husband and my two young boys and my little daughter?"

Lester looked puzzled. Finally he said, "No, were they here? I don't remember any kids coming in. I didn't know you had any family, Jesse, and little kids?"

The disappointment spiraled through my system like one of Isaac's toys where the sand meandered down the curved pathway. Isaac would monitor the time it took for the grains to descend and then chart it.

Lester seemed to be monitoring my sadness. After a fair amount of time he asked, "Why so sad, Jess?"

"Oh, it's nothing for you to be concerned about. I thought maybe my family had dropped in."

"You know, I've been out of it for several days; they could have come in when I wasn't aware."

I know he was desperately trying to relieve my glumness.

"You're right!" I brightened for Lester's sake; no need for him to have worries on his first day "out."

I told him about my plans to visit my mother-in-law and about Maggie staying at the house and Simon's escapades.

He seemed to know a lot about Lone Moon Creek.

"I never knew you lived in Lone Moon Creek, Lester?" I remarked.

"Oh, I never have."

"You surely know a lot about it."

"Yeah, I guess I do," he replied looking baffled.

"Well, I have to go now, Lester."

"I sure want to thank you, Jess. They say you came in every day."

"It was my pleasure."

"Say, Jesse, before you go, can you turn on the radio over there? Our team is up against the Mets. It's going to be a big one today."

"Our team?" I reiterated.

"Yeah, the Atlanta Braves!"

"I didn't know that was your team, too." The sand was beginning to spiral upward through my system!

"I switched to the Braves not too long ago, I guess," he said as he scratched his head in bewilderment.

I left with a quick wave and a quickened step.

Just out in the hallway I stopped to chat with a nurse with whom I had become friends.

As she talked about the excitement of Lester's recovery, I heard and I listened, and I heard and I listened, and I heard Lester singing:

Molly-O and Mommy-O goin' down the path e-o

Molly-O and Mommy-O goin' to see the bird e-o.

I slid down the hospital wall until I was in a slump.

"Jesse! What's the matter?" the nurse asked in alarm.

"Oh," I said weakly, "I think I nearly fainted."

By that time, I had two people helping me to the bench and others taking my vitals. Debbie ran to get juice and cookies.

After a time, I felt OK and started for home. The head nurse said she was calling Sister Agnes to tell her to keep her eye on me.

As I jiggled in the bus seat, I closed my eyes to thank my family for visiting with Lester. I heard Molly's and my little song sail through my head.

Mother Schwartz told me how the trees were just starting to turn. My maples! She said the air was cooler at night, but the days were gloriously warm.

It was time for me to go home.

The ladies of the house gave me a "bon voyage" party. The sisters gave me a beautiful new suitcase. Maggie gave me a lovely new suit! I looked sideways at Maggie; she knew what I was thinking.

"No!" she cackled, "I didn't get it off of a dead lady!"

The sisters looked at her. Maggie and I laughed.

The girls gave me a coordinating shirt, pants, and jacket outfit. It was very stylish.

I headed north on the train.

Jacob and I loved traveling by train. In fact, we met at a railroad station. Every afternoon while waiting for my train home, I saw Jacob waiting for his. Finally, after months of eye contact, he stood a little closer until one autumn afternoon he spoke to me.

That was it for me. I knew from that moment on I would love him forever. It came true! By the next autumn, we were married on the most heavenly of fall days and went to live on his property of many maple trees.

I watched houses and farms and cities speed by—so many people on this earth. Each with their own unique, but not really unique, problems and desires and concerns.

Which ones are content? Which ones want to hurt other people? Which ones are destitute? Which ones feel superior? Which ones have a place to go after they leave this earth?

You have your hands full, don't you, God?

I rested my eyes and tried to feel the same motion of the train that I felt when Jacob and I traveled cross-country during our first year of marriage. The world was ours; each year became better.

My eyes bolted open when flashbacks of the last twenty years pierced through. What a mess I was Lord, but you knew that. You didn't give up. You were so patient; you waited a long time for me. The same God for Jacob's people and for my people waits for us all.

Where was my mind when I went off the deep end, Lord? I remember floating and falling, floating and falling, being in blizzards and being on carnival rides that would not stop no matter how much I begged for the operator to do so.

Why did the street people become my people? How was it I could fit into their way of life?

I know they didn't judge me. They merely let me be; and indeed, during that time, I struggled just to be.

I know God guided and protected me. Now that I am stronger, I can go back home. I need to go not just for myself but for Mother Schwartz as well.

I slept.

She was right—I saw splotches of reds, yellows, pinks, oranges, corals, fuchsias, and magentas!

The train jostled to a stop. I automatically reached for my bag; I panicked when my hand didn't come in contact with it. When will I get over that?

A driver and car waited for me.

It wasn't long before we were out in the country. Oh my, there were many more houses and horse farms and other gentleman-type farms—so beautiful, so peaceful, all in autumn colors.

Our town was soon to come up. Here we go. There were many new businesses, some the same, some with new color schemes; more trees, bigger trees; new sidewalks; more porch box flowers; bed and breakfasts; more houses; newer cars; more black topped driveways; convenience stores; the same library; and the same bank. Out of town there were peaceful rolling roads, autumn colors, and blue skies.

"Driver, can you slow down through this section? Thanks." I saw our stone wall fence, our fields, our woods, our maples, and the empty spot.

This little teardrop went to heaven... This little teardrop stayed home... This little teardrop melted mommy's heart... This little teardrop turned to gold... And this little teardrop brought angels to wipe it away.

"Say it again, Mommy. Say it again."

There was the horse barn, the carriage house, the greenhouse, more woods, the pond, the tree house, the picnic table, more stone walls, the neighbor's property, more road, and more houses.

Jacob's parents' estate.

Oh my stars, she's so old, so tiny, so old, thought Jesse as she saw her mother-in-law standing in the huge doorway.

Oh my stars, she's so old, so tiny, so old, thought Leah as she watched Jesse come up the sidewalk.

"Leah!"

"Jesse!"

They hugged for a long time, feeling each other's history permeate through their skin.

Jesse started to cry.

Leah started to cry.

Mitchell, Frisky, and Levi barked and howled and bayed and cried.

"Well," said Leah, wiping her tears, "we'd better stop crying or these dogs will never settle down."

I leaned forward to pet them.

"Frisky is a daughter from Gabriele; Mitchell and Levi are her sons," Leah explained.

"This is Gab's daughter?" I swooned almost reverently, taking her head and neck into my arms. "And Gab's grandsons?" I petted them as they came for more and more attention.

I started crying again.

Leah started crying again.

"Miss Leah, would you like me to take the dogs out?" Mary asked as she came in drying her hands on a dishtowel.

"What do you think, Jesse?"

"Oh no, I want to get acquainted with them, if it's OK."

"That's fine," replied Leah.

"Jesse, this is Mary. She does so much for me. Mary, this is my daughter-in-law, Jesse."

They shook hands and Mary went back to the kitchen.

"Come in, dear. Let's sit in the living room."

I quickly looked around. I couldn't believe it! Everything was the same! The same grandness, the stateliness, the perfection of the old-world couple who fled to America. There was the doll that Abraham had shipped to Leah on their thirtieth anniversary!

The same gaze for 150 years. Probably a different dress and a different bonnet, but the same face.

What have those brown eyes with the painted lashes seen?

Even though you can just see her little china teeth beyond the petite pink lips, she doesn't smile, just watches.

Her milk white complexion has not shown signs of age, even though she has outlived almost three generations of mommies.

She has quite a place of honor on the window seat. I wonder if she misses her homeland, from whence she came across the ocean years ago?

⟨∾⟩

They left everything to start anew. They fled from near death—to die because their God hadn't shown himself to them yet. To die, not because they were disrespectful people or because they had killed people or broken any of the Ten Commandments, but because they were still waiting for their Messiah.

In America, they worked using the same high standards their parents had taught them; they were successful. Their heroic escape out of the concentration camp had led to a new and prosperous life. They'd raised Jacob. All was well until the devil raised his evil head and took Jacob and his three children. Now Leah waited to see her son, and I waited to see my husband—the same person. Does anyone think God would say no to either Leah or myself?

⟨∾⟩

I knew almost immediately what was missing in the living room—the photographs.

Leah watched as I looked in the "photograph places"—the mantle, the grand piano, the end tables, around the casing of the French doors.

145

"I thought they would be too overwhelming for you at first," Leah said softly.

"They would have been."

"We'll look at them later."

"Yes."

"How did you manage the whole situation after the fire, Leah?" I asked as we had tea on the verandah.

"I didn't know if I was alive or dead during that time," Leah admitted.

"It was Jacob's father who became my pillar of strength. If it hadn't been for him, I would have snapped like..." she stopped.

"Like I did?" I asked.

"I didn't mean—"

"I know. It's OK, Leah. I did snap, and it's been years of me trying to pull myself together. Thank God you did have Abraham."

"Yes," her eyes swelled with tears as she said, "thank God for Abraham."

"During the war we watched our parents, aunts, uncles, brothers, sisters, nieces, nephews, and cousins all led away. Some we know were tortured, some died of disease, some died of starvation, but we escaped. Unbelievable circumstances.

"Then in America after the fire, Abraham had to spoon feed me, take me to the bathroom, dress me, bathe me all the while saying, 'Leah, be strong. Leah, look what we've come through. Don't leave me now, be strong.' And I tried. I tried for Abraham.

"Your Jacob was taken from you, Jesse. You had no one to lean on. I know why you went out of your mind—your children were gone, you husband was gone, your house, your pictures—everything. Sometimes when we hurt so badly, God puts us in a little shell until we're strong enough to come back out. It took you a long time, didn't it?"

"Yes," I cried into Frisky's back.

"It was all right, Jesse; I waited for you. I promised Abraham on his deathbed that I would wait for you. Now you are here! Thank you, God," said Leah.

"Thank you, God," said Jesse.

Both Schwartz women sipped their tea and looked out onto the same autumn trees that Abraham and Jacob had once looked upon.

"Leah, how were you able to forgive the people who started the fire?"

"It was what God wanted me to do," Leah said simply.

Days of reminiscing and reflecting and pondering and meditating went by while the trees turned deeper into their full regalia.

Mitchell, Frisky, and Levi watched the faces of the two women who were sometimes laughing, sometimes crying, sometimes staring. Looking from one to the other, their canine allegiances tried to shelter them both.

"Leah, would you like to hear one of Isaac's favorite stories?"

"Of course."

"We called it, 'The Last Dish.'

The day the last blue, flowered dish broke, not even the air moved. The candles looked at the napkins, the napkins looked at the stemware, the stemware stared at the curtains, but nothing or no one dared to look at Mother.

Everyone knew the dish was the last of the set that had come across the ocean in a wooden trunk packed in straw and carried by Jeremiah and Nathan up out of the harbor to the house on the hill.

Now the last of a legacy was laid in pieces, much like the islands off the coast of Burma where great-great grandfather had once been.

We didn't know what to expect until she quietly said, "Amen."

"I like that story, too," Leah said thoughtfully.

After a whole morning of looking at the hills together, Jesse said, "Leah, I'm ready."

"I'm glad, Jess. Come."

They started in the living room. Mary, with the patience of Job, brought each picture to Jesse.

The dogs had to be taken outside.

Into the night it went. It began again the next morning and continued throughout the day and evening.

For the next three days, Jesse stayed in her room, Jacob's old room, with the picture albums. Mary delivered meals to her.

On Thursday morning, Jesse joined Leah for breakfast.

"Are you all right, dear?"

"I think so; I really think I'm going to get through this. I seem to be getting a lot of strength from God and Jacob and Abraham."

"Ah, yes, three of my main men, too!" Leah's eyes sparkled.

"There's one more thing I have to do."

"I know, I've had my driver on call for two days now," Leah remarked as she spread marmalade on her toast.

"Would you mind if I took Mitchell or Levi with me?"

"Mitchell would be the most cooperative. Just take a leash; if he sees a rabbit, you'll never get him back."

"Just like his Grandpa, Gabriele!" I laughed.

Mary packed a lunch for us. Mitchell and I left, with him feeling mighty proud of himself. I heard Mary saying to the other dogs, "You two have to wait for the next coming."

I was glad I had gotten a good pair of walking shoes before I left Florida. I had forgotten what fields and woods and stones felt like! The smoothness of the city didn't require the agile footwork of the country.

"If anyone saw me, Mitch," I started then began to laugh, "they'd think I was drunk." I think he laughed in dog language.

All day I had Mitchell "look at this" and "look at that." Leah was right; he was most cooperative and really looked. When I cried, he comforted me; when I rested, he rested; when I went deep into the woods and screamed, he waited for me to stop; and when I ate, he ate.

I sat at the picnic table and looked up to where the nursery window once was. I thought of my first boy, Danny.

The sun twinkled in through the lace curtains. The lace curtains that softly billowed by the crib. The crib that I flounced all in blue satin and dreams. Dreams in a little boy's head of someday sailing the seas. The seas of faraway places, where the sun twinkles, twinkles through lace curtains.

I never thought about the work that my father-in-law, Abraham, had to tend to after the fire. The charred debris from the house had to be removed, the ground filled in or smoothed out, or whatever they do. I could see that the lawn had been kept up—for all these years—by someone that Abe undoubtedly hired.

The little trees we had planted with the children were huge. Some of the perennials Leah had given us years ago were still in existence: peony bushes, sweet peas, black-eyed Susans, lilac bushes, and hollyhocks.

Abe and Leah had preserved all of it. They could have sold the property, but they didn't. Land in America meant something to them. Jacob's wife (me) meant something to them. I cried again.

"Oh, Mitch, you are out with a real nutcase today." I laughed and cried at the same time. "Do you want to go back and see Levi and Frisky?"

"I bet that means yes."

"We're home!"

"How was everything, dear?"

"So beautiful, Mother," I answered as I hugged her. "Why did you keep it up for so many years?"

"Why, why, why, you ask so many questions!" She laughed. "I'll tell you why, because that's the kind of people we are. So, are you hungry?"

We watched the sun set on the plush carpet of fall trees. "Winter will be here before we know it, Jesse."

"Winter? I hadn't thought about that."

"Last winter when I was so sick, I asked God to just get me through until I knew you were all right. I think you're going to be all right now, Jesse."

Startled, I blurted out, "What are you saying, Mother Schwartz?"

"Now, don't get upset. I'm just saying I'm glad you're home."

Now it was Leah's turn to look startled, "You are staying aren't you?"

"Oh, Mother Schwartz, when I came north I never thought about staying," I replied sounding apologetic.

"Well, that will be up to you. Everything will be left to you, of course, and Jacob's property is your property, you know."

It never entered my mind that I had property, me—bones-on-the-sidewalk me? I could never handle all the responsibilities of a homeowner or a landowner—Jacob did all of that and Abraham and... How is Leah doing it all?

"Leah? How have you been able to manage all of this since Pop died?"

"He established a lot of help for me. I have lawyers and accountants and lawn maintenance people and snow plowers, etc., etc., etc., which you can utilize if you wish."

I settled deep into thought; my nights were restless, days were spent going back and forth from Leah's to my property. What should I do?

I could establish a house for people like Maggie and Lester.

I didn't want to live by myself; we could all live in a group home and work to keep things running.

I could donate it to a worthy organization.

I could sell it.

I didn't have such worries when I had nothing.

After a week, I couldn't eat, I couldn't sleep, and I had a constant headache.

Leah became worried.

"Do you think you should go back to Florida for a while and think about it?" she asked consolingly.

"Maybe I should, Leah."

Jesse packed for the trip.

At 3:00 a.m. Leah was awakened by someone talking; it was Jesse. She could hear Jesse telling the dogs to lie down and be quiet; they were so excited.

Then she heard Jesse say, almost in a whisper, "Yes, family, it will work! You guys are always watching out for me, aren't you? I love you, too."

"Welcome home, Jesse!" Sister Agnes's generous hug didn't fail the renowned phrase of "Southern hospitality."

"Can I talk to you, Sister?"

"Of course. Let's go into my office."

Three years later a freelance writer's column read:

A WOMAN COULD BE SEEN TRAVELING THE RAILS SOUTH TO NORTH, NORTH TO SOUTH, SEVERAL

TIMES DURING EACH MONTH. ALWAYS WITH A COMPANION HEADING NORTH, ALWAYS ALONE

GOING SOUTH. IT LOOKED MOSTLY LIKE POOR FOLK. THE WOMAN IN CHARGE HAD A GREAT SENSE OF

CONFIDENCE AND PEACE ABOUT HER, ONE WOULD HAVE TO SAY.

"GRANDMA, CAN I GO TO COLLEGE?"

"UM, DO YOU MEAN GO TO COLLEGE?"

"YES."

"WELL, UM, WHAT WOULD YOU DO THERE?"

"FIRST, I WOULD LOOK INTO THE REFLECTING POOL AND THEN I WOULD SIT ON THE QUAD AND WATCH THE PEOPLE GO BY. CAN I GO?"

"OF COURSE, DEAR, LET'S GO THIS AFTERNOON."

Chapter Seven

COLLEGE IDEAS

"Finally," Rena said with a sigh of relief, "we have our son home for the summer. Our very successful, first-year college boy."

"OK, OK, Ma, lay off the bragging. There are tons of college students much more successful than the one standing in front of you."

"But I don't care about them, I only care about you!"

"You see, that's the problem with you; you don't see outside of these walls."

"What on earth are you talking about? No, never mind, I want you to sit right down and taste these desserts, your favorites plus some new ones that I'm sure you'll like."

"Can I invite Carmen over to have some too?"

Rena stopped in her tracks. "Carmen from next door? That disheveled, bearded old hippie? No way! What gets into you sometimes?"

"Maybe life has gotten into me," Ian said to himself, knowing he would never be able to get through to his mother who was now in her dessert frenzy.

"Son, welcome home!" Clark said as he shook Ian's hand while tossing his six newspapers onto the chair.

"Thanks, Dad. Join us for some desserts?"

"Sure, why not; let's celebrate your first year. So give us a little critique."

"Oh, Clark, he loved it. Didn't you, Ian? That's all that matters."

Clark sat poised for an answer, and Ian knew it. Rena knew it too but didn't want to acknowledge it.

"Well, Dad, to get right down to the bottom line, I want to change my major."

Rena interrupted, "Now, honey, you're exhausted from all your exams. You need to rest a few days and you'll get right back to normal."

"Normal? Ma, what are you talking about? You don't even know what I'm thinking."

"I've told everyone that you are in premed, so don't be telling me that you're getting out of that."

"Rena, let the boy speak."

"I just feel different about things since I took that psychology course the first semester and the sociology course during the last. I've done a lot of reading on my own, too. I think I would like to pursue that line or something related to it."

"Clark, say something!"

"Good pie." Clark put his dish into the sink and went to the living room with his newspapers.

Ian and Rena ate in silence. Ian knew it was not a good sign.

"When did you get in, bro?" Shannon half-screamed as she ran to hug him.

"Oh, am I glad to see you!" Ian said.

"And wait until you hear the reason why," their mother interjected as she put another plate on the table.

"What's up, little brother?"

"He—the premed, doctor to be—wants to analyze people's heads and not their bodies. What's the matter with curing the bodies?"

"Nothing, Ma, I just have a fascination with how people think and why. Is that so bad?"

"It's not bad, it just doesn't have the prestige that real doctors have."

"Oh man, oh man, I don't believe you."

"Well, it runs in the family, doesn't it? Clark, can you come out here and talk to your son?"

"Mmm, which dessert should I have?" Shannon asked aloud. "If I choose this chocolate one then I won't be able to have a chocolate mousse later on when Hank and I go out to dinner. If I take this cheesecake thing, oh no, I won't—that has way too many calories. This jelly roll looks good. Ma is this strawberry or raspberry? Ooo, pie. Who's eaten a quarter of the pie already? Wait, if I have just a little chocolate, I still could have a mousse later. But that jelly roll—"

"Shannon! Stop! You always do this; just make a decision."

"All right, all right, jeez. I like to think about things, not like you who at a drop of a hat changes his major."

They heard the recliner crash into the up position. They heard the papers being slammed to the end table. They heard the heavy feet march toward them. "If this nonsense doesn't stop, you're all going to get kicked out of here for the rest of the day. Do you understand me?"

"Yes, sir," was the reply.

Shannon took a piece of jelly roll and went to the door. "Bye, Ma, gotta get ready for my date. Bye, bro."

The two really never said, "Bye," they just sort of waved.

"Snap-o," Ian said softly.

"What?"

"Nothing, Ma, I was just thinking of something one of my professors said. Oh! Carmen's out in his backyard. I'm going over to see him."

"Oh good grief."

"Carmen, nice to see you." Ian spoke with conviction as he shook the Vietnam War veteran's hand.

"Well, you've taken to shaking hands like a man now, pretty impressive." Carm said underneath his whiskers.

"I, well, I mean—"

"Haven't got the knack of speaking though. Right?"

"I'm sorry, Carmen, I don't know why I'm flustered. Maybe because I'm here to apologize to you, and it's a little harder than I thought it would be."

"Apologize for what?"

"I grew up not being very nice to you all those years and I'm sorry."

"I always thought you were a snotty little brat; and now you're telling me that you were?"

Ian could feel his face turning red. "I am sorry."

"What brought this on?"

"Well, I went away to college and—"

"I wondered where you'd gone to."

"And I started learning about life and people and wars and reactions."

"They didn't teach you much about rambling on and on, did they?"

That question took Ian by such surprise and Carmen burst into laughter.

"This is the first time I've ever seen you laugh, Carmen."

"Never saw your face look quite the way it did just then."

"Hey, would you like a piece of dessert with some coffee?"

"Sure, if you bring it over here."

"Oh my ma won't bite."

"You sure?"

"Come on."

Ian could hear a scurrying in the kitchen; he knew his mother was making a mad dash to evacuate the premises.

"Have a seat, Carmen."

Carmen sat like an owl with big eyes darting all around, taking in new territory that had been on the other side of the wall for so many years.

"What are you thinking, Carmen?" Ian asked.

"I never knew it was this nice over here."

"Yeah, my mother is quite the housekeeper with a little OCD thrown in."

"Did you learn about that at school?" Carmen asked.

"I did!"

"I learned about it in the service."

"Learned about what, Carmen, and welcome," Clark uttered as he entered the kitchen.

Carmen stood and the two neighbor strangers shook hands.

Neither Ian nor Carmen wanted to elaborate on OCD in front of Clark, especially since it concerned his wife.

"Just talking about college, Dad."

"You ever go to college, Carmen?"

"Not until I got out of the service. Went in as a boy and came out a N. U. T."

"What's that?" Ian asked trying to think of the psychological acronym."

Carmen and Clark had a good laugh as Ian caught up in a few seconds.

"It was a nasty situation, wasn't it?" Clark asked with much compassion. Ian noted his father's empathy with surprise, not really knowing why he should be.

"I had no idea what I was getting myself into; I was just a kid. Ever have to kill someone, Ian?"

The college boy choked on his cheesecake.

"Whoa, kid, you OK? Didn't mean to make you choke."

"Yeah, I'm all right. What did it feel like?"

"Feel like? Feel like? Are you out of your mind asking a question like that?"

"Don't be too hard on him, Carmen; he's changing his major so he can go into this line of questioning full time!"

It must have been a man-to-man thing, Ian thought, since Carmen calmed right down and the two men laughed.

"So what are you going to do this summer, Ian?"

"Dr. Raymond is going to fit me in with five other students."

"How about you going out to the vet's hospital with me every Thursday? In fact, Dr. Raymond is always out there on Thursdays."

"Me?"

"Good God help us! I'm not talking to your shadow!"

"Well, I hope you're satisfied," Rena remarked as Ian walked through the back door. She was already sweeping the kitchen floor. "Bringing that man into my kitchen."

"Do you know he went to war for you? For all of us?"

"He isn't smart enough to have been in the service, and he's lazy and uncouth and standoffish and—"

"Rena!" snapped Clark from the living room. "That'll be enough!"

"Your professor was right," Rena whispered to Ian as she kept sweeping, "Snap-o."

Ian lay in bed thinking about his family, snap-o, OCD, and roundabout. "Roundabout" was the term he heard in class that related to people who went round and round, not being able to make up their minds. And what was he, a little of each? And Carmen?

"Hi, Carmen, can I ride on the vet's bus with you tomorrow? Dad has to take the car into the garage."

"Sure, if you think you can stand it."

"What do you mean?"

"Some of those guys get pretty wild."

"Can't be any worse than college," Ian said and laughed.

"You might be right. See you at eight."

"You're up early. Where are you going this morning?"

"Out to the vet's hospital with Carmen."

"What? Why?" Rena asked.

"I want to get inside their heads and try to understand what they've been through and what they're still experiencing."

"Why on earth would you care? What's in their heads isn't real, but being a doctor, like I thought you intended, would let you treat real ailments, things you can see."

"You know what you have, Ma? You have AD."

"AD? I pay attention."

"No, not attention deficit, attachment deficit."

"Who has attachment deficit?" Shannon asked as she came in and sat at the kitchen table.

"Well! Apparently I do! I don't know where your brother comes up with these things. I'm beginning to think he makes them up."

"There is an attachment deficit disorder and those who have it feel no closeness, no attachment to anyone outside of their immediate family."

"One's family is all that's important," Rena replied, continuing to defend herself.

"But, Ma, there's a big world out there, and we're responsible for it."

"You know," Shannon interrupted, "I want to join a group that helps others. I was thinking about the Clean Your Park group, but I really don't want to touch some of that stuff out there so I thought about the Be a Role Model group, but I don't want to tie myself down on a certain day of the week. Suzy thinks I should join her group at the soup kitchen, but I don't know. I like going to parks and being outside, but it would be kind of neat taking a youngster around to fun places but—"

"Roundabout," Ian and Rena uttered at the same time.

"What's a roundabout?" Shannon asked.

Ian watched his mother cook-clean, fix-clean, straighten-clean, arrange-clean, stack-clean.

"Why don't you sit for a few minutes, Mom, and eat your breakfast?" Shannon asked.

"She never does," Clark uttered as he walked in.

"Guess what your son says I have?" Without waiting for an answer she blurted out, "AD— attachment deficit disorder."

"Huh," Clark mumbled as he read his paper, "I thought he would have said OCD."

Ian chocked on his toast.

"O what?" Rena asked.

"Doesn't matter," he mumbled.

"How's everything at your apartment, sweetie?" Rena asked Shannon, changing the subject.

"Well, Mom, you know that one neighbor I told you about? He's at it again!"

"He's making that pounding sound?"

"Yes! Sometimes in the middle of the night it starts up."

"I think he's trying to force me to move!"

"Did you complain to the super?"

"I was going to, and then we all got these flyers in our mailboxes."

"And?"

"They sound suspicious, like, 'At our next meeting bring your concerns—we need to make some alterations in this building.' Doesn't that sound like they are trying to get rid of me?"

"Shannon! That's ridiculous! You're just being paranoid," her father exclaimed as he took his coffee and newspapers into the living room.

"That's why our son is going down the primrose path, it's because of you," Rena yelled in at the back of Clark's head, "calling your own daughter paranoid and me—something that starts with an O."

"OCD," both Ian and Shannon sang together. "Obsessive compulsive disorder."

"I'll 'disorder' him," Rena whispered as she rewashed the frying pan.

"You in there!" Carmen pounded sharply on the back door. Shannon jumped, knocked her coffee over, and Rena's frying pan went sailing through the air. "You coming?"

"OK, next one on will be Jeffrey. Don't stare at him; make eye contact for only a second and then look away. But he'll stare at you, sometimes for the whole trip. Just let him, don't make any big deal out of it.

Archie's cool, he'll try to give you coupons. All week he clips coupons and then tries to hand them all out before we go back home. I guess it's sort of a game with him. It doesn't do any harm; even the doctors and nurses take his coupons.

There's robot man; more than half of him is artificial. Got blown up real bad, but he's got a good attitude about things.

"Oh no," Carmen lamented.

"What's the matter?" Ian asked.

"We're supposed to have a thunderstorm this afternoon and here comes Walt."

"Huh?"

"He must have a new caregiver who doesn't know or forgot that you don't send Walt out of the house if it's going to thunder and lightning."

"Part of his PTSD?"

"Hey, you're smarter than you look!"

"What's the matter with that guy?"

"He thinks he's the social director. Pretty soon he'll be singing like Frank Sinatra and motioning the others to join it. Some of them will. If it brings them enjoyment, that's a good thing."

Ian met up with Dr. Raymond and the other students. "What brings you out here, Doctor?"

"I lost my brother in the Vietnam War," he paused before going on. "Just want to give what I can."

Ian changed his major; he went deep into his studies. Home was not on his agenda that second year, but then the second year ended and Ian had to leave the dormitory.

"Oh, my boy, my boy!" crooned Rena. "Here, sit, have some cake, some pie. How about a homemade sugar doughnut? Clark, Clark, Ian's home."

"Son, I think you've grown a couple more inches." Clark laughed, as he had to look up a little higher at Ian. The two hugged.

"Hey, give me one of those hugs, you silly goose."

"So, how's life been treating you?"

"Not bad, Dad, not bad. I've really been studying hard; there's so much to learn. There's so much out there."

"Well, you don't have to tell your dad that; you see how he reads six newspapers every day," Rena proclaimed as she lifted their plates to wipe away crumbs that weren't there.

"How has the change in your major worked out?"

"It was the absolute best thing I could have done, because now I know what I really want to do."

"Yes, yes, yes," Rena cheered as she waved and circled the dishrag above her head. "You're going back to being a real doctor, and that's OK about those other courses because you're going to need those, too. Real doctors, I mean the nice ones, they like to know what the patients are thinking, too! Oh, I'm so happy; wait until I tell all my friends."

Ian had another sip of coffee and two more bites of the sugar doughnut before he spoke. "Mom, Dad, how can anyone heal the person physically or emotionally until the spiritual side of the person is in order?"

"The what?"

"He said the spiritual side," Clark answered.

"I know what he said; I was paying attention."

"What do you mean, Ian?"

"I have taken four theology classes and done a ton of reading on my own, and it has absolutely captivated me!"

"Oh dear God," Rena exclaimed as she slumped into a chair.

"Ian! You're home!" Shannon screamed as she ran to hug her brother.

"Hi, sis! How's everything with you?"

"Ugh, that apartment building, I swear they're out to get me. They want to put a new pool out back. Do you know how many germs are going to be in that community pool? Do they want me to just get sick and die? I found a different building that I think I will like but I don't know. I wouldn't really know who they were and maybe I should just stay—"

"Shannon! Hold on to your thoughts for a bit, Ian just got home!"

"You don't have to snap at me, Dad, jeez."

"It's OK, dear. Have some dessert and listen to this; it'll make your socks fall off."

"I was merely saying that I need to change my major and am thinking about going into the seminary after college."

"The seminary? Like learning about God and stuff?"

"I think that's how I can serve people best."

"Serve?" Rena injected. "Why on earth would you want to serve anybody when you could be a real doctor and make lots of money? They get paid you know!"

"Let's take a break, Ian. I see Carmen in his back yard; let's go over," Clark suggested.

"Good idea, Dad. We won't be long, Mom."

"Don't be surprised if you see the ambulance pull in after I've had my major heart attack," she whined.

"Well, look who the cat dragged in! Good to see you, stranger!"

"You, too, Carmen." The men shook hands all around.

"So what are you now? Doctor, lawyer, Indian chief?"

"According to my mother, I'm a murderer."

"Huh?"

"Rena is just a little upset because Ian announced this morning that he wants to go into the seminary,"

"No kidding?" Carmen asked.

"No kidding," Ian said.

"Man, you don't hear many kids say that! You know, if it wasn't for our chaplain in the war, there would have been suicides all over the place. He had a way of talking to those men and making them see that life was worth living. In fact, it was the chaplain who saved my life."

"What happened?"

"Fire! I was on fire and he grabbed off his coat to smother it. He got burned, too. I had burns on seventy percent of my body, but I lived. Why do you think I wear all these baggy clothes and keep my whiskers? I'm pretty much a mess."

Ian went right to Carmen and hugged him, while Carmen's tears jigged and jagged down into his whiskers.

"Why does everything have to be so noisy?"

"What are you talking about?"

"I don't know, but I hear a lot of noise."

"The only noise I hear is you, now hush."

ᑕᔆ᠑Chapter Eight᠑ᑐᔆ

The Widower

The pounding, teeming, slashing rain was soon to devour his soul, say nothing about the vehicle that she had chosen six months before she died. He hung to the steering wheel as if his fingers could press hard enough to squeeze her pretty fingers out of the arc to replace his. He didn't want his large knuckled appendages to be driving her beloved Lizzy; he wanted her behind the wheel so he could copilot while he sat looking at her beauty.

Why, why, why, his thoughts clicked like a metronome in perfect sync with the windshield wipers. He reached for his five o'clock shadow with his fingers and wiped the tears that wouldn't stop, matching the persistence of the heavens that had opened, releasing the sadness of his world. The highway offered no peace with the agitation of the travelers evident through the jolts and jabs of the accelerators and brakes.

Luke jabbed the radio knob eliminating the noise. "Stupid music," he snarled. And then, for two seconds, he was transported into a world of silence and peace and the tranquility of how his world used to be when she was alive and their world was good. But he could not stay under the bridge; the tightly knit traffic kept him moving. No one would let him stop or go back or turn around; he had to leave the dry, silent haven that lived under the overpass and transcend into the wet, cruel, opportunist, me-first world. There was not one vehicle that encompassed the beloved Lizzy that knew about the man named Luke who was like a caged animal within, living without his Ashley.

He knew there would be another overpass in a mile or two; he and Ashley used to travel that one every weekend when they were courting.

"Courting," he murmured and wondered where that term originated. He pulled into the right lane, wanting to travel as slowly as traffic would allow in order to elongate the two seconds of peace with Ashley. The heavy rain disallowed his view of the bridge until he was almost under it. He took in a huge breath of humid air and held it to make the moment even quieter. Ah, there it was: no beating rain on the car or on his soul, no sadness, no memories of a funeral. They had their life again.

He even heard her voice say, "Luke."

"What?" It couldn't be! He squirmed in his seat as the car behind him blasted the horn because he had slammed on his brakes. He only looked forward when five cars passed, not wanting to see their terse, irate faces.

The scare made the tears cease, so when he stopped at the tollbooth the lady only said, "You look terrible; you better get some sleep."

Ah, yes, sleep. What is sleep? Luke lay on his bed wondering about the word "sleep." As a baby, you love it and do it innately; as a toddler, you cry before sleep; as a youngster, you fight it; teenagers claim they don't need it; the college aged crave it; working people look forward to it; but widows and widowers have no description that can come close to the meaning of the term because it is transparent and ambivalent. Would there be a dream of loveliness or a dream of worry? How many times would the sleep be interrupted? Would terror creep in? But concretely, the spouse is never there in the morning.

"Good morning, Mrs. Stevens," Luke muttered somewhere underneath his neglected whiskers.

"Brought you a warm breakfast, dear," Mrs. Stevens chirped cheerfully after running across the street with her picnic basket full.

"You don't have to do this every day, Mrs. Stevens."

"I know I don't, I just want to."

"You're a kind woman," Luke remarked sincerely.

"Well, Ashley was kind to me and—oh, I'm sorry, Luke. Here, take this napkin."

"I've got to get a grip on my life, but I don't know how. I'll never get used to her not being here," Luke cried into the blue and white checkered napkin.

"You need to grieve, dear, go ahead. Someday it'll begin to ease."

"Yeah, someday."

Luke ate standing up, eating right from the picnic basket. Maybe he would drive out to the highway again. There was no rain like yesterday, the highway would be much quieter, and the underpasses would be very still. He could drive slower; maybe he'd hear her call his name again. Luke shivered.

"Morning, Luke," he heard his neighbor call out. "Want to go fishing with me today?"

"No thanks, Mr. Landow. I'm going out for a little drive."

"Well, anytime you want to go let me know. Remember how much fun we used to have, you and Ashley and me?"

Luke quickly put on his sunglasses to hide his tears and slid into his car. He and Mr. Landow waved to each other.

Luke drove slowly through his little town, the town that Ashley adored. He tried to get her to move to a bigger town, maybe even a city, but it she would always say, "I could never leave Lone Moon Creek—this is home." And home it was. They'd made a wonderfully happy life among their friends and neighbors.

Luke drove to the highway and reached for the ticket. "Have a nice day," the attendant called out. Luke didn't respond as he tightened his grip on the steering wheel.

"There it is!"

Luke was pleased he could see it from a distance; he could prepare himself. It had come up much too quickly the day before. He could feel his breathing pattern shorten. No one was behind him, so he let up on the gas. Under the overpass, he had more than two seconds, much more time; but Ashley didn't call out. It wasn't the same; maybe he needed the torrential downpour to hear the silence.

Under the next overpass it was the same. He wanted that moment of ethereal joy; he needed it.

"Thanks for traveling the highway. Hope you had a good day!" the attendant remarked.

"Yeah, just great," Luke answered sullenly.

Noise—that's what he needed to hear the silence, the silence where Ashley was! Luke's mind searched like a computer for places of noise. The road crew and their jackhammers! The farmers filling their silos! The cheering at the ball game! The train going through town!

Luke turned off the car and there it was. Before his hand reached for the door handle, the silence of the motor brought him his quest. He sat motionless with the warm sunshine streaming through the windows. He put his head back on the headrest and closed his eyes. Comfort spread over his entire body as his mind wandered to the park and the picnic area, to the gazebo, and the fishing hole with Ashley.

"Luke, Luke, are you all right in there?" Mrs. Stevens called as she pounded on the window.

Luke jerked forward, wondering where he was. "Yes, I'm all right. I guess I fell asleep."

"You've been looking like you needed some sleep. See, nature has a way of taking care of the wounded."

As Luke walked into the house, he thought of Mrs. Stevens's word, "wounded."

"Is that what I am, wounded? Hmm, maybe I am. I feel that way."

Luke flopped on the couch as he began his march through the room with his eyes. Somehow he had gotten into a habit of looking first to the roll top desk with their wedding photographs to the open staircase with more of their pictures ascending the wall to the basket by her chair with her knitting things to the houseplants on the bay window that had desperately wilted because he hadn't watered them to the jigsaw puzzle still on the card table untouched since...

Bang, bang, bang! Luke jumped and ran to the back door. *Oh no*, he thought as he wished he hadn't let the old coot see him. Their backyards were adjoining, and for some reason, no matter how pleasant and cooperative he tried to be, the old coot was never satisfied: the grass was never short enough, the shrubs were straggly, their company made too much noise on the patio, the lights were on too late at night, and on and on. It was Ashley who never gave up on John; her kindness was unprecedented. "I wonder what he wants to complain about now!"

"Luke."

"John."

They stood eyeball to eyeball. *What is this? A standoff?* Luke wondered.

Finally John muttered, "Here. This is for you." He handed Luke a large brown shopping bag.

"What is this?"

"Thought you might be hungry—made some for myself, too. Well, take care." John turned and walked through their backyards.

Luke removed a covered casserole dish of stew with potatoes and carrots and onions. "Ooo," he exclaimed, almost drooling as the aroma wafted upward, "my favorite."

Bang, bang, bang! Luke swung around to see the old coot again.

With two pot holders, John handed Luke a warm peach pie. "Couldn't figure how to fit them both into the bag without a big spill. Sorry to bother you again."

"John, wait! Thank you, thank you so much. Did you know that these are my favorite dishes?"

"Well, yes I did. Ashley and I were visiting about food one day and she told me."

Luke devoured the tender pieces of beef and stabbed one vegetable after another as he stood over the casserole dish remembering how his wife would make this very dish on special occasions. The peach pie didn't stand on ceremony and get sliced; instead, it was scooped into as tears rolled onto the counter.

Luke stared at the back of John's house. He needed a moment with Ashley, right now.

He jumped into his car and drove to Hemlock St. where he knew the sidewalk was being replaced. Sure enough, the jackhammers were vibrating in full volume.

He got a thump on his back as an irate worker demanded his attention and motioned for him to "Get back." Luke waited and there—the silence. He closed his eyes and waited for the Ashley moment. "I don't like the looks of you," the same worker expounded. "This is a work area; it's not for loiterers standing around with their eyes closed. Move along."

Luke parked by the train tracks. He lowered all the windows so the clatter would be as loud as possible in order to have the silence of its departure extra quiet. *Please, Ashley, come to me, if even for a few seconds*, he mulled the thought over in his mind as he allowed his head to be cushioned by the headrest.

His mind focused on the buzzing of a summer fly somewhere inside the car. "The windows are all open; you can fly out. Go. What's stopping you? Oh stop, stop that buzzing." And just like that, the buzzing stopped. There was the silence! "Ashley? Say something. I miss you desperately." But it wasn't the sweet voice that Luke craved, it was the blasting of the train's horn that caused Luke to swing to the left with such vehemence he felt his neck crack, even though he couldn't hear it above the unyielding roar of the train.

"Got a sore neck?" Mr. Ambrose hollered from next door.

"Yeah, I guess I do," Luke answered as he continued rubbing it as he sat like a stray dog on his front steps.

"Might have something that'll help. Be right back."

Luke liked his other neighbor, Mr. Ambrose, just as he liked Mr. Landow. They always were very kind when he went to them with a house problem or a lawn problem. He knew they were way beyond his expertise, as he was the new homeowner on the block. And they were so respectful to Ashley. Luke always knew that his new wife would be kept safe with them on either side of the house and Mrs. Stevens across the street. He only worried about the old coot in the back, but apparently Ashley had earned his respect long before he had.

"Here you go; try rubbing this onto your neck."

"But this says it's for horses!" Luke said.

"Right! If it helps them, it ought to help you!" He laughed.

"Can't hurt, I guess. I'll try it."

"What were you doing when this happened?"

Luke was embarrassed to tell his neighbor about the fly and the train and the silence. It didn't even make sense to him. How could anyone else understand it?

"Oh I just turned too quickly, I guess."

"How would you like to come and eat supper with me tonight?" Mr. Ambrose asked.

"Oh, I'm sorry, I can't. The old—I mean John brought me some stew and peach pie that I should finish." Luke was glad he had an excuse; he knew he couldn't get through an evening of small talk.

"That's OK. It took me a long time to want to be with anyone after my wife died, too."

Luke twisted his head too quickly, resulting in him rubbing his neck as he asked, "Your wife died?"

"Yes, thirty years ago and I still miss her."

"Oh no!" Luke whined as he grabbed the horse liniment and ran into the house.

As he warmed a dish of stew, he thought about his neighbor. He had no idea that Mr. Ambrose ever had a wife. He thought it was odd that he'd never mentioned her; but then again, after thirty years without her, maybe he didn't know what to say in front of him and Ashley—the newlyweds.

Wait! He gave Ashley something. What was it? Something about sewing, yes! Luke ran upstairs to Ashley's craft room. He opened the top drawer of one of her supply bureaus. There! That's it! This must have been his wife's. Luke carefully opened the lid of the cloth-covered box and inside were all sorts of compartments for thread and needles and little scissors—strange little notions. It was a long time, like thirty years, before Mr. Ambrose could give this away, Luke reckoned. He must have known that Ashley was a special person.

The young man, smelling of horse liniment, sat on the top step of the stairs and bawled into the sewing box.

"Whew! What's that smell in here?" Mrs. Stevens asked as she came in with breakfast for Luke. "Wait a minute, the closer I get to you the worse it gets."

"Oh, it's me," Luke answered, not trying to deceive his across-the-street neighbor. He lifted the bottle for her to see.

"Ah, I know where that came from."

"Did he have you try it, too?"

"No way, not me, but my husband was a true believer in his tonics."

"Your husband?"

"Yes, and why are you looking at me like you're seeing a ghost?"

"When, I mean, how long, uh, what happened. I mean, did you, uh—"

"Would you stop mumbling and stammering? You must have known I was once married. Ashley and I spent many an afternoon talking about our terrific husbands."

"How long have you been alone?" Luke asked sheepishly.

"Going on twelve years now."

In a slight whisper, Luke asked, "Do you miss him?"

"Of course I miss him!"

"How do you handle it?"

"At first, you don't handle it, it handles you. But after a time, a little bit of peace creeps in for a while and, of course, disappears again. Back and forth, back and forth."

"Thank you for the breakfast. And Mrs. Stevens, did Ashley really think I was terrific?"

"She sure did, Luke; she sure did."

Luke exhaled such a sigh that the crumbs from the toast blew across the table. How had Ashley known more about the neighbors than he had? She was such a chatterbox, why didn't she ever mention Mrs. Stevens's husband or Mr. Ambrose's wife? Maybe the thought never came up; he didn't know.

Luke sat at the kitchen table for the next two hours thinking of his life with Ashley. He looked through the window, gazing at one birdhouse then the next and one birdbath then the next, remembering how she just had to have them. He was so thankful that he'd given in to her; she relished the thought of having birds in her backyard. Looking beyond, he could see the old coot hanging his wash on the clothesline, which reminded him of returning the dishes.

"Am I up to it," he questioned himself? "I guess I better do it," he answered himself. "It was very nice of him to bring me my favorite—there! There's another incidence of Ashley bonding with a neighbor."

"Hello, John," Luke strained to greet the clothes-hanging man as he cradled the casserole dish and pie plate in his arm.

"Howdy, neighbor," John answered after taking a clothespin out of his mouth. "How was the grub?"

"It was the best meal I've had in weeks," he replied truthfully.

"I'm glad. Ashley told me you loved those two things."

"I sure do, but I'm just surprised you know how to cook," Luke responded, hoping he wasn't insulting John.

John laughed. Luke had never heard John laugh! "It was either learn how to cook or starve. After my wife passed away, I was just about starving."

"What? Your wife passed away? When?" Luke asked.

John watched the color fade out of Luke's face. "Here, sit on this bench, Luke. Let me take those dishes out of your arms."

"Thanks. For some reason I'm feeling a little faint."

"Did you have any breakfast?"

"Yeah, Mrs. Stevens brought me some."

"You mean that busybody across the street from you?"

There, thought Luke, *there's the old coot that I know.* "All I know is that she has been very nice to me."

"Humph," retorted John.

"When did your wife pass away?" Luke reiterated the question.

"Well, let me think. Which wife are you referring to?" John said.

"Which wife? How many have you had?"

"Three. I've had three wives, and I've lived past all of them."

That was the sentence that put Luke over the edge He went stark white, and John was sure he saw his eyeballs roll back into his head. "Get your head down between your legs," he ordered pushing it there himself. With the other hand he snapped a cold wet towel off the line and placed it on the back of Luke's neck then placed a washcloth on his forehead.

"There. Are you feeling better?"

"Yeah, thanks," Luke said.

"Think nothing of it. You don't suppose the old busybody poisoned you, do you?"

Luke emitted a limp laugh. "I hardly think so."

"Eeuuu, why do my towels smell like rot?"

"Oh sorry, it's the horse liniment."

"Hey, you know that stuff really works."

"I think I better head home and lie down," Luke said weakly.

"Hey, Luke," John called out, "I'm making meatloaf for supper. Can I make you some?"

"Sure! I love meatloaf!"

"I know."

Luke stared at the ceiling thinking about the old coot losing three wives. No wonder he was so grumpy. Poor guy.

"Hey! Are you here?"

Luke looked at the clock. He had slept the whole afternoon!

"I'm here, I'm coming," Luke hollered down the stairs.

"Brought you your supper: meatloaf, mashed potatoes, and salad. Are you up for it?"

"Oh does that ever smell good. I'm starving."

"OK, enjoy," John said.

Luke savored each mouthful; it was just the way Ashley would fix it. "Oh no," he said aloud as his fork stopped in midair, "I need to learn how to cook!"

"How's it going over there?" Mr. Landow hollered through the holly hawks.

"I feel somewhat normal this morning; something must be wrong."

"Oh, I hope not."

"Could I ask you something?" Luke asked hesitantly.

"Sure, what's up?"

"It's kind of a delicate subject, as Ashley would say."

"Can't be about house repairs or lawn maintenance then."

"No."

"OK, shoot."

"Have you ever been married?"

Mr. Landow howled with laughter as he leaned over and slapped his knees. "Good grief, that's all you wanted to know? The answer is no. Why do you ask?"

"Well, I've been getting to know my neighbors and come to find out they've all had at least one spouse who died. It's starting to freak me out."

"Oh I see, I think," Mr. Landow replied. "Say, Luke, how about you and me go fishing today?"

"No, I better not. I need to stay here."

"Why?"

"I don't really know. I feel like I'm waiting for something, and I don't even know what it is."

"Hm, I remember those days."

"What do you mean?" Luke asked.

"When Ellie was killed in a car accident, I didn't think I could ever go on."

"You said you weren't married," Luke snapped.

"I wasn't, Ellie was my fiancé, and we were to be married in five days."

"Oh my God, I'm sorry. I'm so sorry."

"You didn't know."

"I guess it's true then, I am surrounded by grief," Luke moaned as he buried his head in his hands.

"No, Luke, you are not surrounded by grief. You are surrounded by survivors, and you are going to be a survivor, too."

"Marjory! What on earth are you doing? What are you hiding under your bed?"

"My money."

"Why are you hiding it?"

"I don't know, but Erin told me to hide my money away for a rainy day. Why do we need money when it rains?"

Chapter Nine

Gravy Money

E rin peered over top of the music book while her fingers continued playing the organ. Her eyes scanned the congregation or, should I say, the noncongregation. Of course Luellen Norel was there; why would this Sunday be any different from the last seventy-three years? So she didn't count. And old Dudley Hathborn sat in his pew like a large capital C, curved to perfection. Interestingly enough, when he stood, he still did not uncurl from his designated letter; another "no counter" Erin calculated. Oh well, what did she care? She could play to a full house or to an empty one; it didn't matter to her. This gravy money she was earning went into the pot for her exotic island vacation.

Oh no, thought Erin, *not them*. Erin watched as the three Yalder children ran up the aisle, all of them going in different pews. The mother, not paying any attention, stopped to chat with Luellen. Erin lowered her eyes onto her music to avoid seeing the antics that were assuredly going to transpire. *Forget them,* she lectured to herself. *What do you care what they do? Just keep on playing this God music and earn that good old gravy money—pure profit.* She smiled to herself.

Just as she thought, two of the Yalder's were in a squabble over a hymnal. One boy had the other by the necktie, pulling to supposedly jerk the book out of his brother's hand. *But I don't care, I don't care,* she thought then softly hummed the words to "Amazing Grace."

Ah yes, of course, what would church be without the two spinster sisters wearing their hats and gloves? Why don't those two get real? Do they even know what era this is? Erin stomped on the volume pedal as she called out the year under her breath. She knew Esther and Wilma would jump. They did. Erin bent low behind her music to laugh.

What a cinchie way to make money! Erin entertained herself with the thought as she jazzed up "Blessed Assurance." Her five-day-a-week job of teaching music theory at the college was work, with the entire paycheck going for bills and essentials; but this was easy money, gravy money!

She could see the two prudey sisters raise their eyebrows and whisper behind their white gloves; Erin knew they were complaining about the velocity of their dear hymn. Erin added a few more syncopated stanzas and set the metronome in her head to swing a little faster.

Well, well, well, Erin thought, as she saw Maude Philander pull her hungover husband into a pew. *I wonder how she got him here today. She's probably holding something over his head,* she mused as she played the next hymn without looking at the page or her fingers. Old Jim sat there, green around the gills, probably wishing he was a thousand miles away. *Me too, Jim,* Erin sent out a mental message to him. *It won't be long before I'll be basking on the beach, but how about you, Old Jim? Poor old fool, you'll still be in this crummy little town, sneaking to the bar and having Maude pull you into the church.*

The music continued until the pastor walked to the podium. Erin yawned behind her music. *Easy money, easy money,* Erin began the mantra in her head to compensate for the slow monotonous drawl of the pastor.

She knew how to sit in church and appear to pay attention; she had learned that when she was seven years old. "I never saw a child so well behaved," the women would tell her mother.

"And she listens, too!" her mother would reply. Whatever gave her mother the impression that she listened was a mystery to Erin. Erin never listened. She didn't know why her mother never questioned her about the sermon.

Jim's head bobbed and Maude gave him the elbow. Jim jolted upward. Erin let only her eyes show over the top of the music; everything below was laughing.

Dudley Hathborn, in his "C" position, was looking at his knees. Good grief, why does that man come to church? Doesn't he know how ridiculous he looks? Erin stretched her own back, thinking how svelte she was going to look parading on the beach. She lifted her face and closed her eyes, thinking of the sunshine that soon would melt all over it. She stayed in that pose for several minutes, knowing it definitely looked like a spiritual pose.

The pastor stopped to direct the congregation to a hymn. Erin deemed it a gift to sense when the droning ended and to listen for directions; she never missed a cue! Erin encouraged the organ to resound as if she was in St. Patrick's cathedral, in which she had never been. She wanted her music to be heard down the street to Cagney's little grocery store and clear to Ray's one-pump station to the east. Mainly, she didn't want to hear any of the caterwauling from the parishioners, especially Esther and Wilma, who thought they were eligible for the Metropolitan Opera House. The pastor gave her a few hand signals as if to say, "Tone it down," but Erin pretended he was waving and smiled graciously at him, never looking back in his direction. Her fingers tingled with exhilaration as she thought of the room she had reserved on the beach.

On with the droning and on with vacation plans. She made a list in her head of what she still needed: the sandals were still on sale in Brakeman's; she'd check on more white shorts...

What are they doing? What have they cooked up this week? Erin stopped list making to concentrate on the Yalder kids. The oldest boy had positioned himself in the back pew and the next oldest boy was on the far left in the middle. Erin listened. They were sending some sort of code back and forth. They both were studying their papers and tapping out signals on the backs of the pews! *Oh, how funny*, Erin thought. She wished she knew Morse code. Erin waited to see how long it would take the pastor and the others to notice. Are they deaf? There. Finally, the mother turned, and the boys stopped. Again, knocking, turning, knocking, and turning. Before long everyone was turning except Jim, he was asleep.

That's a good one, boys, Erin thought; she guessed there was hope for them yet!

Dudley Hathborn rose to take the collection; that is, he rose as far as he could. Erin started her money hymn as the man progressed around the church, appearing to have his head in the basket. He laboriously climbed the three steps to Erin, but as always, she shooed him away with her left hand. Someday he's going to fall right on his face going down those steps. *Why does he come up here? He knows I never donate.*

Erin stepped off the plane in heaven. Her six-day workweek had paid off! Her gravy money was sequentially placed in her new wallet, and the taxi was waiting to take her to the hotel. She knew how to make her life perfect, unlike her mother who never had anything and was content to stay that way. Erin opened her purse and gave the driver a generous tip. She felt her pride swell at the thought of being one of the elite on the island. Oh yes, she'd managed her first thirty years of life in a much regimented fashion so that now she could be the princess of the island. *My friends will never get here*, she mused as she looked farther and farther up the side of the hotel. They wouldn't get more than fifty miles away from Lone Moon Creek. They'd keep having those kids who'd devour every cent they earned on foolishness, like carnivals and bowling and camping gear.

Oh well, too bad for them. I don't feel sorry for them at all, she told herself as she tipped the bellboy.

Erin walked out on her balcony to face the ocean. This was it! This was paradise! Paradise certainly wasn't that humdrum jabbering place that the pastor talked about every week. Not that she would ever wish those Sundays away—that's where she earned her spending money!

Erin changed into her new red bathing suit and almost ran off the elevator to get to the beach.

"Ah," Erin moaned, as she buried her toes in the whiteness. How luscious it was to feel the warm, soft sand. She spread out her towel and spent the next hour in complete adoration of herself; she exalted over her industriousness, her stamina, her frugality, her resourcefulness, her motivation...

"Sorry, lady," a little voice apologized as she picked herself up from the sand.

"It's OK," Erin replied, rather vexed that there were children on the beach. The upset seemed to break the spell of the narcissistic litany, and she returned to the hotel for lotion.

"Look at what I have accomplished," she sang to herself as she espied the sparkling chandeliers and the shiny black marble staircase that cascaded into the lobby. She stopped to touch a velvet settee and to stare at a bouquet of fresh flowers that was larger than the meat counter at Cagney's grocery store.

Those poor people back home, Erin thought as she clucked her tongue and rolled her eyes, as if she was actually speaking with someone, *they'll never see what the real world is like.*

Erin bounced on the huge bed and lay on her back looking at the beautiful ceiling. She thought it might be hand painted, maybe stenciled—whichever, it was beautiful. The breeze blew the billowy sheers into the room with the lapping sound of the ocean needing no invitation.

Erin wanted to continue with the litany, but no, she'd hang her clothes in the closet and look over the menu for the evening's meal. She almost drooled as she read about the entrees and yes, she did drool over the desserts.

"This is it!" she sang aloud as she twirled herself and her new gold lamé sheathe around and around in front of the mirror that extended from the ceiling to the floor. "I will wear this little rag picker's dress to the dining room tonight!" she laughed.

It wasn't until Erin walked into the bathroom did she realize she truly was the princess. "Is this real? Am I real?" She turned from one sparkling fixture to the next in a sea of tiny tiles. Her bath water would maneuver down a path of real rocks lined with plants and the closet was stocked with more luxuries than her mother had seen in a lifetime.

Erin didn't need her on sale suntan lotion from home; she selected the exotic bottle from the shelf.

"One more hour of tanning and then I shall luxuriate in that tub!" Erin smiled to herself as she went for her purse. She had seen waiters serving drinks on the beach. Why shouldn't she imbibe?

Back in the bedroom, she giggled and said, "I better get my head about me," as she looked from the dresser to the closet to the nightstand. She stopped to think and then checked the dresser drawers, the top shelf of the closet, and inside the little door of the nightstand. "Oh, come on," she uttered louder. The search accelerated; the search became frantic. The search reached its pinnacle when Erin screamed!

Then came the silence, nothing except the ocean lapping against the land. Erin sank onto the edge of the bed and looked at the empty suitcases and the clothes she had strewn on the floor in the search.

"OK, OK, calm down," she lectured herself. "Put on your beach robe and go downstairs to report this."

"Do you have the serial numbers of your traveler's checks, ma'am?"

"I didn't have traveler's checks."

"Oh, then you'll want this list of telephone numbers for all major credit card companies. You can use this phone to report your stolen cards."

Erin didn't move, and she didn't respond.

"Ma'am?"

"All my cards? My cell phone. My new smartphone. Cash."

"All that was in your purse at the beach?"

Erin stood in front of the hotel with her luggage; she had managed to get some of her reservation money refunded. She hailed a taxi and wept in the back seat as the driver looped around and around on the way (or not the way) to the airport. When she paid the fare, he bounded from the vehicle and screamed into her face when she didn't tip him. She merely turned her back and walked away.

Erin spent an hour trying to find a flight home, but there were none that she could afford. "Can't you call someone at home and have them wire you some money?" the agent suggested.

"My mother certainly doesn't have any money, and I would be too embarrassed to ask any of my friends. Wait! I guess I could call the pastor at my church."

"Is it all set?" the agent inquired, looking up upon Erin's return from the phone.

"No, I'm afraid not," she said disgustedly, "apparently the church is running in the red. It figures," she added flippantly. "Would you know of a hotel that charges reasonable rates? I can stay there while I figure out this whole mess."

"Did you contact the police?"

"Oh yes, the hotel did, they told me there wasn't much hope of finding the thief."

"I'm afraid they're right," she said, nodding compassionately. "Say, why don't you stay at the Mission House? All you would have to do is make a donation of whatever you think you can afford!"

"Really?" Erin asked like a broker studying her prospectus.

Again, with no intention of giving a tip to the cabbie, Erin gave her orders to the driver.

Erin groaned as she looked out the window. "Are you sure this is a hotel?"

"Hotel, no. Mission House, yes," came his reply.

Another stiffed cabbie drove off with his tires kicking dust. She quickly put her lime-green scarf over her mouth and nose as she scurried out of the barrage of ammunition.

Erin looked at the one-story, long, pink, drab structure. A few vines tried to climb its walls, and weeds grew profusely through the cracks of the steps.

"Oh my God," Erin mumbled to herself. "I'm glad my friends can't see this." She walked through the front doorway into the dark. The darkness felt cold—no not cold, maybe cool with moisture. No, a thick warmth with a cold edge…

"May I help you?" came a voice through the black strange air.

Erin turned toward the voice as her eyes began detecting a form. "Yes, I need a room."

"Certainly, follow me."

"Don't you want me to sign or something?"

"That won't be necessary," replied the form with the long white robe and a flowing veil wrapped around her head.

Erin followed in silence noticing the emaciated hallway with the many doors.

"Here you are, dear. You may stay in here."

Erin was surprised to walk into sunlight. Another period of eye adjustment wouldn't let her see the woman leave; it was only through her auditory channels that she knew.

"Good grief," came Erin's first remark when the room gradually focused. This could be my mother's room all over again! She slowly turned the three hundred and sixty degrees to see the same type of sheer white curtains with the shade to pull at night. There was the white bedspread with, yes, white sheets and white pillowcases. The room contained one dresser, one nightstand, one little lamp, one tiny closet, a cross hanging over the bed, and no bathroom. No bathroom! Erin swung around again, knowing the door to the bathroom must be somewhere.

"Oh no," Erin droned as she lowered her limp, defeated body to the bed. There would be a shared bathroom in the hallway, and the thought of it squelched any notion of going to find it. She leaned back and put her hand over her forehead.

Erin awoke to darkness and a woman's voice from the hallway asking her if she wanted dinner. She jumped up, excited to put on her beautiful gold dress that she'd purchased from weeks of saving. Just as her feet hit the floor, she remembered.

Again, the knock came with the same question. Erin felt her way to the door and found the knob. Now the hallway was excreting light, and she could see the woman dressed in the long robe with her head veiled except for her face.

"Are you all right, dear? The dining room will be closing shortly. Don't you want something to eat before you retire?"

"Uh, yes, I guess so."

"Good, follow me." Erin followed the swift moving flow of white, wondering why she thought the hallway was so bright; there were only a few sconces on the wall. "By the way," the woman turned her head without breaking her pace, "I'm Sister Philomena, Sister Phil for short."

"Oh, hello, I'm Erin."

You must be kidding me, Erin said to herself as she entered the dining room. Two long tables with six or seven people scattered here and there was the extent of the facility. As soon as Erin sat in the wooden chair, another woman in the same kind of robe and headgear floated over to her with food on a plate. Erin looked at the "something" that was piled on her dish and asked, "Is there anything else?"

"Oh yes, yes," the woman said with a laugh. "I'm sorry. I'll get your bread and tea."

Erin lifted her eyes; she looked from one person to the next. Each one was centered on his or her food, never looking up. Because of that, she didn't mind staring at them, just as she had stared at people from her organist's perch.

Well, this is a sorry lot, Erin concluded when her inspection ended. *They're worse than that crew from church, which I would have never thought possible.*

Erin poked her fork into the mound of food, separating the grains of rice, looking to see what else was there—beans? Peppers?

"Here's your bread and tea, ma'am," the cheerful woman said as she swished over to Erin.

"Oh gee, thanks," Erin replied sarcastically.

Erin pulled off a piece of bread. *At least this is good,* she thought as she realized how much the man down the table from her looked like Dudley Hathborn; he was bent over with his nose almost in his rice.

Erin stared at the woman with the three children while she intermittently soaked chunks of crust into her tea. The four of them ate in silence; not one kid caused any consternation. *Those Yalder kids ought to see this,* she thought, as she recalled the Morse code escapade.

Erin suddenly jerked herself upright as she realized she was thinking about those stupid people instead of devising a plan to get off the island. As she pushed the rice around on her plate, she knew she didn't want to return earlier than anyone had expected; if she worked it right, she could return with not a person knowing anything about the mess she'd gotten herself into. There, she now had a time frame. She had six days to work on her problem. Besides, she was notorious for getting what she wanted—she just had to set her mind to it. That being settled, she took the liberty of looking at the people again, being the good judge of character that she was, she could analyze them.

Erin looked with great curiosity at a man probably about her age, in need of a haircut, with wire-rimmed glasses, and very tan. *I wonder what his problem is.* She looked under the table at his bare feet. *Probably one of those beach bums expecting everyone else to support him.*

Erin finished her tea and thought about the extravagant dinners she was going to have at the grand hotel. "Damn," she said aloud as every head bobbed up to look at her.

Erin noisily pushed back her chair and stalked out of the room. She certainly didn't need them staring at her. She had amounted to something in life. What had they done? "Nothing," she answered her own question. Erin slammed the bedroom door.

"Oh no," she groaned. She had to find the bathroom.

It turned out to be an easy task; it was only two doors to the right of her room. When there was no response to her knocking, she slowly turned the knob and peeked in. Well, it wasn't so bad, nothing fancy but clean. As she washed her hands, she thought of the tiny tiles and the cascading waterfalls into the sunken tub at the hotel. But there was no tub at the mission, only a shower. *Oh well, who cares?*

Erin opened the door just as a greasy, smelly, disheveled man pushed her aside and made a beeline to the toilet. He vomited. "Oh, my God!" Erin screamed as she ran to her room. She felt like she was going to be sick and quickly pushed the window open to thrust the upper part of her body out into the night air. She breathed deeply, glad she'd only consumed bread and tea for supper. Her queasiness settled just as three men drove past howling and whistling at the sight of a woman leaning halfway out of the window. Erin bolted, bumping her head, and then sank to the floor to get out of the light. When there was no sound of traffic, she quickly shot up to pull the shade.

She sat on the edge of the bed and felt the goose egg that was developing on the back of her head. "Great," she sighed, "what else?"

The restless night was accented with pain every time she rolled from side to side. Sometimes she remembered to lift her head before turning. Erin spent at least two hours telling herself she didn't have to go to the bathroom again; she was not going in there. Finally, she reached the point where she had to get up. In the hallway, it came to her that there must be more than one bathroom. *Of course*, she exalted to herself! The quest was on as Erin quietly walked from door to door. The snores seemed exceptionally loud from some rooms, while there was total silence from others. Someone was coming from the opposite direction.

"May I help you?" one of the women in white asked her.

"I'm looking for a bathroom," Erin whispered.

"Oh, honey, there's one up from your room."

"I know, but there was a man in there who was sick, and I really couldn't bear to go in there."

"That was all cleaned up hours ago, dear; it's sparkly clean again."

"Oh, that's good."

"But let me tell you about two other bathrooms in case you run into a difficult situation again. By the way, I'm Sister Carmangina, but you can call me Sister Gina."

"Thank you, Sister. Thank you very much. Oh, I'm Erin."

Once back to her quarters, Erin began feeling the security of the four walls. She felt herself drifting off to sleep when a sudden crash left her lying paralyzed in fright. She listened to someone thrashing against the door.

Without noticing her own plea, Erin whispered, "Oh dear God, help me." She heard running steps and women's voices. She tiptoed to the door and listened. She knew one of the voices was that of Sister Gina, so she opened the door a crack and whispered, "What's the matter out there?"

"It's Julian; he has had another seizure."

"Is he drunk?"

"No, of course not. Can you give us a hand?"

Erin tied the sash of her robe as she looked down. It was the man she'd seen in the dining room, except now he didn't have his glasses on.

"We're going to help him back to his room; you go ahead and open door six and pull back the sheet if it isn't already down." Erin did as she was told while the two sisters used their shoulders for Julian to steady himself.

"Lift up his feet," Sister Gina ordered after they'd positioned him on the edge of his bed. Erin looked down at the same bare feet that she'd accused of being beachcomber feet, parasitic feet. Maybe they were, she didn't know, but she'd touched them... she'd touched them.

Sister Gina drew the sheet and the cotton blanket up to his chin as the man looked at Erin and whispered, "Thank you."

Erin suddenly had a feeling, which she thought originated in her chest. She stood like a statue as it traveled up through her neck and into her face to her left eye. It was then that the strange feeling trickled out to drip upon her cheek.

"What on earth?" she thought to herself as she quickly wiped it away.

◦◦◦

"My God, I'm not even tired now," Erin mumbled as she turned in bed, keeping her head up. She listened to an occasional car

192

go past, thinking of how she should be listening to the sound of the ocean on her beach. My beach," she sighed.

Erin heard an engine running. She could see a cab driver and two of the sisters helping a woman into Mission House. In a few seconds, Erin heard footsteps coming down the hallway.

"What's the matter now?" she inquired with her head poking out of the door.

"She's beat up pretty badly," one sister whispered.

Erin saw the blood and the dirt and the torn clothes on the dangling woman. "Jesus!" she exclaimed in a loud whisper.

"Here," directed Sister Gina, as she handed Erin a piece of paper, "go to the front desk and call this number. Ask for Dr. Santana. Tell him we need him right now."

Erin returned to screams of pain and crying. "Erin, run past the front desk to the other corridor and get Sister Philomena. Quick, we're going to have a baby here. Room three. Hurry, honey."

Erin never missed a cue, as in her music ministry; she was Johnny-on-the-spot.

"Erin, here, hold her leg the best you can. Sister Phil, I guess you're up at bat."

Erin touched the hot skin of the woman; she felt the muscles inside pull and strain. The three nuns rattled off words of direction and words of comfort to the stranger. *A stranger*, Erin thought; she was helping a stranger. And for all the world, even though she knew the woman was having a baby, it did not register that this was another human being!

"Oh my God," Erin screamed, "it's a baby." The sisters looked at each other and burst into laughter.

"Ah, you Americans are so funny!" the short, little round nun said.

Erin saw the morning sun as she returned to her room. *That's the same sun that my friends are waking to back home*, she thought, but it seems so different there. She closed her eyes.

Erin slept. She slept through the entire day, one that she should have used to formulate her departure plans.

Was this déjà vu, she wondered when she heard the question, "Do you want dinner?" again.

"I've got to take a shower," she told the sister, "but yes, I'll be there. I'm starving!"

The little round one was serving the plates when Erin entered the dining room.

"Good evening, Erin, I don't think I introduced myself last night. I'm Sister Gabriella."

"And I can call you Sister Gabby, right?"

"Sister Gabby? Oh, you Americans are so funny!" She laughed as she put a plate of something in front of Erin.

She didn't play with the food that evening; instead, the hungry woman fed herself. "Sister Gabby, what happened today? Are the baby and the mother still here?"

"Oh no, no they're in the hospital. Sister Phil promised the hospital we'd come up with the money."

"And Julian? How is he?"

"He was out all day. I haven't seen him yet tonight."

Erin looked around to see some different faces. "Where are the three children and the mother?"

"They left early this morning; they are going down the coast."

"Do people come in for breakfast and lunch, too?" Erin asked as she used her bread to soak up the last drop of gravy.

"Oh yes, yes. We had forty-two for breakfast and thirty-five for lunch."

"What?"

"Oh yes, yes. I guess you haven't been around for those meals, have you?"

"I guess not. I slept all day today. Wait a minute, when did you sleep?"

"Oh, I can sleep standing up," she said with a laugh. "Maybe tonight will be calmer."

"I hope so," Erin replied as she rolled her eyes. "Can I ask your advice about something, Sister?"

"Oh sure, sure. Come in by the sink while I wash dishes."

"I need to earn some money real fast, Sister. Can you tell me where I can get a job for five days? A job that pays lots of money?"

"Well, you could go to Lulu's Pleasure House and make all kinds of money in five days?" she said seriously.

"Lulu's Pleasure House? You don't mean? Sister!"

Gabby just about fell into the dishpan laughing.

"See, we can be funny, too!"

"That wasn't funny." Erin laughed.

"Why do you have to make lots of money in five days?"

"I have to fly home by then, and all my money was stolen."

"Oh, you poor girl. I'm sorry."

"Yeah, I'm sorry, too. What am I going to do?"

"Why don't you try to get a waitress job; the tourists usually tip very well."

"What a great idea! Thanks, Gabby and good night."

"Good night," hailed Gabby as she stared at the stacks of dishes yet to be washed.

Erin gave herself a manicure and a pedicure and styled her hair in all sorts of ways as she waited to get tired. Finally she turned out the light. She listened to the traffic and to various footsteps coming and going in the hallway. She heard at least three vehicles stop out front, dropping people who needed a room for the night.

"Oh no, not a crying child," she whined to herself. Erin lay listening to the incessant crying for what seemed like hours. "God, why doesn't it stop?" she said aloud as she jumped to her feet. She pulled on her robe and jerked the door open. "I can't stand this another minute," she fumed as she nearly ran along the hallway to find a nun.

"Sister, Sister, could I speak to you?"

"Certainly. Oh, you must be Erin, I'm Sister Angela."

"Wonderful," Erin commented rudely. "There's a child in one of these rooms, and it won't stop crying. Can you do something about it?"

"Well, let's see."

The two women walked to the sound of the cry. When there was no response, Sister Angela turned the knob. There holding an infant was a girl who looked to be about twelve years old.

"Don't be afraid, honey. Where's your mother?"

The girl did not answer but tried to rock the baby in what must have been painful arms at that point.

"Would you like me to rock the baby for a while?" Sister Angela asked gently. The girl didn't answer until tears came to her eyes and she nodded yes.

Sister took the child and put him up against her shoulder as she swayed back and forth. The girl put her head down on her own skinny knees and sobbed.

"Hold her," the sister whispered to Erin.

"Me?"

"Yes, you."

Erin didn't know whether to sit or stand, talk or not talk, tell her a story or try to joke with her. She didn't know until she touched her arm. She touched her and she knew. The girl cried and cried into Erin's outstretched arms, and Erin gently rocked her back and forth as she stroked her hair and told her everything would be all right.

When the crying subsided, the four of them went to the kitchen. The thin girl sat on Erin's lap while Sister Angela held the boy.

"Food works miracles!" The sister exclaimed with a wink.

"I'll move the children to the room with the two single beds," Angela said on the way back, "and I'll sleep in one bed while the two youngsters use the other."

"That's a good idea," Erin commented. "But wait, let me do it. You should be making your rounds, and when the mother comes back, you will need to tell her where the kids are."

"Would you do that?" Sister Angela asked in surprise.

The pure disgust Erin had been feeling toward the absent mother started to dissipate as she watched Carmelita with little Paulo. The twelve-year-old tenderly readied her brother for bed, saying the prayer that he could mimic, singing his little song, tucking him in, and rubbing his back until he fell asleep. Erin could see that she then said her own prayers.

I guess that mother must have done something right, Erin thought, and for some odd reason tears ran from her eyes as she studied the profile of the girl in prayer.

Erin listened to the breathing during the night: hers, Paulo's, and Carmelita's. The three of them in a world of uncertainty, breathing the same air, using it to stay alive. Alive for what? She startled herself when she thought about asking God for guidance.

Erin rolled over quickly, irritated at her ridiculous idea. "I better get home to reality; I'm getting soft down here on this island."

A gentle touch on Erin's shoulder bolted her awake.

"Erin, the mother is back."

Erin quickly scrambled out of the bed as the mother came in. The woman checked the children, pulled the sheet up a bit as all mothers do, and then turned to Sister and Erin.

"Thank you," she whispered and got into the bed that Erin had exited.

Erin looked at Sister Angela as if to say, "Well, is that all the thanks we get?" She thought of the nice warmth she'd left from her own body that was now being absorbed by the child abuser.

In the hallway, Erin snapped at Sister, "What's the matter with that woman, leaving those children like that and not even thanking us properly?"

"We don't know what other people are going through, Erin. We just do the best we can to keep ourselves on the right path."

"Humph," Erin mumbled as she returned to her own room. "I've got to get out of this place."

She fidgeted as she turned from side to side.

"Chito, bumbito, aye, aye, aye, I love you," sounded someone's voice at full volume.

"You've got to be kidding me!" Erin snarled as she put the pillow over her ear. Crash! Someone bumped against the door and then there was more serenading.

"Who the hell is that?" Erin streamed out of the bed and yanked open the door. There was the barefooted Julian trying to lead the serenader through the hallway. "Are you two drunk?" Erin snarled. Sister Phil came running after them with a bucket.

"Put him in number eight, Julian."

"Why do the rest of us have to put up with this nonsense all night?" Erin catapulted the question at Sister Phil and then at Julian. Neither of them answered, even though she trotted behind them waiting for a reply.

The tenor voice slowly changed his tune of amore to a low bass monotone of a drone. Julian sat him down on the bed, and

Sister Phil positioned the bucket just in time to catch the pleasures of the evening.

"Oh my God," Erin groaned as she turned away. When the echoing of the flash flood against the metal pail stopped, Erin partially looked back to see Julian bracing the man with both arms as Sister Phil leaned over to wipe the man's face with her own white handkerchief.

"Erin, run and get some wet washcloths and some towels and make the washcloths warm."

"Make the wash clothes warm?" she grumbled to herself as she ran to the nearest linen closet. "He should get a cold washcloth for all the trouble he's causing."

Erin returned just in time to witness another onslaught from the man's body, and this time the splatters went out onto Julian's feet. Sister Phil immediately grabbed a washcloth as did Julian. The man groaned and held his stomach as Julian gently cleaned his face. And Sister Phil? She was on her hands and knees washing the feet of Julian.

Man oh man, this is too much for me, Erin thought as she turned to leave. *I'll just call my mother tomorrow; she must know enough people who can send money.*

Erin didn't hear any sounds for a long time as she stared into the night. *The man must have gone to sleep or passed out or whatever they do. I don't know why Julian would bring someone in that condition back here. Does he think we want to put up with that?*

"Erin, I need you," came a voice at the door. Immediately Erin jumped and started for room eight, grabbing washcloths and towels on the way. She hurried into the bathroom to run warm water over the cloths. Julian was at his post with the man who was getting sick all over again. Erin wasn't as fast with the bucket as Sister Phil had been. *Maybe this is why Julian doesn't wear shoes,* she thought as she looked up into his eyes and said, "I'm sorry."

He gave her a little smile while he braced the man's retching body against his own. Sister Phil quietly entered to see Erin on her hands and knees washing Julian's feet.

Erin slept until noon again. When she entered the dining room at the midday meal she stopped.

"My heavens," she uttered as she saw the crowd, "let me help you, Sister."

"Oh bless you child," Sister Gabrielle replied as she scurried through with a huge tray.

"I could be a waitress," Erin complimented herself as she served and cleared. "Where are the other sisters?"

"They're out in the streets begging for money."

"What?"

"Our baby and mother will have to leave the hospital if we don't get some money over there PDQ."

"That's terrible."

"I know. The assault did damage to them both and they need more medical care."

Sister and Erin worked the rest of the shift in silence. Erin was sure Gabby was praying and Gabby thought that maybe, perhaps, Erin was praying too.

The nuns returned just before the two lone workers began preparations for the dinner hour. Bedraggled and solemn, the women in white processed into the kitchen. Sister Gabby and Erin looked for a sparkle in their eyes. There was no sparkle, but there was hope.

"There's always hope," Sister Philomena reminded them.

Erin had intended to canvas the island for work opportunities, but she stayed to help with dinner. As Erin filled the bowls, she wondered what the night would bring.

"Has anyone seen Julian today?" she inquired.

No one had, but that was normal.

"He's out among the people."

The solemnity of the late afternoon was suddenly broken when Sister Phil ran into the kitchen waving an envelope. "I spotted this on the front desk! There's three hundred seventy-eight dollars in it—in cash!" The joy echoed off the cooking pots; thankfulness arose with the aroma of the baking bread. Prayers bounced off the ceiling!

"Oh Erin, this is a miracle!" Sister Gina expounded as she hugged the American.

"It surely is," Erin replied as she looked up to heaven and winked. She felt much lighter knowing her last bit of money wasn't weighing her down anymore.

"Erin, quick! Stir the gravy, honey!"

Oh man, she thought, *I'm really losing it.*

During the night, when Erin returned to her room after helping Julian with a homeless boy, she wrote a letter:

Dear Mom,

I'm having such a great time on the island, I've decided to stay! I love it here, and I'm finding so much to do. Please tell my friends that I might make this my permanent home so I can continue my "swinging lifestyle" with these terrific people.

Maybe you could fly down to see me sometime; you'll be surprised!

Would you please inform the college and, oh yes, the pastor? My gravy money came in handy.

Love,

Erin

"I WANT TO WRITE SOME MUSIC, GRANDMA."

"WONDERFUL! THE MUSIC PAPER IS ON THE SECOND SHELF. DID YOU KNOW THAT IRENE'S DAUGHTER USED TO WRITE MUSIC UNTIL SHE GOT HOOKED ON... UM... JAZZ."

"JAZZ IS GOOD."

"YOU'RE RIGHT, MARJORY. JAZZ IS GOOD."

◦✐Chapter Ten✐◦

AND ALL THAT JAZZ

"I'm sure, Ma. This is what I want to do with my life!"

"Oh, I just worry. How do you know what you want to do for the rest of your life?"

"What happens to people when they don't follow their dreams?"

"Like me?"

"I didn't mean anything bad about it, Ma. I just know you never got to do what you really wanted."

"That is true, but I still had a good life here in Lone Moon Creek, bringing up you kids, being one hundred percent behind my husband in everything I could."

"And you were great through everything! You were a terrific mom and wife and homemaker. All my friends think you are tops!"

"But I didn't follow my singing career, did I?" Irene looked like she was going to cry.

Carli swooped over to her mother and whispered, "But you sang to us kids all the time. You made us appreciate and love music."

"It is true—you kids can really cut a rug when you get going at it." Irene laughed.

"Remember all the prizes we won at the variety shows, and we got the leading parts in the musicals at school and won all the music awards at graduation? Where do you think we got all that talent? From Dad?"

"Now don't make me say anything negative about your dad. He was very talented in other areas, like math and figuring out things."

"I know you two gave us everything in every field!" Carli said.

"My goodness, you really know how to butter me up. If your dad was still alive you wouldn't get past him," Irene remarked as she grabbed a tissue from her apron pocket.

"Mom," Carli again hugged her, "we have to be strong; we have to go on with our lives."

"I know, I know. I just need more time to make decisions than your dad did. He could make split-second decisions."

"Don't take too long. My application has to be submitted in three days."

Carli left for music school with her mother waving from the porch, holding back her tears until the car navigated the corner.

"Can you believe it? We're both going off to music school!" Mickey squealed as she raised her hand to high-five Carli.

"Not while you're driving, thank you," the sensible Carli responded.

"Oh, don't be such a deadhead."

Never having been taught how to handle criticism because there never was any, Carli reluctantly raised her hand.

"I am so happy that you wanted me to live in your apartment, Mickey. I promise I won't bug you upper-class girls."

"We're glad you wanted to! Now we don't have to advertise and perhaps get someone who wouldn't meet our standards."

Carli began her freshman year filled with high hopes and aspirations. Everyone knew that Carli would be the dream student, the success story. Irene didn't worry about her youngest child as she had with some of her other children when they went off to college. She darted a quick look at the picture of her dear departed husband and said, "Thank you, hon, for providing college money for our last one, too. You sure knew finances and how much we would need to be comfortable."

Thanksgiving vacation was filled with all of Carli's enthusiasm. The entire family was entertained with story after story of Carli's classes and professors and projects and accomplishments. She primed them for the semester break when she would debut her "big" project: the musical that she had been assigned to compose. "You're going to love it, and I am going to get an "A" for sure!"

Irene spent many happy hours in her overstuffed chair listening to her gang perform for her. It had now grown to include spouses and boyfriends, girlfriends and little tykes. The wee grandchildren were even more animated and talented than her own had been. Well, maybe not, but they were fun anyway.

Oh the loneliness that will take over when they all leave. Irene wasn't looking forward to it, but she knew it was inevitable.

"Carli, Mickey will be here in five minutes to pick you up."

The mother and daughter faced each other, their eyes froze into a never beginning and never ending love.

"I love you."

"Love you, too."

⌒∾⌒

"Carli? Are you still at it?"

"Yes, this project is so colossal, I don't know when or if I'll finish. I don't know if I'll make the deadline. Why did I include so much?"

"Ah yes, the over exuberant freshman," Mickey said, and she and the other roommates laughed. You've got to do less in order to survive. You don't want to burn out, do you?"

"Well no, but I want to do the very best I can!" Carli looked as if she was going to weep.

"Oh for heaven's sake, here, take one of these. It'll get you through the night so you can work even harder as long as you're hell-bent on doing it. Maybe next time you won't take on such a huge project."

"What is it?"

"I don't know the scientific name; all I know is that it works. Good night. The rest of us are going to bed."

Carli got her *A*. The professor said it was the best musical composition submitted, and now the young composer couldn't wait to get home and assign the parts to her sibs and extended family.

Christmas weekend brought a houseful of family. Carli made sure they all came home with their musical instruments, the same ones they began playing in the fourth grade. She had her mother bring down all the costumes from the attic and handed the piano part to her brother, Hunter. He was a genius at the piano. Two days were spent rehearsing.

"Mom, who did you invite?" Carli asked.

"I asked Agnes and Marjory, Betty, Mae, Lorraine, and Katie."

"Great, I hope they love it!"

"Bye, darling, I'll see you on your next break, and can I thank you just one more time for giving us all the most wonderful production this house has ever seen?" Irene said.

"OK, one more time, but that's all. I'm on to writing something new this semester."

"Hi, Mickey! How was your vacation?" Carli asked.

"Terrible, I broke up with Jer."

"Sorry."

Carli already had a reputation around school of being the rising star. The professors were spreading the news among themselves. "She's someone to watch."

Again, she was doing what her roommates warned her about: working too hard.

Every night and every weekend found Carli working her musical talent to the bone. Her friends were out relaxing while she worked.

"Mickey, do you have any more of those pills that help people work longer?" Carli asked her friend.

"You don't need to work longer."

"I have to finish this. Do you want me to fail the class?"

"Oh good grief, they're on the shelf in my room and only take one. They're very expensive," Mickey said.

"Thanks."

"I don't see where you have joined any clubs, Carli," her mentor criticized. "Participating in various organizations will be very important in you evaluation at graduation. You can't just be in the band and the jazz band and the choir; that looks like you are trying to take the easy road in college and employers won't hire you."

Carli joined the a cappella group, the River Dance troupe, and the Musicians of America.

"Carli, wake up! You're going to be late for class!" Mickey shouted.

❧

"All *A*s! I'm so proud of you, honey! When are you coming home? What do you need the money for? Of course, if you say you need it, I'll wire it to you tomorrow."

❧

"Hasn't this been a wonderful summer? I wish you didn't feel that you had to work, Carli. I didn't get to see you as much as I would have liked to. Your dad budgeted a nice sum of money for your college education, but maybe he didn't realize how prices were going to escalate. I'm glad I'm sending you back looking healthier. When you first came home, I knew you needed some home cooking and proper rest. Maybe it was a good thing I didn't go to college; maybe I wouldn't have made it."

"Oh, Mom, you would have made it," Carli said.

Carli dug into her sophomore year with a vengeance. Over the summer she'd formulated plans for her next musical composing project, an operetta. She was elected president of the Musicians of America and chosen to submit an article every week for the college newspaper.

"I can't, Mom, I just have too many responsibilities here. I'll see you during Christmastime,"

But then Christmastime came.

"What? We can't have Christmas without our little sister," Hunter exclaimed.

"Well, she's not coming; she's got a job out there now," Irene said.

"I have a business meeting after Christmas in that area. I'll try to catch up with her and at least take her out for a nice dinner."

"Thanks, Hunter. Oh! Can you play this? Carli wrote it for our Christmas."

Hunter sat at the piano. "It says it's dedicated to you, Mom."

Irene's gang listened, not saying a word. Even the babies were quiet while Hunter played Carli's composition.

"Oh my! That was beautiful!" Irene whispered as she dried her eyes.

"Hi, Mom, are you home?"

"In here, Hunter. Did you get to see Carli?"

"How about some coffee first, I'm freezing."

"OK, why are you stalling?" Irene asked.

Hunter picked up a cookie. "I saw Carli at her apartment. Well... kind of saw her."

"What do you mean?"

"She looks like a skeleton with black circles under her eyes, and she's a mess. Her hair is oily and her clothes are dirty. I was shocked!" Hunter said.

"Did she say anything?"

"She talked real fast and went from one subject to another. It's like she has a million things to do and not enough time."

"What else?"

"There was a guy there; he looked as bad as she did."

"Did you speak with him?" Irene asked.

"I said hello. He never responded."

"Oh dear God. What is happening with her?"

"Oh yeah, I forgot to tell you, I met Mickey down by the front door. She said she needs to ask Carli to move out; it's just not working between them anymore," Hunter said.

※

"Hi, Mom. It's Carli. How are you?"

"I'm fine. How are you?" Irene asked.

"Great! Just wondered if you could send me a little money? I'm really running short here."

"What do you need it for?"

"Oh, you know, I need some new books and some new music paper and stuff like that."

"How much do you need?"

"Probably about two thousand dollars," Carli said.

"That much?"

"Things are expensive now days."

"I want you to come home. I want to see you."

Click.

※

"Hunter, take your sister Maive with you. Get Carli to come home," Irene said.

"We'll try, Ma."

Irene waited all day for her children to return. She thought of different approaches she would use with Carli. She set up an appointment with their family doctor so Carli could have a complete physical. Together they would get Carli straightened out, even if she had to take a semester off. That wouldn't be so bad. That would be OK, as long as Carli got back on track with her life. Even if she wanted to change majors, that would be fine. Even if she wanted to travel for a while, she would go with her. Yes! That would be wonderful to have all that time alone with her daughter!

"Hi, Ma.

"Where's Carli?"

"We couldn't find her."

"What do you mean you couldn't find her?"

"Mickey didn't know where she'd moved to. The registrar's office had no new address. No one seemed to know who that fellow was that I saw in her old apartment," Hunter said.

"This can't be!" Irene said as she slumped into her chair. "Did you check with any of her teachers?"

"The ones we could find said she hadn't been in class for two weeks. We went to the police station, Ma."

"Good. Are they going to look for her?"

"Yes, but not too seriously; they said college students do this all the time. We filled out all sorts of papers. They'll probably come and talk to you, too, because you have things like her social security number, her passport, more current pictures, etc."

"I gave them her senior picture that was in my wallet," Maive said as she broke down and wept.

"Oh, Maive, don't worry. We'll find her," Irene said as she rose to hug her daughter.

"Are you Mrs. Irene Shapiro?" a policeman asked.

"Yes! Did you find Carli Shapiro?"

"No, ma'am, but can you identify this briefcase?"

"It looks like Carli's, but let me check the bottom. Yes, three of my other children have their initials on it too. Where did you find it? Why isn't Carli with her briefcase?"

"Calm down, ma'am. We found this in a locker at the bus station," the officer said.

"The bus station? Why?"

"We don't know, ma'am, but I think it's a substantial clue."

"What's in it?" Irene asked nervously.

"Just papers, mostly music papers with someone's notations all over the place. Does your daughter write music?"

"Oh yes, yes, she writes beautiful music." Irene smiled for the first time.

"Could you go through it and see if there are any clues as to where she might be?"

"My son is coming over in a little while, can you wait for him? He knows more about music than I do."

"I guess so, ma'am. It'll give me a chance to ask you some more questions while I wait. Was your daughter taking drugs?"

"Drugs? Certainly not," Irene said.

"Was your daughter happy at school?"

"She was thrilled... until... well, I don't exactly know what changed; but she got so busy that she didn't even have time to come home during the breaks."

"Mm," the officer groaned.

"Oh, Hunter, come in here. The police found Carli's briefcase. Can you go through the music and see if there is anything that might be a clue. It's evidence, so we can't keep it."

"Sure. Good afternoon, sir," Hunter said.

"There was no evidence of her taking drugs?" the officer continued.

"Certainly not!" Irene exclaimed.

"Ma, I never told you this, but that time I was in Carli's apartment there were pills all over the coffee table. That man was trying to swipe them into a bag."

"What?" Irene said with wide, dagger-like eyes that Hunter had never seen before. "But why?"

"Maybe because of this," Hunter answered as he grabbed a handful of music written by his little sister. "My God, she's composing for the entire orchestra!"

"And? What does that mean?" asked the policeman.

"She's nineteen years old. Do you think this is typical of a nineteen-year-old?"

"Certainly not mine," the officer answered.

"She was killing herself trying to keep up with her own unrealistic goals!" Hunter exploded. "You know, here's another thing I never told you, Ma, Mickey said Carli would ask for uppers so she could work harder and longer."

"Uppers?"

That was written in the policeman's notebook.

"But why would Mickey have such things?" Irene asked.

"I don't know, but when she refused to give Carli anymore, she knew Carli went out looking for someone who would supply her."

"You've got to find out who that man was!" Irene spoke in a terse tone as she pointed her finger in the officer's face.

"Calm down, Ma. How about the titles or dedication on that music? Do they mean anything, sir?" the policeman asked Hunter.

Hunter went through the music page by page.

"The whole piece is dedicated to our dad. Each Movement has his various characteristics."

"Such as?"

"Do you see the staccato, quick rhythms through here? I imagine Carli was thinking of his quick mind. And here, this is equivalent to a mastermind in mathematics with all the perplexities of rhythms. This movement must be Dad's love for Mom—all legato with swells and arpeggios. Yes, I would say that was what Carli was thinking."

"Has this given you any help, Officer?"

"Not a bit. She loved her dad a lot, didn't she?"

"She loved us all and would never try to hurt us."

"You look like you are deep in thought, Officer."

"Yeah, I was just wondering what kind of music my daughter would write about me. I'll be in touch."

"Hi, Mom, it's Alicia. How would you like me and the kids to come and spend some time with you? I don't want you to be alone through all this."

"Really? I would love it. Is it OK with Robbie? I think having your two little tykes in the house will help us get through some of this terrible doom."

"Oh, Mom, Amy just texted me. She's coming, too."

"It's for you Mom. Shh, kids. Grandma's got to be able to hear on the phone. It's the dean of students from Carli's college."

"Hello," Irene said timidly. "Yes. Oh? When? Oh. Yes. Good-bye."

Alicia and Amy looked at each other and then they looked at their mother. But their mother didn't say anything.

It wasn't until little Sissy said, "Gamma talk," did Grandma speak.

"The dean of students is coming here to show us something he received in the mail."

"What is it?" the two sisters asked in unison.

"I don't know. He thinks Carli sent it to him. See if Hunter and Maive can leave work to come over. I'm feeling very insecure," she whispered as she looked at the photo of her husband.

∽

"Mrs. Shapiro, it's nice to see you again."

"There's nothing nice about it," Irene spoke coldly.

"You're right, please forgive me."

He gave a nod to all the siblings, and they gave a nod to him. He opened his briefcase and removed a manila envelope. They could see that it was not a handwritten address, but a computer generated label.

"Where was it mailed from?" Hunter asked.

"Arizona."

"Arizona?" they chimed in like a quintet with bass, tenor, alto, second soprano, and soprano.

"At least it's a clue," Alicia said.

"What is it?" Irene demanded.

"Actually, it's a piece of music. I had Peter Levoman, the director of the music department look at it, and he said it's a complete mass."

"You mean a mass for a church?"

"Yes, and we think Carli wrote it or else someone wrote it for her or, should I say, dedicated it to her."

"What on earth are you talking about?" Irene displayed agitation that her kids had never witnessed before.

"Here, look at this title," the dean said. The title read, "A Requiem Mass for Carli Shapiro."

"A mass for the dead?" Irene said.

"Ma! Oh my God, she's fainted! Get some water!"

"Get that policeman over here, right now, he's got to see this," Maive ordered.

"Is she going to kill herself?" Amy wept into her sister's long hair.

"She wouldn't do that—but do you think someone is going to kill her?"

"I don't know, I don't know, I don't know. I'm so scared." Alicia cried right back onto her sister.

"Girls, stop it. You've got to be strong for Ma," Hunter warned.

Eleven months passed. Music didn't emanate from the Shapiro household. The little ones were aging, not knowing that their entire family was extraordinarily musically talented.

It was a Monday when two state troopers appeared at the door with condolences.

One year later, Irene, Hunter, Maive, Alicia, and Amy occupied the first five seats of row *A* in the Doninton Auditorium at the college to listen to the premiere performance of "*A Requiem Mass for Carli Shapiro*" by Carli Shapiro.

"Grandma, were my mother and father happy?"

"Yes they were, Marjory."

"Are all people who get married happy?"

"It's hard to say. Unless you live their lives, you never really know."

Chapter Eleven
I Do Not

"What did you do to snag her?" Tony asked as he stood among the eight groomsmen waiting for the bridesmaids to arrive.

"I played it cool, man!" the groom-to-be said as he high-fived his older brother.

"I'm glad I could scrape together enough money to fly out here; I wouldn't want to miss this for the world."

"You better believe it, brother. This is going to be the wedding of the century."

Andy returned to his position and looked from the top of the cathedral to the rows and rows of guests to the flower-banked altar to the hundreds of flickering candles. He listened to the somber pipe organ and thought of the reception where the music would be rocking. He couldn't wait to get the formalities over so he could cut loose in the life that was going to be incredible.

Look at that dress! Andy thought as he first spotted his bride-to-be. *That must have cost the old man a fortune! But so what? He's got it, and got it big time.*

Andy smugly replaced Mr. Panelli in front of the altar. *She's mine now!*

Andy went through all the steps of the ceremony—the long, long ceremony—with impeccable control and patience. He knew how to play the game. He could read Angelique like a book. She wanted a reserved gentleman with manners and decorum and intelligence and that's what he'd given her. After all, he'd had a master teacher—his father.

Ever since Andy was a little boy, he watched and learned from his dad who was a genius at conning people. His other brothers never got the hang of it, including Tony, who married into poverty and would never have anything. He couldn't even bring his wife to the wedding because they couldn't afford two plane tickets.

"Man oh man," Andy mumbled when he should have said, "Amen."

He darted a look at Mrs. Panelli, who was wiping away her tears, and Mr. Panelli, who was trying to comfort her. Andy felt like shouting out, "Hey, your daughter is marrying the 'most wonderful man in the world,' and those are her words."

Andy knew what his father's face would look like: his father would be grinning from ear to ear.

"Yes, I'm right." A quick glance confirmed it, which prompted him to give Angelique's hand a little squeeze; that little extra touch brought about the most beautiful smile from his goddess.

"Now we can have some fun," Andy whispered in his bride's ear as they entered the country club.

Fun it was! Theron Panelli walked through the rooms of guests as a proud father would and Andy walked through as the king of the world. But why wouldn't he? He had a beautiful wife, rich in-laws, and a future that was full of bounty for him.

"Yo, my boy!" Andy's father hugged him. "I always knew you would amount to something, not like your brothers and your mother. Their noses are always sniffing the ground; yours is in the air where it should be."

"Thanks, Dad! It's going to be a ride!" Andy said.

"Andy, I'm so sorry your mother couldn't be here," the lovely and gracious Mrs. Panelli spoke softly.

"Oh, me as well," Andy said, lying. He thought how humiliated he would have been with his mother, dressed in one of her church dresses, trying to have a conversation with those people.

"But I'm sure we'll meet on many occasions as the years go by," Andy's mother-in-law said.

"Yes, as the years go by and Angelique and I are entertaining all of you!"

"Won't that be fun?" Yvonne said as she touched Andy's arm.

The hors d'oeuvres were works of art, the meal sumptuous, and the cake a tower of grandiosity by which Andy could gauge his prosperity.

"Ah, this is living," Andy proclaimed as he toasted his dad.

"Don't get too used to it, sweetheart. After the honeymoon will be reality," Angelique said then laughed.

"I think I can handle it, sweetie."

During the first dance, Yvonne shed a few tears watching her little girl as Theron comforted her with his protective arm around her shoulders. The newlyweds were a perfect couple floating to the music. It was a fairyland wedding.

With the formal dance ending, Andy was ready to cut loose with his style of music, the songs that he'd prearranged for the band to play.

"Angelique! What kind of music is this?" he whispered curtly to his bride when he heard some kind of Bohemian music.

But she was already clapping her hands and running to get her Nana-vonnie.

To the center of the crowd, the bride led her beloved Nana-vonnie. Slowly, slowly the two circled each other, and with their right hands together and raised high, they stomped out the first beat of each musical pulse as many in the crowd swayed and sang the words—words that Andy knew not the meaning of.

"Clap along, son, if you want to fit in. You've got to do this," Pierce interjected.

"I guess I should have invited, Ma. She loves this kind of stuff. I never thought this of Angelique's family."

"Dancing is one thing, knowing how to act is another," Pierce scowled at Andy.

Andy let his bride swing him around as he clapped when they clapped and shouted *something* when they shouted. He noticed that his brother Tony seemed to know what he was doing.

"Of course," the groom said to himself, "he's just like Ma. They like this peasant, old-world stuff." Andy noticed his father wasn't making a fool of himself.

The music finally changed to what Andy liked, and he didn't miss a dance. It didn't matter if Angelique joined him or not, he was out on the floor.

"Honey, don't you think you're getting a little too wild out there? I'd like you to mingle with me and thank everyone for coming," she implored.

Andy almost rebuked her but caught himself. "Of course, sweetheart. Take my hand."

Good-byes were said all around, kisses were thrown through the air, and the happy couple flew off to the island.

"Wasn't it nice of Daddy and Mommy to give us this trip?"

"Absolutely." Andy yawned as he stretched out for a nap.

Island time, island euphoria, island hypnosis, whatever it was, it captivated the newlyweds. Angelique went on and on about the future with their new little home and the children and their pets and, and, and... While Andy played a bigger scenario in his head. He saw a mansion with several cars and vacations and a swimming pool and, and, and... until it was time to go home.

⤸

"Well, kids, where are you going to live?" Theron asked.

"Good question, Daddy. Where are we going to live, hon? In your apartment?" Angelique asked.

"Oh no. You wouldn't like that. I kind of had my eye on your guest house, Theron," Andy coyly answered.

"Sorry, we'll have guests coming and going all summer and fall."

"Daddy, how about your fishing cabin?"

"Sure, if you can stand it."

"I love it there, thanks Daddy. And we can put all our beautiful wedding gifts in storage until we get a real house."

"How is your job, son? Are you moving up the corporate ladder?" Theron asked.

"Actually, I haven't told Angelique yet, but I resigned my position just before our wedding," Andy answered.

"What? Why?"

"There was no room for improvement there. Plus," he said slowly, "I was pretty sure you were going to take me on at your company. Right, Pops?"

Theron tilted his head and stared at Andy. Angelique tilted her head and stared at Andy. Yvonne...

"I guess you don't know too much about me, son. I don't give anything away for free; the people I know work for their money. If you want to start on the bottom and work your way up, you are welcome to join my company. But you'll begin at minimum wage."

"How about you show me the fishing cabin Ang? I'll do my thinking there. And while you're unpacking, I'll take our wedding money to the bank and set up an account."

"So, where is it?" Andy asked.

"It's right in front of us, silly."

"We're going to live in that shack?"

"It's not a shack, it's cute. It's fun being out here in the wild, and I can teach you how to fish!"

"Never, that's too disgusting for me."

Andy remembered Angelique using the word "reality." If this was what she'd meant, he hated it. It was not his dream, and it was not how he was going to live the rest of his life.

"Honey, how can we take a vacation now? You haven't worked long enough to take time off," Angelique asked.

"I got permission, so let's do it."

"Ah, now this is the life," Andy exhaled as he put his feet up on the edge of the motorboat. "See the resort up on that hill? That's where we're going to stay for five days. Like it?"

"Of course I do, but where did you get the money to pay for all this?"

"Don't worry your pretty little head about it. I have everything under control."

And so it went all through the summer. Angelique cooked over the wood stove or the fire pit, creating a home for her new husband while her hubby was away more and more working double shifts and triple shifts, so he said.

Then there were more vacations and a brand new sports car, fancy dinners out, and always new clothes.

"We're doing good, aren't we, babe?" Andy said.

"We are, but you're working almost all the time. You are going to wear yourself out. Oh, we received a notice today that there is a package at the post office. Can you go and pick it up?"

When Angelique saw the package, she exclaimed, "Oh, it's huge. It's from Nana-vonnie! What could this be? Andy, it's Nana-vonnie's complete set of antique dishes. She's giving us her valuable dishes!"

"Very nice, very nice. But, honey, there is no room for all these dishes. Why don't I put them in the storage shed with the other wedding presents, and then when we have our own house, we can use them there."

"I know you're right, honey."

Mr. and Mrs. Panelli often sent cards from their excursions around the globe, a trip that Theron had promised his wife on the day they were married. And now they were finally doing it.

I think Andy is a lot like Daddy, Angelique thought to herself. *They're both tremendous workers; they know they have to work in order to get the things they want. Those are old-fashioned ethics that I'm glad Daddy made Andy realize right from the start. Daddy knew if he babied Andy, Andy would never be a man who would support his own family. Both are also very generous; when they have the money, they like to give their wives nice things. I think it's time that Andy and I get serious about starting a family. Daddy always says, "Family is everything."*

"We received another letter from my folks, honey," Angelique said.

"Where are they now?"

"In Turkey!"

"They're turkeys all right," Andy mumbled. "I've got to go; I'm working another shift today."

"Oh, my sweet husband, it'll be worth it someday. Keep a stiff upper lip." She remembered her mother saying that to Daddy.

Angelique sat on the sunny front porch waiting for the mailman. It was the only sunshine from that direction at that part of the day. It would be shady other than at mailman time. She couldn't see the road, but she would be able to hear his vehicle, which would slow, stop, and then go on. Angelique had discovered many routine patterns from the woods. She knew what time the deer would be at the lake for their drink, when the birds would come for the seeds, she watched for the mother quail to lead her young ones on their daily march, and she even liked to time the dew patterns, having learned that the hotter the morning the quicker the dissipation of the dew. She laughed at herself as she tried to imitate the birdcalls.

Angelique's dad was the best, but she and her mom made valiant efforts, too. She had so many happy memories of them staying at the fishing camp. That's when they got close as a family, and Angelique was sure that was what her dad wanted for the newlyweds when he allowed them to stay in the cabin.

"Guess what, little squirrel? I hear the mailman. Come on, you can walk with me!" She laughed as it ran ahead and scampered up a tree. "OK, see you later!"

"Oh, a big envelope from Nana-vonnie!"

The squirrel and the birds must have wondered what made the beautiful lady run back to the cabin. She plunked onto the top step not wanting to wait another second to discover what her Nana had sent.

The gasp must have caused the doe to raise its head from the sweet grass, the woodpecker to halt its pecking, while the tom turkey invariably would refuse to set another foot forward.

Angie's baby cards! But why? Angelique's hands shook as she found the letter from Nana-vonnie

My dearest Angelique,

I have designated you as the recipient of these precious cards. It was you who loved them the most. It was you, as a little girl, who would sit with me and read through them each and every time you came to visit. You were the one who got me through my terrible grief of losing Angie when she was only eight years old. Imagine a little granddaughter being able to help her old grandmother after years of holding onto so much grief?

So, my dear, enjoy them again, and maybe someday you'll be able to share them with your little daughter or son.

Poor Grandma, losing an eight-year-old child, how dreadful. But she endured, she persevered, she raised her other children—she was a survivor.

Angelique looked at the cards, which were now more than sixty years old. Oh, how beautiful! How could they make such lovely cards way back then?

The first card featured two little cherubs flying over the land carrying a bundle. Nestled inside the bundle was, of course, a baby dressed in pink.

Best wishes for you and the baby! Congratulations! Just heard you've a bundle from heaven who'll share in your love for each other. So here's to a lifetime of gladness. To the baby, her dad and her mother.

With our love and best wishes,

Corinne and Lou

On the next card there was a border of pink roses with white scalloped edges featuring a tiny baby posed on a pillow of pink and white with the word "baby" written in a ribbon effect.

Sweetest little someone, so welcome and so dear. Come to add new meaning to every day and year. You'll be your mother's darling; you'll be your daddy's pride. And, long years through, for all of you, may the brightest joy abide.

Love,

Joe and Ann

A star edged in pink roses floated down from the starlit sky with a sweet baby inside, nestled under her blanket.

To the new arrival. Your mom and dad have waited a good long time for you, and now you'll be a joy to them in everything you do. They planned a lot before you came, and now that you are here, you're sure to help their dreams come true. So welcome baby dear!

Love from Auntie

On another card, scalloped in pink bows was a stork-shaped boat pulling a new baby in its flounced bedding. The bed was also carrying pink roses, and the baby was holding the ribbon that directed the boat in the water.

Rejoicing in your good fortune and wishing you happiness.

Love,

Aunt Bebette and Uncle Charles

Next, a baby on its tummy nestled into a white pillow with a ruffled edging, surrounded by her stuffed animals.

A little one to love and keep, to guard and guide, to hush to sleep. A little one whose love will bring an added joy to everything. May all that's best from year to year bless mother, dad, and baby dear!

Love,

Tessie, Julio, and children

A baby with a pink bonnet.

A babysitting in a pillowed chair surrounded by flowers.

Ribbons and bows and rattles and toys.

"Oh, I must stop for now," Angelique paused to give the envelope of precious cards a kiss.

Yes, she would fix Andy a special dinner and absolutely insist on starting a family right away. She ran to the garden for fresh vegetables, and then she lit the charcoal in the pit so it would be nice and hot for the steaks and carefully rinsed the blackberries that she'd picked. All the while she glanced at her treasure in the manila envelope, her inspiration.

Finally, she heard the roar of the new sports car careening up the dirt driveway. The mountain of dust that billowed behind the car hid the beautiful sunset but it couldn't hide the love she was feeling for her husband.

"Andy, darling, sit down and let me show you what Nana-vonnie sent me." Angelique fanned all of the baby cards across the table in front of him. "Aren't they adorable?"

"What did she send you this junk for? Why didn't she send you something valuable? Your damn family, they're all alike, dripping in money, but they won't even send us anything worth anything! Get these out of my face! And just forget about babies—they do nothing but eat up your money!" With that he scooped up the cards, stomped out to the charcoal pit, and threw them into the fire.

"No, no!" Angelique screamed as he held her back. "No!"

Would the forest ever know what pierced its solitude that evening? Would the night animals not go prowling? Would the young animals cuddle closer to their mothers? Would the lake paralyze itself as if it were winter? How long into the night would the crying ricochet from tree to tree?

Andy wouldn't know anything about it; the mountain of dust followed him far, far away from Angelique.

"Sorry, ma'am, don't mean to disturb you, but your mailbox is full. I didn't think you'd want me to take it all back to the post office. I've got it here for you, if you want it."

"Oh, thank you," the red-eyed Angelique replied, "guess I haven't been to the mailbox in a while."

"Looks like you've got a nice little package here," the mailman said. "Have a good day."

The package sat on top of the pile. "Oh no, it's from Nana. Does she know about the burned baby cards? Angie's baby cards? Is she going to be mad? No, wait, there's no way she could know."

She picked up the package, it rattled. "Oh no, whatever it is, is it broken? What else could go wrong for my grandmother and me?"

"What? The silver rosary? Nana's silver rosary; the one her parents gave her when she made her first communion back in the old country? The rosary that traveled with her to this country? The rosary that comforted her all through her life, through Angie's drowning, through Grandpa's illness and death? Why would she send it to me?"

Angelique found a note.

My dearest,

I have the strongest feeling that you need this rosary.

Remember that God will never abandon you.

Angelique hung on to the porch railing as she wailed to the hills.

Two weeks passed or some amount of days, she didn't really know, when she heard a car come up the driveway, but it wasn't roaring. Her body stiffened.

She peeked out the window. "Daddy! Mommy!"

"Our girl, our girl." The three hugged and cried.

"Dear Lord, Angelique, what has happened? Look at you; you're so skinny. As soon as we got back from our trip I went to my office and found that Andy had quit the job after one week! I went to the bank—you have no account. All your wedding money has been taken out. The police opened your storage shed—it's empty!

Why are you wearing your Nana's rosary around your neck?" Theron asked.

"Grandma somehow knew I would need all the strength I could get," Angelique said.

"Why didn't you try to contact us?"

"I didn't want to be a quitter. You always taught me that life takes perseverance."

"No Marjory, I won't send you there. According to Bea Winchum, you know Bea—the woman with the curly, dyed red hair—well anyway, she lives next door to that place, and she says half of the building is lit up all night. She thinks the staff is in there playing cards instead of working."

Chapter Twelve

GIVE US THIS NIGHT

Twilight now comes in the morning and dawn comes at night.

It is rather difficult to get used to, but manageable. The body and the mind are so habitual; once they have learned something, it's a devil to break.

Babies sometimes sleep during the day and stay awake all night; they don't know the difference. With well-planned manipulation, however, they soon learn to follow suit with the mother, and her mother, and her mother—back to?

What if the mother works all night and sleeps all day? The child still has to conform to society's alarm clock.

Now, it's mandatory for me and for the whole world to reverse our day/night pattern. So I wake up at about 8:00 p.m. and have my coffee and breakfast, read the paper, do my regular chores around the apartment, shower, dress, and meet the girls for lunch around midnight.

Some restaurants here are lit up like the old days of twelve o'clock lunches, trying to encourage their customers to become nostalgic about the times of sunny meals. Others don't fight Mother Nature and use the beauty of the darkness to create ambiance. Candlelight is the norm at lunchtime.

All the tennis courts are well lit so we have, of course, continued our tennis matches and lessons. It's such a pleasure to play now—the coolness at 2:00 a.m. is utterly refreshing. No more are we perspiring profusely to stay in shape.

Golf has become exorbitant to participate in because of the lighting expenses. But those who do play are thrilled to be on the course at night.

Shopping is just the same as it was before. When you're in a mall you really have no idea if it's day or night anyway.

It's in vogue to schedule the dinner hour to coincide with the rising sun. I love it, myself. Some of the very best restaurants have huge windows facing east, so the clientele can dine and be transposed from darkness to dawn. Dancing, they say, goes to 12:00 or 1:00 p.m. I would never be able to stay awake that late! Once I easily could, but not anymore. I'm usually asleep by 10:00 a.m.

So what are you going to do? Life changes. We all have to make changes. Except Robert. Robert would never have been able to accept this. He would have balked against this until his dying day. So it's a good thing he passed away before all this transpired.

The kids, I don't know, they don't say too much. I imagine they're coping with it; they're younger; they're not so set in their ways yet.

Seems like a lot more people going to church these nights. I think it's the allure of the candles. All the churches are breathtaking by candlelight. What's nice, too, is how the intentional beam of light from the outside comes through the stained glass windows. I think they use floodlights. It's very attractive and inviting.

Often my friends and I go for coffee and cannoli after church. We don't feel like rushing home like we used to. The sidewalk cafes are particularly popular after church.

Christmas is grand; the lights are on the entire time most people are awake. It used to be we'd have the lights on for a few hours and then go to bed. Now shoppers can be out all night with the pretty lights! Robert would be fit to be tied about the electric bill for Christmas lights. Our house would probably be the only one dark all night long. What a penny pincher he was on certain things.

Oh, this hair! I've got to get another perm soon. I don't know why I haven't had a permanent in so long? I never used to look like this. Robert wanted me looking just so at all times, day and night. That was when day was the opposite of what it is now, night too.

I love this little apartment; it's just darling. I can keep up with the size of this place, not like before with sixteen rooms! Oh, so much work, my other place, so much work! It had to be just so— clean, scrub, straighten and clean, scrub, straighten, that's all I did.

"Yes, Robert, I worked all day, all day." That's when days were on the other side. I'm not on that side anymore. This is better.

I hope Mary can go out for lunch tonight. We have such a nice time when we're together. I'm glad I have friends now. I didn't have time to make friends before with so many rooms to clean every day. That's when we had day at a different time.

I just need to tidy up my apartment a wee bit, and then I'm free to go out for lunch! I hope Mary can go today.

I'll try brushing my hair to this side. That does look better. Oh, I forgot I can't do that; the scar will show. Back over to this side. Maybe if Mary and I go shopping I will buy a barrette. I don't know why I don't get permanents the way I used to. Well, times change; we all have to change.

I love this little apartment; it's like a dollhouse. I have pretty things on my shelf. Wonderful people live in this building. Out of the blue, for no reason, one of my neighbors might give me something. The other night, George gave me a statue of a mother cow and her baby calf. Isn't it adorable? Robert would not have liked that cow. He would have said it was stupid. I can have things now. I love this apartment; people are awfully good to me here. I can have my cow and her baby here.

Maybe Mary and I can go shopping today. I just need to finish my chores. Everything in my dresser has to be straight, straight, straight, straighter, straighter, and straighter.

Ah, pitch black out there, all black with pretty lights. It looks like it'll be a glorious night. Wake up world, the night is beginning! Don't be a sleepy head.

I just have to straighten the fringe on the bottom of the bedspread, and then I'll see if Mary is going out for lunch. Every string straight, they have to hang straight, straight down, every string.

"Come in."

"Oh, hi, Liza! How are you tonight?"

"Hi, Fran, I'm good. What are you doing down there?"

"Just straightening the fringe."

"I never seen the likes of it, Miss Fran. This room is always spotless; I don't know why I even come in here to clean."

"I don't know why you do either, Liza, except I like to visit with you."

"I like to visit with you, too, but my job is to be cleaning, not sitting around talking."

"We might as well visit, Liza. There's absolutely nothing left to be cleaned. I've washed the floor, the bathroom has been scrubbed top to bottom, and all the dusting is done. Let's talk. I love to have visitors.

"Why do you do all the cleaning when I'm getting paid to do it?" Liza asked.

"I'm just used to cleaning. Every day I cleaned my big house. This is nothing compared to that! Tell me how your boy is, Liza."

"He's doing better, Fran. Says he'll be walking again in a few weeks. I still can't get over him being beat up by his wife. I can't get my mind to make sense of it."

"I never heard of such a thing either, Liza. It's many a time a woman gets beaten up, but the other way around? Do you know yet what the fight was about?"

"Naw, he don't say and she's long gone. I'll tell you, I never would have dared raise a hand to my husband or he'd beat me worse."

"Your husband used to beat you?" Fran asked.

"Oh, you know, once in a while when he was liquored up; he didn't know what he was doing. The next day he didn't remember nothing, and I sure didn't bring it up. Did you ever get a beating?"

"My heavens, no, never a beating!"

"What then?"

"Well, he would strike me, just one strike though, one hard strike."

"Why'd he hit you?"

"It was my fault; I'd do something wrong."

"Something wrong?"

"Oh, you know, not having my hair fixed just so or forgetting to put the butter on the table, you know."

"Well," Liza said pushing the mop bucket with her foot, "I guess I don't know. However, I have to get back to work, can't be losing my job."

"No, we can't have that. I look forward to our visits."

"Where are all your friends from when you lived in your big house?" Liza asked.

"Oh my, Liza! There was never time to have friends. Besides, I wasn't smart enough to pick the right kind of friends," Fran said.

"Is that what Robert said?"

"Why, yes!" How did you know that?"

"Just smart, I guess."

"I guess you are."

Mary must be wondering where I am! I hope she's still in her apartment.

"Oh, good! Mary! Mary! Wait for me!"

"Hi, Frannie. Where've you been?"

"I was visiting with Liza."

"Oh. I finished the letter to my folks quicker than I thought, so I decided to start out for lunch hoping you'd catch up to me."

"I'm so glad I did."

"Me too."

"Where shall we go tonight?"

"How about the café right over there and then to a matinee?" Fran said.

"Great."

"So when do you expect your folks to arrive?"

"Any night now. I'm so excited. It's been quite a while since I've seen them. I have everything ready; we'll have such fun."

"We're lucky to have gotten such nice apartments. I love it here, Mary. Isn't this fun since night is now our time, everybody's time. It's so much better. Now I have friends, friends everywhere. Everyone is so helpful; they're always asking if they can help me!

Imagine Liza wanting to clean my apartment. What friends! So many friends. Did I tell you about my new statue for my shelf?"

"When my folks come, I'll definitely bring them by to see your collection!" Mary said.

"Oh yes, yes! I can't wait."

"Me neither! I haven't seen them in quite some time now. I'll write to them after supper."

⁂

"This meal is delicious!"

"Isn't it though! When my mother comes, she'll want to cook for me, but I'll invite you over."

"Wonderful, I love other people's cooking. I only ate my own for all those years and got a little tired of it, if you know what I mean."

"I do. Wait til you taste my mother's cooking!"

"Hi, Mac."

"Where are you ladies going to tonight?"

"We're going to a matinee."

"What's playing?"

"South Pacific."

"Oh, there you go! Enjoy!" Mac said.

"Isn't he a nice man?"

"Indeed, he is. What do you suppose he does for a living?"

"He sometimes asks a lot of questions. I think he might be a census taker."

"I bet you're right!"

"Lucy! Edna! Yoo-hoo! Hello! Edward!"

"There's quite a few people here tonight, Mary," Fran said.

"I should say as much. My folks and I always went to the matinees back when they were in the daytime. They're coming to visit me soon. I haven't seen them in quite a while now."

"Oh, that's good. Don't you just love matinees when it's dark outside?"

"I do. I really do!"

"I'm glad people decided to make this change—it's a good change."

"Wasn't that a wonderful movie, Fran?" Mary asked.

"It certainly was! Want to do some shopping?"

"Of course! I'm looking for a little welcome sign to put on my door; my mother will get a kick out of it. Did I tell you my folks are coming to visit?"

"Yes! Isn't that nice," Fran said.

"This way, Mary. Remember, it's the blue path to the stores. Don't take the green path; that'll get you into the bad neighborhood. We don't want to go there, do we?"

"I should say not!"

"Good evening, ladies. How are you?"

"Wonderful! Life is just plain wonderful!"

"Can I help you with something today?" Janice asked.

"I'm looking for a little welcome sign," Mary said as her eyes beamed back and forth across the shelves. "My folks are coming soon. I want everything to look perfect."

"Take a look over here, Mary. Aren't these adorable?"

"Oh! Yes! Frannie look! Look at this one and this one! How will I ever decide between Sunbonnet Sue or teddy bears or flowers or cats?"

"Well, what would your mother like best?" Fran asked.

"Cats! She loves cats! I'll take it!"

"Sure enough, Mary," Janice said. "Hope you enjoy it!"

"Oh, my mother will love it!"

"I'll have to get Bill to hang this up for me," Mary chirped as she walked along peeking into the bag every few seconds.

"Let's go to the front desk and enter your request into the maintenance book right now, before we forget it," Fran suggested.

"Good idea."

"Not that way, Mary. We want the yellow path to the front desk, not the green path; that'll take us into the bad neighborhood. We don't want to go there, do we?"

"No, that's for sure," Mary said.

"Hello, ladies!"

"Good evening, Bennett."

"What can I do for you?"

"I need to make a request for Bill," Mary spoke proudly.

"Here you go," Bennett said, swinging the maintenance book around for her.

As Mary filled out the form, Fran and Bennett chatted about the building.

"I'm so glad you like it here, Fran."

"This simply is the highlight of my life, Bennett. Everyone is so nice here and everything is well maintained."

"You sure made my counter look much better," commented Bennett.

"What?" Fran asked with a bewildered look.

"You've straightened everything here since we've been chatting!"

"I have?" Fran laughed. "I didn't even realize I was doing it. I guess I'm just so used to cleaning and fixing, I do it automatically!"

"You can come to my house and do it every day," Bennett suggested facetiously.

Fran's face darkened. She began scratching her wrist. "No, Bennett, I couldn't do that. I can't clean a big house anymore. No, Bennett, no, not anymore."

"Fran, Fran," Bennett said quietly, "I was teasing. I was just kidding."

"Oh," Fran sighed, "I thought you were serious."

"No, no."

"You know how happy I am here now that day is night and night is day. I don't have to clean a big house anymore!" Fran's face brightened.

"You are right, Fran, absolutely right!"

"There," said Mary. "I hope Bill can do it soon."

"According to the book," said Bennett, scrutinizing the list, "he has a few jobs to do before he gets to you. But it won't be long, maybe a couple of days."

Mary looked worried. "I hope it's before my folks get here."

"I'll put the rush on him," Bennett said and smiled.

"Thank you!"

As the women walked back to their apartments, Fran said, "Can you believe the sun will be coming up in about two hours? Where has the day gone? Are you going to eat dinner in?"

"I think I will," Mary said. "I need to write to my folks before I go to bed."

"I'm going to order in, too. I want to be home when Mac comes. He says he has a few more questions for me."

"Him and his questions!" Mary laughed. "What do you suppose he does for a living?"

"I don't know. Maybe he does surveys for different companies."

"Oh, that could be. Will I see you tomorrow?"

"I certainly hope so. Check the sunrise; we'll discuss it tomorrow. Sleep well," Fran said.

"You, too."

Fran hung her blue tag out by the door, which meant she would be expecting a meal to be delivered.

Imagine that, Fran thought, *living in a place where they cared enough to bring three meals a day if you wanted it.* She remembered being sick at her big house and nobody brought her even one meal. This was living!

Fran sat in her chair looking east, waiting for the sunrise.

Fran recognized the knock on the door; it was Sebastian's.

"Come in, Sebastian, come in."

"Ready for your dinner, Frannie?"

"I sure am, Sebastian! How are you?"

"Good, thanks. How's the world treating you?"

"Never better. What do you have for me tonight?"

"Spaghetti and meatballs, garlic bread, salad, and cake," Sebastian said.

"Yummy, my favorite!"

"Everything's your favorite." Sebastian smiled as he put the tray down.

"Isn't it though? As long as I don't have to prepare the meal, I love it!" Fran clasped her hands together.

"Weren't you a good cook, Frannie?"

"Apparently not. Robert never said it was good."

"But what about you, Fran, did you think it was good?"

Fran walked over to Sebastian whispered into his ear, "I thought it was delicious."

"There, that settles it; it was delicious!" Sebastian exclaimed gleefully while giving Fran a hug.

"Oops, I've got to get settled in my spot; we're going to have a beauty of a sky," Fran said.

"Enjoy! See you tomorrow."

"Bye, Sebastian."

Oh my, oh my, look at that!

Thank you, God, for this sunrise. Another day is ending for me and a night is beginning. Thank you for allowing us to change things around. I know I really needed it. I am most grateful for such a major change in your grand scheme of things. It was very kind of you.

"Fran, its Mac."

"Come in, come in."

"Are you washing your dishes again?"

"Yes, I would never put them out on the cart with food on them," Fran said.

"Other people do."

"I know, but they didn't live with Robert."

"I'm sure you washed your dishes at home."

"I thought I did," Fran said looking into the distance, "but one night Robert saw a speck of something on his dinner plate. Say! Let's talk about happy things!" Fran said rebounding to the present.

"Yes, let's," Mac agreed.

"Here, let's sit by the window. What's the topic tonight?" Fran asked.

"Reach into the bag and pull out a paper. We'll talk about whatever is on the paper."

"OK, here goes. And the topic is—hair. Hair? I was just thinking about hair today."

"Do you mean tonight?" asked Mac.

"Mac, I know it has been hard for you to adjust to changing our days to nights, but you'll get it."

"Thank you, Fran."

"You're welcome. Now, what can I say about hair? Oh yes, I was wondering why I don't get permanents as often as I used to?"

"Why did you have a permanent so often, Fran?" Mac asked.

"It had to always look good for Robert."

"Did Robert like your hair?"

"Well, you know, I don't think he did." Fran tilted her head, looking into the past again.

"Why do you think that?"

"It never suited him."

"And you thought getting a permanent would help?"

"I thought so," Fran replied.

"How about the color?"

"Oh heavens, blond, it always had to be blond."

"Why was that?"

"Robert liked blondes. He wanted me to look like a movie star."

"What happened to your hair, Fran?" Mac asked.

"It started to fall out," she whispered.

"Was it caused by the permanents and the dying?"

"Mostly, probably, I think." She started scratching her wrists.

"Did Robert pull on your hair?"

"A little, it didn't hurt," she said hurriedly.

"Look at my hair, Fran. Now you can ask me any questions you'd like about my hair."

Fran started to giggle. She sat back in the chair and folded her hands.

"Let me see. Were you a good boy when you got your hair cut?" Fran asked.

"My mother said I hollered and screamed bloody murder for the first four times," Mac laughed.

"Did you comb it like a movie star?"

"I remember trying to comb it like Elvis Presley, all slicked back!"

"Did somebody ever pull your hair out?"

"No."

"Why is my hair so short and curly now?" Fran asked as she ran her fingers through it.

"I think this is your brand new hair, Fran. Just think, it doesn't have to be permed anymore, and it doesn't have to be colored. It's beautiful this way, Fran."

"It is?"

"It truly is!"

"Oh, thank you, Mac."

"You're welcome. Well, you must be tired; you've had a long—was it night or day?" Mac asked.

"Oh, Mac, it was night, but it was my day."

"I'll get it straight one of these days."

"I'm sure you will."

"Good, uh, night?"

"Good night, Mac."

Oh, what a character he is, Fran thought. *I guess he works for a hair products company, probably something to do with customer service.*

It's ten o'clock? No wonder I'm tired, Fran thought to herself.

Fran looked in the mirror and fluffed her short little curls.

She dwelled on Mac's words about her hair being beautiful. *Must be living here that's doing it*, she reasoned.

"Good night world, see you just before sunset," she whispered.

I can hardly stand reading the paper anymore, Fran thought to herself as she sipped her coffee and finished the scrambled eggs. Such fighting between countries and cruelty everywhere, it's terrible.

Fran thought the eggs were delicious and remembered how she would add a dollop of sour cream and fresh chives to add a bit of zest. But then again, what did she know about cooking?

Fran read another article and concluded that God was going to get totally fed up with people and bing, bang, boom, that would be the end of the whole shooting match.

Oh! I better get my work done before the cleaning lady gets here, Fran thought. I want Liza to sit and visit, not work; I love having company.

Fran fluffed her brand new hair as she passed in front of the mirror.

"Come in!"

"Oh my, God! Get away from that window! Miss Fran, get down," Liza screamed.

"What's the matter?"

"What are you doing up there?" Liza reached for Fran's hand.

"I was washing the window, for heaven's sake!"

"Oh, Jesus, Mary, and Joseph, save us," she exhaled wiping the sweat from her eyebrows.

"I wanted to get everything done before you came in. Here, sit," Fran said.

"Golly, Miss Fran, you make me feel like a lady come a visiting here."

"That's good! You are a lady and we like to visit, don't we?"

"Well, yes, I guess we do." Liza giggled.

"So how long is your son going to stay with you?"

"I don't know. My husband takes him for his physical therapy every day. He can't live in his house. It has to be sold according to the separation agreement. What a mess. You think you raise your kid to be out on his own and then something like this happens. You got any kids, Fran?"

"I think so, I mean, yes! I have a boy and a girl."

"That's nice. They live around here?"

"No, one is in Texas and the other in Colorado. My daughter came once, didn't say much. She said she had to get back."

"Fran, did you hear anything about Dorothy?"

"You mean Dorothy next door with the poodle skirts?"

"Yeah."

"No, I haven't heard anything about her. I saw her yesterday playing cards. Why, what's going on?"

"I don't know, I only heard she has moved to green," Liza said.

"The bad section of town?" Fran asked.

"Yeah."

"Well, I wonder why she'd want to move there."

"I don't know. Well, I'd better go, got a make a living. See you tomorrow."

"Bye."

Isn't that something about Dorothy, Fran thought to herself? *I'll ask Mary if she has heard anything. Hate to see Dorothy move away, she was great fun; what a live wire. She just says anything that pops into her head. Boy, I wish I had that nerve. When I lived with Robert, I didn't hardly dare say anything. I could have made people laugh like Dorothy could.*

Fran straightened the fringe before she went to see Mary.

What's this?

Gone to the front desk—yellow path—to check the

maintenance book. I'll wait for you there.

"Hi, there, Mary! Good to see you!"

"You, too, Fran. Did you sleep well?"

"Fine. How close is Bill to your request?"

"I see he has crossed out the three jobs ahead of me; I don't know why he hasn't come to hang my welcome sign yet. I told you my folks will be coming soon, didn't I, Fran?"

"Yes, that's wonderful!"

Oh, Mary," Bennett interrupted, "Bill had an emergency situation in Dorothy's room. He had to drop everything and go there right away."

"Dorothy's room? I hope she's all right."

"I heard she moved to the green area," Fran whispered to Mary.

"Oh dear," Mary uttered as she wrinkled her brow.

"I'm sure Bill will get to you as soon as he can, Mary," Bennett said.

"Do you want to go to the restaurant at the other end of the building?"

"Sure," replied Mary. "Maybe we should go down the green pathway and see if Dorothy's OK."

"No, I don't think it's safe. We'll see her at Carnival Night or maybe a dinner/dance. You know Dorothy; she'll be where all the fun is."

"That's true, she's a live wire!"

"Oh, Mary, I think I know what Mac does for a living. He's a sales representative for hair products!" Fran said.

"Really? He has made an appointment with me for tonight at six. I told him I'd eat dinner early so I'd be all ready for him. Oh, I can't wait! Does he give out free hair products?"

"I didn't think to ask him, darn it! I will next time."

"Hi, ladies. I'm looking for someone to play pitch with Shawn and me. Any takers?"

"Mary, do you want to beat Roger and Shawn at cards tonight?" Fran asked.

"Sure."

"We'll meet you in the game room at about two. How's that?"

"Fran, do I have time to run back to my apartment and see if my folks are there?" Mary asked.

"Sure, I'll go with you."

"What on earth are they taking out of Dorothy's room?"

"I don't know," said Mary edging closer to Fran. "It looks like a crocodile."

"Well, it can't be a crocodile!"

"I know that," whispered Mary as she edged herself behind Fran and peered over her shoulder. It looks like venetian blinds wrapped around something."

"That does look like venetian blinds that have been woven together."

"Move along, ladies, move along," snapped a policeman who suddenly darted out of Dorothy's room making Fran and Mary jump two inches off the floor.

The women clasped arms and ran into Mary's apartment.

"What do you suppose is going on?" Mary panted into her hands, which were covering her mouth.

"I have no idea! What do you think was wrapped in the blinds? Why did Dorothy suddenly move?" Fran fired questions at Mary, knowing her friend couldn't answer them.

"Maybe we'd better stay in here tonight."

"Let me peek out," whispered Fran.

"What do you see?"

"Nothing. The hallway is clear."

"Should we go?"

"I think we can, but we'll run past Dorothy's room."

"OK."

"You girls look like you've seen a ghost! What's the matter with you two?" asked Roger as he showed off his shuffling techniques.

"We don't know. We saw something strange going on by Dorothy's room."

"Yeah, the whole building is talking about what might have happened. Haven't heard one story that's probably true though. Oh well, isn't our business anyway. Let's play cards."

"Shawn, you want to cut the deck?"

"OK, Mary, it's your bid."

"I'll say, two."

"By me, I ain't got nothin'," Shawn said.

"Pass."

"We can't let you have it for two. Three!"

"Take it away, partner."

"Well, the kitty didn't do me much good. Here we go on a wing and a prayer."

"Ah! You fell right into my hand, Roger Dodger; we got it in the bag!" Shawn exclaimed.

"The jack! You sneaked it in and saved it, Fran. I think we've got the low, too!"

"Oh, you damn women," Shawn mumbled.

"That's OK. Three in the hole means nothing to us," Roger spoke admirably. "We'll be out in no time."

"Who do you think came out of Dorothy's room?" Mary asked.

"We don't know it was a *who*," Fran said.

"Well, you said it wasn't a crocodile!"

"That I did."

"What do you mean 'came out?' And Mary it's your deal."

"Something was carried out horizontally, wrapped in woven venetian blinds."

"I'll bid three!" Shawn yelled.

"Wrapped in woven venetian blinds?" Roger reiterated.

"Fine by me, I'll pass."

"Me too."

"Me too."

"Damn it, I was expectin' more in the kitty!" Shawn growled.

"What do those people on the green hallway do anyway?" Mary asked. "Dorothy's there now."

"Read 'em and weep, Shawn. I don't have a thing to help you," Roger directed.

"Damn, damn, damn, I was countin' on my king to be high!" Shawn hit his fist on the table.

"You saved the deuce, Mary!" Fran exclaimed.

"I don't really know what they do on green," admitted Roger, "All I know is that there's always trouble down that hallway."

"I was sure I could pull it off," Shawn groaned as he slouched in his chair hitting his head with his fist.

"Why would Dorothy want to move there? She doesn't like trouble, she likes fun."

"Six in the hole is nothing, Shawn, we'll pull her out," Roger spoke confidently.

"I'll tell you, if she was here now, we would be howling, splitting our sides open. Did I tell you my folks are coming to visit?" Mary asked.

"Oh, that's nice. Thanks for a great hand, Fran, I'll bid three!"

"Too rich for my blood. Pass."

"Four! I'll bid four."

"Shawn, what are you bidding against me for?"

"This is unbelievable, wait until you see this! Throw the cat away. I don't even want to look at it!" Shawn was standing like a jockey on a horse, bobbing up and down.

"Here's my ace!" He slammed it down.

"Here's my king!"

"Here's my queen!"

"Here's my jack!" He was screaming now.

"And these two don't matter because they're both aces!"

"But I have the deuce of trump, right here," Fran said impishly.

"That's it! I quit, I quit, I quit," yelled Shawn.

"Don't be a poor loser, Shawn, sit down," Roger said sternly.

"Hi, guys, what's happening?" asked Mac as he sauntered over.

"These women are cheatin'!" Shawn hit his head with his fist.

"Let's go have a cup of tea, Shawn. I'll tell you a funny story about women."

"There's nothin' funny about women," Shawn snarled.

"Oh, you'd be surprised. Come on."

Mac looked back at Mary. "Don't forget our appointment at six."

"Oh! That's right. I have to have an early supper. You ready to go, Fran?"

"I thought I'd stay and play gin rummy with Roger."

"But I don't want to go alone, Fran, especially by you know where," said Mary, pointing behind her other raised hand.

"OK, do you want to walk with us, Roger?" Fran asked.

"Sure."

"Well, the door is wide open; it's absolutely empty. There's not a thing in it!" Mary said in amazement.

"Probably all set for the next tenant," Fran remarked.

"I wonder who it'll be." Mary suddenly looked joyful. "I hope it's someone nice!"

"Oh, I'm sure it will be. This building attracts the most wonderful people," said Fran dreamily. "Even Shawn! His little temper tantrums don't upset me one iota. They are such mild little spasms."

"I think you like everybody," Roger said pensively.

"I think I do, too! Well, nowadays I do! OK, Mary. Have a good evening. Let me know if you get any free hair samples."

"Free hair samples?" Roger asked as they started toward Fran's room.

"Yes, Mary is meeting with Mac this morning."

"Oh. Say, Fran, do you want to eat dinner at the Patio Restaurant? We can watch the sun rise."

"Oh, I'd love to!"

"How do you like the change in days and nights, Roger?" Fran asked.

"I like it very much. After my wife died, I couldn't face the daytime. But now that I can sleep during the light of day and have my *day* at night, I can deal with it. Something so simple solved the problem. How about you, Fran?"

"I love it! I'm not exactly sure why, but it does fit my whole system of being. I'm at complete ease with it. God forgive me, but I remember hating the days. It got so I never looked forward to another one. Maybe it was a combination of living here and having new hours that has brought peace to my soul. It's an awful feeling when you wake up dreading the day."

"It sure is," agreed Roger, pointing to the horizon. "Here it comes!"

"Miss Fran, what's the matter? Why you crying?" Liza asked as she knelt on her knees by Fran.

Fran handed her a photograph of a baby girl.

"Aw, how cute! Who is she?"

"She's my granddaughter," sobbed Fran.

"Did something happen to her?"

"My daughter just decided to tell me about her. She was born six months ago!"

"Is your daughter married?"

"Oh yes, that I knew. She was married about three years ago in Texas. I never met her husband, and I certainly didn't know about the child. Why didn't she tell me?"

"Who knows about kids, Miss Fran? Look at the situation my son is in. I don't know half of what's going on with him. When they're ready, then I suppose they talk. Who can figure them out?"

"I think she wanted to punish me—holding back something as sensational as this. I could have been enjoying this child for the last six months and even in the expecting stage.

"'You need to be punished,' her father said so many times to me. I think my own children feel they should punish me too."

"What would they need to punish you for, Miss Fran?" Liza asked, putting her arm around Fran's quivering shoulders.

"I don't know, I don't know. I tried so hard with them."

"Well, never you mind now. You have a nice life here with all of us. Your daughter will come around. In fact, it looks like she already has! Now you know you have a beautiful granddaughter, and you can show everybody her picture! What's her name?"

"It says 'Elizabeth' on the back of the picture. Her name is Elizabeth!" Fran said.

"Well, congratulations!"

"I can't wait to tell Mary!" Fran said as she hugged Liza.

"Mary, yoo-hoo. Are you home?"

"Come in, Fran. How do you like the welcome sign?"

"I love it!"

"My mom is going to get a kick out of it, too! I'm glad Bill got here to hang it before my folks arrive."

"Mary, look! It's my granddaughter!"

"Aw, she's so pretty! When was she born?"

"Six months ago."

"I didn't think babies looked this big when they were born. When are you going to see her?"

"Gee, I don't know. I'll write to Jean and see when they can come. Oh I can't wait! Elizabeth looks just like Jean did when she was this age, so cute."

"Excuse me for interrupting, Fran, but do you want to eat in or out?" Mary asked.

"What do you want to do?"

"Well, I was thinking if we stayed here we could finish the Scrabble game we started a week ago."

"You saved it? Oh Mary, you didn't have to do that. It has probably been in your way all this time."

"It was OK. I worked around it. Let me hang my meal tag out by the door with a number two on it. Doesn't my new welcome sign look great? My folks should be coming any day now."

"I love it! Maybe I should put one out for Jean and Elizabeth!" Fran said.

"Oh yes! OK, which side of the table were you sitting at? Do you remember?"

"Yes, I was looking at the words upside down," Fran said.

"Do you want to trade sides now?"

"Oh no, that's OK."

"I need to take three more letters," Mary said.

As she reached into the bag, she said, "Oh, by the way, Mac and I didn't talk about hair last night."

"You didn't?"

"No, he wanted to talk about fire," Mary said.

"Fire? I wouldn't want to talk about that!"

"Well, I didn't either, but I think Mac is a fireman of some type, maybe even a fire safety officer for our building. I know how important safety rules are, so I didn't tell him I'd rather talk about hair. Oo, I can make the word help. H-E-L-P. There."

"That's good, let me think a minute."

Mac could tell you things about fire but what could you tell him?" Fran asked.

"Hardly anything, to tell you the truth. I told him I was very afraid of fires and never wanted there to be a fire in this building. I also told him how good I was during fire drills and that I knew where the alarm box was out in the hallway. He seemed pleased about all the rules I know."

"That's good, Mary! Oh, here, I can make the word *food*."

"Well speak of the devil, here's our lunch!" Mary laughed.

"Are you calling me the devil?" Sebastian laughed as he brought the trays in.

"Oh no, no, no, Fran was just making the word *food* when you came in."

"Ah, Scrabble. Great game!"

"What did you bring us?" Fran asked as she peeked under the lids.

"Homemade broccoli and cheese soup with egg salad sandwiches and peach pie."

"Mmm," the ladies replied as a duet.

"I never got to have egg salad at my big house, and it's my favorite!" Fran said.

"Why not?" Mary and Sebastian asked together.

"If Robert so much as smelled egg salad, he would go nuts. Once he threw everything out of the refrigerator onto the floor claiming he could smell it."

"Good grief."

"Sebastian, did you hear anything about Dorothy?" Mary asked.

"Just that she's living on green now. She must have done something really bad."

"Done something bad? What does that mean?" Fran asked with a wrinkled brow.

"That's where they send people who have... Oops, I'm not supposed to be talking about the residents," Sebastian said as he drew himself up straight.

"I thought it was the bad section of town?" Mary interjected.

"You could call it that," Sebastian replied. "Darn, I'm going to be reprimanded again if I don't learn to shut my mouth." He hit his lips with a *whack*.

"See you, ladies. Enjoy your lunch."

"That's the oddest thing, isn't it Mary?"

"It certainly is," Mary agreed as she spooned into her soup.

Fran started with her egg salad sandwich.

"Did I tell you my folks will be coming soon to visit me?"

"Yes, isn't that wonderful?" Fran said.

"What did you do when your husband threw everything on the floor?" Mary asked just before she took a bite of her sandwich.

"What could I do? When he finished smashing everything, I cleaned it up."

"Were your kids there?"

"Yes, they watched the whole thing."

"What did they do?"

"Nothing. When the tirade was over, Robert said, 'Come on kids, let's go out to eat.' I saw that Bobby was crying, crying without making a sound. I knew he wanted to stay with me."

"Here, Fran, let me fix your tea for you," Mary said sympathetically. "Never you mind. We have a good life now. This is a nice building; everyone is so kind. Plus, everything is better with day and night reversed, right?"

"Yes," Fran said weakly, still scratching her wrists. "Did Sebastian mean that if you did something bad around here they'd send you to the green section of town?"

"Gosh, I don't know," Mary said looking scared. "We'd better not be bad."

"I guess not!" Fran agreed. "We haven't done much with our game except *help* and *food*! Maybe we should go to a matinee tonight."

"I guess we just can't think very well right now. I'll leave it here. Maybe we can continue later."

"Fran!" Mary shouted as she grabbed Fran's arm so hard it hurt.

"What's the matter?" She pulled away from Mary's clutches.

"Look at that welcome sign!"

"It's the same as yours," Fran said.

"My folks might go to the wrong apartment. Maybe they won't be able to find me! Fran! Who moved into Dorothy's apartment? Why do they have the same welcome sign? My folks won't know where I am!"

"Mary, Mary. The numbers on the doors are different."

"Maybe they won't look at the number. Maybe they'll just look at the sign. I described it in detail in my letters. Oh no. What if they come and I'm not home. I don't want to miss them."

"They'll inquire at the desk, Mary. Don't worry, they'll find you," Fran said as she put her arm around Mary's shoulders.

Mary got her little pack of tissues out to wipe her tears.

"I think I'll change my sign to make it look different," Mary said.

"That's a wonderful idea, Mary. You could add a little something to it to make it look unique!"

"Yes, that's what I'll do! Let's go to the arts and crafts room."

She livened her step and Fran was glad for the quickened pace. It meant Mary was happy.

"Alicia, has your class started yet?"

"Oh, hi, Mary. Hi, Fran. No, not for another hour. Are you coming tonight?"

"Well, maybe, but actually I wanted to know if I could have some craft materials. I need to make my welcome sign look different."

"Sure, what would you like?"

Mary's eyes darted around the room.

"How about some ribbon and beads and some of those feathers! Feathers would make it look different!"

"Here's an empty container. Put what you need in it," Alicia said.

"You know, Mary, that's quite a project you're planning. Why don't you bring the sign to class some night and I can help you with it."

"Why, thank you, Alicia. If Fran and I can't figure it out, we'll be back."

"OK. Bye, girls."

"She's so nice, isn't she?"

"She sure is. Remember those ornaments we made? We spent months on them but it was worth it!"

"Oh darn," Fran said.

"What's the matter?"

"I forgot to show her Elizabeth."

"Do you want to go back?" Mary asked.

"No. I'll show her the picture next time. I wonder what Elizabeth is doing right now."

"Yeah," said Mary dreamily.

"Oh! I'm sorry, Mary," Mac apologized as the three of them bent down to pick up beads and feathers. "What are you doing with all this stuff?"

"I have to make my welcome sign different. The new person in Dorothy's room has one just like mine. I don't want my parents to be confused when they come to see me."

"Oh, I see."

"Mac, look," Fran said as she put the photograph in front of Mac's eyes.

"Well, who's this little cutie?"

"It's Elizabeth, my granddaughter!"

"Really! How nice."

"Excuse me, Mac, but do you know who lives in Dorothy's room?"

"Actually, I do know. Her name is Ann Marie. She's very quiet and shy, so I want you girls to make her feel welcome."

"Oh, we will," Fran said excitedly. "We're good neighbors. Will you be giving her the fire safety rules?"

"Fire safety rules?" Mac looked puzzled.

"Yes, like you and I talked about yesterday," Mary piped up.

"Oh that." Mac hesitated then said, "Ann Marie and I will have our little talks, too."

"Mac, is it true that we can be kicked out of our apartments for doing something bad?"

"Where did you hear such a thing?" he asked.

"That's what Sebastian told us," Mary divulged.

"Oh he did, did he?"

Fran could see the cords in his neck pull upward.

"You ladies don't need to worry about anything like that," Mac said.

"We really don't want to end up in green."

"Of course you don't. But like I said, that is something you don't have to worry your pretty little heads about. Go on now, make a beautiful welcome sign."

"Isn't he nice?"

"He certainly is!"

"Did you hear him say 'pretty little heads'? Robert never said I was pretty or that I had beautiful hair," Fran said.

"Never you mind about that Robert; you forget about him," Mary said.

"I wish I could."

"All right, let's see. How should we do this?" thought Mary out loud.

"How about we string the beads on the ribbon with one knot in between each bead. Remember how Alicia showed us?" asked Fran.

"I have no idea what you are talking about," Mary said blankly.

"Watch."

"Oh yes, now that I see it, I remember!"

"Then we can loop them down in this area by the cat. What do you think? That'll make it look different. Now, what shall we do with the feathers?" Fran asked.

"Don't tell me it's going to be the cat that ate the canary?" Mary laughed as she spoke.

Fran suddenly ran to the sink and splashed cold water on her face.

"My dear God, Fran, what's the matter?" Mary asked as she jumped up, spilling her beads.

"Oh, I'm sorry. I'm OK."

"What happened?"

"I just had a vision of my poor canary, Aria."

"What? Your cat ate it?" Mary asked.

"No, Robert killed it after—"

"After what?"

"After he let it out of its cage for six days so it could mess all though the house. And Robert wouldn't let me clean up the mess for the entire six days! It was everywhere, Mary. On the drapes, the bedspreads, and the carpets.

"Finally he said, 'and this is why I have to kill your bird. It messes all over the house. Now clean it up.' It felt like it took forever. Imagine sixteen rooms. I know my kids were disgusted. All I could do was clean and cry, clean and cry."

"Well!" Mary said. "That's it for the feathers; they are going right into the garbage!"

"Oh, you don't have to do that, Mary, I'm OK now. In fact, I realize I hadn't thought about that episode for a long time."

"You poor thing. I'll make you a cup of tea and put in a spoonful of honey, just like my mother did when I was feeling blue."

"Thanks, Mary."

"We do nice work, don't we?" Mary stood back admiring the sign.

"We certainly do! Let's see if we can get it hung up."

"Hello, ladies," said Bennett. "What can I do for you? What are you fixing now?"

"I need Bill to hang my welcome sign."

"Again?"

"Yes, again." Mary laughed.

Bennett swung the maintenance book around and said, "This dinner/dance notice just went up. Are you interested?"

"Oh, maybe. Will Dorothy be there? Won't be any fun without her," Fran said.

"Dorothy? Well, uh, uh... I'm not at liberty to discuss the people who live in the building."

"Oh, since when?"

"Since always, really."

"Oh."

"Bennett, this is my granddaughter! She might come to visit me!" Fran said.

"Frannie," Mary interrupted as she stopped writing, "wouldn't it be wonderful if Elizabeth came the same time as my folks?"

"Wouldn't we be in seventh heaven?"

"I should say as much!"

"This way, Mary. Stay on the yellow path until we get to our hallway."

"Oh yes, yellow. I hope my folks don't get here before Bill hangs my sign. Oh my heavens! I need to write a letter home describing the renovations. They need to look for the sign with the beaded, looped ribbon," Mary said.

"Should we stop and invite Ann Marie to go to dinner with us?" Fran asked.

"That's a wonderful idea, Fran!"

"I guess she's not home. Well, maybe tomorrow."

"I'll meet you at the Patio Restaurant in an hour. How's that sound?"

"Great! See you there," Mary chirped.

"Fran, sit with us!" hailed Roger.

"OK, Mary is coming, too. Hello, Shawn."

"Hello," Shawn said gentlemanly.

"What have you guys been doing tonight?" Fran asked.

"We played poker with Fred and Louis."

"And they didn't cheat!" Shawn inserted abruptly. "Oops, sorry, Fran," he apologized.

"We found out that our new neighbor is Ann Marie. We're going to try and catch up with her tomorrow."

"Guess what we heard about Dorothy?" Shawn asked.

"First of all, who told you?" Fran said.

"We're not allowed to say," Shawn answered arrogantly. "Anyway, Dorothy made this mannequin with pillows and sheets and wrapped it up with her venetian blinds and had a funeral for it. Crazy old bat."

"Why do you say that?" Fran snapped at him. "You don't know the whole story. Maybe that was her mother who never had a proper burial. Maybe that was Dorothy's way of bringing some closure to her life."

"It must have been a bad thing to do or else why would they take her to green?" Retorted Shawn.

"Fran is right, Shawn, we don't know the whole story or any of the stories for that matter. We just hope Dorothy is OK."

"Women think they know everything," grumbled Shawn.

"I wonder where Mary is," Fran said as she checked her watch again.

"Probably wanderin' round lookin' for her *folks*. Like how long has she been sayin' they were comin'?" Shawn laughed and rolled his eyes.

"Shawn, stop. Why do you have to degrade everybody? Do you think you're perfect?" Roger spoke with red escalating on his neck.

"Well, I know—"

"Mary! Oh my Lord, Mary, honey, what happened? Sit, sit," Fran said.

Mary took her napkin and cried into it for several minutes.

The three waited. Fran remembered Bobby and Jean waiting after "Mommy did something bad."

Finally, Mary lifted her puffy face and said, "I got lost. I couldn't remember the colors."

"Oh, Mary," Fran whispered as she put her hand on top of hers, "I'm so sorry. I should have waited for you."

"Well, what stupid color did you go to?" Shawn asked as he turned sideways and crossed his legs.

"Green."

"Oh," the three said.

They waited for Mary to speak.

"What's the matter?" she asked, when she realized they were all staring at her.

"Was it bad?" Shawn asked leaning inward.

"No, not at all. It was a quiet hallway. The only difference from our hallway that I could see was that their doors had little windows in them, cute little windows. I wish we had little windows. Then when someone knocked, we would know who was at the door."

"That's a good point, Mary," Roger said with authority.

"Humph," Shawn snorted.

"Well, let's look through the menu," Fran said, reminding them of the meal they were gathered for.

"Seems like a hundred years ago since you told me about this," Mary said as she held up her menu so just Fran could see her finger pointing to egg salad.

"Ugh," Fran replied and rolled her eyes.

Roger and Shawn didn't ask.

"Look everyone!" Fran exclaimed as she pointed east.

When Liza knocked on Fran's door around 9:00 p.m., Fran thought of the windows on green. Was she sure it was Liza out there?

"Come in," Fran yelled. "Liza! Blessed Mary, what happened to you?"

Liza touched her swollen eye. "Oh, my old man and my boy got into a big hullabaloo. I'll tell you, all hell broke loose."

"Here, sit down. Talk to me."

"I guess it all started when Tom sassed me. Old Tom jumped up and told him to pack his things and get out of the house and that we weren't there to be sassed at. Tom pushed him and Old Tom popped him one, and I jumped in to stop it and Old Tom accidentally landed one on my eye.

"You know what, Miss Fran?" Liza said as her face began to blush. "I know Old Tom really loves me."

"That's nice, Liza," Fran said thoughtfully. "When Old Tom hit you—you knew it was love. When Robert hit me, I knew it wasn't love."

"What us women go through," Liza groaned as the pair sat in silence pondering two decades of thoughts.

Another knock at the door brought more thoughts of the little windows.

Liza jumped up, grabbed her broom, and whispered, "It might be my supervisor!"

"Come in," Fran said.

"Fran, I can't believe it. I can't believe it!" Mary cried.

"What, Mary, what?"

"Come, let me show you."

Liza and Fran ran down the hallway after Mary. They stopped short at Ann Marie's door.

"I'll be darned," Fran said slowly.

"What? What is it?" Liza whined.

There it was: beaded, looped ribbon placed exactly by the cat on the welcome sign!

"This is strange," Fran said to Mary.

"What, what is strange?" Liza continued.

"Go and look at the sign on my door," Mary said weakly.

"Now settle down, Mary. Try and think why Ann Marie would do this."

"I don't know, I don't know, I don't know," she repeated, raising her voice and swinging her arms.

"Mary! I thought I heard your voice," Mac said as he hurried over to them. "Is there a problem?"

Mary didn't speak, only pointed to Ann Marie's welcome sign. She then pulled him down the hall to her doorway. They went inside.

❦

Fran put her newly delivered hanging clothes into the closet, making sure there was an inch of space between each garment. She took her flashlight and checked each corner of the closet, even though she knew Bobby wouldn't be there. Somehow, however, she wished for the first time that the light would bring his face back to her. She knew Bobby loved her. Fran turned off the flashlight and wiped the tears from her face.

Her letter to Jean was ready to be mailed. When Mary finished talking with Mac, maybe they'd go the mailbox at the front desk and then to lunch.

Fran sat in the dark looking at the twinkling lights of the city, how beautiful. She wanted to hold Elizabeth on her lap and share the sight with her baby girl.

She thought of her wooden box on the top shelf of the closet, the box that held the returned letters to Bobby, no forwarding address.

"Where could he be? Where could he be? Where could he be?" she sang to the motion of the rocking chair.

"Come in."

"What are you doing, sitting in the dark?"

"I'm just enjoying the lights. Here, sit with me."

"I know why Ann Marie is copying my sign," Mary said.

"You do?"

"Yes, she wants to belong and be like us."

"Well, that sounds right! Did Mac tell you that?" Fran asked.

"Actually he did! He said he had a little brother who copied everything he did. It used to make him so mad until his dad explained how much the little guy wanted to be like Mac and feel joined to him."

"Firemen know a lot, don't they?"

"They sure do!"

"Are you going to write to your folks about the situation?" Fran said.

"Yes, I need to tell them about the pencil."

"The pencil?"

"Mac stuck his pencil right in by the cat. It looks like the cat is holding the pencil. It's so cute. Plus Mac said my folks could use the pencil to write me a note if I wasn't there!"

"Great idea."

"Isn't it though?"

"I need to mail a letter to Jean, want to go?"

"Sure. Blue?" Mary asked.

"Yellow."

"Did you ask Jean to come with the baby?"

"I sure did. Won't it be fun to have a baby around?"

"I should say as much!"

"I was so happy to have my children. Why did Robert make it so difficult for me?"

"What do you mean?" Mary asked.

"They had to be spotless at all times. He would become furious with me if he saw their hair out of place or a spot on their clothes. If they spilled something on themselves, he would rationalize it to be my fault. He would ream me out in lavender. The children would sit and listen to his raving. As they got older, it seemed as if he was on a real mission to brainwash them against me. He tried to make them think I was stupid and I had to be punished, punished with more work and no freedoms.

"He treated the kids very kindly, bought them everything they wanted, took them on nice vacations. I guess that's what kept me going—knowing he treated the kids nice."

Fran used the wall to lean against as Mary dug out a tissue from her little pack.

"There, there, don't cry, Fran. Won't be long before Jean and Elizabeth will be here to see you. Time heals all wounds, you know."

"I hope so," Fran said as she wiped away her last tear.

"I wonder where those elevators go," Mary said.

"I have no idea, but I see the people who use them have a special card to get the doors open."

"Yes, I've noticed that, too."

"Hi, Bennett, how are you?"

"Fine! Did you decide to sign up for the dinner/dance?" he asked.

"No, not yet. We have to find out if Dorothy can go, too."

"Well, uh, uh, well... don't wait too long."

"Say, Bennett. Where do those elevators go?"

"Up to the next floor."

"I surmised that! What's up there?"

"It's basically people who—I think I can say this—have kept their old ways of having day in the daytime and night during the dark hours."

"Oh, those poor souls."

"Oh," Mary said sympathetically, "I feel so sorry for them."

"You like working during the dark hours, don't you, Bennett?" Fran asked with a concerned tone.

"I sure do. It's a lot more peaceful on this floor."

"See! We knew it. It brings peace!"

"Yep, Mac had a good idea to have one floor just for night owls," Bennett continued.

"Night owls!" the two ladies uttered together and laughed.

"Is that what we are?" Mary continued to laugh.

"I think Mac is some kind of a genius, don't you, Mary?" Fran asked.

"I certainly do!"

"Oh, Bennett," Mary remembered to say, "if my folks come in, tell them it's the welcome sign with the beaded ribbons and the pencil by the cat."

"Will do, Mary. Will do."

"Fran, look! Bill and the other maintenance people are doing something down on that hallway. Yoo-hoo, Bill, Bill," Mary motioned him to come over.

"Hello, ladies. We're not making too much noise are we?"

"Oh no, I just wanted to thank you for hanging my sign, twice."

"You're more than welcome. Anything for you two!" Bill said.

"What are you working on down there?"

"It's going to be a new area with just café's and little restaurants. We thought it would be better to get them all in one area. Better for the visitors, too. They don't want to walk all over the building looking for a place to eat."

"How marvelous! What color will the pathway be?"

"Purple."

"Oo, purple!" the ladies exclaimed.

"Well, we're off to have our lunch. See you again, Bill."

"That'll be exciting to have new eating places! I'll take my folks, for sure, and you and your family can meet us there!"

"Great!"

"Oh, Fran, there's green. Let's just walk down and peek in the little windows. Maybe we can find Dorothy."

"It sure does look quiet down the hallway."

"It is! It's not a bad section at all!"

"OK."

"What do you see?"

"Nothing, this person must be out."

"Do you see anybody in there?"

"Yes, but she's sitting in her chair looking at the night lights. She's just like us!"

"How about in there?"

"A man is laying on his bed."

"Looking for someone, ladies?"

"Eeks!" the women jumped.

"Mac! You scared us half to death," Mary panted.

"I'm sorry. I didn't mean to scare you."

"We were trying to find Dorothy," Fran explained.

"Dorothy is resting. Have you girls had lunch yet?"

"No, we were just about to do that."

"If you let me go with you, I'll treat!" Mac said.

"It's a deal," Fran said.

"A big dinner/dance is coming up, and we wanted to know if Dorothy was going," Fran said as she placed her napkin in her lap.

"I don't think she can go this time," Mac replied, "but maybe next time!"

"Isn't she well?" Fran whispered, leaning toward Mac.

Mary leaned in to hear.

"She's very sad about her mother passing away," he said.

"Oh, we can understand that. Can't we Mary?"

"My soul and body! If my mother ever passed away they'd have to put me in the loony bin."

"Well," said Mac robustly, "what shall we order?"

"The special looks good," Mary remarked.

"I think I'll have an egg salad sandwich," Mac said.

Fran and Mary looked at each other and burst out laughing.

"What's so funny?"

"Actually," said Mary, "it's not funny, not funny at all, but laughing is better than crying, right?"

"Right!" he said.

"Isn't it sad about the people upstairs?" Mary said directing her statement toward Mac.

"Upstairs? What do you mean?"

"Them! Still having to live with day and night the way it used to be."

"Now where did you hear that?" Mac stopped eating and folded his arms across his chest.

"Bennett told us."

"Oh, he did?"

"If there's anything we can do for them, please let us know. We are so sorry they still have to live like that," Fran said sympathetically.

Mac resumed eating while shaking his head.

"Thanks for lunch, Mac."

"You know what I'd like to do, Mary?" Fran asked.

"What's that?"

"I'd like to go shopping and buy a few things for Elizabeth!"

"What a grand idea!"

"Yellow?"

"Blue."

"Mary, look at this!"

"Oh, how cute! Baby things are so adorable."

"Look at the sweater sets! They're handmade! My mother made sweater sets for Jeanie, and she made the hat and booties to match. They were so soft and sweet, all pink for my little girl.

"Mother died before Bobby was born; he never got any sweater sets from Grandma. I was devastated when she died, so I know what Dorothy is going through. In my mind I had years and years of sharing planned with her and my children.

"I tried to knit a sweater for Bobby but it infuriated Robert so I gave it up."

"Why did it infuriate him?" Mary asked.

"He said it was a waste of time. I should be cleaning the house, not knitting. The next day he came home with five sweaters for Bobby. He threw them at me saying, 'There, these are a lot better than what you can make.' But they didn't have the love in them like the homemade kind."

"Why don't you buy one and... I'm going to buy this one. It'll be from her great auntie Mary!"

"Are you sure?" Fran said.

"I certainly am," she professed as she walked to the counter with it.

"I think I have decided on this pink teddy bear, too!" Fran said as she joined Mary at the counter. "Listen as I shake it."

"Oh, how pretty! It sounds like chimes."

"So many things for babies; babies are special. You know, it doesn't cost anything to look. Let's stay awhile and look at everything!"

Fran and Mary spent the early morning hours looking through the wares in the baby section and even wandered into the toddler department for more memories. There were ohs and ahs and sighs and giggles mixed in with a few tears and sniffles.

"Let's stop and ask Alicia if she's going to have a class on picture frame making. I'd like to make a homemade frame for Elizabeth's photo."

"What a nice idea, Fran!"

"Hi, Alicia!"

"Hi, ladies. How did the welcome sign turn out?"

"Great!" Mary responded. "We didn't use the feathers though." She looked apologetically at Fran.

"What can I do for you?"

"Are you going to have another class on frame making? I'd like to sign up if you are," Fran said.

"Let me see. We were going to do quilling next Monday, but I'd just as soon change it to frame making."

"Oh wonderful! I'll see you on Monday!"

"Do you want to get back to our Scrabble game after supper?" Mary asked.

"Yes, let's do," Fran said. Then, "Mary, you won't believe it!"

"Won't believe what? What? Stop laughing and tell me what. Fran, stop, stop before you split your britches!"

Fran couldn't stop, so she pointed.

Ann Marie's welcome sign had a pencil in it!

Mary's "Oh" went from high *C* to two octaves below middle *C*.

Fran went into her apartment, still laughing.

"See you after supper," she managed to get out before she closed the door.

Oh to laugh. It's delicious, almost delirious, Fran thought. At one time, she reckoned she would never laugh again. It must be the place and the night being day and the day being night.

She set Elizabeth's picture on the shelf leaving the cow and calf there for her granddaughter to enjoy. She placed the teddy bear on the other side of the photo after shaking it first, of course. On one end she laid the sweater set neatly wrapped in pink tissue paper.

It wasn't long before Fran had the pink paper unwrapped and was holding the baby's sweater in her lap.

She rocked in the dark as the lights twinkled like stars. The darkness would soon fade and there would be a new sunrise.

Would Elizabeth be ready to get up or go to bed, she wondered?

Fran suddenly stopped rocking and sat motionless with fear emoting from every pore.

What if Jean and Elizabeth haven't gone on the new schedule yet? What if they come at the time I sleep? What if Jean thinks my sleeping during the daylight is stupid and goes back to Texas?

Mac, I've got to find Mac, Fran reasoned as she started running.

"Bennett, where's Mac? Where's Mac?"

"Fran, Fran, calm down, my God, what's the matter? Fran, stop, stop, you're making your wrist bleed. Fran!"

Bennett grabbed a hold of Fran's hand and reached for the intercom with the other.

"Mac to front desk, STAT! Mac to front desk, STAT!"

"It's OK, Fran, shh, OK, shh," he quietly said as he embraced the frantic woman.

"I'm here, Fran, it's Mac."

He led her over to a chair where she sat and wept into her lap.

"Shh, Frannie, everything will be all right," Mac quietly said as he rubbed her back, trying to bring comfort to her soul.

"I had such an awful thought," she uttered as she sat up.

"What was it?"

"I thought of Jean and Elizabeth coming to visit and them being on the old day/night schedule and us never getting together and her angrily returning home without me seeing the baby."

"Oh, Fran." Mac held out his arms for her to come in for a hug.

"When we know that Jean is coming, I will set up a schedule that will be perfect for you both."

"You will?"

"I will."

Such relief came to Fran's body that Mac had to steady her for a few steps.

"We're going to stop at the nurse's office before I escort you home," Mac said quietly.

"Why?"

"She needs to give you a little first aid on your wrist."

"Well, how did that happen?" Fran asked.

"Were you scratching a mosquito bite?"

"May be, I don't remember."

⌒

"I guess your supper was delivered while you were out. It must be cold by now. I'll get you a replacement," Mac exclaimed, ready to pick up the tray.

"No, no, it won't bother me a bit. Things like this have absolutely no consequence for me. I like food cold, hot, warm— anyway they serve it. I'm not Robert. I never want to be a Robert."

"Don't worry, you won't be," Mac said. "Are you going to be all right now?"

"Oh yes. Mary and I are going to play Scrabble for a while then I'll be sound asleep by ten."

"Guess what? So will I!"

"Thank you, Mac."

He left, giving Fran the thumbs-up sign.

"Who is it?"

"Mary."

"Come in, Mary."

"Are you coming over to my apartment to play Scrabble?" Mary asked.

"Yes, I just finished dinner."

"Just finished! What have you been doing?"

"Oh, I needed to tend to a few matters."

"Your shelf looks cute!"

"Thanks."

⌒

"Hooray! I can finally make a word—S-M-O-K-E." Mary spelled out the word slowly.

"Very good. Last time you made *help* now it's *smoke*. Are you trying to form a story called 'Help! Smoke!?'" Fran used her voice in a theatrical way, making the title sound real.

"Say that again," Mary said.

"What?"

"My two words and make them sound real like you just did."

"Help! Smoke!" Fran said.

"My dear God," Mary said as she broke out with perspiration.

"Mary, what's the matter?" Fran inquired with such intensity she rose off the chair.

"I just went back to when I was a girl. I heard those same two words when I was a girl."

"Do you know who said them or where you were?"

"No, I don't remember," Mary said softly as she slumped in her chair.

"Do you think we should call it a day and get some sleep?" Fran asked.

"I think we better. I feel exhausted."

"You know, I do, too," Fran said, remembering her scare earlier.

"I'll see you in the night."

"Sleep well."

"Don't forget about church."

"I won't."

Oh I can't wait for church, Fran thought. She loved the little chapel with all the candles and stained glass windows that were

277

illuminated at night. The windows were in memory of a man who used to live on Fran's floor, Mac said. *He must have needed church at night, too*, Fran thought.

"My best dress, my just for church dress, I love how it feels," sang Fran.

A lot of people attended the service, residents and staff. There was almost something magical about the hour and the darkness that drew them. *When you're there, your very soul tingles*, Fran thought.

Fran remembered taking her children to church but never felt peace as she did there. Of course there Robert wouldn't be outside honking the horn if they were late.

Every week brought a different preacher. Protestant, Jewish, Catholic, it didn't matter to Fran as long as they spoke about God. And they always did. She marveled at how they could say words that brought comfort and hope. She especially liked to hear how God would be waiting for them when they went "home" to their eternal reward.

Fran often told people how she wouldn't want to sit in her apartment for weeks on end and not hear a sermon because she was too uppity to listen to what other pastors had to say. Each one had a way of saying something with just a little different slant, she would explain, and sometimes the slant was the only way you could understand it.

"There, Elizabeth," Fran said to her granddaughter's photo, "how does Grandma look?"

"Did you just say 'nifty'? You are a pretty smart little girl for only being six months old!"

Fran laughed as she went to get Mary.

Now what? Fran thought to herself as she spotted something different in Mary's welcome sign.

Well, that makes sense! There was a little memo pad edged in behind the cat.

"Yoo-hoo, Mary. Are you ready for church?" Fan called.

The door opened to a replica of a girl on her way to church in the '50s: white gloves, a hat with ribbon streamers dangling off the back rim, flats with white anklet socks, a little pocketbook carrying a packet of tissues and a coin for the collection, and the nicely ironed dress that was belted at the waist with a Peter Pan collar.

"You look very nice, Mary!"

"As do you. Did you notice my addition?" she asked as she looked at the sign.

"I did and I think it's a very good idea."

We both stopped to look at Ann Marie's door.

"I guess she hasn't come out of her apartment yet tonight."

"I guess not!"

They both giggled.

Sure enough, people were already filing in for the 11:00 p.m. service. It sounded like organ music was playing, but there wasn't any room for an organ. Someone was in charge of pushing the button for music, even though Fran could never discern who it was. Fran tried not to look around at other people too much; her mother had told her to concentrate on God and not to look around the church. Sometimes she couldn't help it though.

Oh darn, thought Fran, *we should have invited Ann Marie. That would have been a nice way to start a friendship. Next week we will.*

I'll bet my bottom dollar Mac will come in, just under the wire, and sit by Mary, Fran reckoned to herself. Mac always sat by Mary in church. Fran thought it was a habit.

The pastor entered and everyone stood. He asked the congregation to sing hymn number fourteen. Somebody pushed the button, which started the music, and Mac entered.

Fran leaned forward to give Mac a little wave.

He smiled and sang robustly, looking on with Mary.

Ten candles, all straight in their ascending candelabra's were on the left of the pastor and ten candles starting high and descending in steps were to the right of the pastor. With the lights off, it was striking.

The pastor talked about patience and tolerance. Fran had tried to have patience with Robert. When he told the children they didn't have to help with the housework, she tried to explain to him how important work and jobs and responsibility were to children. After a while, she stopped trying to make him understand and remained quiet.

She thought of how nice it was for that family to donate the windows in their beloved's memory. She wondered if Jean and Bobby would donate something nice in her memory.

In a way, she thought, *it was too bad Robert passed away before he could see me as my happy self.* She also wanted Jean and Bobby to see her as she was now. She remembered the sad times they witnessed and wondered why Robert insisted the children see her at her worst?

Well, Fran thought, *what's over is over. We can start all brand new and fresh—*

"Help!" Mary suddenly screamed.

Everyone swung in their seats to look at Mary.

"Fire!" she screamed again and pointed.

One of the candles was bending and leaning. Wax was dripping profusely.

The pastor blew out that particular candle, but by then Mary had fainted. Mac scooped her up and out they went with Fran scurrying behind.

Mary lay on the cot in the nurse's office mumbling and moaning. Mac tried to get her to talk, but she covered her mouth with her hand and began coughing. She cried for her mother and father. Fran sat with two purses in her lap.

"Maybe you should go now, Fran. I'll sit with Mary. I'll drop by after a while and tell you how she is," Mac said kindly. "Sandy, can you get someone to walk with Fran?"

"Sure."

Ann Marie had added a note pad. It didn't seem funny anymore. Nothing seemed funny with Mary going through some kind of a situation and Fran not knowing what it was.

Fran sat in the dark nibbling on her chips and dill pickles while the city twinkled without a sound. The egg salad sandwich hadn't brought her any comfort. The strawberry shortcake had made her cry. She had made strawberry shortcake for Bobby's fifth birthday—his favorite dessert. Robert threw it in the garbage, even the homemade whipped cream, and ordered a sickeningly sweet cake from the bakery. Bobby only ate the ice cream.

"Come in."

"Fran, is that you over there? Sebastian asked.

"Yes. Hi, Sebastian."

"Are you OK, Fran?"

"Just a little worried about Mary; she's not feeling well."

"I just saw Cheryl in her room getting some of Mary's things."

"Some of her things? Why?"

"Cheryl said Mary was going to green."

"Green? Oh no, they can't take Mary and Dorothy! No, no, no." She started crying.

"Got to get back to work. Have a nice day," said Sebastian as he hurried out.

Fran reached up to get baby Elizabeth's sweater. She laid it on her chest and rocked to the silence of the distant lights.

The warmth of the sweater reminded Fran of Robert's "masterpiece." Robert called it *his* masterpiece, even though Bobby wrote it. Many years ago, Bobby presented it to his dad on Father's Day and Robert had it framed.

FATHER'S TIES

His ties held my wooden swords together.

His ties were reins for my horse.

His ties pulled my sled up the hill.

His ties were lassos pulling my sailboats in.

I used them for jump roping, magic tricks,

Fishing poles and dog leashes.

I made flags out of them, rugs,

Snake homes and gun powder horns.

And on stormy nights,

I emptied my whole bottom drawer of ties

And laid them one by one

Across my frightened chest.

"Robert would not allow me to go to Bobby during a storm. ' He has to grow up to be a man,' he would say."

"Hello, Fran, its Mac."

"Come in, Mac."

"I wanted to tell you that Mary needs a lot of attention right now. We're putting her on green where someone can watch over her day and night."

"Yes, I heard that about half an hour ago."

"What?"

"Sebastian told me." Fran could see his face tensing in the dark.

"Would you mind if I turned the light on?"

"It's OK."

"Oh, Fran, you've been crying." He handed her a tissue. Mac glanced at the baby sweater.

"Is she going to die?" Fran asked.

"No, she won't die; she just needs time to adjust to some things. And guess what? When Mary is ready, you're going to play a big part in her recovery!"

"I am?"

"Yes, she is going to need you. You're good for Mary."

Fran suddenly felt important. What Robert had said was not true; she was needed!

As Mac was leaving, he said, "Don't forget about Ann Marie."

"Oh, I won't."

Fran decided to take care of business right then and there. She freshened up and went to call on her new neighbor.

There was no response to her knocking. Ann Marie was out again? Or was she? The only thing Fran knew for sure was that Ann Marie left her apartment to look at Mary's welcome sign. Maybe Fran could track her down through the sign!

Let's see, what can I add to the sign, Fran thought?

She went back to her apartment and folded a tiny piece of paper like a fan then out to Mary's door she went with the cellophane tape. *There, a little fan in the cat's paw!*

It was Monday! Time for picture frame class!

Fran quickly ran down the hallway to check on Ann Marie's sign. Darn! She'd missed her. Ann Marie's cat, too, had a fan. *So she's out earlier in the night is she*, thought Fran? *All right. That narrows it down.*

She knocked on Ann Marie's door to invite her to lunch and the craft class. No answer.

Fran was just returning to her room when Liza followed her in.

"Well, hello there, come in!"

"Hi, Fran."

"Sit, sit. How are things at home?"

"Pretty good."

"I see your eye is turning all those lovely colors of the rainbow," Fran said. "Liza, what does Ann Marie do when you go into her room to clean?"

"Why, she doesn't even talk to me! I try and try to get her to open up, but she won't. I don't know what the matter with her is. Maybe she's just antisocial."

"Or maybe shy."

"Could be."

Fran walked alone to her mailbox.

She missed Mary.

"Hello, Fran," Bennett said as he put his magazine down. "Are you going to the dinner/dance?"

"I don't think so; Mary and Dorothy won't be there," she said sadly.

"Yeah, that's too bad."

"Have you heard anything about them, Bennett?"

"Uh, uh, no… not a word."

"Oh, look, Bennett, look! I got a letter from Jean! It's from Jean!" Fran exclaimed. "Bye, Bennett," Fran said as she nearly ran back along yellow.

She leaned against the inside of her door, panting as she stared at the envelope.

Such beautiful penmanship. Fran remembered sitting with Jean as she learned to print and then in the third grade when script was taught. Jean was such a perfectionist; every letter had to be perfect. Robert had walked in on them when Fran was telling Jean that her letters were fine and to stop fussing over them so much. Jean had erased so much, there were holes in the paper.

"How dare you tell her not to work for improvement," Robert had bellowed Robert. "Do you want her to grow up to be stupid like you?"

Fran certainly didn't want Jean to do sloppy work, but it looked like she was neurotic over it. Of course, she didn't say anything to Robert or Jean about that thought.

Bobby, on the other hand, required a lot of help from Fran so that he could improve. She couldn't remember how many times Robert would look at his handwriting and shake his head. "Your mother certainly doesn't know how to teach you anything."

Fran looked at the stamp. Jean had touched that stamp. It looked like a "Jean stamp." She probably had the postmaster display what was available and chose the prettiest ones. Everything with Jean had to be the best, the prettiest, the most perfect, the cleanest, the most expensive, the most alluring. Everything of hers was that way—except her mother. Robert and Jean were like two peas in a pod. Bobby had feelings, but he was too afraid to go against Robert and Jean.

A loud knock on the door made the letter fly across the room.

"Hello in there. It's Roger and Shawn. Do you want to go to lunch? It's just about midnight."

"Uh, just a minute," Fran said.

Fran rushed for the letter and darted to the closet to put it into her wooden box.

She took a quick look in the mirror. Her eyes scared her; they looked wild. Fran took two deep breaths before opening the door.

"Thought you might be a little lonely without Mary. Do you want to go to lunch with us?" Roger asked.

"Yes. I'd love to," Fran said as she glanced at the closet.

"How's your new neighbor?"

"I don't know. I haven't seen her yet."

"She has quite an interesting welcome sign on her door."

"Doesn't she though."

"So Mary went off the deep end, did she?" Shawn abruptly said after they'd settled into reading their menus.

"Shawn!" Roger said disgustedly.

"She did not!" Fran bolted to Mary's defense.

"My God, I was in church. I saw her and heard her!" Shawn retorted.

"She just needs to rest!" Fran insisted.

"She needs more than rest!" Shawn jumped to his feet.

"People, people, people," Mac called out using a booming voice. "Shawn, sit down."

Shawn sat.

Mac reached over for Fran's hand when he noticed she had started to scratch her wrist.

"You people are going to have indigestion, calm down. I have a nice report for you! Mary is asking for you, Fran. Would you like to visit her tomorrow?"

"I certainly would!"

"Great. How about one in the morning?"

"One in the morning would be fine," Fran said.

"And how's the other nutcase? Dorothy?" Shawn asked sarcastically.

"Dorothy is doing well; in fact, she didn't use your name, but she asked how the village troublemaker was. I assumed she meant you," Mac replied.

"Ha, ha, very funny," Shawn said as he put his menu up in front of his face.

Fran wasn't much of a conversationalist during lunch. She had two major events coming up to think about: reading Jean's letter and visiting Mary.

She did ask, "Are you going to the framing class tonight?"

"We sure are," Shawn said quickly. He reached into his pocket and took out a plastic bag. "I got my idea for a frame right here."

"What is it, Shawn?" Fran leaned forward to see.

He dumped the contents for her to see. It was a collection of miniature baseball bats, mitts, and balls.

"Where did you get these?" Fran asked inquisitively.

"Every year when they decorate my birthday cake, they put on baseball stuff 'cause they know I love it. I've been savin' these for, I think, five years. Now I have enough to decorate a picture frame for my son. He loves baseball, too."

"Well, Shawn, I am surprised!" said Fran kindly. "I didn't know you had a tender heart."

"Nothin' tender about it. I ain't no woman," he retorted sharply.

"Let's take the early class," Fran suggested. "I need to tend to some things later on."

Alicia exclaimed with delight, "Shawn, what a wonderful idea."

The others thought they saw Shawn blush.

"What would you like to create, Fran?"

"I want to make a frame for a baby picture."

"Do you have any ideas?"

"Yes. I want to make a collage of baby pictures all around the frame and then shellac them down. The shellac will make them shine, right?"

"Right! What a cute idea! Do you have a picture to put in the frame?"

"I sure do. My granddaughter's!"

"There's a pile of magazines and catalogs over there. Help yourself," Alicia said.

It was fun for Fran to look up and see everyone intent on their project. She remembered her own children sitting at the table creating all sorts of things. Their father always praised their work. Unfortunately, the cleanup was left entirely to her.

"This will be dry by tomorrow night, Fran. You can pick it up then. You did a beautiful job!" Alicia told her.

Fran wondered what she could put on Mary's sign next. She knew it was a way of communicating with Ann Marie.

She recalled Bobby and her communicating without saying a word, also.

What could she use? The thought of the little umbrella that comes with the iced tea made her conclude that it would be perfect! She hoped Ann Marie had one; Fran didn't want the line of communication to break down over a silly umbrella. Out she went with the umbrella.

Fran looked at her watch and then at the closet door. Maybe she'd wait closer to dinnertime. Or she could read it with dinner. Or, better yet, wouldn't she enjoy it more after dinner?

No! She would read it now!

Again Fran looked at Jean's perfect penmanship and at the stamp.

With trembling hands and no sign of breathing, Fran read:

Mother,

It has come to my attention that

our summer schedule will be very busy;

>*henceforth, our visit must be delayed until*
>*fall.*

Jean

"It has come to her attention? Henceforth? Busy? Fall?"

Fran curled up on the bed with the letter in her hand, first looking up at the shelf and then closing her eyes to look further outward—outward to eternity.

She started to pray:

When I'm with you, God, I won't be lonely, I won't be sad. Help me to remember this life as a mere drop in the bucket. If I can get through it in a decent fashion, I'll be there with you, Lord. You know how desperately I tried with the kids. I know I made mistakes. I should have stopped Robert from the ruination of my motherly image; I couldn't save my own image in my children's eyes. Forgive me, Lord. Give me strength to forget about my own sorrow; take it from my mind and let me be of some use to you.

"Fran? Fran? Are you home?"

"Oh, oh yes, Mac, come in. I guess I must have fallen asleep."

"No one saw you for dinner, and you didn't hang your meal tag out. I thought I'd stop in and check."

"My goodness. I can't believe I slept so long. I guess I needed it."

"Are you hungry?"

"I guess I am!" Fran laughed.

"Looks like you received a letter." Mac looked down at Fran's hand.

"Here. Read this," Fran said.

"Well! She lays it right on the line, doesn't she? How do you feel about this?" Mac asked.

"I am disappointed, but I'm not hurt by it, thank God. I remember being so hurt by everything and that hurt nearly ate me alive. I don't want that feeling to come back again. I need to be at peace."

"Ah, yes, peace." Mac took a deep breath and let it out slowly.

"Fran, would you mind if I telephoned Jean? I would like to tell her how well you're doing here at this building."

"Call her if you want to; she never answers the phone and never returns messages."

"I see you've been stocking up on baby things."

"Yes, they're for Elizabeth!"

"Come! Let's grab a bite to eat."

"Oops, wait a minute." Fran took something out of her dresser drawer.

"This is for Ann Marie, in case she doesn't have one."

Fran laid the little umbrella at her neighbor's doorstep.

"You don't know Jean, do you, Mac?"

"Actually, I do. We met when you first came to this building," he said.

"You did? I simply don't remember a lot about that time. I guess I was nervous about moving to a new place and all."

"It's hard for everyone when they have to leave their home, their family, and their friends."

"I was glad to leave my house—I should say Robert's house. That place had become a prison to me. Both kids were away at college, so I wasn't really leaving them. And I had no friends. So I don't know why I was nervous when I moved here. It was just something different, I guess. Did Jean come home from college to bring me here?"

"Well, both Jean and Bobby were home for the funeral."

"The funeral?"

"Robert's funeral."

"Did he pass away just before I moved into my new apartment?" Fran asked.

"When did you think he passed away?"

"Hmm, I don't know. I thought it was a long time ago."

"It probably seems like a long time ago, doesn't it?"

"Like a hundred years ago," Fran said slowly as she sipped her tea. "Did you meet Bobby?"

"No, he didn't come here with you that day."

"I wonder where he is. I want to see him," Fran said decisively.

"Didn't you tell me he was in Colorado?" Mac asked.

"I thought that's where he was, but all my letters have come back."

"I'll try to find out for you."

"Thanks, Mac."

"Well, this has been a lovely dinner," Mac said as he smiled at Fran, "and if you're finished, I'll walk you back before I head home to my wife."

"I'm going to try and get out early tomorrow morning to see Ann Marie. That seems to be her time to check out Mary's sign."

"Don't forget your meeting with Mary tomorrow at one."

"I can't wait!" Fran exclaimed joyously.

"Mary has recalled some things about her past that she is trying to cope with. She might tell you and she might not. Don't say too much about it, just be a good listener."

"Oh, I will."

"I know you will," Mac said fondly.

Fran woke, remembering part of her dream. She had been running alongside a train, trying to reach Bobby, but the train kept going faster and faster until there was no way of keeping up. She could see Robert and Jean up front; they were the engineers.

Oh why am I lying here? Fran thought. She remembered she had to go out into the hallway. She pulled on her robe and slippers and quietly opened her door. She looked both ways down the empty hall. Fran walked to the right to Ann Marie's door. The umbrella wasn't on the floor—the cat had it! Fran went left to Mary's door. What could she put there next she wondered as she surveyed the conglomeration. *What is this?* Fran pulled the note pad out.

Thank you for the little umbrella, I didn't have one, was written on it! Fran was quick to follow suit. She padded down to Ann Marie's door and wrote:

You're welcome.

Please come to dinner.

6:00 a.m. today.

Next door to your left.

I'm Fran.

"There's my Mary," Fran said to herself as she peered through the tiny window.

When Fran entered, Mary jumped right out of her chair and ran toward her friend.

The two women hugged like the war was over.

"Fran, sit here. I need to tell you something. I found out why my mother and father haven't come to see me." Tears started their trail down Mary's face. "You see, Fran, when I was a little girl there was a fire." The trail led to her jaw. "They never got out, Fran, they never got out." From her jawbone, the tears dropped onto her folded hands. "All those years I waited for them to come." The trail of tears went from wet hands back to her cheeks where it received more droplets.

"Oh, Mary, Mary," Fran cried.

When she could, Fran spoke. "Mary, in one way they have left you but in another way they have been in your heart and mind and soul every single day since I have known you."

Mary was silent for a long time, and then she said, "Fran, you are right; you are absolutely right! I have constantly felt their love! They didn't leave me! Oh, Fran, you came to me when I needed you most!"

God sent me, Fran thought to herself.

"Here it is, all dry and shiny! Isn't it just darling?" sang Alicia.

"It's perfect for my little girl," Fran said.

Fran held the frame close as she walked home.

Fran's eyes darted across Mary's sign just as a teacher would check the bulletin board in the main office.

There was another message!

I'll be there at six.

Ann Marie

Such anticipation!

Fran wondered why she missed such excitement when Robert was alive. She thought of the joy he denied her and wondered why she'd permitted it.

Her friends were not allowed in the house, and his friends caused Fran to be terrified; she remembered working for days to make everything ready for his dinner parties. What caused her not to run away? So many times, that was what she wanted to do.

Fran inserted Elizabeth's photo into the new frame and stepped back to admire her exquisite shelf.

She put out her meal tag with a note, "For two."

Since she had time, she dashed out for special napkins and fresh flowers from the gift shop.

Fran noticed a lot of commotion down on green but stayed on the blue hallway to the gift shop.

"Hi, Fran," Ashley said excitedly. "Did you hear?"

"Hmm?" Fran murmured as she looked through the beautiful assortment of floral napkins.

"About Dorothy."

"What about Dorothy?" Fran stopped her search.

"Come here," Ashley whispered as she motioned Fran closer. "Dorothy killed herself tonight."

"What?"

"Yes, she did. The first night she wasn't on twenty-four-hour watch and she did it. Can you believe it?"

"Why?"

"She wanted to be with her mother, the note said."

Fran grabbed the counter.

"Are you all right?" Ashley punctuated the words as she rushed around the counter to steady Fran.

"No."

Ashley caught sight of Mac rushing past the store.

"Mac! Mac! Come here! I think Fran is going to faint."

Mac rushed in and grabbed Fran.

"Do you know what triggered this?"

"I just told her about Dorothy, that's all."

"That's it! Ashley you're fired. Stop in the business office tomorrow morning."

Mac helped Fran to a chair and dialed for a nurse.

"I'm sorry you had to hear about Dorothy like that, Fran," Mac said.

"Oh my, it was such a shock!"

Fran went to the nurse's station.

"I'm sure you're with your mother now, Dorothy," Fran said to herself as she started down her hallway. She had gotten her release from the nurse's station.

"Oh no! Ann Marie!" she said aloud.

Her watch said 6:30.

Fran rushed into her apartment, there sat the two dinners. She turned and went to Ann Marie's door. *Please answer, please answer*, she said to herself. But knocking and calling brought no response. Like a sink stopper being taken out, all of Fran's energy ran out and she crumbled to the carpet, sobbing into her knees.

"Fran?"

"Oh Bobby, I'm so glad you're here. Don't let him hurt me anymore."

"Fran, its Ann Marie."

Fran looked beyond the haze she'd fallen into and saw long blond hair streaming down to her. Through her hurt-pelted skin, Fran felt the warmth of kind hands.

"Come, Fran, let me help you."

As an adult who resembled a child, Fran went to Ann Marie with no fear or apprehension. A youthful frame bolstered the shaking woman into Fran's apartment.

A cool wet cloth devoured the beads of perspiration and left a refreshing breeze much like Fran remembered from her grandmother's beach house.

Ann Marie rubbed Fran's hands, bringing comfort through her palm lines of life and love. The touch brought Fran to say, "Bobby?" once more.

"No, Fran, its Ann Marie. Here, drink some tea; let me put some sugar in it for you."

"Oh my," said Fran weakly, "what a night this has been. I'm sorry I was late, Ann Marie. My good friend passed away unexpectedly, and I kind of fell apart."

Fran sipped the tea feeling better with each swallow.

As she started to focus, she looked at Ann Marie for the first time.

"Ann Marie, you're so young!"

"I am?"

"And beautiful! You're very beautiful!"

Ann Marie looked down. She hurriedly said, "I must go now."

"No, no, please, stay awhile; I'm still a little shaky."

Ann Marie sat down.

"I'm so glad to finally meet you. Don't you just love it here? This has been the happiest place I've been in a long while."

Ann Marie looked at her pensively and said, "I don't want to sound disrespectful, Fran, but didn't I just find you out in the hall crying?"

"Well, yes," Fran chuckled realizing the paradox of it all. "What I meant was, other than the few calamities that have happened, life here is a heaven on earth."

"A heaven on earth? Isn't that a little strong?"

Beauty and brains, Fran thought to herself.

"Well, maybe that's not the right expression, but this is much better than my other life."

"My other life was a nightmare, too," Ann Marie confided.

The two women looked at each other. They were a few decades apart. One had long, silky blond hair, the other short curly hair with a few curly grays. One had supple, creamy skin, the other dry, tough skin with a few wrinkles. Both women had caring and compassionate eyes.

"How do you like the day/night change?" Fran asked.

"I love it!" Ann Marie exclaimed.

"That's my girl!" The older woman beamed. "It'll bring you peace, believe me."

"Oh, I hope so," Ann Marie said quietly.

"Does it matter if your dinner is not hot, hot?"

"Not at all," the statuesque girl replied.

"I think we both need to eat something. Do you mind eating with an old lady?" Fran giggled.

"I actually think I'll enjoy it more than some of the posh dinners I've had with men."

"Oh," said Fran pensively.

Indeed, it was a pleasant dinner with the beginning of a new friendship. Fran drew from Ann Marie the youthfulness she missed from Jean, and Ann Marie drew from Fran the maturity she never received from her mother.

"How's the lady who has the cat sign?" Ann Marie asked, looking a little sheepish.

"That's Mary. She'll be back soon."

"I was somewhat confused as to who was changing the sign every night," Ann Marie admitted.

"I took over for Mary. I was almost sure it would be a way to meet you," Fran said.

"I'm glad you did," said Ann Marie, "but I'm not worthy to have friends." The young beauty hung her head, causing her hair to swing like a pendulum—a pendulum that echoed the age-old problem between women and men.

Fran suddenly thought of the clock at her grandmother's beach house:

The tick of the clock ruled the afternoons... perched grandly on the top shelf of the buffet perfectly centered with everything matching to the right of it and everything matching to the left of it. The hand-carved wood became a castle for the pendulum that marched back and forth in precision to guard the "tick" and the "tock" that lived somewhere inside.

In the afternoons when all the little ones were taking their naps and all the big ones were out of the house, except Nanny and me, the old clock ruled supreme.

It was louder than Nanny's knitting needles clicking together, the apple pies sizzling in the oven for supper, the cat snoring on her chair, and me building houses of cards at the kitchen table.

I never heard the clock during any other time of the day, but Nanny said she heard it at night sometimes.

"We all want to eliminate some aspects of our pasts, Ann Marie. Maybe we can't erase them, but we can leave them in the background and go forward. We don't have to repeat our pasts. In a way, those nightmares can serve as a reminder of where we never want to go again."

"Hmm, how come that makes sense to me?"

"Maybe you're ready to have it make sense," Fran said.

"Maybe I am."

"Say, neighbor, would you like to go out to lunch with me tomorrow?" Fran asked.

"Would you want to be around me?" Ann Marie replied.

"I'd be proud to have you at my side!"

"Thank you, Fran."

"Sleep well, sweet princess."

Ann Marie left with a swelling in her heart and a mist in her eyes that weren't put there by misuse.

Fran ate her breakfast while watching the sun set. It was a brilliant display across the west! *What a lovely way to start the day,* Fran thought to herself.

"Come in."

"Hello, Fran."

"Oh, Mac, welcome!"

"How are you doing after yesterday's episode?"

"You won't believe how well the night ended for me."

"What do you mean?"

"After hearing about Dorothy, I came home to realize I had forgotten my dinner engagement with Ann Marie. I broke down, Mac, but guess who came to my rescue?"

"I honestly don't know," Mac said with curiosity.

"Ann Marie!"

"You're kidding!"

"No, she comforted me; we ate dinner together. We're going out for lunch around midnight."

"Oh! There is a God!" Mac looked upward.

"There sure is!"

"Well, now I have good news for you. I think Mary will be ready to return to her apartment in about a week."

"Oh, Mac," Fran squealed, covering her mouth with her hands.

"I would like you, and Ann Marie, to visit Mary every day," Mac said.

"We certainly can do that!"

"Thanks, Fran. Oh yes, and I'm going to call Jean tomorrow to persuade her to visit, with Elizabeth, before autumn."

"That would be wonderful! Don't forget to ask about Bobby. I mean, please, don't forget to ask about Bobby."

"I won't." Mac laughed as he went over to give Fran a hug.

"Well, well, who's this?" Shawn asked as he looked at Ann Marie with teenage eyes.

Roger darted him a look and Fran replied, "This is Ann Marie, my neighbor. Ann Marie, meet Roger and Shawn."

She muttered, "Hello," but did not make eye contact with them.

"Do you want to join us?" Shawn asked, permitting his stare to descend upon Ann Marie like an elevator.

Fran could feel the young woman edging closer to her.

"No, thanks, Shawn, maybe another time."

After they ordered, Ann Marie said, "Thank you, Fran. Thanks for not having us sit with those two men."

"Shawn is really harmless, he just acts like a..." she leaned closer to whisper, "jerk. Roger is very nice."

"I guess you could say I hate men," Ann Marie said nervously.

"All of them?" Fran asked.

"Well, probably not all of them. Just the ones who try to talk to me."

"Do you hate Mac?" Fran asked.

"Oh no, I like him a lot. He's the type of man I've looked for—forever. However, I always end up with men who—you know."

Fran didn't actually *know*, but she had a pretty good idea.

"Don't worry about them anymore, honey. Now you can make a fresh start."

"So many times I've tried, Fran, so many times. Every morning I would wake up and say, "That's it! No more of that kind of lifestyle."

"But, Ann Marie, just think, now you wake up at *night* and it can be different!" Fran said with as much hope in her voice as possible.

The beauty put down her fork as her eyes widened. "My gosh, Fran, you're right! I do have another chance."

"You sure do, sweetie! God is always there with one more chance if we're alert enough to take it."

"Why was I lured to men who didn't care about me, except superficially?" Ann Marie asked.

"Well," said Fran as she straightened each piece of silverware, rearranged the napkin on her lap, and repositioned the water glass, "God's adversary and God are great competitors. God's love for you is so strong, his adversary needs to play every card in the deck to try and win you over."

"Are you talking about Satan, the devil?"

"I am."

"You mean he wanted to win me over for pernicious ways and God wanted me for goodness?"

"That's about the size of it," Fran said.

"Why did I choose evil?" Ann Marie looked horrified.

"Because Satan makes everything look glamorous, fun, inviting, exciting, fulfilling, etc."

"Why doesn't God make us do what's right?"

Ann Marie was sitting so far forward, Fran hoped she didn't tip the chair over.

"Because God gives us free will. We are free to choose."

"And I didn't make good choices, did I?" Ann Marie said.

"Well, probably not, but God knows you're worth waiting for and he's waiting."

"I'm worth it?"

"You sure are, Ann Marie; you're worth it!"

The beautiful face became enveloped in her napkin as her past soaked through the cotton fibers; it was the same cotton that ruled the South with the age-old problem between women and men.

While they visited Mary, Ann Marie was very quiet. Mary, on the other hand, was barren of news and soaked up every bit of information Fran could think to tell her.

Ann Marie seemed to drift in and out of listening to the local news; Fran knew she had a lot to think about.

Mary was most excited to hear Mac was going to contact Jean.

Fran and Ann Marie walked home in silence. The young woman was thinking of her worth, the older one wondering about the hold Satan had had on her own household when Robert was alive.

"Would you like to come in?" Ann Marie asked.

"Oh!" Fran uttered, thoroughly surprised by the invitation. "I'd love to!"

Fran's head revolved around the room much like Earth orbiting silently in the great span of outer space.

"These are beautiful! How long have you had them?"

"Since the day I painted them," Ann Marie answered humbly.

Fran went from one to the other in a slow methodical march while Ann Marie waited quietly in her chair.

"They are exquisite!" Fran spoke in a hushed tone.

"Thank you."

"Do you still paint?"

As Ann Marie said, "No," her gaze plummeted to the floor.

"Somewhere along the line, Fran, when my soul died, I couldn't paint."

"I wouldn't say your soul was *dead*, but I know what you mean."

"Maybe when I get life back into my soul I'll be able to paint again!" She spoke as only an artist could speak.

"That could very well be," Fran said quietly. "Well, my dear, even though I could stay and look at your work forever, I must go. Mac may come with news of my Jean."

"Au revoir."

Fran studied her own walls. If it wasn't for her shelf, she'd have no richness in her soul either. She remembered the sterility of her home with Robert. There had been no creative "aliveness" anywhere. That's what it was, an empty, soulless house.

Her own words to Ann Marie reverberated in her ears. "But God gives us another chance."

"Hmm, painting class for the artist and the novice?"

"Come in?" Fran sprang forward with anticipation.

"Mac?"

"I got through to Jean, it was seven in the morning her time, but she said she was awake."

"Yes?"

"She's not sure about visiting."

"Why? Why won't she come to see me?" The furrow in Fran's brow deepened. "Did she say anything about Elizabeth?"

"Jean said she wasn't sure if her daughter should be exposed to the kind of people who live here."

"The kind of people? What did she mean by that? She is so much like Robert: self-righteous, pompous, and arrogant."

"Calm down, Fran, she didn't say no. She's going to think about it."

"And Bobby? Where's Bobby?" Fran asked.

Mac took her hands in his.

"Bobby's in a penitentiary in California."

"What? Why?"

Mac paused to ask for God's guidance.

"Fran," he said softly, "on the last day of Robert's life, he attacked you and Bobby shot him. Bobby killed his father, Fran."

"Oh, Mac, no."

"MARJORY, DON'T TELL ME YOU ARE WATCHING THAT MOVIE AGAIN?

YOU LIKE THAT LITTLE GIRL, DON'T YOU?"

Chapter Thirteen

THE CHARIOT

MARJORY'S FAVORITE MOVIE

They said it was black.

She touched it. It didn't feel black. It felt rough and it felt tight, but not black.

Yolanda slowly rubbed her fingers over her arm as the August heat fought to escape what her mother said were "pores" or "poors," one or the other. Yolanda guessed it didn't matter.

Brown. She could see brown. Why did they always say "black?"

Yolanda turned on her back, feeling a twig under her left rib, but it didn't hurt much. It was too hot to get rid of the little vexation. "Endure, child, endure," she could hear her mother's words, not that her mother was there now. No, they were just words that meandered into her mind at a quicker pace than any molecule of air moving that afternoon.

She stretched her arms upward, letting the shade of the peach tree make black patches on her skin. There! She thought, that's black—black on brown. Yolanda rolled off the twig, not because she couldn't endure, but because she wanted to reach the patch of sunshine in which to place her arm.

"Oh," she gasped, "I'm hardly even brown."

She kept her arm in the spotlight even though the rays seemed to pierce her very soul.

"Yolanda, come now," the bass voice of her mother filtered through the thick air.

"Oh," groaned the nine-year-old as she pulled her arm into the shade. "Oh no," she panicked as she bolted upright, "is it black?"

"Landa!" Her mother called again as she stopped and turned abruptly, making her long dusty skirts twirl like the skirt of the woman who danced in the big house. Yolanda smiled to think of her mother dancing with beautiful, shiny skirts.

"What's the matter with you, child? We don't have time for you to be standing around 'musing yourself." Yolanda felt the big, prickly fingers grab into her sunny-brown-black arm. The girl jounced along the dusty dirt trying to endure the vice grip as the skirts twirled.

She saw the others converging onto the field; she didn't know how they all knew when to return to the picking place. Yolanda managed to wriggle out of her mother's grip when she saw Amisha looking over at her. Amisha was older; Amisha was real pretty. Yolanda wanted to be Amisha.

Yolanda averted the pretty one's eyes when she felt her mother pulling up the back of her collar and plopping a hat down over her forehead. She guessed her mother didn't want her go get black, even though when she asked, "Why this?" and "Why that?" her mother always said, "Because you're black."

Yolanda put the bag's strap over her head and looked down into the emptiness of the pouch. It felt good now. The girl grinned as she used her thumb and little finger to heft the bag.

"Pick!" The low roll of her mother's voice somersaulted across the plants to her daughter's ear.

Yolanda could hear Amisha's high, snickering voice somewhere to her right. Janzee's low, man voice embarrassed the young girl. She never asked her mother about it, but thought it had something to do with the long scar across her neck.

Yolanda put the first sweet potato into the sack. *It couldn't feel heavy already*, Yolanda thought. *No, no, that's just my 'magination*, the girl consoled herself. It didn't take long to fill the sack; now she knew heavy. She looked to the side of the field for Sonny and the tater cart. There he was, tipping the wooden, two-wheeled cart so that the potatoes rolled to the front to hit against the wide boards. Old Mule Babe grunted every time Sonny tipped the cart.

"Well, well, what you got there, ugly girl?" Sonny laughed as he grabbed for the slouched girl's bundle.

"Sweet cherries and molasses cakes," Yolanda taunted him in return.

Sonny slung the bag up onto the cart as if it was a feather from an oriole. Yolanda stared at the big lumps on his arms. She knew his muscles were inside those lumps.

"There you go, ugly girl." Sonny laughed as he threw the dirty bag into her face.

"Amisha! Let me help you," Sonny said, suddenly brightening as he saw the pretty one hauling her sack out of the field. Yolanda tried to rub the specks of dirt out of her eyes as she watched Sonny carry Amisha's satchel like it was a bag of spinach leaves.

"What happened?" The low growl exploded above the sound of the shovels striking into the dirt. The skirts jumped over the tops of the plants until the hands could grab the girl's shoulders. Again the voice demanded, "What happened?" Yolanda looked into her mother's wild eyes and pulsating neck.

"I got some dirt in my eyes, that's all," the girl answered blankly, having no idea why her mother hurdled the five rows of plants.

Janzee pulled out her sweaty handkerchief and roughly wiped the dirty streaks from Yolanda's face. The girl pulled away when she thought she heard someone walking toward them.

Janzee returned to her digging after staring across the field at Sonny. She and the other big people left the yams on top of the ground for the children to pick up. Yolanda didn't know that her mother's back ached. She only knew that her mother was doing what she was supposed to do—work. Work, because she was black. Yolanda gave a quick glance at her arm—it wasn't. It was a beautiful brown.

ᐤ

That night Yolanda listened to the river frolic unceasingly past the row of houses. Where does it go? Where has it come from? Someday she would go with the river. She was not going to stay and—like her grandmother—work herself to death.

She heard her mother lie down on the mat next to hers. She heard the guttural sigh and the moan, every night the same. *The river wouldn't do that; the river knew how to be happy*, Yolanda thought.

They lay in stillness as the heat spread across their bodies like brown lard. Water poured out of the skin exuding the salt into the lard. Yolanda jumped when Janzee reached over and grabbed her arm.

"Come on," she uttered as she pulled her daughter to her feet. "Hush," Janzee whispered sounding like a rasp being rubbed against a tree trunk. Janzee led Yolanda into the dark river.

Yolanda listened to the ripples. She heard the river bustling by. But her mother? Where was she? She lurched forward to find her but was met by a huge burst of a splash and a woman who—

laughed? It had to be! Janzee splashed her again and again—they laughed!

Yolanda thought of the water far into the night as she listened to her mother sleeping.

By midmorning, the heat and the dusty soil reigned supreme over the potatoes. As Yolanda stooped to pick the strange vegetable out of the dirt, she wondered if her own salt and lard would season the heated potatoes. The girl looked over to her mother. Was that the same supple, playful woman who frolicked with her in the river? She didn't think so. The woman with the shovel was stiff and hard. Yolanda stopped her staring when the voice like gravel snarled, "Work!"

Yolanda squatted lower to retrieve the last of the jewels from the hill. She lugged the bounty across the field to Sonny and Old Mule Babe. She wished she didn't have to see Sonny; she wished it were just Babe by the cart.

"Hey, ugly girl, you're uglier than you were yesterday!" Sonny smirked as he grabbed for the bag. Yolanda hung on long enough to make Sonny sail backward into the cart when she released her grip. Hundreds of potatoes rolled like an avalanche to the ground.

Yolanda ran. Sonny cursed and fired a barrage of yams at her back. Yolanda put her arms up over her head and watched several bullets sail past. It was when she took a blow to the center of her back that she fell on her face.

"Landa!" her mother screamed, as again the skirts flew but not in melodic three-quarter time. Janzee turned her daughter over and picked her up.

"I'm all right, I'm all right," Yolanda whispered, fighting back the tears when she saw Amisha and some of the others gathering near.

"Here, Tahinta, take Yolanda to the shade," Janzee said slowly as her steel eyes looked across the field at the tater boy.

"Mama, no! We were just foolin'."

But Mama didn't stop. Yolanda turned her face away. This wasn't the water mother from last night; this was... was the "because we're black" mother. Her tears made her think of the river and how she was going to get away someday.

The turnip field was next. Everyone worked about the same, everyone except Sonny. No one talked about him much; but people thought he had run off.

"Good!" Yolanda thought to herself until she came to the realization that when she ran off she might encounter him. "Oh no," she moaned every night as she sat staring at the river.

"What's the matter with you?" the bass voice questioned.

"Nothin', Mama."

Janzee was glad when Tahinta started her singing; she hated Yolanda's sighing. Every night Tahinta's voice rolled out of the huge woman and cascaded across the water. Tahinta said the river would carry her song to God and God would come for them. "You just wait, girl; you be patient, and he'll come for us." They all listened to the old woman's music until the children fell asleep across their kins' legs and the fires were nothing but hot ashes.

"Is he, Mama?" Yolanda asked through the blackness.

"Huh?" came a low rumble that Yolanda at first thought was thunder.

"Is he coming for us?"

"If Tahinta says it's true, it's true."

The young girl faded into sleep with thoughts of her water mother and herself on a raft.

"Because that store is not for us, you know that," Janzee exclaimed, feeling frustrated with her daughter's repetitious questions.

Yolanda cupped her hands like Old Mule Babe's side blinders as she peered in at the display of dolls and lace and ivory hair combs. She didn't move until her mother walked back to grab her by the arm. "Walk," came the directive. Yolanda walked with her head on a swivel until Janzee threatened not to let her come with her the next time.

The tall woman waved the paper to get the attention of the merchant. "All right, wait in the back," the man proclaimed as he turned to gather the wares for the woman in the big house.

Janzee and her daughter walked through the alley to the rear. There were other people with beautiful brown skin waiting also.

"Why—"

"Hush." Her mother knew what she was going to ask.

The merchant's son snapped a whip over the horse's ear and everyone in waiting jumped back. The young man laughed as he vaulted off the wagon and ran into the mercantile.

The store-bought wares rode in the wooden wagon as the people walked behind. The women and girls put their overskirts across their mouths and noses to keep out the dust. The men and boys endured the grit.

At each homestead, the entourage lessened, as did the load. Silent farewells passed among the troupe.

"Well, get on," the driver snarled at the last two shoppers, "but don't you dare tell my father."

Yolanda and Janzee sat on the wooden floorboards just as the whip cracked and the horse jolted forward. The two riders pulled themselves upright as they heard the young man's laughter over the clopping of the horse's hooves. Yolanda watched her mother touch the scar on her neck.

Silence lay upon the evenings by the river as Tahinta lay dying. The women took turns tending to her while the children idly poked sticks into the campfires and waited for Tahinta's chariot to come out of the sky. The men passed the whiskey bottle among themselves.

"What are you doing in here, child? You go on out with the others."

"I have to see her, Mama."

The little girl slowly walked to the old woman on the mat. She stared at the still figure, wondering why Tahinta looked so small.

"What's she doing, Mama?" Yolanda asked.

"She's not doing anything, child. She's just waiting for the Lord to come for her."

Yolanda pondered that thought.

"You stand right there, child. I'm going to fetch more water."

Janzee left the door open, allowing the full moon to gaze in upon Tahinta. The girl looked at her own shadow lying across Tahinta's bed.

It was when the girl was studying the woman's old, gnarled hands that Tahinta's eyes opened.

"I'm ready, Lord," she uttered suddenly, startling Yolanda. "I'm ready."

Then the old woman smiled and closed her eyes.

It came up on two weeks after the passing that Yolanda whispered through the black, hot night, "Mama, Tahinta thought I was the Lord."

There was a long silence.

Yolanda gave up on getting an answer and changed her thoughts to being pretty like Amisha.

"That was all right, wasn't it?" the low voice whispered across the dirt floor.

"But I'm black."

"Yes, you are."

"How come some people can't talk?"

"Maybe they were born that way."

"Why else?"

"Maybe something happened that took their voice away."

"Aren't you glad I can talk?"

Chapter Fourteen

It's Over

"Come on in, Julie. I'll get us a snack."

"Thanks, Levi."

"Oh no!" Levi exclaimed when he heard the moaning from the living room.

He hurried to the trembling man whose fingers dug into the arms of the chair while the sweat poured from his forehead. "Grandpa, it's all right; you're all right. The war is over."

"The war is over?" repeated the man who instantly released his fingers to wipe the liquid ammunition from his brow.

"Yes, Grandpa, everything is OK."

Cy breathed a sigh of relief that everyone in every profession could understand.

"Grandpa, do you know where Mom and Jarett are?"

"I think little Jarett had another doctor's appointment."

"Oh, Grandpa, this is Julie."

"Nice to meet you, Julie. Are you and Levi in the same grade?"

"We're both seniors." She spoke nervously, not knowing if the man was going to have another episode.

"Hi, everybody, we're home," Marcia called out as she laboriously stepped over the threshold carrying Jarett, the diaper bag, and sacks of groceries.

"Here, let me help you. Come here, little buddy. Come to your big brother."

"Thanks, Levi," Marcia smiled. "How are you Julie? Cy, were you OK all by yourself this afternoon?"

"Oh sure, I was fine," Cy responded with his pat answer.

Levi let his mother know with his eyes that all was not fine.

Julie extended her arms for Jarett. "Come here, little fellow. Can you say, 'Julie?' Come on, don't be shy. Say 'Julie.'"

Jarett didn't respond to her command but wriggled out of her arms and ran to the kitchen.

"Well, we know who's hungry!" Marcia laughed.

"I really have to go, Levi. I'll see you in school tomorrow," Julia said.

"OK, Julie, see you then," Levi said with a tinge of teenage sorrow as he wished his grandpa hadn't had a war reflection in front of Julie and that his mom and little brother hadn't come home until later. But the thought was gone in the next instant, as all self-centeredness was when it came to Levi.

"That boy has been blessed," his grandmother used to say.

Everyone in the family held the fondest memories of their dear, departed Caroline, especially her husband Cy. It was at the point of her passing that the veteran first showed signs of post-traumatic stress disorder. He never crumbled to the ravages of war memories when Caroline was alive. Was it she who had held him together?

Whatever quiet thoughts were going through the heads of the household inhabitants, they were suddenly jarred from the universe by Chase coming home and slamming the door nearly to the point of causing it to be hingeless.

∽

Marcia ran from the kitchen, Grandpa stood up from his memory chair, and the two Dillet boys jounced to the noise.

"Chase! What on earth is the matter?" his mother called out.

"Nothin'," came the middle child's "pat answer."

"Nothin', shmothin,'" she rhymed, as she did over many occurrence. "Look at you! Who have you been fighting with?"

"Nobody," Chase said as he brought his voice to a lower pitch. Their house did that to them, nobody knew why, but there had always been noticeable calm and quietness within.

Little Jarett walked over to Chase and patted his leg as if to console him. He didn't say a word, just gave him a few pats.

"I'll go upstairs and clean up."

"Good idea, Chase, we can talk about this later," Cy said quietly to his grandson.

Cy had always been good with the boys, Marcia and Linden knew. He had seen a lot in his lifetime and knew how to relate to them. *But now,* Marcia thought as she returned to the kitchen, *without Caroline he's reliving the war, Chase is fighting with other kids, and Levi... Hmm, I think Levi takes after Caroline; he's a good influence over everyone.*

Marcia looked down when she felt the familiar tug on her slacks. "Hey, little guy, what would you like?"

Jarett held out his sippy cup for her. "Oh, you'd like a drink. Can you say 'Drink, please?'"

Jarett gave his mother that million-dollar smile that only mothers can treasure. She remembered her mother-in-law saying, "Don't worry; he'll talk when he's ready."

But Jarett never spoke. He could make noises, he could cry, he could hear—but no words. Marcia and Jarett went to many appointments with nothing given as the reason for his inability to speak.

Was Grandma right? Are you going to talk when you're ready? Jarett took the cup with another award-winning smile.

"Levi, could you and Grandpa put in Jarett's new sing-along tape and sing right out. Maybe Jarett will join in with you guys. I'll get dinner going here."

Linden walked in to the aroma of something Italian, maybe spaghetti and meatballs, maybe lasagna. He didn't care; he was famished. But his stroll to the kitchen stopped immediately when he saw his father, Levi, and Jarett sitting in a little group, each using hand motions to go along with the words. The hale and hearty voices crooned out the words—except for Jarett. Jarett watched their faces and moved to the music with a smile that melted his father's heart.

"Come on, son, join right in!" Cy directed. Linden did just that. Jarett scurried to his father's lap and began staring at his father's mouth.

Linden caught a glimpse of Chase sitting on the staircase watching. He motioned to him to join them. Chase shook his head.

Up popped Jarett who pleadingly looked at Chase and held out his arms for his brother. It worked the magic; Chase came over.

"Caroline, keep them together, always keep them close," Marcia prayed to her mother-in-law as she poured the extra sauce into the gravy boat.

Into the night Marcia lay awake wondering if Jarett had dreams. *Was he talking in his dreams?* What about Chase? She heard Grandpa talking with him after dinner. She heard him tell his grandson how bad fighting was. Chase retaliated with questions about soldiers in the war and why they joined up knowing they were going to be trained to fight and then fight. What did Chase dream about? *Did he fight in his dreams? Was he the victor or the loser?* She smiled as she thought about Levi having nice, peaceful dreams, him being blessed with good-heartedness and tranquility. *Does he ever dream about Julie?* Marcia looked over at her husband. *Does he ever have a dream about me like he used to?*

It didn't much matter as she jolted upright! Linden reacted the same way as they heard Cy scream to his men.

"Get down, get down, cover your heads. Loomis, get out of there! Grab Half-Pint, Oh no!"

"Dad, Dad, you're all right; it's OK. The war is over."

"The war is over?" he mumbled, trying to shake the fogginess out of his brain. "That's good; I hated the war."

"Is Grandpa all right?" Levi asked as he poked his head into the room.

"He's fine, son. Go back to bed."

"You better stop in and see if Chase is OK. I heard him mumbling or crying about something."

"Linden, stay with your father awhile. I'll check on Chase," Marcia said.

By the time Linden returned, Marcia was already under the covers with the report that Chase was sound asleep. "It must have been a nightmare."

"Too many nightmares around here," Linden sighed.

"OK, let's count off around the table. Everybody call out your number when it's your turn," Marcia announced, in hopes that she could get Jarett to speak.

"One."

"Two."

Jarett held up three fingers.

"OK, now let's go around this way."

"One."

"Two."

"Three."

"Four."

Jarett held up his whole hand.

"That's five for sure. Can you say five?" Marcia asked.

Jarett smiled.

"How was school, Chase?"

"OK."

Marcia knew that the last six months had gotten harder and harder on Chase. She and Linden, Grandpa and Levi had all tried to talk to him to find what was troubling Chase. What was making him more and more angry. There had been meetings with the guidance counselor and the superintendent and the teachers. Marcia tried to make their home life as pleasant as possible.

"Chase, it's a beautiful day out there. Would you mind going out to the backyard with Jarett and Grandpa? Have some fun. I'll make some refreshments and be out to join you."

"There," Marcia complemented herself, "I can come up with some pretty good ideas, just like Caroline could." She reminisced as she bustled around the kitchen deciding to take out a plate of fresh fruit cut into fun-sized pieces.

She dropped the knife when she heard the consternation through the open window. Maybe she shouldn't have taken so long with the fruit; maybe she should have just grabbed some ice pops. Jarett was crying, actually screaming, as Chase rolled in the grass with the boy from next door who was pounding on his face. Marcia screamed at the neighbor boy as she yanked on the back of his collar to pull him away from Chase. The boy's father ran out and marched his son into their house.

"What happened?" Marcia implored. But no answer could be conveyed because Grandpa was suddenly in the war.

He tipped the sandbox over and yelled for everyone to get under. He picked up Jarett and put him under the green domed turtle. Marcia grabbed him out as Cy grabbed Chase to force him under. Chase wouldn't budge.

"Grandpa, it's OK; everything is all right. The war is over," Levi announced as he ran out from the house.

"It is?" Cy uttered as he looked at the backyard in puzzlement. "Oh thank God; we were in real danger!"

"I know, but everyone is safe now."

∽

"Chase, can you tell us why you were fighting with the neighbor boy?" Linden asked as he tried to sort through all of Marcia's tales of the day.

Immediately Chase was angry. "You didn't hear what he said about Grandpa and Jarett!"

"No, I didn't; I wasn't there. What did he say?" Linden asked.

"He said Jarett was retarded and Grandpa was a lunatic!"

"Well, is that true?"

"No!"

"What were you going to do? Make him eat his words?"

"I had to do something!"

"How did the fighting pan out?"

"Not that good," Chase admitted sadly.

"Would you be on top of the world if you had beat him to a pulp?"

"Oh yeah." Chase smiled as if that had been his dream.

"Now I know we have a real problem," Linden sighed as he looked as his wife.

"We seem to have more than one problem," Marcia replied as she added another sigh to the living room.

Could Caroline's departure from the family have caused this crumbling? It definitely was the beginning of Cy's PTSD and possibly the beginning of Chase's anger. What of little Jarett? Watching his brother getting pounded and seeing him come home disheveled every other day must be having some effect on him. Seeing his grandfather going into a tirade can't be healthy. Marcia and Linden were also being harnessed with heavier and heavier burdens as the months went by. And Levi? Had he truly been blessed as Caroline had said? How could he maintain his composure and always be there to counsel? Was he the rock of the family?

Marcia couldn't be the rock; she felt more like silt as she ran from appointment to appointment. She took Cy to the Veteran's Hospital and Chase to his psychologist and Jarett to the speech therapist. Linden couldn't be the rock; he felt more like the chiseled piece of marble after working all day and spending his evenings trying to sort through the incidences that Marcia relayed to him. Chase and Grandpa? They were loaded with explosives—don't hit those rocks! Jarett? How could he be a rock? He was a shiny little pebble, a treasure to his family.

"Oh no," Marcia said aloud as she opened the letter from Chase's psychologist. He wanted to set up a meeting with her and Linden and Chase.

"Levi, I've cleared it with the school. You'll have to stay with Grandpa and Jarett while we have a conference."

"Sure, Mom."

"Do you know what he is going to say?" Marcia whispered to Chase as they waited their turn at the clinic.

"I have no idea."

"Thank you, everyone, for coming in. Chase and I have been having some great talks, right Chase?"

"If you say so."

Linden leaned forward and stared at Chase. "You change that attitude right now and apologize."

"I'm sorry," he said, obeying respectfully.

"Thank you, I appreciate that," Dr. Vogler uttered. "Well, let's proceed. I understand you also have a son named Levi."

"Oh yes," Marcia swooned and smiled.

"Yes," Linden added, "my mother used to say he was blessed."

Dr. Vogler noticed Chase's face squelched into a craggy rock filled with explosives.

"We need to end our session for today, but we'll get back together very soon. Thank you for coming in and Chase, we'll have our regular appointment in two days."

"What was the purpose of that?" Linden snarled as they left the building.

"I don't know. I can't imagine him calling us in for a two-minute session," Marcia snarled as well.

"I didn't know that you guys ever got angry at anything!" Chase proclaimed in utter amazement.

"What do you think we are? Zombies?" His dad asked. "Everybody gets angry sometimes."

"Not Levi," Chase said.

The parents stopped dead in their tracks.

"What on earth happened to you?" Marcia gasped as she saw Levi sitting on the couch with an ice pack on his forehead.

"I stumbled on the stairs and did a few somersaults all the way down."

"Why? What was going on?"

"I went upstairs to use the bathroom when I heard Grandpa yelling and screaming about the hand grenades. I heard a crash, so I went running. I must have tripped, and when I came to, Jarett and Grandpa were playing pat-a-cake. The lamp was still on the floor but the war was over."

"That's amazing! There was no one here to tell him the war was over. I wonder what got him to calm down," Linden said.

"I don't know, but I'm taking Levi to the emergency room. Look at that lump; he might have a concussion," Marcia announced.

"OK, Chase, take charge. I'm going to start supper," his dad said as he peered at him with a different outlook, a new outlook.

It was ten o'clock before Levi and his mom returned.

"Whew!" Marcia exhaled as she plopped into the chair. "What an ordeal."

"What's the news Levi?" Linden asked.

"It's not a concussion. I'll just have this lump for a while and a headache."

"How was your evening?" Marcia asked after she and Linden had gotten everyone to bed.

"You know," he said pensively, "things were different around here."

"How so?"

"I've begun to see Chase in a new light—something I should have done a long time ago. That poor kid has been falling through the cracks and none of us saw it."

"You mean that remark Chase made after the psychologist shooed us out of his office?"

"Exactly! Chase thinks Levi has no faults, that Levi is perfect, and that he can't live up to his big brother."

323

"Oh dear Lord. No wonder he has been so angry."

"Yeah." Linden let his voice trail off into the night, maybe to mingle with the thoughts of other parents from around the world who were trying to make sense of their own families.

Marcia and Linden started their campaign of "Getting to Know Chase." The boy didn't disappear into his room anymore with all the attention going to Linden's dad and little Jarett, even though everyone knew that the old one and the young one needed much attention. Levi was seeing more of Julie and their friends so he wasn't always in the house. Without Levi there, it seemed like Chase had more breathing space. Linden never knew how intelligent his second son was until he had to succumb to defeat almost every time they played chess. Linden saw how Chase was always teaching Jarett under the guise of play. Who knew he had a sense of humor? Who else could make Grandpa laugh like that?

"I knew I loved him, but I didn't know if I liked him," Linden confided to Dr. Vogler. "I'm so ashamed of myself."

"Parents and kids drift apart, Linden. The important thing is that you get back together so you start *liking* each other again."

"Thank God it is happening. I imagine there are many incidences when it doesn't."

"Yes, that is the sad part of my job."

Levi leaving for college in August became more and more real. Had they all been in denial? It couldn't have been that. College visits had been made, financial aid papers had been filed, supplies and dorm items had been purchased, but... Was Levi really going away?

The doctor appointments continued throughout the spring, even those for Levi. He, however, had been discharged with a clean bill of health after his tumble down the stairs. The others were not released.

Linden and Marcia received an invitation from Dr. Vogler.

"Do you think we'll be in there more than two minutes?" Marcia whispered to her husband.

"Thank you for coming in. I wanted to share something with you. Last week when Chase and I were visiting he started to cry."

"Cry? He's fifteen years old," Marcia stammered.

"Don't you ever cry?" the doctor asked.

"Oh yes, I guess I do," she replied meekly. "Why was Chase crying?"

"He said he wanted to be *blessed* like everyone says Levi is blessed. I asked him if he knew what it meant to be blessed. He said no."

"It's just a word that my mother used to describe Levi," Linden contributed.

"How can we make him feel blessed?" the doctor asked.

The parents looked at each other. "If we make him feel special, like we do now, will he feel blessed?"

"Or make him feel important, like we do. Will that do it?"

"I went over all that with Chase, and he said that was not like being *blessed*."

"I don't know what we could do."

"I'm going to suggest something. If you want no part of it, don't be afraid to say so. I asked Chase if he'd been baptized and he said, 'What's that?' I told him I would speak to you, and it would be your decision as to what you wanted to do about it."

"Gee," Marcia finally spoke, "I think you've shocked us."

"I'm rather speechless, to tell you the truth; but we do want to tell you, doctor, that you have been doing a good job with Chase. He is really calming down."

"Thank you. I sense more tranquility every time he comes in. But I think it's what you are doing at home that is the real key."

"I don't know about that *blessed* thing, however," Marcia confessed. "I wish Caroline was here to advise us."

"You know what she would say," Linden spoke quietly to his wife.

"Yes. I do."

As the windshield wipers worked at the job of rain removal, the thoughts of the parents didn't cascade nearly as smoothly or precisely as the robotic duo up front. The people's thoughts jerked along, sometimes streaking, sometimes stopping, or sometimes sticking before they jolted forward.

"So why didn't we get Chase or Jarett baptized like we did Levi?"

"I don't know. I guess life got in the way."

"Yeah, life."

"Well, this conversation with Chase ought to be an eye-opener," Linden said.

"Here we go again." Marcia scowled as she listened to the premature July Fourth firecrackers going off from next door.

"I thought they learned their lesson last year when the neighborhood folks rebelled and called the police," Linden said as he looked at his father.

Jarett seemed to like it. He listened and then copied the pattern on his toy drum. Chase appreciated Jarett's talent the most. "This kid is good!" he proclaimed as he laughed.

For some reason, no one came banging on the door for the posse to congregate and walk next door. There were no phone calls about getting someone to call the police. Because Cy was calm and Jarett was having a good time with the booms and the bangs, Linden let it go.

∞

"Well, there, it is nine thirty and everything is quiet," Marcia sighed. "Good, now we can get this little fellow to bed. He's going to have a big day tomorrow. Grandpa, you about ready to go up, too?"

"Me too!" Chase hooted. "Starting tomorrow I'm going to be *blessed*!"

"I hope Levi doesn't stay out too late."

"I don't think he will," Linden replied with a yawn. "I don't think we're going to be awake to welcome in Independence Day, so I'll say it now: Happy Independence Day, dear."

Marcia didn't get any more words out other than "Happy."

∞

The founding fathers would have been well pleased with the little neighborhoods around the country, Linden surmised. No fighting, no trying to shoot one's way to independence, no bombings in the night... just something calm and peaceful nestled into the little towns. Their efforts had been successful. Everyone would enjoy the holiday. Linden was asleep for maybe two hours when, as the soldiers used to say, all hell broke out.

"Fire! Fire! Everyone evacuate your homes, now. Fire! Evacuate now!" The voice from the fire chief's car broadcasted throughout the neighborhood. Red lights flashed into the windows of the houses. Thousands of firecrackers from next door exploded; flames shot from the neighbor's house.

Chase was the first person out of bed. "Mom! Dad! Wake up! There's a fire next door. I'll get Jarett! You get Grandpa. Where's Levi?"

"Dad, wake up, we've got to get out of here!" Linden shouted.

Cy swung his legs over the edge of the bed, and the war was on.

"Go downstairs, Dad! Go with Chase! Find Chase!"

"Where's Levi?" Marcia cried.

"I don't know!"

"Here, take Jarett! I'm gonna run to the basement; maybe he's sleeping down there!" Linden panted with fear.

"Jarett sit right there, I've got to help Mom get Grandpa down the stairs," Chase ordered.

"Tell the men, there's too much bombing ahead! Have them go around the other way! Don't let them go that way! Loomis, bring those men back this way! We're surrounded. Jump into the ditch!"

No amount of them saying "The war is over" worked.

Linden ran up the basement steps. He could see Marcia and Chase trying to get Cy to descend the stairs. The old soldier wouldn't budge as he held onto the railings. Linden ran to scoop Jarett into his arms, but Jarett somehow wriggled out of his grasp and ran to the stairs. He grabbed the leg of his grandpa and said, "Bampa, it's all right, it's over; the war is over."

Just as the statue of Teddy Roosevelt and his men marching up San Juan Hill doesn't move, Linden's family didn't move.

"Mom, Dad, everybody! Get out!" Levi hollered as he burst through the front door. "Don't just stand there! What's the matter with you? Move!"

"Come on, family," Grandpa said quietly, "let's go."

"Why don't we get our hair done at Mitzi's?"

"Because we can't afford it. You like Molly, don't you?"

"Yes, she's really nice."

Chapter Fifteen
Mitzi's Models

"Of course I go to Mitzi's! Can't you tell?" Bobby Jo drawled as she patted her newly coiffed hair. "Don't you think you should try to get an appointment with her?"

Sharon inadvertently stroked her long straight hair, wishing she hadn't drawn more attention to it by letting her fingers cruise through the strands. "I've tried, but the appointment has always been so far in the future, I had to go to Molly's."

"Mmm, it looks like a Molly," Bobby Jo enunciated with her red pouty lips. "Too bad but keep trying; she only works three days a week, but she's got to fit you in at some point."

Sharon looked down into her fruit plate, totally aware of the swinging locks in her peripheral vision.

"Don't brag about her too much," Ronnie Rae interrupted as she gave her head a shake. "This isn't exactly what I asked her to do!"

"What did you ask?"

"I asked her to do a mild streaking, with blond highlights overtop of a bronze underlay with a sculpted side sweep and a short crew on the opposite side with a layered short back."

"Is that all?" Sharon asked, wondering what words she would use if she ever obtained an appointment with Mitzi.

"Does this look anything like what I asked for?" Ronnie Rae said.

"Well, no, but it's very becoming and it's modern!" Bobby Jo persisted. "Now don't take offense, Sharon, but Molly is not up with the times."

"I know, but she's nice," Sharon uttered weakly.

"Niceness doesn't make you walk out like a model," Bobby Jo expounded as she raised her just-waxed eyebrows.

"Never mind them, Sharon. With your naturalness you look younger than any of us," Missy remarked as she spoke behind her beautifully sculpted nails.

"Don't encourage her, Missy, she needs a new look to feel better about herself."

What is she talking about? I feel fine about myself, Sharon thought.

She wished she had ordered something other than a plate of fruit; she never ordered enough to eat when she was with this "thin" group.

"Sharon, you're in luck. I got you in!" Bobby Jo regaled in her accomplishment. "I was having a pedicure when I heard the receptionist dealing with a cancelation. So you're in."

"When?" Sharon asked with trepidation.

"Tomorrow at ten. OK?"

Sharon didn't dare tell her that she had other plans, not after Bobby Jo had been insistent on the appointment for weeks and weeks. "OK."

"Well, aren't you happy?" Bobby Jo asked.

"Oh yes, thank you."

"So you're Sharon. Welcome, I'm Mitzi. I have heard so much about you, I feel like I know you already. Now you come right over, sweetie, because I am going to pamper you like you have never been pampered before!"

All Sharon could think to say was, "Oh."

"We're going to start with this luxurious new shampoo; you will just love it. Can you feel the bubbles just tingling on your scalp and the scent? Don't you feel like you are right on one of those tropical islands with the fruit and the sand and the breeze? A quick rinse here, and it's going to happen again so get your beach towel and flip-flops; we're at the ocean again.

"Lynn Ann, get Sharon's tropical drink ready. We're going in for the conditioning experience."

"Oh no thanks, Mitzi, I don't care for a drink at this hour of the morning," Sharon said.

"Of course you do, sweetie. I want you to have a relaxing, pleasant experience just like you would if you were on vacation. Now, back you go. This conditioner will be nothing like you have ever experienced. The girls are wild about it and you will be too. What this is going to do for your hair, you just won't believe! I can tell you are just luxuriating, aren't you, sweetie?"

"Um, well, I'm not exactly sure yet."

"That's OK. Sometimes it's a slow process. But it's guaranteed to make you feel like a new woman."

Sharon sat with a turban towel on her head and a drink in her hand. Mitzi got her cutting supplies ready but never stopped talking. The new client looked around the salon. The posters were of models displaying the latest hair styles, the rows and rows of products were eye-catching with a lot of sales appeal, fresh flowers were here and there, and music, maybe tropical, played in the background. The two other chairs were now occupied.

"Everybody, this is Sharon. Now tell me, dearie, what did you have in mind for a style?"

Again she scanned the posters. "Maybe something like that one, the third from the left."

"OK. Just relax."

In a few seconds, the first "Have you heard?" comment came from the redhead two chairs down the line. Of course, the "Have you heard" person had the floor .

"Did you know that Betty Jonalin has left her husband and taken the kids to where her boyfriend lives?"

"What? You must be kidding?"

"No, my kid is in the same class as one of Betty's kids, and she was absent yesterday and the day before. So you know it must be true."

"Well, for heaven's sake, I saw Betty and her husband at the movies Saturday night."

"This must have happened very quickly."

"That's nothing, listen to this: Larry Mitchell has been promoted but he has to go to Germany, and Lisa says she refuses to go with him. Some of the kids want to go and some don't. She says she won't let any of the kids go."

"Sounds like they're heading for a divorce, doesn't it?"

"I've heard of couples having to live apart for a while."

"I wondered why I saw the two of them going into the lawyer's office last Tuesday."

"Yep, there's a sure sign."

"Mitzi, what are you doing?" Sharon asked.

"I'm just giving you a little pizzazz so you won't be so dull looking."

"I don't know what this world is coming to. Did you know that the kids are now the teachers and the teachers are the kids?"

"What?"

"Yes, last Friday my son was the teacher in history class and Mr. Achinson sat in his seat and gave him a hard time. My son said it was terrible how Mr. Achinson interrupted him and kept doing crazy things. I'm telling you, as soon as my hair is done today, I am marching into that school and I'll set them straight."

"Mitzi, what is that?" Sharon inquired.

"It's a new product, sweetie; people will think you have sunshine coming right out of your hair."

"Have you seen those people moving in over on Clover Street? My goodness, I've seen better furniture at garage sales."

"I heard they're related to Nellie Orwell."

"Well, there you go."

"Lynn Ann, see who needs a refill," Mitzi said.

"No, no more for me," Sharon insisted.

Sharon listened to the snipping of Mitzi's scissors.

"Listen to what happened to me. I was in the grocery store choosing some apples when all of a sudden this gorgeous man walks into the store. I had no idea who he was and you know—I know everybody. Well anyway, he came right over to the apples and there we stood side by side. I thought I should be a good neighbor, so I said, 'Hi' and guess what? He said, 'Hi'!"

"I think I know who he is because I saw a real hunk in the diner the other day and guess who he was with?"

"Who?"

"Ellen Idelberg!"

"You've got to be kidding. What is she doing with a good-looking guy?"

"I don't know, but they were pretty chummy."

Suddenly Sharon realized that it wasn't snipping she heard anymore but the buzzing of an electric razor. "Mitzi, can I look at what you are doing?"

"Not yet, sugar, I'm almost done."

"Have you seen Belinda? Doesn't she look great?"

"What do you mean?"

"Oh, don't you know? She's expecting!"

"What?"

"Yes, in eight months."

"There, a little mousse, a little pomade, and you are done! Take a look at your gorgeous self, Sharon."

While everyone in the salon clapped and cheered, Sharon stared into the mirror wondering who the person was. Because she never made a single utterance, Mitzi asked. "Do you like it?"

"I don't know; I'm in shock. I've never seen myself look like this. I don't even have the right color hair."

"Hey, girlfriend, you look dynamic," started the swirl of comments around the salon.

"Really chic."

"Now you're in the right century."

"Wait until your husband sees this!" And that was the comment that made Sharon gasp.

"Ted, oh no, Ted. I was supposed to meet him for lunch an hour ago."

Sharon ran to the receptionist's desk. That will be $230 today."

"What?"

"That includes your bag full of products that Mitzi used on you. Once she opens a product, it's yours. Isn't that great?"

Luckily, Sharon had a credit card.

Sharon ran out of the salon with her goody bag sailing through the air.

"I believe my husband is already here; has there been someone waiting for maybe an hour? Wait, maybe he left."

"No ma'am, no one today came in alone."

"Could I have a table? I need to collect my thoughts," Sharon said.

Sharon sipped her coffee as she tried to be as inconspicuous as possible in touching her new hairdo.

"Excuse me ma'am, but that gentleman has been standing there for ten minutes waiting for his wife. He claims she's not here but is there any chance he can't see you over here in this dim light?"

Sharon lifted her head to see her husband.

"You can tell him I'm over here."

She watched as Ted slowly walked her way, tilting his head to one side as he does when he's perplexed. "Sharon?"

"Ted, for heaven's sake, it's me!"

The hostess looked perplexed also as she placed a menu for Ted.

"New hairdo," Sharon felt obligated to explain to the girl.

"Oh!" she felt relieved to know. "It's cute."

"Sorry I'm late. Have you been waiting long?" Ted asked.

"No, I just got here. Can you believe I was at the hair salon for three hours?"

Ted took his time looking at his wife's new do from every angle possible, from his seat that is. "Yes, I can believe you were there for three hours. She did a lot of stuff to it, didn't she? And it wasn't Molly, was it?"

"Are you upset?"

"Not at all. I'll need to get used to it, but like the hostess said, it's cute."

Wow, Sharon thought, *he's never said my hair was cute.*

"Yes, this seductive lady and I are ready to order," Ted replied as he winked at his wife.

"Tomorrow?"

"Yes, meet us tomorrow for lunch; we can't wait to see your new hairstyle."

"OMG!" Ronnie Rae squealed as she ran to the table, "Are you kidding me?"

"Ronnie, shh, everyone is looking," Sharon said.

"Let them look, baby girl, they've got something to look at now."

"Don't you just love it?" Bobby Jo catapulted into the conversation.

"I hardly knew it was you, Sharon!" Missy added to the accolades.

"What was I before? A dish rag?"

The girls knew they had gone a little too far, and it was understandable that Sharon was on the defensive.

"Oh, we're sorry, Sharon. You've always been a lovely, lovely person," Bobby Jo said with all sincerity.

"Well, OK, I forgive you. Oh, before I forget, I wanted to ask you why I have this lottery ticket in my goody bag from Mitzi."

"She always does that for her customers. I personally have never won anything, have you girls?"

"No, but someday."

"How do I do this?" Sharon asked.

"We'll show you later, let's order."

"You know, Sharon," Missy said slowly in between little bites of spinach salad, "I have a complementary coupon for a manicure and pedicure at Mitzi's. Would you like it?"

Sharon quickly pulled her fingers into her palms knowing that her fingernails were nothing but ordinary. She didn't mean to, but she quickly scrutinized the nails of her luncheon comrades even though it wasn't necessary because they always had sculpted, polished nails.

"I guess it would be OK, seeing how it would be free, right?"

"Yes, silly, free!" Missy laughed.

The girls forgot to take Sharon into the store to see if she was a lottery winner, so after she made her appointment at Mitzi's, she went there by herself.

"Excuse me, sir. I'm not familiar with lottery tickets. How do I know if I'm a winner?" Sharon asked.

"Where have you been? On the moon? Never mind, give me your ticket. I'll run it through. I'll be darned. Hey, lady, you're a winner! You won a thousand dollars!"

Sharon immediately felt better about spending $230 on her hair.

"Yes, I do like this color," Sharon exclaimed as she fanned her fingers and lifted her feet to wriggle her toes. For some reason the wriggling, painted toes made her giggle.

"That's the first time I've ever heard you laugh, Sharon. You're always so serious."

"I didn't know that," she said seriously.

"Now you will have to buy some cute open-toed shoes to show off your cute little toes!"

"Oh, I have a complementary coupon from Missy," Sharon explained as Lynn Ann started ringing in numbers on the cash register.

"That's fine. I'm charging you just for your products, which are right here along with a lottery ticket. Your total is $67 dollars today."

Sharon gulped thinking that the service was going to be free but quickly paid, remembering her windfall. "Good luck with your lottery ticket," the receptionist called after her.

Sharon had decided not to tell anyone about her thousand-dollar win; after all, she needed a little money of her own.

"Oh my, I like those," she said aloud as she stopped in front of the department store window. Open-toed shoes for her new little toes. The very thought made her smile.

"Sharon Naviare, is that you?" the clerk in the lady's department asked.

"Why yes, it is. Hi, Heather."

"Where did you get your hair done? Don't tell me—Mitzi's. Right?"

"Right."

"You mean I won't see you at Molly's anymore?"

"Um, Heather, could I see those open-toed shoes that are in the window?"

"Sure, Sharon. You know, there's a purse that matches."

Sharon was ready when Ted came home from work, "All set? I told Caleb we'd meet him and his wife at six. Wow! Look at you! Painted nails?"

"Missy gave me a free coupon."

"Nice."

He likes them!

The next day Sharon held her breath until the clerk said, "You sure are lucky!"

"I sure am!" she exalted.

Five hundred more dollars but no one shall know. She giggled to herself.

"Girlfriend, where did you get those shoes? They're cute."

"Right across the street in the department store."

"Really? I didn't know they had anything good in there. Let's go in, shall we?"

"Sure," Sharon agreed as she felt the heft of her purse.

"Look at this sundress, it's adorable. And this scarf—I have to have it," Bobby Jo swooned.

"Ted is taking me on a cruise, I really need some new clothes," Sharon said.

"When did all this come about?"

"I think it all started when I got my new hairstyle. Can that be possible?"

"Didn't I tell you? I knew good things would start happening to you."

Sharon left with shopping bags full of new clothes and shoes. She enjoyed opening her wallet so that Bobby Jo could see her one hundred dollar bills.

"I might see you at Mitzi's. I'm scheduled for a facial."

"Me too!" The two hugged like they were teenagers.

Sharon frantically searched through her products bag for the lottery ticket. Where was it? Would it be rude to go back in and tell Lynn Ann it wasn't in the... ah, there it is. She looked up and down the sidewalk; she didn't want anyone to see her giving the piece of paper a good luck kiss.

"You look gorgeous, sweetheart. What have you done to yourself?"

She didn't want to tell Ted about the facial. "Nothing, dear. I'm just much happier now."

"And you are going to be even happier when I spoil you on our cruise."

Sharon put on her sunglasses and searched for a different place to take her lottery ticket.

She rubbed the ticket and whispered, "Be good to me, baby."

"OMG—five thousand dollars!"

She loved her new world. She called the girls and invited them to go out for lunch.

"But you don't have to pay for our lunches," Ronnie Rae pleaded.

"My dear, I want to. If it wasn't for the insistence of you ladies, I would still be the old Molly girl."

"I will take five of those lottery tickets please," she said behind her sunglasses.

"I have to run out for a few minutes, Ted. I forgot to buy the new color in nail polish."

"Oh, we can't have that! A model needs her accoutrements," he said and laughed.

A model? Is that what he thinks I am?

"Sorry, ma'am, no win today."

"Are you sure?" Sharon asked.

"The machine doesn't make mistakes, ma'am."

That's OK, that's natural, not to worry; tomorrow is another chance.

The cruise was fabulous but Sharon had to get back to Mitzi's. Mitzi had the winning tickets!

Sharon listened but didn't hear who was dating whom or who was seen with whom or who whatever. The shampooing and the coloring and the snipping and the nonsense seemed to last a lifetime. Sharon almost grabbed the bag out of Lynn Ann's hand as she waved good-bye and began searching the bag as she ran down the street.

Here you are baby, come to mama.

Sharon knew she had a winning ticket; she could feel it. She spent the morning shopping on the computer, getting a head start on Christmas. OK, she felt the magic hour had arrived. Now, now was the time to redeem the winning ticket. She dressed in one of her new outfits, including the high heels, and off she went.

"Tell me it's a winner," she said, laughing with confidence.

"Sorry."

"But this ticket came from Mitzi's!"

"Sorry."

"Honey, Caleb asked us to go to the casino with them. Do you want to go?" Ted asked.

"No, not really, I've never gambled, and I don't even understand what they are doing."

"Well, why don't we just go for the fun of it? I think you would like the slot machines. I can show you how to play. Plus, I would like to show off my beautiful woman. We don't look like a boring married couple anymore, do we?"

We don't look married? What is he thinking? Sharon thought.

"OK now, that's all you do. Pull the lever. Put in another quarter. Pull it again. I'm going to the blackjack game and to check up on Caleb and Candy."

Sharon did just as she was told when suddenly all the bells and whistles screamed and a barrage of coins rushed at the novice. People all around clapped and yelled, "Good for you," and "Congratulations."

"How do I carry all these coins?" she asked the player next to her.

"The attendant will be around; ask for a bag," she answered never missing a beat with her coin dropping.

"There! Oh, excuse me again. How can I get them changed into bills?"

"Three hundred dollars. Woweee!" Sharon regaled. She lined her wallet with the three nice bills.

"Hi, hon, did you have any luck?" Ted asked.

"No, not really, but if you guys are still occupied here, I guess I'll go back and put in a few more coins. Maybe I'll do better this time."

"You again? This must be your lucky day!"

Sharon added another $200 to her wallet.

"Are you ready to go into the boutique?"

"I sure am."

"Say, darlin', why don't you buy this little number? You've never worn anything like this. You can pretend you are my—"

"Shh, do you want people to hear you?" *What is the matter with this man? He's not the dear, innocent man that I married.*

"Sharon, we're going out to the casino for something to do, do you want to go with us?" Bobby Jo asked.

"Sure."

Sharon bought her lottery tickets before the girls picked her up.

"They seem to know you here. Do they?"

"Ted and I come out here sometimes."

"Sharon! Are you going to play those slot machines all day? I'm exhausted, let's go."

"One more try, Missy."

"What a sad sack! Didn't you have fun, Sharon?"

"I didn't win anything today," Sharon said.

"Well, you don't go thinking you are going to win, you go just to have fun!"

Sharon rushed into her house; she needed to win on a lottery ticket. She had no money left.

"Oh no."

"Hon, these credit card bills are outrageous. What on earth are you buying?" Ted asked.

"Oh, just this and that, you know how you like me looking just so."

"Yes, but we can't go into debt over it. Contain your urges, will you?"

She knew she could win; she'd done it before, lots of times. All it would take were the right numbers. Yes, she needed a Mitzi ticket—they were the best.

"Can you believe I forgot my wallet today? I'll just take my products bag and pay you tomorrow or the next day. Is that OK?"

"Sure, you're a super client. Have a good day."

"Oh, I will," Sharon responded with all the confidence in the world.

"No, no, no," Sharon wailed when she was told she didn't win.

The front door slammed. "Sharon!" Ted shouted, "Bills are coming in from all over the place. What's going on?"

He didn't even wait for an answer; he stormed out.

I just need a break. I know I can win. I did it before. I can do it again. I just need some seed money. I'll go out to the casino and I'll win. I know I'll win.

Sharon twirled her engagement ring around and around. She could get some money for the ring and then when she won big she could buy it back. She could do that.

She also had several other expensive pieces of jewelry. Yes, a win was coming, a big win. She was due; she was overdue.

"Sharon, there's three hundred dollars missing from my wallet. Do you know anything about this?" Ted asked.

"Sharon, it's Lynn Ann from Mitzi's. You are way overdue for a hair appointment. When are you coming in? And, in case you have forgotten, there is the little matter of the last payment. This is just a friendly reminder."

"Sharon, it's Ronnie Rae. Where have you been? Nobody has seen you in ages. We are going to the racetrack. Do you want to go? Call me."

Sharon ran out to the car. "Sharon? Um, have you been sick? You look, well, you look sort of haggard and disheveled and... I mean, are you going to get your hair done soon and... and your nails? Oh, never mind. Let's go and have some fun. You look like you need a fun day."

As they waited in line for their racing tickets, Sharon tapped Missy on the shoulder. "Missy, I'm so embarrassed, I forgot my wallet. Do you think you could loan me some money?"

"Of course, sweetie. How much would you like?"

Sharon felt the blood and the pulse coming back into her body; she felt the exhilaration building in her hands and in her temples. Now she would win; she had new blood swirling around her heart. The outdoor air filled her nostrils, the smell of the horses surged even into her ears. This is what she needed—to be out doors!

"I'm sorry, Missy."

"Don't think a thing about it. I know you're good for it. You can pay me back any old time you see me."

"Where have you been?" Ted asked.

"At the racetrack," Sharon replied.

"Did you win?"

"No."

"Is that why you don't have your engagement ring anymore or the jewelry from my grandmother and why we're in debt up to our necks? And look at you? You're the ugliest woman on the earth. I'm washing my hands of you."

Sharon lay on the living room floor weeping into every fiber of the carpet until 6:00 a.m. when she left the house. She aimlessly walked the sidewalks of her little town wondering how she had gotten so off track. She found herself in front of Molly's Hair Salon when a sudden wave of nostalgia swept over her. The newly formed tears ran from her eyes as she slid down the door and sat weeping with her head on her knees.

Wouldn't Ted be disgusted or her thin friends horrified if they ever saw her sleeping on the sidewalk? But it was she who felt horror when a large, strong hand grabbed her arm, yanking her to her feet and shoving her into the salon. From the floor she looked up to see someone with a head scarf, sunglasses, and a long trench coat.

"Sharon?"

"Who are you?"

"Never mind me. Why were you out by my door?"

"Your door?"

The person removed her scarf and sunglasses.

"Mitzi?"

"And I'm madder than a wet hen at you."

"Why?" Sharon asked.

"It's been eighteen years and no one has ever caught on to this."

"To what?"

Mitzi removed her wig, took off her makeup, removed her red fingernail polish, slipped on the white sneakers, and donned the old black apron.

"Molly? Have I gone crazy?" Sharon asked. "Are you both Mitzi and Molly?"

"I am."

"And who are you?" Mitzi asked.

"I don't know anymore," Sharon cried.

"THERE'S ANOTHER FOR SALE SIGN. THE PEOPLE MOVE OUT, NEW ONES MOVE
IN, AND THE HISTORY FLIES OUT THE WINDOW."

"THAT HOUSE HAS AN OPEN WINDOW UPSTAIRS. WILL HISTORY FLY OUT OF THAT
WINDOW?"

ᴄ✑Chapter Sixteen✑ᴏ
Dashed Memories

"**W**hat the hell is this?" Derrick gasped as he drove onto the circular driveway of his parent's home.

"Lord Almighty, what has she done?" Conrad pummeled the question as he looked from left to right to take in the nonexistent curb appeal.

"You mean what has she not done," the horrified Constance said with a need to perfect her brother's question.

"Why?" Emily questioned, with her customary naivety. "What's the matter?"

"Ouch!" Constance yelled as she rubbed the top of her head. "Why are you driving in those pot holes?"

"Well excuse me, but I can't seem to miss them," Derrick snapped in retaliation. "They're every six inches."

"This driveway used to be so smooth you could roll a Hula-Hoop on it for a good three hundred feet," Conrad interjected.

"I wonder where my Hula-Hoop went," Emily said in all earnestness.

"Derrick! Stop the car!"

"What's the matter?"

"Take a look at our house."

Three of the Carson children stared at the house as if they were in a trance. One of the Carson's said, "Oh, it's so good to be home!"

Constance stepped out. Her foot was eighteen inches from a weed patch. The driveway had always been outlined with two neat rows of geraniums with nary a weed between them. Now the driveway was outlined with two rows of solid weeds.

"The fountain!" she cried as she saw the graceful lady lying on her side with birds walking on her face. "Why is the fountain tipped over? Father would be horrified."

"You think that's bad, look at our front porch!" Conrad commanded his siblings.

Eight pair of eyes took at the broken porch swing, the dead plants in the huge urns, the rusty metal chairs, even the piles of bird droppings from the nests above. "Why did she let things get like this? Father never would have allowed it."

"Oh my little baby chair!" Emily squealed as she ran to the rusty structure still showing a trace of a spotted doe painted on the back of the seat.

Derrick reached for the huge brass doorknob. Of course the front door was locked, much to the relief of the Carson's. Without saying a word, they turned in sync, just as they had as kids, and headed for the side door.

"The trellis! The clematis!" moaned Constance. "Where is it?"

"Look down into that weed patch. You can see some of the wooden cross-hatching of the trellis."

"Yeah, right."

"Why is that caution tape around the side porch?"

"Undoubtedly those steps aren't safe, nor is the floor of the porch. Look, hasn't something gone through the boards?"

"Listen," Emily announced, "I hear kittens."

"Oh great! There's a family of cats living under the porch. Let's try the back door and watch out for those pavers, they're loose."

"Judas Priest," Conrad yelled as his big strapping body lay on the sidewalk. "Why didn't you tell me sooner?"

"Sorry, Bud," Derrick apologized as he hefted his football-sized brother to his feet while Emily handed him a tissue to dab the blood from his scraped hand.

"Oh no! Don't look out back," Constance warned without meaning it.

"Ugh!" The three older Carson's groaned as they saw the green pond.

It was only Emily who said, "We've got to get that cleaned up!"

"Father must be rolling over in his grave," Derrick replied as he surveyed the site of their childhood, their paradise. "Why wouldn't she take care of that grape arbor? Remember when we would sit under there on the hottest days of summer and eat ice cream?"

"How about all those blueberry bushes Daddy planted because Mother wanted them? Remember how we would pick for hours and then help make the pies? I used to love that; now I don't even see the bushes with those sumacs taking over." Constance lamented.

"Look! Here are some strawberry plants," Emily chirped trying to appease her big sister.

"What, five of them?"

"Even St. Francis hit the dirt!" Conrad spoke sympathetically as he brought the heavy statue to an upright position. There he was, their good old St. Francis, still eager to feed the birds with his arm outstretched.

"Remember when Dad brought those birdhouses back from Germany? Mother's entire garden club came here to see them."

"This one is still pretty!" Emily brought their attention to the chalet sanctuary. Her siblings finally agreed to something being pretty.

It didn't last long. Derrick was quick to point out the arrogance of the grass on the patio that had pushed its way up to surround every stone. Conrad looked at the big oak tree to see two boards still suspended across the branches, once their tree house. Constance looked in the raised flowerbeds to see wild daisies and weeds, not the annuals and perennials that once glorified their backyard. Emily turned around and picked up a kitten.

"You look just like a cat we used to have. Are you the grandchild?

Each Carson stood in the backyard/field and let their memories play while they tried to get momentary relief from reality.

"And to my four children I leave love. Lots and lots of love."

The lawyer paused to look at the Carson children. Three looked as blank as white sheets frozen to the clothesline in the dead of winter. One smiled sweetly.

"You mean the house, the property, the belongings—nothing was left to us?" Derrick questioned.

"That is correct. I'm sorry," the lawyer replied.

"Why would she leave everything to a woman named Mrs. Selma Frederick? We don't even know a Mrs. Frederick."

"I'm afraid it won't belong to Mrs. Frederick much longer; it's going into foreclosure."

"Where is that woman?"

"Oh, I thought you knew; she lives at the house."

"Our house?"

"Derrick, slow down; I don't want to bump my head again," Constance ordered as her older brother hit the potholes in the circular driveway with no caution.

"You'll live," he muttered with no sympathy.

They followed the commander on his march to Selma. There was no assessing the flower gardens, the cat-hole porch, the pea soup pond, or St. Francis. It was all business as the oldest Carson strode unwavering to the back porch and pounded on the door.

"Where the hell is she?" His agitation mounted with each knock.

"It doesn't look too bad in there," Constance reported as she peered through the window.

"Who's out there?" a low voice asked.

"It's the Carsons. We lived her once; it was our father and mother who owned this place. What the hell has happened here and why are you in our house?"

They heard the dead bolt slide and an eyeball peered at them.

It was Emily who screamed, "Sellie, Sellie it's us!"

"Well, land of mercy, the children!"

"Sellie? Is that you?"

"Sellie, my stars, how long has it been?"

"My babies, by babies are home!" she sobbed.

"Sellie! What has happened to the place? What happened?"

They followed the old woman into the kitchen. The wallpaper that they remembered, the curtains, the appliances—all outdated—were there. Conrad's eyes focused on the table. He had so many memories of doing homework there. He could hear his father say, "You get a good education; believe me, I've seen what it is to be poor, you don't want to be there. We came to America with nothing, nothing, and we worked our fingers to the bone to get all of this."

Constance looked at the oven, the same oven where she learned how to make pies and pastries and potica. It was those skills that landed her the job of pastry chef at the Continental in New York City.

Derrick, too, centered on the table; the table where he heard the stories of the newlyweds who risked everything to come to America and the work that his father did to support his family. Daily his father commuted to the city to work in an office while his mother did everything at home with the children and the house and the grounds. That's when Selma came to help his mother. Derrick went to an Ivy League school as did Conrad. They learned their lessons well around that table.

Emily concentrated on Sellie. Emily's brothers and sister were grown and out of the house when she was born. Mr. Carson died of a massive heart attack when the little girl was only five years old. So she got to spend a lot of time with Sellie.

"Can we look through the house, Sellie?" Constance asked.

"Of course you can; you have a lot of memories here."

"I don't think we should go through—"

"Derrick, here, you walk with me." Sellie smiled as she offered her arm to the oldest boy.

"Where are Mother's beautiful Tiffany lamps, Sellie?"

"One by one your mama had to sell them."

"Why? She loved them; she would never sell them?"

"She did love them, but she had to pay the bills."

"What?" Derrick interrupted. "Dad left her plenty of money, didn't he?"

"Well, he did leave a goodly lump, but he didn't trust the banks and the insurance companies and the... I don't understand all about that street."

"Do you mean Wall Street?"

"Yes, Wall Street. He didn't trust what they would do with his money. I guess he thought what he left your mother would last her a lifetime."

"Wow, I didn't realize all that!" Derrick wiped his sweaty brow.

Conrad approached Sellie and took her little, wrinkled hands into his. "Sellie, did the money run out?"

Sellie went to her knees and sobbed. "Yes, there was no more money no matter how we scrimped and saved and did without. I worked for free just to be here; I didn't want her to be alone. She started selling things that were dear to her heart and she cried and cried and cried."

"Why didn't you call us?" they all asked at once as they found themselves on their knees with Sellie. The old floral carpet wasn't even thick enough anymore to cushion their knees.

"She didn't want you to know. She thought you would think of her as a failure."

"Oh dear God, that's why she always said no to our visiting her; she didn't want us to see."

Emily's eyes grew larger and larger as she saw for the first time ever tears falling from her oldest brother's eyes.

The house was a hollow skeleton of what they remembered. The crystal chandelier over the dining room table was gone, there were very few dishes in the china closet, the walls were barren of artwork, the porcelain globe was missing from the library, and the bedrooms looked like that of orphans.

The five of them walked through the house as if a dirge was underway. "Sellie," Derrick spoke quietly, "how did the bank come to own the house?"

"Your mama went there one day for a loan. I don't think she understood the conditions; she didn't know they were going to own her house. She told them she wouldn't be able to pay the money back, and they said it was all right because the house was in her name."

"Hmm, no wonder Dad didn't trust them," Conrad interjected.

"How did the grounds get in such disarray?"

"Do you remember the men who used to come and work on the landscaping?" Sellie asked.

"Yeah, we loved watching them."

"Your mother had to discontinue all that. She and I would go out every day to try and keep up with it, but it was impossible."

"And me too!" Emily added.

"Yes, and you, too. Did you know that your little sister worked as hard as we did on this place?"

"You did?"

"Yes, and I can teach you guys how to plant bulbs and care for the perennials and clean the pond and—"

"She's right," Sellie agreed. "She knows how to do a lot of the outdoor chores."

"Why—"

Sellie knew what Conrad was going to ask. "Your mother didn't want you to know how bad things were."

"But, Sellie," Emily cried, "things weren't that bad. The three of us had a lot of fun, too."

"We did baby. I guess it was after you went off to college that we really felt the hopelessness. Mr. Carson wanted nothing more than to have his children go to college and get a good job. Your mama knew that; she would never have any of you come home and ruin your dreams."

"But those were Dad's dreams. I definitely would have come home to help out," Conrad revealed.

"Me too," piped Emily.

"We all would have," Derrick agreed.

"Sellie, how would you like to go to a nice restaurant with us after we all pay a visit to the bank?"

Mr. Carson was right; the good education brought the good jobs, which brought the good pay, which brought the house back into the Carson name. It was not a foreclosure house anymore.

"Now the work begins." Derrick toasted his siblings and Sellie. "How are we going to handle all the jobs that the house is in need of?"

"You know," drawled Constance slowly, "I'm going to have four teenagers home for the whole summer with nothing to do. I wouldn't mind if they actually learned how to do something."

"You mean to come here to spend the summer?"

"Yeah, what do you think? I could help Sellie with the kitchen work."

"Being a teacher, you know I have the summer off. I could teach the kids lots of things about gardening and landscaping," Emily said, beaming.

"I can come on weekends, and I'll bring Sharon and the kids. They'll love it," Conrad commented.

"I'll take my four-week vacation in Lone Moon Creek this year! I never thought I'd be saying that!" Derrick laughed.

"I see Sally walking down the sidewalk pushing the carriage with the three babies inside. The puppies are all on their leashes! Can I run out and take their picture?"

"Sure."

ᴄ◊Chapter Seventeen◊ᴐ

THE FUNDRAISER

"The meeting is adjourned. Don't forget, next time come with ideas for a fundraiser."

"Oh no, another fundraiser," at least half of the members groaned as they walked to their cars.

The other half immediately forgot the assignment long before they got to their cars. After all, whatever was fine with them.

Danica earnestly tried to think of something unique. "Hmm," she uttered as she turned from Main Street and started her familiar trek to the countryside. "Not another bake sale, please," she sang to the tune of the song on the radio.

Alberta maneuvered onto the bridge, and as always wondered how long the old structure was going to sustain itself. Once across, she lowered her foot, as she had to get over a long and steep hill. Her mind went through a list of things the club had done in the past: bake sales, cookie sales, pie sales, garden produce sales, and... A sudden vista of newly foliaged trees caught her attention, distracting her from the mundane list of fundraisers.

Annette drove to the vegetable stand before going home. She almost missed the driveway as the captivation of the colorful display, like a postcard, took her attention. Slamming on the brakes, she slowly maneuvered the car down the driveway, enthralled with the old hay wagon filled with pumpkins and cornstalks. The mum plants spiraled upward into a clever design with a black cat placed on the very top. Upon getting closer, she could see antique hay rakes and milk cans intermingled with jars of jams and hundreds of tiny gourds. Annette thought of how something like that would be a good fundraiser.

The sparkling bracelet brought a smile to Bobby Jo's face as she sailed past the houses and barns on her road. Her dear, thoughtful husband always added a charm to her bracelet during that time of year; after all, they were married in the fall. But anyone could see that the charms were not all of autumn. Winter, spring, and summer were also included because he loved her in all the seasons.

Bobby Jo placed one hand on the bracelet as she steered with the other. She could feel the love emanating from it. "Oh how pretty!" she said aloud as she drove past a tree with a curious hue. "I've never seen leaves that shade of red before," she mused to herself. The charms on her bracelet jingled a wee bit as she turned into her driveway. "Jewelry! We could have a jewelry sale! Everyone has jewelry that they don't wear anymore!"

"Fundraiser, fundraiser, fundraiser," Eunice tapped the beat onto the steering wheel as she spoke the words as a litany. "What can we do; what can we do; what can we do?" The tapping and chanting went on. "Oh! Maybe a talent show!" Those words brought her car to a stop as she looked out across her lake. The water was as blue as the sky and the trees encircling it were beginning to show their talent. "That's where the *talent* is," she proclaimed to herself as she slowly pulled away from one of her favorite vistas.

"Well, ladies, I think our new business is the fundraiser. Let's hear your ideas!"

"We can always be guaranteed to make money with a bake sale," Priscilla spoke confidently. Bonnie noticed several women nodding their heads in agreement.

"We have done very well with bake sales," the president agreed. "Any other ideas?"

"This is sort of like a bake sale but maybe more artistic," Annette added. "I got the idea from the vegetable stand as you go out of town to the west. It is so eye-catching; among the food are really neat antiques and props from nature, like cornstalks and bales of hay, even Chinese lanterns and silver dollar plants. They really know how to set up a display."

"Oo, that sounds interesting," Bonnie replied. "Are there any others?"

"I have one," Bobby Jo answered as she raised her hand while her charms jingled. "We all have jewelry boxes full of items that we don't wear anymore. Right?" Almost 100 percent of the group nodded in agreement. "Well, why don't we have a jewelry sale? Costume jewelry is really a hot item right now. And we can set it up artistically like Annette just described."

"We've never done a jewelry sale before. That certainly is a new idea. Thank you, Bobby Jo. Any others?"

"I really tried to think of something, and because I always do my best thinking while I'm driving, I've been in the car a lot." Everyone laughed. "Anyway," Alberta went on, "do you know what kept distracting me?"

After a few seconds of silence, Bonnie sputtered, "Oh me? No, I don't know what kept distracting you."

"Nature's beauty!" Alberta said emphatically.

"Me too!" Danica squealed. "It's so beautiful out there; it's hard to think of anything else."

"This is true," Bonnie agreed, "but that wonderful thought isn't going to replenish our coffers."

"How about a craft sale?" Rachel asked.

"I had a thought that flip-flopped," Eunice volunteered. "I started to think that a talent show might be a good idea until I too was halted by my favorite vista. In that moment I thought, it's not our talent that's so fantastic but the *talent* of nature's beauty that is phenomenal."

"How about a photo contest?" Shiloh asked.

"Time is fleeing, so we can't spend any more time on this; but think about the ideas and we'll discuss it again next time," Bonnie directed.

This time upon adjournment, all of the members had something concrete to think about and were much more productive in their assignment.

Could it have been the time of year? The breathtaking view around each corner? The colors cascading across every body of water no matter how big or how small? The effort the home dwellers put into decorating their properties using native products?

It was unanimous that the club would sponsor a photo contest. A committee was formed to set up the details. The goal was to show the beauty of autumn in the area. Black and white, sepia, and colored shots would be allowed that were no larger than eight by ten inches. There could only be one picture per entrant. The entry fee would be $10, with a $50 first prize, $30 second prize, and $15 third prize.

"Who are the judges going to be?"

"Where are we going to set this up?"

"What's the deadline?"

The committee put in their due diligence on the arrangements.

"Is the committee ready to introduce the details for the group?" Bonnie asked.

"Are there anymore question?"

"Would someone like to make a motion to accept this proposal?"

"Spread the word, everyone. Get those posters out and put the release in the newspapers. Be sure you give special attention to our famous judges. They all have degrees in photography, have books published depicting their photographs, and have had showings all over the world. This should be fun!"

"Can you believe the involvement from the community?" Eunice whispered to Bobby Jo as they worked quietly in the hardware store. "Mr. Hardy was so kind to give us floor space plus construct panels for the display."

"We are getting some great pictures!"

Mr. Hardy's business was booming. He hadn't had so many people through his doors—ever!

"Does everyone in this area have a camera?" Alberta laughed

"I've been in here every day with more and more pictures!" Danica exclaimed.

The day of the judging came and so did Mr. Brekinstein, Ms. Shantell, and Mr. Hubert, three professional photographers staying at Alberta's husband's sister's aunt-in-law's cousin's B and B over in Rockport. The artisan's hamlet was now hosting the annual photographer's convention.

The club members converged outside the hardware store and peeked in the windows expecting the judges to have made their decisions. They saw the three walking back and forth in front of the display; going around to the other side, navigating sideways along the makeshift panels that Mr. Hardy had to erect during the flurry of last minute entries.

"Thanks to Alberta's connections, we have real judges," Bonnie reminded everyone.

Without taking their eyes off of the inner sanctum, the ladies mumbled, "Yes, thank you, Alberta."

An hour later, two hours, three—finally! The ladies rushed in to find that the judges hadn't made any decisions.

"Why? Why didn't you select the winning photos?" Bonnie demanded.

"There is nothing here worthy of a prize," Mr. Brekinstein huffed as he raised his fisted hand while his blood pressure obviously rose based on the look of his face.

"We are sorry, but Mr. Brekinstein is right," the tall, blond-haired woman uttered as she swished her hair off of her shoulders. "These have no merit."

"And you, Mr. Hubert? What say you?"

"I agree. These don't represent the beauty that is out there."

"What do you think you are talking about? Are you crazy?" Bonnie shouted as she advanced toward the judges. Annette and Eunice pulled her back.

"Please, tell us your reasons for this decision," Bobby Jo pleaded.

"Have you been out in the countryside or even gone outside?" Mr. Brekinstein asked as the redness in his face surged again.

"Of course we have; we all live around here and our countryside is gorgeous, just gorgeous!" Now it was Bobby Jo who flared as the charms on her bracelet jangled more than usual.

"You people apparently see nothing," Ms. Shantell murmured aloofly as she donned her huge sunglasses.

Mr. Hubert walked to the display. "Do you think an old hay wagon sitting in a field laden with cornstalks is of any interest? Or this pond with two ducks? Who cares?"

"Or that baby walking in the leaves, is that anything special?" the hypertensive judge mocked.

"Come," Ms. Shantell ordered as they walked out.

The ladies were probably more tense than the rows and rows of unplugged power tools that Mr. Hardy had hanging on his pegboards.

"What are we going to do?" Rachel whispered.

"I don't know. We're supposed to announce the winners tonight at the town board meeting," Bonnie whispered in return as her face matched the whiteness of the chalk Mr. Hardy had on sale.

"Mr. Hardy, run up to the apartment and get your sister."

The ladies listened to the footsteps ascending the back staircase. They heard the banging on the door, and the two sets of footsteps descending all laced with colorful expletives from Louey.

"Why are you pulling me down here, you damn old fool."

"Shh," the hardware man directed, "there are ladies in the store."

"What the hell am I, a flamenco-feathered fence post?"

She could have been a flamenco-feathered fence post the way she stood looking at the flock of women standing stiff-necked like they had no intention of buying anything.

Her long pink robe was adorned with matted pink feathers that matched her slippers. Half of her hair was wound tightly around rollers and half was dangling out of the rollers bouncing onto her feathers.

Bonnie ran to the woman, wondering if she was going to stand on one leg, which she didn't.

"Louey, we need you!"

"Huh?"

"Everyone, this is Louey, Mr. Hardy's sister."

The group began to buzz with, "Who?... Where'd she come from?... I didn't know his sister lived up there?"

"Sounds like you better spray some of that wasp killer, Elmer. I think there's a drove in here."

"Louey, we want you to judge these photographs for us, you and your brother! Will you both do it?"

Louey and Elmer looked at each other.

"What in the Sam Hill is she talking about?" Louey tried to whisper behind the back of her hand.

"They've got these pictures here of the whole area, in and around Lone Moon Creek. It's a contest and they want us to pick the best one."

"The three best ones, Mr. Hardy."

"What do you say Louey?"

"How the hell do I know what's best? I haven't been out of this building for thirty-eight years. I don't know what's out there."

Bonnie and Elmer knew she hadn't been out in the community since her husband died.

"Here, just take a look over here," Bonnie almost begged.

The ladies stepped back as the frenzied feathered woman swooped past.

Her aging eyes forced her to put her face close to the photographs. She bobbed up and down as her eyes went from one countryside photo to the next.

It wasn't much longer before passersby did double takes as they peered in to see the women sitting on cement bags and lawn mowers and piles of birdseed bags. After all, they had been on their feet for hours.

Danica and Annette went to the diner and came back with coffee and doughnuts. Everyone watched as Louey scrutinized each photo.

"Isn't this old Fred Logan's place?" she asked.

"Yup, sure is," Elmer answered her.

"And this, this has to be Bringman's pond, right?"

Louey was going back thirty-eight years! She hadn't seen those places in almost four decades.

"Elmer, where is this? I can't quite... Wait a minute! Holy crap! I know!" she howled and swung around making one roller hit the hardware entrepreneur in the face. He jumped back as she screamed, "My husband and I used to go there to pick blueberries!" And without missing a beat she belted out, "I found my thrill on blueberry—" She halted as she quickly looked at the two horrified ladies propped up against the roof sealer buckets.

Around and around she went.

Unfortunately, because of the long, long day, one by one, the ladies excused themselves, telling Bonnie that they must be going home. She understood.

Louey continued her journey. "Oh, the colors... How beautiful... I'll be damned; the bridge is still standing. By God, Feldman tore down his old ramshackle barn and built a new one. Nice! Look at the size of those trees in front of the school. I can't believe it! Somebody's house is missing; there's a gap here... Isn't this cute with the mother walking through the leaves with the carriage full of kids and puppies on their leashes... Ah, a nighttime picture of the harvest moon shining across the creek. What the hell is this?"

Her head bobbed back and forth much like a flamenco when she hollered out. "Elmer, is this the same manure spreader that Lincoln Zim abandoned in his field when he ran away with that hussy? Oops, sorry, ladies." She suddenly remembered where she was. "What are we supposed to be doing here?"

The three remaining ladies chorused in unison, "Judging!"

"Oh yeah," she uttered as she got her eyes closer to the subjects.

"Ooo, now this is pretty! Are these Lorenzo's grape arbors?"

"Yup," Elmer answered feeling proud that he knew the whereabouts of about every picture on display.

"Look how the sunshine is sailing through those curved arches making the grapes look like silhouettes! Many a night we sat in Lorenzo's back room and polished off a bottle or two. Best damn wine this side of the creek," she cackled.

"Well, piss and moan my britches off! Look what we have here." Louey didn't notice Bobby Jo and Rachel nearly rolling off the bales of insulation in fits of laughter.

"What are you looking at?" asked her brother.

"Here she is, standing right out in front of her house like she was the center of attention instead of the gorgeous foliage."

Elmer looked in close, "Ah yes, Isadora."

"Yeah, Isadora! The wretch who tried to steal my fiancé away. But did she do it? No blankity-blank-blank-blank way!"

Bobby Jo and Rachel were so giddy with exhaustion that the string of blankity-blanks accompanied by Louey's hip gyrations and roller rotations nearly put them on the floor.

"I'll tell you right now, I'm not giving that one any prize," Louey announced loud enough to send two pink feathers sailing to the dangling, sticky roll of flypaper.

"You really need to make your decisions now; I have to announce the winners in thirty minutes," Bonnie said. Her face as solemn as the picture of the cow on the tin of udder balm.

"Well, I know what I choose."

"Me too."

"All right, take them down. I'll wait for you by the counter."

"They are never going to agree," Bonnie whispered to the last of the club survivors. "We'll be here all night."

"Here they be," Louey proclaimed proudly as she plopped the three photographs on the old wooden counter.

"And yours?" she dismally asked Elmer.

"Same as hers."

"Halleluiah!" the three club ladies screamed and hugged.

"Thank you both so much. There will be a remuneration for your kind service."

"Hells-bells, we don't need any ammunition in this store, not after Simpson nearly blew a hole through my upstairs floor!"

"Girls! We have to run! Thank you so much."

"Good evening everyone and thank you for letting us announce our Autumn Photo Contest winners at this meeting. I know a lot of you have stopped at the hardware store to look at the entries. Weren't they all marvelous?"

Everyone clapped.

"We have been blessed to see every photo as we hung each for showing. I think I fell in love with our beautiful area all over again. What the camera saw was often nothing I had ever seen or even noticed before. We had shots of a chipmunk peeking out from under an oak leaf and a mouse dining on a pumpkin that had split open. There were kids in all adorable poses and involved in antics that took us back to our own childhoods. We saw the elderly fall in love with the season of their lifetimes—the autumn of their lives. The acute eye of the photographers captured mystery and mystique, haze and glaze, hues and dew—all right here in our God-given area. We have been so blessed.

"But you know what? We ran into someone late this afternoon who hasn't seen the countryside in thirty-eight years. You can't imagine what those photographs meant to her. She was enthralled with what she saw... And the things she could remember! Believe me, we were well entertained.

"So with no further ado, here are the winners! Third prize goes to: *Blueberry Hill* by Theodore Magin."

Bonnie looked over at Bobby Jo and Rachel. They both had their hands over their mouths undoubtedly stifling a laugh.

"Second prize is for *The Historic Bridge over Lone Moon Creek* by Sissy Deloise."

Bonnie waved the envelope high in the air trying to create some drama.

"And here is the first prize winner, *Mother and Babies and Puppies* by Marjory Lane!"

Everyone clapped.

A week later, Bonnie saw Louellen (Louey) and Elmer driving slowly down her road with Louey hanging out the window not wanting to miss a thing.

"Is Odelia coming today to help me with my scrapbooking?"

"Yes, she is!"

"Oh good, she is nice. I like her. Do you think she is an angel?"

Chapter Eighteen

Bored as a Board

"**I** think there is something wrong with them," Vince whispered to his wife as he turned out the light.

"They are just overwhelmed; give them time," Tricia whispered in return.

Vince stared at the black ceiling wondering how much time his two stepsons would need to return to the living. Their father had passed away three months ago, and they had come to live with their mother and him. Ten years ago, Vince had gotten Tricia back on her feet and had been more than gracious in taking in her two boys every weekend and now on a permanent basis.

On the weekend visits, Tricia had planned every moment of her sons' time; she wanted them to have wonderful and meaningful memories. She regretted her time of falling to addiction and vowed to make it up to them. They had no memory of anything wrong in their family and lived happily with their father and his wife during the week and with their mother and her husband, Vincent, on the weekends.

"We wish we could be with you boys over your winter vacation, but we have to work all week," Tricia said sadly as she said good-bye at their bedroom door. Judson grunted and Jay yawned as he turned toward the wall and pulled the blanket over his head. Two cars pulled out of the driveway, one taking Tricia and one taking Vincent to another workday.

The two teenaged boys stayed in bed to almost noon. It was basic hunger that brought them to the kitchen. Judson hung on the refrigerator door, staring at the covered bowls as Jay clicked the television to attention. It wasn't long before every bowl and platter was on the kitchen table with the lids removed. Cold fried chicken, macaroni salad, pickles, apples, Jell-O, and milk made an acceptable lunch. They put the dishes in the sink and lumbered to the living room television with fists full of cookies. The afternoon wore on with naps and video games and television.

"Hi, boys, I'm home!" Tricia hailed.

"Hey," they both droned.

"What did you do all day?" their mother asked with high expectations.

All she got was, "Nothing."

"Nothing? That's terrible."

"We're on vacation, remember?"

Vince came home with the same question and received the same answer.

"Come on, honey, let's start dinner."

Their eyes first went to the sink. "At least they put them in there today," Tricia murmured.

Vince raised his eyebrows, and his wife spoke quickly so as not to give him the chance to say something negative. "What would you like tonight, hon?"

"We'd really like you boys to eat with us at the table," Vince responded after the boys announced that they wanted to eat in front of the television.

"So, what do you fellows have planned for tomorrow?"

"Nothing."

"A lot of kids go to the ice skating pond. Wouldn't you like that?"

"Nah."

"In fact, Albert said they are looking for some young people to keep the ice swept and shoveled when necessary. That would give you guys a little spending money!"

"Nah."

"That's OK," Tricia interjected quickly, "you guys don't have to do anything. I've got some great things planned this weekend for us to do." Vince darted a look of disapproval her way.

"Tricia, now that the boys are with us full time, they have to learn what life is like on a normal, daily basis. They have to be a part of our family, playing and working. They can't just sit around and wait for us to entertain them like we used to when they visited only on weekends."

"But they are only thirteen and fourteen. What are they supposed to do when we are at work every day?"

"They should have jobs in the house and maybe for some of the neighbors and develop some skills to keep their minds active and creative! I think their minds go dormant except when you spend a fortune on entertaining them."

"Excuse me?" Tricia questioned as her dishwasher loading came to a dead stop. "What are you saying? Haven't you always enjoyed our weekends with the boys?"

"Yes, I enjoyed our activities, and I participated fully because I knew how much it meant to you. Truthfully, I did it more for your benefit than theirs. I was so proud of how you beat the addictions and turned your life around. You did more for your boys than most mothers do in a lifetime. Judson and Jay never knew your accomplishments, they just took it for granted that they were special and deserved all the attention you showered on them."

"I wanted to make up for the few bad years, and I'll never forgive myself for not being there for them. They deserve all I can do for them," Tricia said emphatically as she wrapped the dish towel around and around her hand.

"But, sweetheart, it's time we showed them how to live a normal life, or they'll grow up not having the foggiest notion of how real people live!"

For the first time, her shepherd, mentor, crutch, advisor, sponsor, advocate, friend, strength, shield, companion was not getting through to her. She stared into his eyes, not knowing him, not wanting his advice, not even loving the color of his eyes.

"I have worked out a plan that I'm going to present to them this evening," Vince said.

Tricia could not speak and only felt a strange feeling in her heart. Was she even breathing?

"Boys, I'd like you to consider something. Do you mind if I turn off the television?" Vince didn't wait for an answer. "We know that your lives have been turned upside down with the death of your Dad and then coming here to live with us," he continued. "We know that you miss Kathi, too; she was very good to you boys. But her life changed also. So basically you've gone from four adults in your lives to two. We love having you with us and feel we've given you the time that you have needed to acclimate yourselves. No major change is easy for anyone. With that said, as you are developing into young men, you'll need to start thinking and acting as responsible adults."

The boys looked at each other with facial expressions that said, "What's this dude talking about?"

"Tomorrow you'll get up when we do and have breakfast with us. Throughout the day there will be some chores that we'll call, everyday chores. Things like washing the dishes, making your beds, vacuuming, laundry, shoveling snow, helping Mrs. Johnson across the street with her sidewalks, taking out the garbage and walking to the store for things on your mom's shopping list. As time goes by, we are going to show you how to prepare some of the dishes for our dinner. How's it sound so far?"

"Us?" Judson responded.

"Us?" mimicked his brother.

"Them?" Tricia joined in the litany.

Vincent laughed. "Yes, you guys! Are you surprised by this?"

"I've heard other kids talk about jobs, but I never thought it would happen to me."

"Yeah."

"Just think," Vince continued, "this is the schedule for your vacation days. During school days, you'll get to do all this after school and in the evening!"

Two pairs of puppy dog eyes peered at their mother. Vince looked for her approval only to see sparks flaring from the slits underneath her furrowed brow.

"Gee, I bet you wish I was finished. But I'm on a roll, boys. Something is going to change about your schoolwork, also. I'm thoroughly ashamed of the report cards that were transferred from your last school. Both of you have *D*s in at least three subjects; that is not acceptable." Vince watched as they both slunk farther down on the couch. "Your mother and I are going to tutor you every single night until you can do your homework by yourselves."

"And the weekends?" Jay whined.

"Of course we'll have our fun weekends," Tricia tried to smile beyond her fury.

"Excuse me, dear, but those weekends will have to be earned. If we see that the boys are living up to their responsibilities and improving their grades, we will have nice weekends. I think that is enough for now. Tomorrow starts a new day. Does anyone have a comment before we work the crossword puzzle?"

"Good night, boys. See you for breakfast and, gee, I forgot to mention that your room has to be cleaned tomorrow, too."

Tricia waited in the kitchen for Vince. "What do you think you are doing?"

"I'm being the man of this family," Vince said.

"Since when did you become the boss over my children?" Tricia asked.

"Aren't they my children, too?"

"No, they are Jim's children and he is dead."

"Haven't I been their dad for nine, going on ten years?"

"Just weekends."

"Which I gladly gave up anything I wanted to do for the boys and for you."

"Well, why didn't you say there were things you would rather have done?"

"Because I love you."

"And I think I'm beginning to see the real you," Tricia shouted as she ran out of the room.

Vincent held his breath as he walked in the door after work.

Ah, the dishes were done, the kitchen was neat, and the boys' room looked much better.

"Nice," Vince exclaimed. "Very nice."

"Jud, Jay," he called, "where are you? What a great job you did today!"

The door flung open with gleeful boys and a smiling mother. "We're home!" Tricia called out happily. "We've got pizza for dinner!"

"Pizza?"

"I left work a little early, and when I saw what a good job the boys had done, I thought it might be nice if we treated them to a pizza."

"You're right, hon, this is a celebration!" Vince said.

"Wow, look at the snow coming down."

"Be prepared, boys. Mrs. Johnson will be calling for your help tomorrow and don't forget our driveway and sidewalks. Now, let's get into our crossword puzzle, and then your mother and I will show you how to get everything ready for a nice crockpot dinner for tomorrow night. If you are going to do all that shoveling, you'll be glad to have a hot, delicious dinner, and so will we. Right, hon?"

"Oh, sorry, I guess I'm dozing over here," Tricia said.

"That's OK. The boys and I will carry on."

Vince didn't see them rolling their eyes in disgust.

"Let me use that word in a sentence; maybe then you'll get the meaning of it," Vince said with concern. He was shocked at how little they knew about words and synonyms. Consequently, he was compelled to continue the crossword exercise each evening.

"Hold the carrot like this and swipe the peeler away from you. Good. The potatoes can be cut into chunks about this size. Now, since this part is all done, in the morning you'll just have to put in the ingredients that I circled and turn the pot to the directed setting. By dinnertime, we'll have a great meal!"

"Good job today, boys. I'll see you in the morning for breakfast."

"I see some hope, hon; the boys did a lot of chores today, and we had a good session in the kitchen. You see, they don't need to be bored out of their minds every day. They'll really be busy tomorrow with all the snow that's coming. I better set the clock an hour earlier so I can get up and shovel the end of the driveway so we can get to work."

Vince stomped the snow from his boots as he came in the backdoor of the kitchen.

"Oh! Did you do all the shoveling?" Judson asked hopefully.

"Sorry, buddy, I just cleared away the three-foot mountain of hard snow that the plow left across the edge of the driveway. The rest is all yours and your brother's."

"Gee, thanks," Jay mumbled.

"So long, fellows. See you tonight. Don't forget to get the crockpot going. We'll be slaving away making the ole do-re-mi so we can do something fun this weekend," Vince said.

"What was he jabbering about now? Do-re-mi? What do you suppose that was?"

"How do I know? He knows all those weird words, we don't."

"Hi, Mom, you're late."

"I know. I couldn't leave work until one o'clock today." She quickly cleared the breakfast table and started the dishes."

"Did you stop for our burgers and fries?"

"They're in the bag on the table," Tricia said.

As she ran down the hall to make the beds, she saw them juggling their food on their knees with their drinks and feet on the coffee table. They played a video game and they hooted and hollered over the scores.

"Did Mrs. Johnson call?"

"Yeah, about five times."

"You two go over there, and I'll start shoveling our place and don't tell any of this to Vincent."

A half hour passed when suddenly Tricia bolted upright from her shoveling and hollered across the street, "Did you turn on the crockpot?"

"Oops, forgot."

Tricia ran to the kitchen and dumped everything into the pot. She swung the dial to fast cooking.

"Wow, look at this!" Vince said, admiring the shoveling feat of his and his neighbor's domain. "Good job, boys," he called out as he entered the kitchen. There was enough of an aroma streaming from the dinner that he complimented that too. "Where is everybody?"

He walked into the living room to see his wife sound asleep on the couch, Jay sleeping in the recliner, and Judson stretched across the area rug, snoring. Vince smiled. *I guess they need a little nap before dinner*, he thought. *They've all worked hard today.*

"Vince, it's eight o'clock. Why didn't you wake us for dinner?" Tricia asked.

"There must be something wrong with our crockpot; the meat and vegetables were nowhere near done."

"Um, I realized that, too, so I turned it right up when I got home from work."

"Everything is done now. Wake the boys and we'll have a feast."

"This is delicious, boys. Thank you for a nice dinner and guess what? We're getting more snow tonight!"

It was not the younger ones who moaned, "Oh no!" It was Tricia.

"Honey, you don't have to worry about it, we've got it covered! Right, men?"

"Yeah, right," the brothers answered as their faces drooped nearer to the plates.

"By the way, do you have any school assignments to do over the vacation?"

The silence was broken by the same voice that asked the question. "Well?"

"Just to write a short essay on what we did over vacation."

"Yeah, me too."

"I'm sure you can squeeze that into your work schedule. Better get it started tomorrow so you'll have time to do a good job. We've got to get those grades up, right?"

"How can you expect those boys to do all that work and do school work, too?" Tricia said in an angry whisper.

"You're kidding of course!" Vince laughed as he helped his wife put the dishes in the cupboard.

"No, I'm not kidding. You're asking way too much of them." She continued to whisper like the north wind.

"Tricia, I think you've lost track of reality. I'm sorry, that Jim and Kathi ended up with the boys during the week and we just got them on the weekends, but that's the way it was and we can't go back and change it. Now is our chance, though. We have full custody these days, and we have to play catch-up to get Jud and Jay to know what normal is."

"Just what is normal?" Tricia responded, no longer whispering.

Now it was Vince who was saying "Shh" as he glanced toward the living room.

"I suppose you are blaming me for losing custody because I had a problem. You think it's my fault for having boys who aren't normal. Right?"

"Tricia, stop. You know I've always supported you and helped you give the boys their wonderful weekends. I'm just saying—"

"Yeah, you're just saying. You're saying that you were my savior. That I wouldn't be anything without you and now… Now you want to save my boys. Well, I don't appreciate it one bit."

Tricia marched past her sons and slammed the bedroom door. Vince stayed in the kitchen, and the boys continued on with their video game.

Snow again. Tricia rushed home early from work and shook the boys awake. "Why haven't you been shoveling?"

"We were waiting for you"

"Ah, that's sweet," she said, fawning.

"Did you pick us up something to eat?"

"Yes, chicken fingers."

"You're the best."

"I'll get the laundry started and do the vacuuming while you go over across the street."

"I'm going to tell that old lady to stop calling the house; she woke me up three times."

"Is there any dinner tonight?" Vince asked.

"I am just too tired to cook. Why don't you cook something?"

"OK. I'm starting to worry about you, Tricia. You're looking so tired lately."

"Just let me rest before dinner."

"Come on, boys. I could use your help. Plus you can tell me how your papers for school are coming along."

"I've been pulling it together in my head," Judson fabricated.

"Yeah, me too," Jay added.

"You guys cut up the vegetables for the tossed salad. I'll brown the hamburger meat for the spaghetti sauce and put on the water to boil the pasta. So what are you going to include in your essays?"

"Just junk like how we have to work around the house and shovel snow."

"Same here."

"There'll be some fun things, too! Your mother has been planning things for two months!"

"Really?"

"Why don't you start writing after dinner, that way I'll have a chance to help you if you need it."

"Sure" and "yeah" came with dismal acceptance.

"No, I'm not hungry. I'm going to bed," Tricia murmured as she shuffled down the hallway. Vince shook his head in silence.

"I'll do the dishes while you both sit at the kitchen table and start your essays," Vince directed.

"There! All done. Let's see what you've written! Jay, there's nothing on the paper!"

"I'm thinking," Jay replied.

"I see something on Jud's paper. Let me see what you have."

sonetimeswegotta getuperlyand shovlsno

"What on earth is this?" Vincent asked. "What does it say?"

"Sometimes we gotta get up early and shovel snow," Judson answered.

"Oh! Does your teacher let you use the computer?"

"Yeah."

"I think that might be a good idea. OK type it. Do you know what those red squiggly lines mean?" Vince asked.

"No, do they mean something?"

"Yes, the computer is telling you there is something wrong, such as a misspelled word. OK, type the word *sometimes* again. Did you see how the computer changed your lowercase 's' to a capital letter?"

"I did see that. Why did it do that?"

"Because you are supposed to start a sentence with a capital letter. Now you see how the red line is still under your first word? That means it is misspelled."

"Well, I don't know how to spell it."

"The computer does. Click on 'Review' and then 'Spelling and Grammar.' There is a list of words. Click on the first word and 'Change.' See if the red line goes away."

"It did!" Judson declared with his first inflection of enthusiasm.

"The computer is not going to like it if you don't leave a space between your words," Vince said.

"Picky, picky." He fell back into his ordinary bleakness.

"Keep going and see how far you get with that sentence."

An hour later, the sentence was perfect!

"Fantastic!" exalted Vince. "I'll save this for you, and we'll continue tomorrow night. Jay, are you ready to begin?"

"What's going on out here?" Tricia mumbled as she shuffled through the kitchen. She didn't wait for an answer; she swung open the refrigerator, grabbed a fork, and started eating the spaghetti out of the bowl.

"Do you want me to heat that for you?" Vince asked.

"No, I'm starving. I don't know why you didn't call me for dinner."

"OK, Jay, why don't you start on the computer? Write your first sentence. Do you know why some of your words are underlined in red?"

"I heard what you said to Judson," Jay said.

"Good for you, Jay! That's how we learn; we listen to others!"

"Yeah, you listen to Mr. Know-It-All. He'll go blah-blah-blah all night long. Well, you don't have to listen to him anymore because you have me and... ooh, I don't feel so good... uh, I'm going to be sick."

"You boys go to your room. I'll take care of your mother."

"What happened last night?" Tricia asked her husband.

"You were very sick. I know it wasn't the spaghetti; we all had that for dinner."

"Spaghetti? I had spaghetti?"

"Good-bye, boys. See you tonight. Do your chores," Vince called out as he drove away.

Tricia whispered to her sons, "I'll be back in ten minutes. I called in sick today. Don't tell Vince."

The three of them slept until noon.

"What's to eat?"

"Isn't there spaghetti?"

"Not after you got sick in it!"

"Oh, sorry."

"Why don't we go out for lunch?"

"Mom, you're the best!"

"I am, aren't I? You guys wait in the car. I'll be right there," Tricia said.

"Mom, you are so funny! When you said that to the waitress, I thought she was going to kill you."

"And when you sent that coaster flying through the restaurant and hit a man in the back of the head, I thought we were going to get thrown out of there."

"But nobody knew it was me, did they? Your mother knows how to have fun, doesn't she?"

"Mom, you better slow down. Mom, please."

"Where's your sense of adventure?" Tricia said.

"Yeah, Jay, don't be such a baby."

"Whoa, I almost missed our street. OK guys, we're home, and I declare that this is our day off—no work today!"

"All right!" the two boys shouted and plunked down in front of the TV.

"I'm exhausted. I'm going in for a nap."

"Tricia, are you sick again?" Vince said quietly as he placed his hand on her shoulder.

"Oh, I'm afraid so," she said weakly.

"The boys must have it too. They are sound asleep in the living room."

"Oh no. Could you make us a light supper?"

"Sure."

"Were you guys sick all day?" Vince asked.

"Mostly."

"Tomorrow is Saturday. Are you going to be well enough to go on our trip?"

"We think so," Judson moaned as he winked at his brother.

"This is how a family should act," Tricia whispered into Vince's ear as she kissed his cheek. "This is how I want our boys to remember us."

Vince watched the boys go from game to game as lights flashed and whistles blew. The music shook the huge indoor arena with the hundreds of vacationing kids running wild with the freedom of no school.

"Well," Vince said slowly, knowing she wasn't going to like what he was about to say, "this is fine for a day, but the rest of the days have to be devoted to responsibilities and hard work. After that, there's always time for fun."

"Ugh," she erupted, as she pulled her hand out of his, "you always have to ruin everything!"

"I'm not trying to ruin anything, Tricia. I'm looking ahead so that the boys will have a successful future!"

"Let the future take care of itself. This is the time for the kids to have fun."

"Hey, Mom, can we have some more money? We found some new games!"

"Sure. Oops, I forgot. I didn't get my paycheck this week. Vince, give them some money."

"Ten dollars each and that's it," Vince said.

It wasn't long before they were back asking for more money. "Sorry, boys. That was it. But you can walk around and watch the others or we can go outside and go ice-skating. That's free."

"No way," Judson snarled as he yanked his brother away.

"Now you've done it. You've ruined their day!" Tricia shouted above the raucous music. "Stay here. I'm going to the lady's room."

Vince slumped onto a bleacher seat. "Not a good day?" a voice asked.

He turned to see a man about his age bouncing a toddler on his knee. Vince smiled to be polite, but also because he saw understanding in the man's eyes.

"Having a hard time with my two stepsons and their mother. Now that she has full custody, I'm too strict and I have rules and on and on and on. Sorry, I don't know why I'm telling you all this."

"That's OK. Everybody needs someone who will listen to them occasionally."

Vincent had a tremendous longing to sit and talk with the man, maybe for the rest of the afternoon. And maybe he would have if a loud raucous hadn't lured his attention to someone on the floor striking another woman with her purse. They were both screaming at each other.

Vincent suddenly bounded from the bleacher and ran to Tricia. He pulled her away from the red-faced woman and wouldn't allow the two to merge again.

"She tried to steal my purse; she was going to take it!" the stranger screamed as people started to clap and yell, "Cat fight, cat fight."

"Drop dead, you hag; you don't know what you're talking about," Tricia shouted, making sure she cuddled close to her husband to garner his sympathy.

"Tricia, come on, we're getting out of here," Vince commanded as he ushered her to the door.

"Mom, was that you out there?"

"Pretty cool, Mom; you could have creamed her!" Judson laughed.

"I'm going to bed," Tricia announced.

"Come on, boys, we have to make dinner," Vince said.

"We don't work on Saturday!"

"You do now," Vince proclaimed assertively, "and bring the laptop."

"Jay, you go to your essay first. Jud, slice this cabbage very, very thin for coleslaw. Read what you have so far while I mix up the ranch burgers."

"I don't have anything yet. Remember Mom got sick and we had to leave the kitchen."

"Oh yes, that's right. OK, what is your first sentence going to be?"

"On my vacation I watched my mother beat up another woman."

Judson laughed and sliced his finger. Blood spurt over the cabbage.

"Get over to the sink!" Vince ordered as he ran to hold Judson's hand under cold water. "Jay, run for the band aides and bring a wash cloth."

"Oh!" Tricia said as she came to the kitchen. "Are you putting on a play? Jay said there was blood all over the kitchen. I love to watch plays," she droned. "I'll sit in the front row so I can see everything. Ah, blood on the cabbage, nice touch. And I see you are pretending to be bleeding in the sink. Was it a murder or an intruder? I love murder mysteries!"

Jay ran in with the box of band aides and the washcloth.

"There's my little actor." Tricia clapped as the three looked at each other perplexed.

"Ma, what's the matter with you?"

"Why nothing my little southern julep," she drawled as she left the kitchen telling them she would be in the big house."

Vince stopped the bleeding and bandaged the wound. "There. I think we'll change the menu."

"Wow!" Jay said excitedly, I have another exciting thing to put into my essay: my brother was almost murdered on the plantation.

"Jud, would you go in and check on your mother. I'll make dinner."

"She's sleeping," Jud reported when he returned to the kitchen.

"OK, sit with your brother and help him figure out why he's getting those red squiggle lines."

"I've got blue squiggles, too!" Jay announced joyfully.

"Don't you guys have computer classes in school?"

"Yeah, but in our old school we just sat and played games."

"You've got a lot of catching up to do; maybe I could get you a tutor."

The boys faced each other and made faces at the thought.

"Tricia, what are you doing? It's three o'clock in the morning."

"I am wide awake and I'm starving. I'm eating this meatloaf."

"Do you remember what happened last night?" Vince asked.

"Of course I remember. We went to the movies."

"Do you want me to stay up with you?"

"No, I'm going to watch a movie. Good night."

"Good night."

But it wasn't a good night for Vince. He was terrified. He remembered twelve years ago when Tricia was addicted. Had she started using again?

"OK boys, you're off to school and we are off to work. Start going through the list as soon as you get home and that will help out a lot. Have a good day everybody."

"Mom, you're home?"

"I left work at two so I could start the list. I can't believe he'd make you guys do all that work," she said.

"It's not that much—" Jay started to say when Jud coughed loudly.

"Thanks, Mom. We have a lot of homework anyway. Do you mind if we play video games until Vince get home?"

"Of course not; you've had a hard day. I'll start dinner."

"You're the best, Mom."

"I know," she laughed.

"Wow, this is impressive!" Vince smiled as he looked through the house and smelled the aroma coming from the kitchen. "You guys are remarkable. Aren't they Tricia?"

"They sure are!"

"Did you hand in your essays?"

"I did!" Jay said proudly. "And the teacher said it was the most creative essay of all."

"I can understand that!" Vince laughed. "How about you, Jud?"

"My teacher said she'd give me one more day to turn it in or I'd get an *F*."

"How dare she say that to my son? I'm going in there tomorrow and set her straight," Tricia said.

"Mom, no!" Jud pleaded.

"I'll help you tonight. Now do you see why you have to be responsible?" Vince asked.

"Yes, I guess."

"Tricia, have you been depositing your checks?"

"Why?"

"Because we have to pay the bills, and there isn't enough money in our account."

"I'll put them in tomorrow."

"Maybe you'd better sign up for direct deposit."

"Are you saying I'm not responsible? I'm not a kid you can boss around. I'm surprised the boys take it like they do. They'll probably run away from home someday because of you."

"I can't believe you're saying that. I'm going to bed."

Vince heard her car leave the driveway and return in thirty minutes. "Oh no," he muttered as he pushed his face into the pillow.

"Vince, guess what? My English teacher said I'm doing much better!" Jay said during dinner.

"That's terrific! We're proud of you!"

"Where is Mom?"

"I'm not sure, maybe she had to work late."

"And Judson, I talked to the guidance counselor at school, and she recommended a nice young lady to be a mentor to you. What do you think?"

"A nice, young lady?" Jud said.

"Ooo, a nice, young lady," snickered Jay.

"Shut up, creep."

"OK, OK, settle down. Will you give it a try?"

"Do I really need a mentor?"

"Yes, you do, Judson. If you fail your grade, you are going to be in the same class as your brother."

And that rang a bell with Jud.

"So, Jay, the after school list won't be as long because Jud will have to stay in school until five."

"Thanks, Vince."

"You're welcome. It's only fair."

"Why are you vacuuming, Jay?" Tricia asked.

"Because it's on the list."

"That doesn't mean you have to do it. I'm home; I'll do it."

"No, I want to help out," Jay said.

"Where's your brother?"

"He's at school with his mentor."

"With his mentor? When did this happen?"

"Just today."

"We'll see about that!"

Jay heard the car roar up the street. *Oh no. I hope she doesn't beat up the nice, young mentor.*

Jay and Jud peeled the potatoes while Vince got the pork chops ready for baking.

"So, tell us, how did the mentoring session go?" Vince said.

Vince was sure he saw Judson blush. "It went really well. She is really smart, but she is nice, too. She doesn't laugh at me when I don't know something."

"Good! I thought about you all day and hoped it would be successful."

"What did Mom say when she went in?" Jay asked.

"Mom didn't come in," Judson said.

"Why do you think she did?" Vince asked.

"She told me she was going to 'see about that,'" Jay said.

"Tricia, it's eleven o'clock. Where have you been?"

"Out with my friends. I have friends, you know."

"Don't you think you should be here with us?" Vince asked.

"Why should I be? You've got everything under control. You even go behind my back and get my son a mentor because you don't think he's smart enough. You think you're smarter than everybody else. Well, you're not, you're…"

And that was all she said. Tricia had passed out across the bed.

"I think I better call your mother's boss this morning and let him know she won't be in; she'll have to take a sick day. Get your backpacks loaded up."

"Oh? No, I didn't know that," Vince said into the phone.

"What's the matter?"

"Your mother doesn't work there anymore."

"Why are you here?" Tricia asked.

"I wanted to talk with you without the boys."

"Oh goody. Here comes the lecture."

"Tricia, what's happening? You have been clean for over ten years."

"And it hasn't been any fun. I'm ready for some *fun*."

"But you had it conquered."

"It can never be *conquered*," Tricia said. "It always has you by the throat."

"Haven't we had a good life?"

"It used to be good until you decided to change my boys. *My* boys."

"Sweetheart, we're learning how to be a family. We didn't have to be so rigorous when they only lived with us on weekends."

"You just know everything, don't you?"

"We need to get into counseling, honey. We need help."

"Why don't you just say it? I need help. Right? And go back to work. One of us has to earn a living."

"Why did you quit your job?" Vince asked.

"I didn't quit; they fired me!"

"Why?"

"They didn't like me taking off early every day."

"Early? For what?"

"I came home to do those stupid jobs that were on the list," Tricia said.

"They weren't for you, they were for the boys!"

"My boys aren't slaves."

"No, they're not; they are a part of this family."

"Where's Mom?"

"She's out, but I'll help you with the jobs until Jud gets home," Vince said.

"They're all done! I started as soon as I got home from school!"

"Wow! You're the man!"

"Can I do my homework on the laptop while you're starting dinner?" Jay asked.

"You sure can."

"In the kitchen, by you?"

"You sure can."

"Hi, buddy, how was the mentoring?"

"Really good. Odelia knows everything," Judson replied.

"Odelia?" Jay giggled.

"Everyone calls her Odie for short. She wanted to know if I could go to her youth group on Friday night."

"Judson has a date," Jay sang.

"It's not a date, dummy; it's a group for kids."

"Where is it going to be held?" Vince asked.

"Over at St. Andrew's Parish Center."

"St. Andrew's?" Vince questioned, even though he heard clearly.

"Yeah, can I?"

"I don't see why not. You need to associate with other kids."

Jay stopped his typing. "Thanks a lot! What am I? Chopped suey?"

"Vince, can you drive me over there?" Judson asked.

"Sure."

Vince sat in the car looking up at St. Andrew's steeple. He knew the church well. It was his home away from home when he was growing up.

"Vincent! Is that you in there?"

Vince jumped out of the car and shook hands with Fr. Booth.

"Hello, Father. How are you?"

"I am fine. How are you? And Tricia?"

"Well, I'm afraid all of your hard work is unraveling."

"You mean?

"Yes, Tricia is going back to her old ways," Vince said.

"Oh no. What can I do?"

"Ever since her two boys moved in with us, she hates me."

"Do you think you can get her to come in and talk?"

"I don't know, but maybe Judson can! I just dropped him off. He's a guest of Odelia."

"Ah, Odelia! That girl can work miracles!"

"That's what we need—a miracle!"

"Hi, Mom."

"Where have you been?"

"Over at St. Andrew's youth group."

"St. Andrew's! I forbid you to ever to go there again. Do you hear me?"

"Mom," Judson whined as Tricia's bedroom door slammed in his face.

"Vince! Why did she say that?"

"I'm not sure. I'll try to find out later. Right now, let's go to the kitchen for hot chocolate and you can tell us what you did at the group."

"Well, they did some weird things and some interesting things," Judson said.

"Start with the weird things." Jay laughed as he rubbed his hands together.

"They prayed to God."

"What's weird about that?" Vince asked as he stirred in the chocolate.

"Who is God?"

Vince went numb or maybe he was paralyzed or maybe...

"Oh no," he muttered as he broke out into a cold sweat, "you don't know, do you? You were with us every weekend, every Sunday—the day of the Lord. We did this to you." Vince slumped into a chair.

"Vince, do you want me to take over the stirring?" Jay asked timidly, not knowing what to make of Vince's near collapse.

"I guess you better. I just had an awful shock."

"I don't get it. What shock?" Jay questioned and stirred.

"Odelia is a miracle worker! Father Booth was right; if it wasn't for her, my eyes might not have been opened."

"Marshmallows?"

"Yes."

"Yes."

"Your mother and I used to talk about taking you guys to church on Sunday, but she said she wanted to take you to *fun* places, not church. And I went along with her. Wow, how could I have been so off base?"

"Why? What do you learn at church?" Judson asked.

"First tell us about the other stuff you did at the youth group."

"We talked about bullying and how we can defend the kids who are picked on. Then we did some role-playing; that was fun. Then we heard about some of the newest movies and which ones were objectionable for kids our age. Then we had refreshments. I loved that!"

Jay and Vince laughed.

"Then we copied down some addresses for soldiers that we can write to. And that's about it. Can I go next week?"

"I'll talk to your mother about... What was that?"

The three ran from the kitchen to see why they heard a crash. Tricia was lying on the floor with the lamp and the end table tipped over beside her. She wasn't moving.

"Tricia!"

"Mom, Mom!"

She was barely breathing. "Judson, call 911." Vince rubbed her hands and grabbed a blanket to cover her. "Jay, grab that pillow."

"We'll follow you in the car," Vince told the ambulance workers.

"Vince, what happened to her?"

"Let's wait to see what the doctor says."

"Father Booth, what are you doing here?" Vince said.

"I was called in for one of my parishioners. What are you doing here?"

"It's Tricia, and we haven't heard yet. Oh, Father this is Jay and—"

"Judson!" Father Booth extended his hand. "You were just at the youth group."

"Yes, with Odelia."

Father Booth and Vince looked at each other as they both thought the same thing: the miracle worker.

"Are you the husband?" a doctor asked.

"Yes, sir."

"Could I talk with you over there?"

"Go ahead," Father Booth said, "I'll stay here with the boys."

"Mr. Griffith, your wife almost died tonight."

"Oh dear God," Vince gasped. "What was it?"

"A drug overdose."

"Oh no. Do you think she was trying to end her life?"

"I don't know, but she's in critical condition. This is serious."

"Vince, what did the doctor say. Is she going to be all right?" Jud and Jay both wanted to know.

"It was a drug overdose."

"Our mother takes drugs? No way."

"That can't be true; bad people take drugs, not mothers."

"Have you noticed how erratic her behavior has been lately? She hasn't acted like that in years."

"You mean she did this before?"

"A long time ago when you were very small."

"Is that why we lived with Dad and not her?"

"Yes."

"But she must have beat it; she has been fine until lately."

"She worked very, very hard to get away from her habit; she wanted to be a good mother to you boys."

"What got her going again?" Jay asked.

Vince looked at Father Booth and felt like he was going to his first confession after years of being away. "I'm afraid it was my fault. I felt if we were to become a real family, we had to get away from that weekend-fun mode and start having rules and responsibilities."

"You did this to her?" Jay snapped.

"Jay, all children need to do well in school and help around the house and eat dinner as a family," Vince tried to explain.

"He's right, Jay," Father Booth interceded. "Vince only wanted the best for your futures; he wanted you both to grow up to be fine young men."

"He's right, little bro. Vince only wanted the best for us. I think Mom was scared of change and scared that we wouldn't like her if she gave us rules," Judson said.

"Thank you, Jud, and thank you, Father," Vince uttered as he hugged Jay.

The four men stood as stiff as the marble statues just inside the door of St. Andrew's as they watched a flurry of nurses and doctors push some sort of machines into where Tricia lay—dying?

"Father Booth, call Odelia! Tell her we need her at the hospital right now," Judson begged as he hung on to the pastor's arm.

"Jud, you can't expect—" Vince attempted to say.

"I will, Jud. I know her mother and father will bring her here."

"Vince, pray!" Judson begged his stepfather. "You know how to pray. Do it please."

Vince went right down on his knees with the boys following suit. He folded his hands; they folded their hands. He said, "Dear God," and they said, "Dear God."

Vince said, "Please help Tricia."

The boys said, "Please help Mom. Please let her live; please let her live."

The praying went on and on mostly led by Vince but sometimes led by one of the boys. Vince didn't think they even realized they were sometimes leading. It didn't matter because their hearts and souls were totally immersed.

Just as Odelia knelt with them, the paralyzing fright drained from their muscles. They were cognizant of relief, some sort of relief. As she took over the praying, they looked at her face. Her eyes were closed, her face was lifted upward, and her words were real.

"How long do you think Mom will have to stay at that rehab place?" Judson asked as he chopped the celery.

"It's too early to know yet," Vince said slowly as he searched through the drawer looking for the meat thermometer.

Jay looked up from his bread cubing. "I can't wait until we can go and visit her."

"Me too."

"Me three."

"Grandma, remember our New Year's reso-lotion? We better get busy."

"You mean resolution, and yes, Marjory, it's time we sat and wrote our cards to the people in the home; they don't have much to think about as they sit there day after day."

ᴄᴏᴘChapter Nineteen

Morning Snow

"Now she's all set for the morning," the director of nursing told the young nurse's aides. "Isabelle likes to sit in the quiet room, but remember to always put her in the lounge chair that faces the window; she likes to look out."

And there sat Isabelle, called Izzy, on various occasions.

Isabelle saw unruly snowflakes skitter past the window. She felt the cold windowpane on her forehead as she puffed short hot breaths, making mysterious movable clouds on the pane.

"Isabelle, stop, I don't want to see fingerprints on that window. Spring cleaning won't come for three months you know."

Well, she didn't know exactly, but she wasn't making any pictures in the cloud; she remembered her mother's warning the last time.

"No, I'm not letting you go to school today either; it's treacherous out there, and your father is not going to hitch up the horses; it's not fit for man nor beast."

"Run Isabelle, run, the beast is coming to get you!"

The little girl could feel the hot prickly hay sticking to her sweaty body. She watched the thick barn boots plod past on the haymow floor. She wondered what kind of tree was brought out of the woods to make such wide boards. The boots stopped. Isabelle didn't breathe.

"Keep stirring, Isabelle, or it's going to burn. Stir, stir, stir around and around. Me too, Izzy, I love to do Ring around a Rosie with you. We'll be best friends forever, right, Izzy? Now look what you've done. I'll have to throw all this milk out, and we'll have to start over."

"One, two, three—go! You cheated. You started before I said go. No I didn't. Yes, you did. I'm telling Ma."

"Today we're going to tell a story, class. I won't be reading to you and you won't be reading! We'll just be plain telling! Won't that be fun? Isabelle, would you like to start?"

"Once upon a time…"

"Class! Stop laughing! She has every right to start her story like that if she chooses."

"Their rights have been violated. Matthias, don't go into town and join that group; there's going to be trouble. I think they set that fire over at Wilber's farm."

"Jenny, your hair is so pretty. I wish my hair was like yours. Isabelle! Pull that hair back. It's going to catch fire. And stir without stopping this time."

"I can teach you a new game, Jenny. Wanna do London Bridge?"

"It wasn't my fault, Ma. I told her not to get so close to the edge. Stop crying, Isabelle, you're only wet, not dead. Poor girl, getting soaked on her wedding day. Too bad we had to have a storm. Stay here in the haymow until the storm is over, and then you can run to the house."

"Pa, don't fall asleep, I want to count the big boards again. I want to learn how to count."

"Three, two, one—run. Ha, ha, fooled you. I won."

"We have rules in school and rules are not to be broken, right class?"

"I don't know, Isabelle, he should be home by now. Go to sleep, it's late. This is adult business; it's not for children. Wilber's son died in the fire?"

"And don't come back in until this bucket is full. Now get out there and pick, pick, pick."

"Ouch, ouch, ouch these briars hurt. My hair! It's tangled in the blackberry bushes."

"Izzy's a boy; Izzy's a boy! To the corner with you, mister. Girls with short hair are lovely, dear. Can I brush your hair for you, Jenny? Why isn't Pa home yet?"

"Pray, Isabelle, pray."

"I'm looking for you, God."

"We're taking all this to Wilbur's house and don't ask questions; just help me carry..."

"And I'll carry you over the threshold and love you forever. Jenny wanted forever, too, but she moved away. The train was a beast; it snorted and snarled and took her away. Pa came home, he always did. Milk and sugar on a bowl of blackberries—heaven with Pa."

He went off to the army and Isabelle needed to catch the horses. Where did they go? They weren't heading for school, were they?

"Rub them down good, they're soaked with sweat. That snort wasn't from the train with Jenny. She could see down into the barn through a space between the wide boards. Pa and Wilbur were talking justice and rights."

"Just checking on you, Isabelle. Do you need anything?"

"No, dear, I'm fine."

"Are you watching the snow?"

"Yes, I guess I am."

"It's been quite a winter."

"Yes, quite a winter."

"Well, don't forget that your bell is right here by your side. If you need anything, you just ring."

"Yes, I'll just ring."

"Grab hold of that rope; with a blizzard like this, you'll never find your way to the house. Don't you let go."

"People have rights; if they don't want to be roped to the horse, they don't have to be. If they want to jump off the train, they can."

"Late again, Isabelle? The bell rang two minutes ago. Go to the office and tell the principal why you were late."

"Pa is going to buy an automobile? A horse can go faster than an automobile. No it can't. Yes it can. No it..."

"Why did your cats spill the milk bowl again? They don't give Pa much money for the milk and your cats are wasting it. Shame, shame, shame."

"You can choose if you want to be the cow or the horse or the cat."

"There is a change in the performance, Jenny will play the cat and the horse because poor Isabelle has fallen and broken her wrist."

"Ouch, ouch, ouch these boots are too tight. You let go of the rope after I told you not to. Stop that crying. You're frozen; you're not dead. Wait until I can carry those heavy baskets out to the clothesline; in your condition, you don't need to be lifting."

"Yes, I baptized the baby myself."

"The army wanted men, real men—a war?"

"What fun, being in town on a Saturday night. That's barbed wire; don't ride your bicycle down that way. Listen to the band. Look whose holding hands."

"An old lady could peel apples faster than you. Peel, now spell the other kind of peel."

"Why haven't you made your book cover for your spelling book yet?"

"Are you ladies talking about fires?"

"God, is that little Wilbur boy with you? The horses got up into the haymow and one has fallen through."

"Oh dear Lord. Stir those onions, they're burning."

"The baby and I will ride in the backseat, and you go slowly. Yes, I want real candles on the Christmas tree."

"But I didn't mean to let go of the rope."

"Clap, clap, clap everyone."

"Take the carrots to the root cellar and bring up more canning jars."

"Don't look over at that group of men."

"The Wilbur's lawyer is coming in on the train."

"The blackberries are grandioso this year. Did you know that you can sell them for twenty-five cents a quart at the restaurant down in Lone Moon Creek? She'll take all you can pick to make pies."

"It's a good thing your head was sticking out above the snow or you would have been dead. Your father had to stop the milking to search for you. He never finished up until eleven o'clock that night."

"Did you dance? Did anyone ask you?"

"The squirrels worked all day transporting those acorns."

"Isabelle, here is your midmorning snack. Doesn't this pudding look delicious?"

"Do you have any blackberries I could stir in?" Isabelle asked.

"Oh, Isabelle, you are so funny. This isn't the time of year for blackberries!"

"Didn't we preserve some to be eaten in the winter?"

"Um, I'm afraid we don't have any, Isabelle."

"Well, that's too bad; we'll do better next year."

"Work, work, work or we'll have nothing for the winter. Is that what you want—nothing?"

"This calf can be yours."

"Oh no, the school bell is ringing."

"The cover tore; it was an accident, teacher."

"That's all right, you can make another one."

"Izzy is in trouble."

"No, I'm not."

"Yes you are."

"No..."

"Why do you have to move away, Jenny?"

"We'll write and we'll use our best penmanship."

"Will that lawyer sit in the same seat on the train where Jenny sat?"

"Why is the creek water so cold when it's hot outside?"

"A new child! This one I can hold forever!"

"Duck down, Izzy, duck down so he doesn't see you."

"Yes, you may pedal to the neighbors but stay over to the side of the road."

"There's a disease going through everyone's barn. Matthias, go into town and talk with the men to find out what's going on."

"Don't be lazy; pull every bit of that silky hair off the ears of corn. Do you want to open a jar next winter and see that stuff floating around?"

"The veterinarian is coming; it's serious."

"That is beautiful, Ma."

"Your father gave it to me on our wedding day."

"How many hundreds of acorns do they need?"

"Pull all of those buckets out of the shed; it won't be long before we can tap the maple trees."

"Three cows dead and more sick."

"Put that back in my jewelry box."

"Ski down the haymow hill, I dare you. See, you can't do it."

"Yes I can."

"Oh no, now it's your wrist."

"Pray, Isabelle, pray. It's serious."

"You'll give your lives to each other forever and ever and ever."

"Jenny's coming for my wedding!"

"Stop crying, Isabelle. It's all part of nature. Calves are born and some calves die."

"Of course you'll graduate, stop being such a worrywart. Worrywart, worrywart, Izzy is a worrywart."

"Why don't we have enough money to pay Mr. Jonberg?"

"You were supposed to scald the tomatoes, not yourself. You'll be all right, you're not dead."

"Take little stitches, Isabelle. That looks like a two-year-old did it."

"Ma, you won the blue ribbon at the fair! Jenny had the bluest of eyes and the most beautiful hair. And God bless the twins!"

"We'll ride into town and go to the picture show."

"Lone Moon Creek has a few new businesses."

"Time to go into the dining room for lunch, Isabelle."

"Oh already?"

"Yes, my dear, it's twelve o'clock."

"Land of mercy, the time flew by."

"You always say that. What makes the time fly by?"

"I don't really know! It just does."

"Guess what? There's going to be strawberries for dessert!"

"Just picked strawberries?"

"Well, I don't know about that, but they're going to be delicious."

"OK, so we're all in consensus?" asked the social worker at the afternoon meeting.

"We're all for it," piped in the activity director.

"Of course we can try it, but senior citizens don't like to be busy just because we think they should be," the nursing director interjected.

"I'm tired of walking by and seeing people staring out the window or dozing in their chairs; they should be keeping their minds active. What are they thinking of as they sit there? Probably nothing," the social worker insisted. "Five times this morning I walked past the quiet room and there sat poor Isabelle staring out at the snow. All morning she did that. We're forcing her mind to become lethargic at best."

"WHAT ARE SUPERSTITIONS?"

"THEY'RE LIKE WHEN YOU SPILL THE SALT AND I TELL YOU TO THROW SOME OVER YOUR LEFT SHOULDER OR YOU'LL HAVE BAD LUCK."

"THEY'RE PRETTY FUNNY, AREN'T THEY?"

"SOMETIMES."

Chapter Twenty
THE LAST WISH

"Well, well, well, what's this?" Florence said aloud as she opened the paper. "Our county has gotten a grant for senior citizens to fulfill their lifelong wishes."

"What wishes?" Elroy peered upward from his toast.

"I don't know. Just something that they've always wanted to do and never did."

"I've got a ton of things like that," Elroy snorted.

"Not the stupid little things that have been on your honey-do list for fifteen years—but something big."

"Mmm, something big," Elroy reiterated as he licked the jelly from his knife. "Something big."

Florence continued reading. "The school is going to be open for six months in the evenings and Saturdays. Mentors and teachers will be available as needed. Call the school to apply."

Again Elroy mumbled, "Something big."

"I wish I could give you some more vocabulary," Florence snapped at her husband as she snatched his dishes from the table.

"Never you mind my vocabulary," Elroy retaliated as he pushed his chair away from the table. "I just might get my unfinished novel out of my footlocker and get it finished."

"Your what?" Florence laughed.

"The novel I started when I was in the service. I always wanted to finish it and get it published."

"Well, now I've heard everything."

"And what's your big wish?" Elroy asked.

Florence twisted her mouth around like she always did when she was deep in thought. She started slowly. "I wish I had learned how to tap dance."

"Tap dance!" Elroy howled and continued howling all the way to the back shed.

"Gabby, did you see what was in the paper about doing something you always wanted to do?"

"I did! Maybe I can finally learn how to swim!"

"Oh, wouldn't that be wonderful. And guess what? Maybe I can learn how to tap dance!"

"Really?"

"Do you want to hear something funny? Elroy wants to finish the novel he started years ago!"

"Well that's nothing. Siggie said he wants to learn how to cook! He has never even boiled water. What a riot!"

"Opal, did you see the paper today?

"Yes! And I am so excited! Maybe now I can learn how to make all those wonderful yeast breads and fancy cakes that my mother and grandmother from Eastern Europe used to make for the holidays. I could have learned when I was young but I was too busy playing with my cousins. Plus they were always shooing us out of the kitchen."

"And you?"

"Tap dancing!"

"Oh. And listen to this—George wants to take public speaking!"

"George?"

"Yes! Can you imagine George getting up in front of a group and talking?"

"No, not really, but that's great. I wish him well."

And so it went. This program seemed to inspire lots of folks in Lone Moon Creek. Could it have been that it prompted a "One last chance" and "You better do it now or never" type of chord? How many people have had longings their entire lives but continued to put them on the back burner? Probably almost everyone.

The following week's headlines read "Gov. Program Rethought."

"Oh no," Florence mumbled to Elroy. "I bet they have canceled our senior citizen's agenda."

"Figures," the man with limited vocabulary uttered.

"Wait, wait, it's still on. It says, 'Because of an overwhelming interest from all over the county, the location has been changed to the community center in Jackson. With the number of people who want to participate in swimming, a building with a pool has become mandatory.'"

"That'll be a forty-mile round trip for us. Will that be worth it so you can learn how to tap dance?" Elroy laughed and tried to conceal it in his bowl of oatmeal.

"Don't you laugh at me, Mr. No-Novel."

"Yes, George is saying the same thing—forty miles at night is too far to learn how to speak in front of people. He says he's never done it up to now, why bother. But I want to learn how to make potica for Christmas this year."

"Here is my perfect chance to learn how to swim and old stick in the mud says he doesn't really need to learn how to cook with me around anyway."

Florence heard all sorts of last wish aspirations from gardening to quilting to stained glass making to car repairs. There was woodworking and jewelry making and Indian artifacts. She chuckled at Anna Belle's desire to learn how to sing (Anna Belle sits behind her in church) and Linea's quest to "Make sense of the stock market." Everyone seemed a need to push the envelope before it was too late.

Everyone except Phoenicia, that is. As quickly as one's wish was uttered, she was right there to say, "Don't you realize what will happen to you as soon as you fulfill your last desire?" Some people thought they might have an idea of what she meant and didn't ask her to qualify it. For those who had no idea, she wasn't shy in blurting forth, "You will die!"

"Ooo, that woman," Florence mumbled as she put down the phone.

"Why do you need peanut butter on your toast every day now?" Florence quizzed her husband as she reached for the paper.

"I've got my reasons."

"'County Provides Bus for Seniors,'" Florence read with exuberance. 'Because of the great demand from senior citizens, transportation will be provided for programs at the community center in Jackson.'"

"Yahoo," Florence exclaimed as she twirled and tapped her heels and toes while knocking over the jar of jam with her over exuberant arm thrust.

"Lessons wouldn't hurt," Elroy said behind his sport's section, trying not to let the paper jiggle as he silently laughed.

"Hadn't you better find the draft of your book? Classes start next week," Florence said.

"Done."

"Where is it? Let me see it."

"Sorry, old girl, not until it's published."

"You mean never?" Florence mumbled under her breath.

"I heard that."

Sure enough, the county bus pulled in front of Chester's Deli and was soon loaded with high-spirited senior citizens. The noise level was even higher on the return trip when everyone had their lists of materials needed and/or expectations of their classes.

"I get to buy a bathing suit!" Gabby bragged to everyone around her.

"And I have to take an apron," Siggie commented as he put his arm around Gabby.

"Oh, an apron?" Opal said. "Me too, except I'm in a different class where I'm to catch up on my ancestors' breads and cakes. I can't wait."

"Do-re-mi-fa-sol-la-ti-do," Anna Belle sang out in not perfect pitch. "Does anyone know what I have to take in?"

"A bushel basket?" Elroy said softly as Florence elbowed him. "Ow! This is just like our school bus days," he moaned.

"Linea, do you need any equipment to understand the stock market?"

Whistles could be heard throughout the bus. "Settle down back there," the bus driver yelled.

Only a few unobtrusive lights were exposed inside the bus as it jounced through the dark night. The students calmed their anxieties after surviving their first day of school and breathed easier, except maybe for George, who didn't know how he was going to cozy up to public speaking and Elroy, who was starting to panic about exposing his novel to the public.

Florence's feet were silently moving to a tap routine she'd seen her instructor perform; she couldn't wait to buy her tap shoes. "Who is that woman?" she whispered as she nudged the dozing Elroy. They watched a woman wearing a trench coat and scarf that made it impossible to see her face hobble down the aisle grabbing onto the back of each seat. She made sure she was the first one off the bus.

"Don't know," mumbled the man of few words.

The next week the bus stop was ablaze with excitement. Florence was wearing her tap shoes on her hands like gloves, doing a click-click routine in midair; Jonah broke into song with "Standing On the Corner Watching All the Girls Go By" as Anna Belle continued singing the next phrase out of tune; Siggie was already wearing his apron, which made everyone laugh when they read the words printed on it: Great Cook in the Making—Beware; Linea was approaching people with her three-year-old grandson's blue and orange calculator asking them what they thought about who knows what? And Gabby was holding up her new bathing suit while William began singing, "It was an itsy, bitsy, teeny, weeny, yellow…" Gabby responded by hitting him over the head with her retro beach bag. There was no silence in front of Chester's Deli until George called out in a deep authoritative voice, "Hear ye, hear ye, the bus is coming!"

It was his wife, Opal, who first realized that he was mentally preening himself for public speaking."

"Oh, George!" she said as she hugged and kissed him, "that was wonderful!"

"Hey, you two, no making out on the bus!" Milt laughed as everyone followed suit.

With a quick jab to the ribs, Florence whispered, "There she is, way in the back with her manila folder in front of her face. Who is it? Don't turn around."

"Don't no."

"Well, I hope your book is more exciting than you are."

"Ow, ee, uh, ooo," Florence moaned the next morning as she put the coffee on the table.

"What's the matter with you?" Elroy asked.

"I can barely move."

"Out of shape, are ya?"

"Telephone. Bring it to me, will you? Hi, Gabby. Oh, you too? I know. I am so sore. I think it was those exercises we had to do first. At least you could do yours in the water. I was out there on the hard floor. Oh, and tomorrow it'll probably be worse. What? Siggie burned your breakfast? That's too bad. Phoenicia already called you this morning? She is critical about everything; don't listen to her. Yes, try soaking in the bathtub. Bye."

Florence could hear the faint tap tapping from the computer. Elroy was hard at work transposing his handwritten unfinished novel from the yellowed, wartime paper to the computer.

Better him than me, Florence thought, as she didn't tap her way to the sink.

"Florence, I think George is going to quit the class," Opal sighed into the phone.

"Oh no, I hope not. What happened?"

"He said the teacher went around the room and asked each student to say a few sentences about himself. When it was George's turn, he completely froze. He said it was awful; he was so embarrassed."

"Did the teacher give him any suggestions or support?"

"No, he just went on to the next person, and at the end of the session he told George he was going to call him at home.

George is afraid he's going to tell him not to come back. Poor George, he is so depressed. I don't know what he is going to do."

"Have faith that it is going to work, Opal, and by the way, how was your class on Eastern European baking?"

"Well, so far not that good. She keeps rattling on and on about the people and the geography and the customs and traditions. I don't want to hear all about that, I want to get my hands in the dough and stretch it paper thin and load it down with luscious goodies like my mother and grandmother did."

"That's probably coming down the pike, be patient. OK, call anytime. Bye."

"How are you going to practice tap dancing when you can barely move?" Elroy uttered as he entered he kitchen.

"Don't worry about me; I'll be fine in a day or two," Florence remarked as she braced herself against the pain until she got beyond her husband's line of vision.

By the next week's bus time, Florence and Gabby bounded the vehicle's steps like junior high girls. George lumbered upward like a disgruntled student who didn't want to go to school. Anna Belle theatrically sang "School Days" to the bus driver while he covered his ears. Siggie sported a few bandages on his novice cooking fingers, the golfers talked incessantly about Sunday's Open, and Dennis cursed as the trench coat– and scarf-wearing woman pushed him out of her way to get to the back of the bus.

"Watch you language," the bus driver snarled as he glared into his rearview mirror.

Linea cuddled her juvenile calculator in her arm as she sashayed onto the bus with a new hairdo, polished nails, and a striking outfit.

"Are you in fashion design class?" Harriet asked as they sat side by side.

"Oh no, I'm in the stock market class," Linea answered sweetly.

"What would be interesting about that?"

"The cute instructor."

"Oh."

"Elroy, sit over there with George. I want to talk to Opal."

"Opal, did George's teacher call him on the phone? What did he say?" Florence whispered.

The two women huddled with their whispery voices like eighth grade girls talking about boyfriends. "He didn't say anything threatening. He just visited. After four days and four phone calls, the two of them were talking like lifelong friends. I don't know what that was all about."

"Do you know who that woman is way in the back? Don't turn around! She's wearing a big cover-up like she's trying to be anonymous."

"Elroy, you can come back now," Florence dictated. "What did you and George talk about?"

"Oh nothing really."

"That figures. Do you have all your papers?"

"What papers?"

"Your book! Your book!"

"It's all right here," Elroy announced as he held up his laptop.

"Elroy! I'm proud of you!" Florence said in utter shock.

The novelist-to-be was even more shocked to get a compliment and couldn't think of one word to say to his tap dancer.

"One hundred bottles of beer on the wall, one hundred bottles..." Immediately the entire busload emitted a groan that could have swept the vehicle off the road if the driver hadn't had his hands securely on the wheel.

Anna Belle didn't sing another note.

Poor Anna Belle, just really loves to sing, Florence thought as she felt guilty about wishing the woman didn't sit behind her in church.

"Evening, George," his instructor called out.

In barely a whisper, George gave him a mumble.

"Tonight, folks, we're going to use the podium and each person will just say a few words about—maybe their ride in or the day they had, whatever."

George began to sweat and twitch and countdown in his head how many people were ahead of him. Of course the inevitable came: he had to go upfront.

George couldn't lift his head to face the audience. He mumbled "something" and was set to return to his seat when his teacher said, "Wait a minute, George, you have a phone call."

Carl handed him a phone. Of course it was obvious to everyone that it wasn't a legitimate phone, as the wire dangled to the floor. Carl hung on to the other receiver with the cord dangling.

"Hi, George, how are you today?"

George didn't say anything.

"Thought I'd give you a call. Wait until you hear what happened when I went fishing today. I was standing on the bank of Lone Creek when this kid came right up to me and threw in his line. The father soon followed, laden with poles and fishing baskets and nets. He was all apologetic that maybe his son had been bothering me. Once I assured him that he hadn't, he settled down and threw in his own line. The kid was so funny; he kept calling me "partner." He'd say, "How are you doing over there, partner. Got any bites yet?""

George laughed. The class laughed.

"Then it was, 'Been fishing long, partner?' Of course, you might know who caught the first fish!"

"Carl, that was funny, it reminds me of my nephew who was a real rip snorter of a kid. He had a way about him that was like a miniature John Wayne; he could just go anywhere and capture the whole audience."

"Do you mean like you are doing now, George?"

Suddenly George faced his audience and they clapped! *They clapped for me!* exclaimed George to himself.

⸎

"Tonight, class, we're going to begin by melting butter in a frying pan."

Oh good grief, thought Siggie. *Everyone knows how to do that.*

Siggie turned his burner to high and went to the refrigerator for the butter. He peeked under the pan to see that it was nice and red. In went the butter while Siggie turned to nod to the teacher to let her know that he was on top of things.

Bonnie ran toward Siggie with a potholder. *I wonder what she's up to,* he thought. He soon found out when she grabbed the handle of the smoky frying pan.

Siggie's shoulders visibly drooped. "Don't worry, Siggie. Let's start over by putting your burner at a very low temperature."

The class made delicious fried eggs that night, with toast and coffee and bacon.

⸎

"Gabby, would you like to put your face in the water tonight?"

"I don't think so, Celia."

"That's OK. Just practice in your mind what you would do if you did put your head under."

"That's easy. I would take a deep breath, hold it, and go under."

"Very good. Perfect. How about you practice your back float? You're getting really good at that."

"Hey, Celia" another coach called from the upper level, "Here's your good watch; you left it in the locker room."

"Thanks. Toss it down here, I'll catch it."

She didn't and it went down into the water in front of Gabby. Without a moment of hesitation, Gabby took a deep breath and went to retrieve it.

"Here it is Celia."

"Thank you, Gabby." She laughed.

"Why are you laughing?"

"Who just went underwater?"

"I did! I did it!" Gabby yelled as she bounced in the water.

"What's the matter Elroy?"

"I can't seem to write without my old, yellowed war-time paper."

"You know, everybody writes in a different manner; some write in longhand, some with an old-fashioned typewriter, some with a computer, some dictate into a recorder, to name a few. If that paper inspires you, by all means use it."

"Thanks, Mr. Willard, I will."

Elroy was glad he had tucked three sheets of paper into his coat pocket. As he flattened the creases, he stared at the spatters, maybe coffee, maybe blood. That paper had seen it all. Out of his pocket, too, came a stub of a pencil that had been sharpened with his weapon. A shiver ran the length of his spine, and there he worked for the duration of the time.

"Where is he?"

"I don't know. Has anyone seen George?"

"Here he comes. He's on the run."

"Hey, everybody, let's all cheer when he gets on."

The cheering startled George but maybe not as much as the bus driver handing him a note. "Read this announcement to everyone," commanded the driver.

There stood George at the front of the bus with his hands trembling as he held the paper.

"Hurry up," snarled Gary, "I want to take off." But George couldn't get the group's attention; they were still in their cheering mode.

"Excuse me, excuse me," he managed to say softly.

The 6' 6", 300 pound Gary, who lived two doors down from Florence and Elroy, stood to face the crowd and yelled, "Hey, listen up! This man has an announcement."

If the fashion design people had dropped a pin, it would have been heard.

Everyone stared at George. He looked at Opal who was praying with all her might that her husband would be successful in this public speaking order.

He cleared his throat and enunciated. "Because of the Monday holiday, there will be no classes that night."

"Good job, George, I'm proud of you," Opal whispered to him as he took his seat.

Florence leaned forward to ask Linea why she had a handheld calculator instead of the huge blue and orange one. "Oh," she said as she tapped in three numbers, "my cute instructor gave it to me."

"Really? Can I come up and sit with you for a while? I'll be right back, Elroy."

"So tell me about this teacher of yours," Florence said coyly.

"No changing seats, ma'am," the bus driver called out.

Florence whispered, "I'll call you tomorrow," as she slunk back to her seat, wondering when the seat rule came into being.

"You'd think he'd be considerate of me, seeing how we live two houses apart," mumbled Florence to her dozing husband.

"Psst, Florence. Do you think I could get into your tap dancing class?"

"Griffin, is that you?"

"Yeah. I'm not very happy with that line dancing; maybe tap would be better for me."

"Sure, I don't see why not; but be sure you exercise every day, or you will be sore and stiff as a poker after the first class."

"Gotcha."

"So did you write anything tonight?"

"Are you talking to me?" Elroy asked.

"There's nobody else to talk to."

"As a matter of fact, I did write quite a lot."

"Do you still remember way back to the war time?"

"How could I forget?"

"Gang way, there she goes," Florence moaned.

Everyone who wasn't dozing watched the woman secure her place at the front of the bus to disembark.

"Good morning, I just had to tell you about the beautiful breakfast Siggie made for me."

"That's wonderful, Gabby!"

"And guess what I did in my class? I went underwater!"

"Wow! You two are really making progress."

"And you?"

"I'm tapping my way to success." Florence laughed. "Oh, by the way, do you know Griffin? He wants to switch to the tap dance class; maybe I can get him caught up to where we are now. Did you know that Linea has some sort of infatuation with her teacher? I have to find out about this. And congratulations again! Bye."

"Morning, Linea. So what's going on in the stock market class?"

"I have no idea about the market, but Mr. Monroe is yummy!"

"Oops, I have another call, we'll talk again. Yes, hello, Opal. Are you crying? What's the matter?"

"It's that class; I hate it."

"Why?"

"Now she's going to show us videos from Eastern Europe. I don't want to sit and watch videos and hear about the demographics. I want to bake the breads and cakes of my ancestors. I've heard enough about customs and traditions; I want something real. I'm going to quit."

"Don't quit, Opal, stay with it at least two more weeks."

"OK, got to go. George's teacher is calling in."

Florence was practicing her tap dance routine in the kitchen when Phoenicia called.

"I'm just a little winded from practicing my dancing, Phoenicia, I'm not sick. No, I don't think I'm too old for tap dancing. Yes, I'm getting quite good, if I do say so myself. Yes, it's always been a wish of mine to learn how. What do you mean if I fulfill my wish then I'll drop dead? You're horrible. Good-bye."

"Who was that?"

"Ooo, that darn Phoenicia. Do you know that when you finish your novel you're going to drop dead?"

"Whoa, I didn't know that." Elroy laughed.

"How Great Thou Art"—beware, Florence mused to herself. *She's clearing her throat behind me, and this has to be her favorite hymn.*

Florence waited for the onslaught to begin. Hmm, maybe she wasn't listening hard enough. She ceased her singing so she could better hear the off-key Anna Belle. Gee, what happened? Could she really have improved this much?

The pastor made it a point to look at Florence when he said he'd like everyone to sing out in praise.

"Of course, I'll help you," Florence replied. "Yes this afternoon at two will be fine. See you then."

"Elroy, Griffin is coming over today so I can get him caught up with the dance routines," she hollered through the three rooms.

"I don't have the music that the teacher uses, but we'll wait until I hear something on the radio that sounds similar. There, that's close enough. OK watch my feet. That's it! You're a quick learner."

"Elroy, can you go to the attic and bring down my old record player and bring the forty-fives too. I can't stand finding tunes on the radio."

Florence and Griffin worked for over an hour until Florence said, "I think that's enough for one day."

"Me too, and thank you so much. See you in class."

Florence sunk into the kitchen chair and let the music continue. One by one the forty-fives dropped to the spinning platter, bringing back wonderful memories.

"That's our song!" Elroy shouted as he literally ran to the kitchen. He swooped Florence to her feet; engulfed her in his arms the way that brought the chaperone out on the gymnasium floor to tap the boy's shoulder, which meant, "Get some space in between you two"; and slowly guided his first love around the kitchen floor.

"Elroy!" Florence whispered as he gave her the last dip, another move that raised eyebrows years ago.

"I've still got it." He winked as he went back to his novel.

The bus stop gathering was not as large as it had once been. "Where is everybody?"

"I heard the flu is going around."

"I know of four people who are away."

"Maybe they are getting disgruntled with the program," Opal remarked, sounding like a disgruntled one.

As George filed on, the bus driver handed him a paper. "We have some more rules to follow on the bus. Would you mind reading them to everyone?"

George felt himself almost go into total collapse as he went from calm to shock in a split second. He had to delve into his reservoir of support that his mentor had slowly been developing for him and the others in his group. He cleared his throat and said, "Sure."

That one word, "Sure," when he heard himself say it, was like the gate to heaven had opened and there was sunshine on the other side.

He didn't have to worry about how he was going to get their attention, because the bus driver gave a whistle that almost blew out the windows.

George began, "New Rules for the Bus from the County: 1. Once you are in your seat, stay there. 2. No getting out of your seat until the bus stops. 3. No standing to lean forward or back to talk to other people. And this is the bus driver's number if you have any questions..."

For some reason, Elroy jotted it down as Florence clucked her tongue in disgust, knowing her husband would post it in the kitchen by the phone.

"Thanks, George."

George smiled.

Florence slouched in her seat and mumbled, "Oh good grief, more rules."

"Welcome, Griffin, and just follow along the best you can," the teacher directed. He stood next to Florence.

"You must be a natural, Griffin. I've never seen anyone catch on that quickly!"

Florence thought he would mention that she had been helping him, but he didn't.

"All right, choose a partner for the next routine. This is something new," the teacher dictated.

Griffin grabbed Florence's arm. "Do you mind?"

"I guess not."

Opal sat to watch the video.

This is such a waste of my time, she thought to herself.

She watched the Eastern European landscape sail by as the flowers on the hillsides opened and the spring animals appeared for the first time with their offspring. She saw people dressed in their native costumes walking across the hills and dales to their churches and the women taking platter after platter of wonderful looking food to the tables of their families.

There! There are the breads and cakes that I want to learn how to make!

"OK, class, I hope you enjoyed the video and all the background information I have given you so you can better understand where these people come from who are notorious for baking some of the most delicious breads and delicacies in the world. Today starts our real work in the kitchen, and to help us are actual descendants of the women we've been learning about. Please welcome Tatianna, Margaret, and Katrina. As they work alongside us, please feel free to ask them questions and converse just like they were your sisters or mothers or grandmothers or aunts or... Well, you know what I mean."

Ah, this is what I have been waiting for!

If someone walked through the building they might have heard:

"We're going to learn how to tread water tonight, gang."

"We're going to learn how to introduce people remembering that it's all about them, not us."

"I would like each of you to read one paragraph from your manuscript."

"We're going to discover how easy it is to make a gored skirt."

"Let's see how you can take five strokes off your golf game without even trying."

"Are you ready to harmonize?"

"Let's go through these statistics and make a graph."

"How can asparagus survive the winter?"

"Who's up for a nice steak dinner tonight? Put on your aprons, class."

"Being critical is going to make you more pessimistic and more superstitious. Why is that?"

"Good morning, Florence. I wanted to tell you about the wonderful experience I had last evening. We started the baking segment with real people! It was just like I remembered when my mother and grandmother got together. They laughed and told stories of their mothers and aunts. Sometimes one of them would break into song and soon they were all singing while they chopped and ground and sifted and mixed. The history that our teacher was trying to get us to appreciate came to life! Thanks for encouraging me to hang in there. Talk to you tomorrow or so."

"It's Phoenicia, are you still sore from tap dancing? I don't see much sense in a lot of those programs. I think the county is wasting its money with a lot of foolishness. You can't talk this morning? All right. Good-bye."

"Good morning, it's Griffin. Do you think you can help me with a few of the new routines? I can come over at two, is that OK?"

"I don't think you need extra help, Griffin," Florence said.

"Please, Florence, you are so good at explaining things. I would feel more comfortable with additional practice before I go into next week's class. Please?"

"All right, today is OK."

"Hi, Florence. Thanks for letting me come over. I didn't see your car in the driveway."

"I think Elroy went to the hardware store. Well, let's get started."

"This music is great!" Griffin smiled as he followed Florence's moves.

"There's nothing like the oldies. Move back, Griffin. I'm going to end up kicking you."

"You can kick me anytime you want."

I wish I never let him come here, Florence suddenly thought just as Griffin grabbed her and pulled her to him.

"What are you doing?" she uttered in complete shock.

"Come on, I know you like me."

"Get away from me! Elroy! Help! Elroy, help me!" she screamed as loud as she could.

"But he's not here and I am," Griffin hissed.

Florence struggled; but she didn't struggle for long.

Elroy ran into the kitchen and knocked the man to the floor. He stepped on the man's chest and told Florence to call the police.

"Now call Gary to get over here fast. I might need a little help here."

Within two minutes, the 6'6'', 300 pound Gary charged through the door, allowing Elroy to hold Florence in his arms with her need pouring into his heart. This is what his heart had been missing for a long time.

"What were the sheriff's cars doing at your house?"

"Who is this?"

"Phoenicia. I heard they took someone out in handcuffs. Is that true?"

"Good-bye, Phoenicia."

"Sit down, Florence. Let me make you a cup of tea."

"Just hold me, Elroy, and never let me go. I'm not going tonight. I can't face anyone. I never want to tap dance again."

"Sweetheart, you didn't do anything wrong, and all your friends are one hundred percent behind you; they care about you."

"I know they do. I just need a little more time to settle my nerves."

"That's understandable—wait! I have an idea. Let's take the car tonight, and you can sit in on my class. Would you like that?"

"Yes," Florence said meekly.

"Certainly, welcome, so nice to meet you. Class, as you know, everyone is going to have a chance to read one paragraph from their manuscript tonight."

"Are you sure you want me to be here?" Florence asked shyly. After all, she had not seen or read one word of the book that her husband had started before they were married.

"Yes, I want you here," he responded as he reached out to hold her hand.

"Who wants to be first? OK you're on."

Tempe went to the front of the class and read:

Far into the night, the trees trembled and the birds hid their heads farther under their downy wings. The soft sounds of the footsteps were like thunder to the wildlife who had been scavenging for prey. The coyote stared, keeping his body as a statue while the deer remained in the thicket of evergreens.

Tempe gave a little bow as she returned to her seat and everyone clapped.

"Very nice, Tempe. It makes me want to read on to find out who or what is approaching with soft footsteps!"

Kim-Lu read:

Skimming across the yellow water, Len-shu eased the oars through the reflection of the moon. This was the only night that the delivery could be made. Fully exposed to the world, Len-shu had hoped for a thick-clouded sky, even a rainy night. As the oars dove down and back, the navigator's eyes traveled side to side, hoping not to see another craft on the water. On the distant shore he could see that they had arrived. They were there to take the package that was wedged securely between his bare feet.

"Nice, Kim-Lu. Who's on the edge of their seat?" Everyone raised their hands and then clapped.

"Next, anyone?"

Elroy gave Florence's hand a little squeeze and went to the front.

I counted three pebbles in front of my left eye and watched an earthworm crawl in and out of the dirt in front of my right eye. I didn't know if my knees had any blood running through them anymore, and I knew my back was not of the human kind but of the wooden kind, the kind I had to lean against when I did my school lessons. The tops of my combat boots were digging into my legs, and I visualized my rifle burning into the side of my face. Six hours with the command of "Don't Move" left America's bravest to rot in foxholes. This soldier would have rotted if it hadn't been for his thoughts of the lovely Florence.

Elroy lowered his eyes and walked back to his seat as the applause began. Florence jumped up to hug her soldier, feeling the tears flow.

"And this, ladies and gentlemen, is the lovely Florence from the story! Good job, Elroy."

As the two traveled home, they eyed the bright sphere in the universe all the way to Lone Moon Creek. "This has been one of the best nights ever," Florence whispered to Elroy.

"Good morning, Florence and Elroy. I made something for you," Opal chirped as she entered carrying a platter covered with aluminum foil. "It just came out of the oven so it's nice and warm."

"It smells heavenly!"

"Where's George?" asked Elroy.

"He's out in the car."

"Have him come in. We'll all enjoy this heavenly delight together."

"We missed you guys on the bus last night."

"We decided to have a private, romantic night." Florence grinned as she looked at Elroy.

"That's great. Let me think if anything exciting happened, oh yes, Gabby did something phenomenal in the pool; Siggie said they made some kind of flaming dessert; Anna Belle invited us all to a concert; and, listen to this, Linea is engaged to her teacher!"

"Did that incognito woman go through the bus?"

"Yeah, I think I saw her."

The heavenly warm walnut cinnamon raisin sweet bread was sliced and the coffee poured as George raised his cup and announced that he would like to make a toast.

"To Florence and Elroy. May their lives be filled with love and memories. May they be present for each other in pleasant and pleasing ways and may their presence for each other be a blessing."

"Here, here," Opal added.

"Thank you, George. That was a wonderful toast."

"We've been working on such things in my public speaking class. I am so thankful that I signed up."

"And I'm so glad you signed up, Opal. This bread is delicious! I just wish I had never had the harebrained idea to learn how to tap dance." Florence's whole demeanor plummeted.

"Don't think any more about it, sweetheart. Today is a new day," Elroy said lovingly.

"You want to hear something funny? Phoenicia called early this morning and said because there was a full moon last night there would be something suspicious in our mail today!"

"Oh, that woman; she is so superstitious."

"And critical."

"And ill willed."

"I can't believe there are only three weeks left to our program!"

"Me neither!"

"Here comes the bus."

Plans were underway for the culminating festivities. Every group would flaunt its talents and skills. People from each town in the county were invited to attend and observe, participate, evaluate, and enjoy. Crafts, food, and paintings would be on sale. There would be free concerts, sports demonstrations, and a fashion show. There would be free gardening tips and potted plants. The children were invited to the puppet shows and given an opportunity to make their own puppets. The public speakers would be the emcees. Authors would read and give pointers to hopeful new authors. People were invited to use the computers and explore all the latest electronics. Chess, golf, bowling, and ping-pong competitions would run all day. A quilt show with sewing demonstrations promised to be spectacular.

"You know, Linea," Phoenicia said gloomily into the phone, "all that grandiosity will only lead to failure."

"Phoenicia, hush!" Linea retaliated, "And good-bye."

Elroy and Florence started taking the bus again, even though Florence didn't go back to her tap dancing class. She just couldn't.

Maybe next year, she thought. *If they have this program again.*

Florence followed her husband into his writing class and thoroughly enjoyed listening to excerpts of the student's manuscripts. It gave them lots to talk about on the way home.

Phoenicia was wrong—the ending festivities were a huge success! The evaluations were returned with positive remarks and hopes for more such activities in the future. She was also wrong on another note: nobody died from fulfilling their lifelong wish.

Wait a minute! What!

Phoenicia Williams from Lone Moon Creek passed away at her home. A full obituary will appear in Thursday's paper.

"Yes," answered Gabby, "I saw that in the paper. What on earth do you think happened? She wasn't ill was she?"

Opal also responded, "I saw it, too! Creepy, right?"

Most of the town waited for Thursday's paper. They noticed cars from out of state at her house.

"Can you imagine growing up with a superstitious, critical woman like Phoenicia?"

"I can't imagine them having anything good to say about her."

The notice in Thursday's paper read:

Phoenicia Lilac Williams died Monday at her home. She was ninety-one. Phoenicia grew up on the levees of New Orleans, the oldest of eleven children. They have all predeceased her.

Phoenicia came to Lone Moon Creek with her new husband sixty years ago. During that time in Lone Moon, she brought up her children and got to know many of the locals.

Phoenicia's last wish came true when she took the bus every week to join in on the class How to Stop Being Superstitious. Even though this was very difficult for her—because of her memories of the tour bus tragedy that took the lives of three of her siblings—she told her children it was the most wonderful class she ever attended and hoped it would help her.

"Are you kidding me?" Florence whispered to the newspaper. "Elroy, read this."

"Wow," Elroy muttered in total disbelief. "I am wordless."

THE END

About the Author

Teresa's first published work ***Stories from Lone Moon Creek*** was released in 2015. ***Stories from Lone Moon Creek: Ripples***, is a follow-up to that popular work, providing more of the heartfelt stories demanded by her readers.

Teresa was born in Cooperstown, NY and lives in Worcester, NY. She attended the K-12 Central School in Worcester and graduated with eighteen others in her Senior Class.

Continuing her education, she received her degree in Elementary Education from SUNY at Oneonta, New York.

Teresa taught Kindergarten and First Grade at Worcester CS for twenty-five years developing the love of reading and writing.

She has always had a fondness for the arts and has delved into painting, piano education, creativity, garden sculpting, quilting, and writing.

She says rural life has a kindness and goodness with a touch of mystique which she tries to describe in her stories.

Teresa has three children and nine grandchildren.

CPSIA information can be obtained at www.ICGtesting.com
Printed in the USA
BVOW04s2023071016

464499BV00001B/1/P

9 781621 833567